JUST
BEYOND
TOMORROW

JUST BEYOND TOMORROW

BERTRICE SMALL

KENSINGTON PUBLISHING CORP.
http://www.kensingtonbooks.com

For Ethan Ellenberg, my agent, and Walter Zacharius, my publisher,
and for Steven Zacharius, who could probably charm a duck into a
roasting pan. Thank you, gentlemen.

Prologue

GREAT BRITAIN, 1642–1650

In the summer of 1642 the king and the parliament began preparing for war, each raising an army of its own. The crisis had been coming for some time now. The parliament wanted Charles Stuart to consult with them in his choice of government ministers and other official appointments. They wanted complete control of the army put into their hands. They wanted to reform the English church, abolish all bishops, and allow the final authority in church affairs to rest with them. They wanted a say in the raising of the king's children. They quoted from the Bible extensively in order to justify their demands, but like most politicians they forgot one of Christ's strongest directives to "render unto Caesar that which is Caesar's; and unto God that which is God's." A very clear warning to the human race to keep church and state separate, but parliament, believing they alone spoke for God, wasn't listening.

The king, however, firmly believed that his authority came directly from the celestial actuary. He held fast to the Divine Right of his Stuart and Tudor ancestors. Unfortunately the parliament also believed God was on their side. But, had the king given in to parliament's wishes, they would have become the sole governing power of England. With all civil, military, and religious authority firmly in their hands, and backed by the landed wealth of certain of the nobility in the House of Lords, they sought to rule England. Had

Charles Stuart yielded to the parliament, he would have found himself rendered little more than a figurehead. It was an intolerable position for the king to accept, but neither side was willing to compromise.

The first English civil war was fought. When it was over in 1647, the queen and her children had fled England for France. The king found himself a prisoner, first of parliament, and then of the Roundheads of Oliver Cromwell. He managed to escape, fleeing to the Isle of Wight, where he attempted to bargain with the parliament and, at the same time, with his possible allies in Scotland. The king, who loved intrigue, also loved to barter. From the relative security of Carisbrooke Castle, he sat like a spider in the center of his web attempting to wheel and deal while his royal agents brought him the encouraging news of the people's discontent with parliament's army, which had grown overpowerful and abusive.

Pleased with what appeared to be a growing discord among his enemies, the king played his usual game of delay, behaving as if all of England were still firmly in his royal grasp and under his personal control. Winter came. The Scots sent envoys to Carisbrooke. Their army would rise in support of Charles Stuart if he would but guarantee the safety of their Presbyterian church and take some of the Scots nobility into his government. Parliament, suddenly realizing that the king was not bargaining fairly with them, feared a Scots alliance would renew the civil war. So the moderates in parliament appealed to the Scots Presbyterians to form an alliance with them. The king thereupon signed an ill-advised treaty with the Scots.

Parliament angrily voted to disenfranchise the king, refusing to offer him any more terms for compromise. Throughout England, however, the anger grew, and directed itself not toward the king, but toward parliament and its military, both of whom were ruling with too heavy an iron fist. Now it became parliament against the people. Many of the gentry who had originally supported reform grew hostile.

In April there was a revolt in Wales. The king, in the meantime, had managed to stitch together an alliance between his English supporters and the Scots, both of whom objected strenuously to the military's involvement in the civil government. A second civil war began. It consisted of small local uprisings as in Wales and an invasion of the Scots into England.

The king and his adherents, however, had underestimated their opponents. In Scotland a separate confederation had to be worked out between royalists, Presbyterians, and the Convenanters, those Scots who supported the national covenant, which had been signed in 1643 with the English. By the time it had all been settled it was July. The Welsh uprising had been brutally quelled. Had the Scots moved faster, they could have obtained a great victory, for their forces outnumbered the English three to one. But disorganized and poorly provisioned, they gave the English time to regroup. A battle was finally fought at Preston in Lancashire, on August 17, 1648. The well-trained English troops decimated both the Scots foot soldiers and their cavalry. In a driving rain they doggedly chased after them until the Scots could run no farther. On that day General Oliver Cromwell took ten thousand prisoners, and many were killed.

Outraged by King Charles I's behavior, the fanatics in the English government and the army now took total control of the parliament. They immediately removed those men believed to be moderate in their thoughts. They ousted the entire House of Lords. Then they boldly brought the king to trial for his alleged crimes against the English people. Charles Stuart was quickly found guilty on all charges. He was beheaded on the thirtieth day of January in the year 1649. The heir to England's throne learned of his father's execution several days later while at his sister's court in Holland, when his chaplain came forward to address him as *"Your Majesty."* The second Charles Stuart promptly burst into tears and could not be consoled for several days. The new king was just eighteen years of age.

Charles II was, however, almost immediately pronounced king of Scotland by the Scots parliament. While in sympathy with the English, the Scots Covenanters didn't like the idea that a Scots king of England had been executed without their permission. They would take back their own Stuart king under certain conditions, none of which could be acceptable to the royalists. Almost eighteen months of haggling ensued. Charles II landed in Scotland on June

23, 1650, barely escaping the English fleet sent to capture him and bring him home to face his own execution.

The delay in his arrival had been caused by his reluctance to sign the National Covenant, a thing his father would not do. The Covenant called for, among other things, the imposition of the Presbyterian form of worship on all the king's subjects in England, Ireland, and Scotland. It denied any other religious faiths, the Anglican and the Roman Catholic faiths in particular, legitimacy. It prohibited a church hierarchy, and enjoined the creation of all bishops, present or future. The king, an Anglican, signed with reluctance, having absolutely no intention of following through, something many suspected, but he needed a power base if he was to retake England.

Charles II needed firm control of an army. He would do what he had to in order to obtain his goals. The members of the Scots parliament were extremely obdurate, and very short-sighted, but they were not stupid. They kept a tight rein on the young Stuart king. They went so far as to banish his personal chaplains and his personal friends. They kept four ministers of the kirk sermonizing at him almost round the clock. Only when Oliver Cromwell was foolish enough to attempt an invasion of Scotland that autumn in an effort to regain control over that land and custody of its king; only then did the Scots parliament act to raise an army of defense. Only then did Charles Stuart, the second of that name, see a tiny ray of hope. He was, unfortunately, to be doomed to disappointment.

Part One

The Heiress of Brae

Chapter

1

Scotland, 1650
Late summer and autumn

She remembered the argument well as she sat by the early after-noon fire, assailed by her memories. "Have you lost your wits entirely, old man?" the Duchess of Glenkirk demanded of her husband of thirty-five years. Jasmine Leslie could not remember ever having been so angry. Her turquoise blue eyes flashed with her indignation as she confronted James Leslie. "What the hell have we to do with the royal Stuarts? I cannot believe you would even consider such a venture as you now tell me you are planning."

"The young king needs the help of all loyal Scotsmen," the duke replied stubbornly, but in truth she knew his conscience had troubled him over the matter.

"We do not even know this king," Jasmine recalled saying in an attempt to regain a firm grip over her emotions. Drawing her husband to the settle by the fireplace, she had sat beside him and affectionately ruffled his snow-white hair fondly. "Jemmie, be reasonable. It has been over thirty years since we had anything to do with the royal Stuarts or their court. King James ruled us then. There was peace. Then he died, and ever since poor Charles Stuart has made one mistake after another. He has plunged not only England, but Scotland as well, into wasteful fighting. How many innocent lives have been sacrificed in this battle over religion? If it could be settled, then perhaps it would have been worth it, but it will never be resolved. The Anglicans want it all their way. The Presbyterians want it all their way, and God save us from the more fanatical Covenanters among them! No one will win in this matter! Is it not better to follow the cardinal rule of the Leslies of Glenkirk, to *not* get involved? The survival of this clan is paramount. You are responsible for your people."

"But our parliament in Edinburgh has taken King Charles II as their own," the duke told his wife.

"Hah!" Jasmine said. "Listen to me, Jemmie Leslie, we knew King James well, both of us. You, since your birth. He was well named the wisest fool in Christendom, for he was a canny, clever man who knew how to play the various factions around him against one another and thereby guarantee his own comfort and survival. His son, our late King Charles, we have not seen since he was a young and untried youth, but I remember him well as a boy, standing in his older brother Henry's shadow. That Charles was stubborn, stiff-necked, impressed with his own importance, and absolutely certain of his own rightness. This is the man who brought us to civil war."

"The Covenanters could nae compromise either," James Leslie reminded his wife. "They were just as difficult as the king."

"Agreed," Jasmine replied, "but it was up to the king to show them a way to compromise, but no, he would not. The Divine Right of the royal Stuarts once again overshadowed all common sense of the common good."

"But this king is a different Charles Stuart," the duke said.

"Aye, yet he is the first Charles's son, with a French princess for a mother. I know that after the Duke of Buckingham's death, the late king and his wife became quite a love match. Their devotion to each other has set a fine example for the kingdom, but the queen has not been noted for her intellect, or her cleverness, Jemmie. This second Charles is the child of their love, but I question his character."

"Why?" the duke asked.

"Because he has signed the Covenant, and we both know he damned well has no intention of honoring that shameful document," Jasmine said bluntly. "He wants a power base from which to reconquer England and thinks to get it in Scotland. He will not. *Not now in this time. Not ever!*"

"But now," the duke replied, "the English prepare to invade the sacred soil of Scotland. All loyal Scots are called upon to aid our king and country. God's blood, Jasmine! I hae been called by my distant cousins to raise a troop of both cavalry and foot soldiers. How can I refuse them? It would bring dishonor upon the Leslies of Glenkirk, and that I willna do."

"*Your distant cousins?* Now, would that be Alexander Leslie, the Earl of Leven, and his brother, David? Those Leslies who turned King Charles I over to the English when he fled home to Scotland a few years back? 'Twas shamefully done, and you know it! Why would you even listen to such men? Besides, Glenkirk's earldom is far older than Leven's. If you seek an excuse, my lord, plead your years. You are, after all, seventy-two."

"Alexander Leslie is but two years my junior. Besides, he willnae lead the armies of the Covenant. It will be his brother, the lieutenant general, and David Leslie isnae much younger."

"*You are mad!*" she accused him. "Do you think I have not heard the rumors that the fanatics who hold sway in this land, who call themselves the Kirk Party, are purging the army of those they deem ungodly? They interfere with military affairs and weaken our defenses, all the while claiming it is in the name of God. Had they any sense they would put the *ungodly* in the front lines and rid themselves of them for all time, but no! They will have a *godly* army go to war. What nonsense! You cannot, must not, be a part of this, Jemmie Leslie. You are a white-haired old man, and I do not want to lose you, damnit!"

"Do ye think my years hae rendered me incapable, madame?" he demanded, suddenly angry. "Ye didna think so last night in our bed!"

The duchess flushed then, but she pressed onward with her case.

"We have had no dealings with the royal Stuarts in years. We owe them nothing. This foolishness over religion is ridiculous. Bigotry only breeds more intolerance, my lord, and well you know it."

"The king is the king, and he hae asked for our help," James Leslie answered his wife. "Yer own father would hae nae put up with such disrespect, and disloyalty, from his subjects."

"My father," she replied evenly, "knew enough not to endanger himself or his family. May I remind you, my lord, that your first wife, her two sons, and her unborn child died at the hands of the Covenanters when they raided the convent she was visiting? They raped, tortured, murdered, and finally fired the buildings, killing all those innocent women and your children. And now, all these years later, you would pick up the Glenkirk banner and march out to war for them?"

"It is nae for them. It is for Charles Stuart. The king is my kinsman," the duke answered his wife implacably. "What of yer own Stuart son? Will he desert his cousin's cause? I dinna think so, madame. We must all rally about the king so those men who are attempting to institute this so-called *Commonwealth* will see that we dinna want it. These rude republicans must be taught to gie way to their betters, darling Jasmine. Besides, here at Glenkirk we hae accepted the Covenant for expediency's sake. Let me show the government that the Leslies of Glenkirk are loyal. Then they will continue to leave us in peace. They will probably decide I am ungodly and send me home anyways," he finished with a chuckle.

"Don't you darling Jasmine me, Jemmie Leslie," she told him. "The king is a royal Stuart, not a Leslie of Glenkirk. *You owe him naught!* If you go, however, you go alone. I will not let you take Patrick to a certain death! Thank God Adam and Duncan are in Ireland, safe from this madness!"

"Ireland is scarcely a place of great safety right now," the duke remarked dryly. "Besides, both Adam and Duncan sincerely accepted the Covenant, although I will wager they are yet loyal to the king."

Jasmine shook her head wearily. There would be no dissuading her husband from his foolish course, she suspected. "Do you not remember," she began in a final attempt to turn her husband's heart, "that every time the Leslies of Glenkirk have become involved with the royal Stuarts disaster ensues?" Her eyes went to the portrait above the fireplace. It was a very beautiful young girl with red-gold hair. "Janet Leslie was lost to her family when her father was in the service of a Stuart king. Her father returned home to mourn her his whole life."

"Yet that Patrick Leslie gained us the earldom in service to King James IV," the duke replied. "And when Janet Leslie returned home many years later, she obtained the Earldom of Sithean for her son."

"Her brother, his heir, and that same son along with many other members of the family, and the clan, died at Solway Moss in service of James V," Jasmine answered him promptly. "The family would have been lost had not that same Janet lived into old age to protect them all. And what of your own mother? Driven from Scotland by a Stuart king's lust! Never able to return, dying in Italy with little family about her. And have you forgotten the debacle the king made in our lives when, having betrothed me to you, he then promised me to his current favorite, Piers St. Denis? I did not enjoy having to hide my children from that madman and to keep on the run for months after Patrick was born. None of it would have happened but for a Stuart king's meddling!" she concluded heatedly.

"Yet when the king saw St. Denis's treachery, he rewarded me with a dukedom," James Leslie countered.

"As I remember," Jasmine retorted, "he said at the time it cost him naught as you already had wealth and lands. It was an empty title and nothing more. Do not make generosity out of nothing, my lord."

They had argued into the night, but Jasmine could make no headway with her stubborn husband. In the end she had reluctantly accepted his decision, but she could not reconcile herself to it. She knew he was going headlong into disaster. She was angry that she could not stop him short of killing him herself. The duke raised fifty horsemen and a hundred foot soldiers. His wife kissed him lovingly, knowing with a sure instinct that it was the last time she would ever see him alive again. Remembering it now on this chill October night, Jasmine wept.

What had happened next had been related to her by her own personal captain, Red Hugh, who had gone with the duke. James Leslie, first Duke and fifth Earl of Glenkirk, had marched south in the service of his God, his country, and his king. He was not, however, sent away as one of the ungodly, for little was known of him by the men who now controlled Scotland. They knew what they needed to know. He had accepted the Covenant when it had been first offered him. He was faithful to his wife, there was no evil gossip about him, and he had raised a family of God-fearing sons and daughters.

He then presented himself to his distant cousin, the lieutenant general of Scotland, Sir David Leslie.

"I dinna know if ye would come," David Leslie said. "Yer the oldest Leslie of us all now, and ye hae nae come out of yer hills for many years, my lord. Yer older than my brother, are ye nae?"

"Aye, I am. I will be seventy-three my next natal day," the duke answered him. "I didna bring my heir. He is nae wed yet, and my wife would nae hae it."

David Leslie nodded. "'Twas wise, and 'tis nae shame, my lord. Come, and meet the king. The parliament dinna want him here; but he came anyway, and the commons love him for it."

The Duke of Glenkirk bowed low to his king, but looking at him he did not see a Stuart. Charles's great height was his only Scots feature. His eyes were black as currants as his mother's were. His hair was black. His face was very saturnine and French. He looked like his grandfather, King Henry IV, not at all like a Stuart. There was nothing at all familiar about him, Red Hugh told his mistress. Visibly troubled, James Leslie had a second qualm of conscience. Why had he come? he now wondered. Was it out of sentiment? Duty? He had ignored the cardinal tenet in his family, not to become associated with the royal Stuarts. Jasmine had been right, he told Red Hugh, that every time the Leslies of Glenkirk became involved with the royal Stuarts, difficulties abounded. When the king spoke, however, even Red Hugh's fears vanished. He was mesmerizing.

"My lord duke," Charles II said in a deep, rich, and smooth voice, "your loyalty does not go unnoticed, though we have not met before today. You have not come to court in many years, but my cousin, the Duke of Lundy, speaks of you and his mother often and lovingly. Please convey my felicitations to your duchess."

"I am grieved for your father, Your Majesty," James Leslie answered. "I knew him from his birth and pray for his good soul."

"In the manner prescribed by the kirk, I hope," the king said, but there was just the faintest twitch of a smile on his lips.

"Indeed, Your Majesty," the Duke of Glenkirk replied, bowing, his green eyes twinkling with their shared conspiracy.

During the month of August the English sought in vain to breach the Scottish defenses. David Leslie made certain that his troops held the stronger defensive position, and the English were finally forced to retire to the coast to restock their dwindling provisions. Hunger and illness plagued them. Their numbers fell to eleven thousand while the Scots had grown in strength to twenty-three thousand fighting men. Cromwell retreated to Dunbar to find more supplies. The Scots followed, trapping them.

On the second of September the Scots departed their position of strength on the hills surrounding Dunbar, camping boldly before the English that same night on Dunbar Plain. Their plan was to attack their enemy on the morrow, but instead the English attacked earlier, and first. The Scots Covenanter army of Charles II was ensnared on impossible terrain and badly defeated. Fourteen thousand men were killed that day, among them James Leslie, the first Duke and fifth Earl of Glenkirk.

Jasmine Leslie was stony-faced on their return. She buried her beloved husband dry-eyed, though she personally saw his body was lovingly washed and dressed in his finest clothing. It was placed in its coffin, candles burning about it. The Reverend Mr. Edie came from the village kirk to preach the long and extemporaneous service. When he had gone away, Jasmine brought forth the Anglican priest who had once had a comfortable living at Glenkirk. Upon imposition of the National Covenant, he had been forcibly retired for his own safety and theirs. Father Kenneth now interred James Leslie in the family tomb with the beautiful words from the King James prayer book and the elegance of the Anglican sacrament.

Jasmine closed herself off from her family for the next few days. "I wish to mourn in private," she told her son, but she went one day to BrocCairn to see her seventy-seven-year-old mother.

"Now we are both widowed," said Velvet Gordon.

"I came to say farewell," Jasmine told her quietly. "I can no longer bear to remain at Glenkirk. Perhaps I will return one day, but I do not want to be there now."

"Will you desert your son?" her mother demanded. "Patrick needs you now. He must find a wife, marry her, and settle down. The line must be secured, Jasmine. It is your duty to remain by his side."

"Patrick is thirty-four, Mama, and quite capable of finding his own wife. He does not need me, or heed me, but I must escape Glenkirk lest I die of sorrow. In every room, and every corner, there are memories of my Jemmie, and I cannot bear it! *I have to go!* You have had your five sons and your many grandchildren about you. They helped you to overcome your sorrow when Alex died five years ago. I have only Patrick here. My other children are scattered to the four winds. Patrick does not need me. He needs a wife and heir, but he will not find them if I remain to keep him in comfort. I intend to take Adali, Rohana, and Toramalli with me."

"Patrick should have been married long since," the Dowager Countess of BrocCairn said irritably. "You and Jemmie spoilt him and allowed him to run wild. What will happen when you are gone, I do not know, but I do not think you should run off, Jasmine."

Jasmine bid her mother, her half-brothers, and their families farewell. Then she returned to Glenkirk, having firmly made her decision. She called the servants who had been with her her entire life and told them of her resolve to depart Glenkirk. "I want you with me."

"Where else would we go if not with you, my princess," her steward, Adali, said. He was very old now, but still very active and in complete charge of the household as he had been since coming to Glenkirk. "We have been yours since your birth. We will remain with you until the great God separates us from one another."

Jasmine blinked back the mist she felt rising in her eyes. It was the first true emotion she had shown since her husband had died. "Thank you, Adali," she said softly. Then she turned to her two maidservants, who were equally ancient. "What of you, my dearest Rohana and Toramalli?"

The twin sisters chorused as one, "We will go with you, lady. Like Adali, we are yours till death."

Rohana had remained a maiden all her long life, but her twin had married a Leslie man-at-arms. They had no children, but had raised a niece.

"Toramalli," her mistress asked, "are you certain? Fergus may not want to come with me. He has scarcely left Glenkirk lands all of his life. You must consult with him before you give me your answer."

"Fergus will come," Toramalli said firmly. "We have no bairns or grandchildren to leave behind, and Lily is already in England with Lady Autumn. We have just our little family made up of my sister and our good Adali. We have been together too long to be separated now."

"I am grateful to you all," the Dowager Duchess of Glenkirk said to her faithful retainers. "Tomorrow we will begin to pack."

She ascended to the top of the castle that afternoon, clambering up a ladder that led to the parapets of the west tower. Breathless, she reached the roof and climbed out onto it. Behind her the skies were darkening. In the east was the evening star, large, and bright, and cold. Before her the sun was setting in a glorious spectacle of blazing colors. Fiery red-orange was streaked with deep slashes of purple. Above it the sky was still a rich cerulean blue and filled with gold-edged pink clouds that floated all the way to the horizon.

Jasmine sighed as she looked out over the forested hills that surrounded Glenkirk. She had been truly happy these many, many years at Glenkirk. She had lived here longer than anyplace else in her whole life, *but she had lived here with Jemmie.* Suddenly, with his death, Glenkirk seemed foreign to her. She knew she had to get away. She didn't know if she would ever come back, whatever she might say to others. Glenkirk would never be the same for her without James Leslie. She sighed deeply again and turned back to the trapdoor leading into the castle. If she stayed here too long, poor Adali would attempt to climb up to find her. With a final glance at the majestic scene surrounding her, Jasmine began her descent. She wanted to talk to Patrick now.

She found her son in the Great Hall, seated by one of the two fireplaces. "I have come to a decision," she told him. "I am leaving Glenkirk as soon as my belongings can be packed." She sat herself in the high-backed chair opposite him.

Patrick Leslie looked up at his mother. He was a handsome man with his father's dark hair and green eyes. "Where will ye go?" he asked her. "I dinna want ye to go, Mother. I know I am a man long grown, but we hae just lost Father. I dinna want to lose ye, too." Reaching out, he took her hand in his and kissed it tenderly.

The Duchess of Glenkirk swallowed back the tears that threatened to break forth. She had to be strong now for her son, as well as herself. "The dower house at Cadby is mine," she said. "I intend making it my home. You must remember I am the Dowager Marchioness of Westleigh as well as the Dowager Duchess of Glenkirk. I like England, and God only knows the climate at Cadby is far more suitable for my old bones than here at Glenkirk."

"What of the civil war, Mother? I dinna want ye rushing headlong into danger just because of yer grief," he said.

"Your brother, the Marquis of Westleigh, has been wise enough to avoid all factions in this dispute. He is loyal to the government in power. Besides, like the rest of us, he has kept from court for many years now. As Glenkirk and Queen's Malvern are isolated to a degree, so is Cadby. Besides, who would disturb a widowed and grieving old woman?"

"Ye are nae old!" he exclaimed. Then he smiled. "Ye begin to sound like my great-grandmother, the formidable Madame Skye, Mother."

She laughed and gave his hand a little squeeze. "I am sixty," she said, "and certainly past my first bloom. Patrick, you are the only one of my children left in Scotland. Two of your brothers are Englishmen. The other two are lost to me in Ireland. India and Autumn are in England, but Fortune is in the Colonies. It is past time that you were settled. The responsibilities of Glenkirk have fallen, suddenly, but hardly unexpectedly, upon your broad shoulders. You should have married long ago. You need a wife, *and* you need an heir."

"I need my mother," he told her.

Frowning, she withdrew her hand from his. "No, you do not, Patrick. You are Glenkirk and must take your responsibilities seriously. Try to understand. I have to go to England for several reasons. Firstly, Scotland is too sad a place for me now. Secondly, I must be absolutely certain that Henry, and India's Deverall, and my grandsons do not become involved in this religious and political folly. Charlie, my not-so-royal Stuart, I know, debates the wisdom of taking up the banner for his kingly cousin. I must dissuade him if I can, which brings me to something I must say to you.

"You must *never, ever,* become involved with the royal Stuarts, Patrick. Even without meaning to be, they are dangerous to know. You do not need to hear the history of the Leslies and the royal Stuarts repeated, for you know it well. Your father did not heed my warning, or his family's own chronicle, and disaster has once again been the result of this association. We deliberately kept you from the court to protect you, and Glenkirk.

"You do not know the royal Stuarts. They are charming, but treacherous. Please God you shall never know them! Your first loyalty is to God. Your second is to this clan, to Glenkirk. Do only what is best for them and for your family. The Stuarts have great charisma, but they are heedless of everything and everyone but their own desires. Remain at Glenkirk where you will be safe."

"What will I do wi'out ye, Mother?" he asked forlornly. He was going to be alone. He had never been alone.

"You must find a wife, Patrick. Glenkirk needs a new, young duchess, not a grieving old dowager," Jasmine sighed. "Find a bride, making certain that you love her. Perhaps one day I shall return home to you."

"I am nae happy wi' yer decision, Mother," he attempted to argue with her.

"That is unfortunate," Jasmine said softly, "because, dear Patrick, my decision is not yours to make. I have always run my own life to suit me, as your father well knew. You cannot stop me, nor, I know, would you even attempt to do so. It is time, my son, that you accepted the less joyous responsibilities of your manhood. Why is it you have never found a woman you wanted enough to wed? God only knows there have been enough women in your life. Although I will not ask it, I suspect that more than one Leslie bastard of your loins resides hereabouts." She gave him a faint smile.

"It was nae important that I wed and hae a legitimate heir until now," he said frankly. "Women can be troublesome, Mother."

"Indeed, we can. Especially when our men are being such stubborn fools," she told him seriously. "The world would be a far safer and better place if men would listen more often to their women, than to the sound of their own loud, braying voices. If your father had listened to me instead of being so stubborn . . . but 'tis water beneath the bridge now, Patrick. *I am leaving Glenkirk.* Find a wife. Get on with your life, remembering to avoid the royal Stuarts and their ilk.

"Unless I am very mistaken, this son of the first Charles will not be able to stomach those narrow-minded and falsely pious fools who currently attempt to control him. I know the Stuart mind well. This laddie has come to Scotland to regain a foothold and obtain an army so he may go down into England to avenge his father, to take back what is now his very tottery throne. He will not succeed. At least not now. These fanatical bigots will hold tighter to what they have stolen, destroying, or attempting to destroy, all who stand in their path. Beware of them, too. Be wise and take no side in this. Support the legitimate government by not rebelling against it, but neither publicly cry for it. It is the best advice I can give you. You would be wise to heed me."

A week later the dowager duchess departed Glenkirk, accompanied by her faithful servants, including Fergus More-Leslie, who was a good man and went for not just her sake, but his wife's, too.

So it was that Patrick Leslie found himself alone and bereft of a family for the first time in his life. The parents he had loved were dead or gone; siblings all scattered to the four winds. There had never before been a time like this for him. He quickly learned that he didn't like it. Sprawled in a high-backed, tapestried chair before one of the two fireplaces in the Great Hall of Glenkirk, he contemplated what lay ahead.

The hall was silent but for the sharp crackle of the dancing flames, the occasional scratching of sleet on the windows. The candles flickered spookily as tendrils of the late autumn wind managed to slip through the thick stone walls. At his feet, two dogs, a rough-coated, dark blue-gray deerhound and a silky-coated, black-and-tan setter, lay comfortably sprawled, snoring. In Patrick Leslie's lap, however, there was ensconced a large, long-haired orange cat, a descendant of his mother's beloved Fou-Fou and some wandering orange tom. The cat, its eyes no more than golden slits, purred softly as the duke thoughtfully scratched it between its shoulder blades with the fingers of one hand. In his other hand was an ornate silver goblet which he now raised to his lips. The smoky whiskey slid down his throat like an unrolled length of burning silk, hitting the hollow pit of his belly like a hot stone, spreading its heat throughout his long, lean body.

His mother was right. He should take a wife and raise a family. It was what was expected of him. Glenkirk had always, in his memory, rung with the shouts of children and the laughter of family, not just Leslies, but Gordons of BrocCairn, too, his maternal grandmother's family. Since the wars had begun, however, most people kept to their homes, not just simply to protect themselves, but to protect their property as well from marauders. It was not as it had been in his grandparents' day when families and friends knew each other all their lives, visiting back and forth regularly. They had arranged betrothals for their children when they were barely out of the cradle, thereby allowing those children to grow up experiencing each other's company, so that by the time the marriages were celebrated, they were comfortable with each other. No, it was different now.

For one thing, many of Scotland's noble families had gone south into England when King James had succeeded the great Elizabeth. Many had remained, thereby gaining or increasing their fortunes. Others had returned to Scotland disappointed. It was true that after the death of his first wife and their sons, James Leslie had served King James down in England in matters relating to England's burgeoning trade. He hadn't wanted to be a Glenkirk with its unhappy memories.

To his family's distress, he had remained unmarried for a number of years until King James I had personally chosen Patrick's mother to be James Leslie's second wife. His wealthy widowed mother had resisted being told whom to wed. It had been several more years before James Leslie had been able to convince her that they had to obey their king. It had been a love match, however, and his parents had sired three sons and two daughters, of whom four had survived into adulthood. And they had done it at Glenkirk, rarely leaving Scotland once they had returned home all those years ago, but for summers in England at his great-grandmother's estate of Queen's Malvern, and once to France for the late king's wedding, and one year to Ireland.

It was his duty, Patrick Leslie realized, to take a wife. Duty was something that the Leslies of Glenkirk understood very well. *But duty to whom?* His mother believed that a man's duty lay first after God with his family, and she had been absolutely right, the second Duke of Glenkirk decided as his gaze swept his empty hall. *I will owe my loyalty only to this family*, Patrick vowed silently to himself. *I hae never met this king. I dinna care what happens to him.* The duke looked up at the portrait over the fireplace. It was of the first Earl of Glenkirk, his namesake. Turning, he looked across to the other fireplace and the portrait hanging above it of the first Earl of Glenkirk's daughter, Lady Janet Leslie. He knew their history well. It was Janet who had gained the Earldom of Sithean for her descendants.

It was Janet with her strong sense of duty who had saved both the Leslies of Glenkirk and the Leslies of Sithean after the Scots' terrible defeat at Solway Moss in 1542 against the English. All the adult men in the family had died in that battle, but Janet Leslie in her old age had gathered their sons and daughters about her, raising them until they were old enough to take their rightful places, teaching them how to rule their small domains, making the most advantageous marriages for them all.

Unfortunately, too many of the Leslie descendants had become careless with wealth and success. They had forgotten the cardinal tenet of the family and suffered by it. *But I will nae forget*, the second Duke and sixth Earl of Glenkirk promised himself. *I will nae forget. To hell wi' the royal Stuarts and all their ilk!*

Outside the hall, the wind rose, rattling the windowpanes noisily. The duke drained his goblet, his other hand stroking the great orange cat whose rumbling purrs were now quite audible. Suddenly the beastie opened its eyes and looked up at the duke. Patrick smiled down at the creature who now kneaded the duke's thighs so contentedly.

"Ye'll hae to stay wi'in the castle tonight, Sultan," he said, "but I'm certain ye'll find a nice mouse or rat to amuse ye, eh? As for me"—he arose from his chair, gently setting the cat upon the floor— "I'm off to bed, old friend. If the weather clears by morning, then I'll hunt early. We could use a deer or two in the larder for winter."

The cat shook itself, sat a moment to contemplate the two dogs, vigorously washed its paws, then stalked off with great dignity into the shadows. The duke chuckled. He knew it wasn't considered manly, but he actually liked cats better than dogs. Dogs, God love them, were loyal creatures to any who fed them. A cat, however, had to actually like you to be your friend. As he made his way up to his own chamber, the deerhound and the setter arose to follow him. The castle was so very quiet. One could actually sense there was hardly a soul in residence.

He had sent his servant to bed earlier, for he was quite capable of taking his own clothing off and washing himself. Pulling on his

nightshirt, Patrick Leslie lay down in the big bed in the ducal bedchamber. Until several months ago these had been his parents'
apartments, and this his parents' bed. His mother had insisted upon
his moving into it after his father had been buried. He was still not
quite comfortable in the great bed. Still, he was soon asleep this
night, and his sleep was dreamless.

Chapter

2

When Patrick Leslie awoke the following morning, he found the day very gray and overcast. There was neither rain nor snow, but the wind had disappeared as he discovered standing in the open window of his bedchamber. "Tell the stables I will hunt today," he told his manservant, Donal, who had been his boyhood companion and was distantly related to him. Donal's family, the More-Leslies, had served the lords of Glenkirk for many generations.

"Cook thought ye'd be out early, m'lord," Donal said. "There's a fine meal awaiting ye in the hall. Will ye be wanting to take food wi' ye? 'Tis deer we'll be after, and apt to be gone the day long."

"Aye, ye're right," the duke replied. "We'll want oatcakes, cheese, cider. Tell the men to provision themselves in the kitchens before we go, Donal."

"I'll see to it, m'lord," Donal said, handing Patrick his drawers and breeches first, then a white shirt with full sleeves and a drawstring neck. He held the leather jerkin with the horn buttons in reserve while Patrick pulled the breeches on over his heavy, dark knit stockings.

The breeches were wool, dyed a nut brown color. After tying his shirt at its neckline, Patrick sat down to draw on his brown leather boots, which covered the stockings and rose to his knees. Standing, he put on the jerkin and buttoned it up. Taking the fur-lined cloak and leather gloves Donal handed him, he exited his apartment, descending into the hall where his breakfast was awaiting him.

Solitude had not deterred his appetite. Patrick wolfed down the oat stirabout with honey, several poached eggs in a cream sauce flavored with Marsala wine, three slices of ham, and a whole cottage loaf he spread with both butter and bits of hard cheese. There was a steaming mug of tea, a brew from his mother's native land that he had grown to favor in the morning. It set better on an empty belly than ale or wine. His two youngest brothers had often teased him about his habit of wanting a hot drink in the morning, for they, like their father, had favored brown ale with their breakfast. He smiled at the memory, wondering how well Duncan and Adam fared in Ireland with its constant sectarian violence and warring. They, too, were yet bachelors. He sighed, resigned. It was certainly up to him to set them a good example.

Finishing his meal, he noted uncomfortably that his cook had quickly learned to do for just one. He found it disquieting. As he rose from the board, his eye swept the hall, seeing the thin layer of dust on the ancient oak furniture. The castle definitely needed a woman's touch. Without his mother's majordomo, Adali, the servants were grown slack. They had no one to guide them. He needed a wife, but where the hell was he to find one?

Glenkirk was well isolated deep in the hills of the eastern Highlands. His holdings stretched for miles in all directions, which was good, but it also meant that he had no near neighbors. The nearest, in fact, were his Leslie cousins at Sithean and his Gordon cousins at BrocCairn. He was on good terms with both families, which gave them all an added measure of safety. His paternal grandmother's family had sold their lands at Greyhaven to the lords of Glenkirk and gone down into England with King James I to seek their fortunes. Their old manor house, not in particularly good repair, had been demolished.

He rarely saw his cousins now, and he couldn't recall if there were any lasses of marriageable age among them. So how did one go about finding a wife these days? Perhaps he would go to the games this summer and pick out a pretty girl. He would ascertain before-hand, however, that she knew how to keep house. Almost any lass could be cajoled into being good bedsport, but if she couldn't rule his servants, or at least delegate authority among them, she would be of little use to him.

While isolation was preferable in these dangerous times, it did leave him with certain disadvantages. He considered again if there were any female unmarried cousins at Sithean or BrocCairn. Nay. His generation had been all males, and they were all, he recalled, wed. Where the devil had they found suitable women to marry? Mayhap he could get some of them to go with him to the games and advise him in this delicate matter. He suspected they would all find his plight amusing, but there was no help for it. He needed assistance. He shook his head wearily as he put on his cape.

In the courtyard of the castle, his stallion was waiting, saddled. The great gray beast pawed the ground eagerly, anxious to be off. Half a dozen of his clansmen were mounted and waiting to accompany him. The duke swung himself up into the saddle, pulling on his riding gloves, his cloak spreading across the gray's dappled flanks. They clattered across the heavy oaken drawbridge and into the forest, the dogs yapping with excitement. Because there was no wind, the mist still hung among the bens and in the trees.

Here and there a flash of tired color remained, startling amid the dark green of the fir trees. By mid-morning they had managed to flush a large stag from amid the wooded copse. The well-antlered creature fled through the trees, twisting and turning with a great skill born out of long experience, the baying dogs in quick pursuit. Leading them through the forest, the stag finally reached a small loch and, leaping into the water, swam away into the fog, success-fully evading its pursuers. The belling of the dogs could be clearly heard, echoing through the air ahead of their riders. Then came the whines of their defeat and frustration.

The hunting party arrived, their horses coming to a nervous stop, dancing about while the dogs milled about their legs whimpering. The stag's trail through the water could be faintly seen in the still loch, but the beast was quite lost to their sight.

"Damn!" the duke swore lightly. "Half a morning wasted finding it, and the other half wasted chasing it only to lose it." He dismounted. "We might as well stop here and eat before we go on, laddies. I'm quite ravenous, but we've only oatcakes and cheese."

"We've caught some rabbits along the way, m'lord," his head huntsman, Colin More-Leslie, Donal's brother, replied. "We'll skin 'em and cook 'em up now."

When they had eaten the more substantial meal, the duke looked about him. "Where are we?" he asked of no one in particular.

"'Tis Loch Brae, m'lord," Colin More-Leslie said. "Look over there. Ye can just make out the old castle on its island, in the mist. 'Tis deserted. The last Gordon heiress of Brae married a Brodie many years back. She went to live in Killiecairn wi' her husband."

"These lands abut Glenkirk lands," Patrick Leslie said thoughtfully. "If nae one lives here any longer, and the castle is a ruin, mayhap I should purchase it from the Brodie of Killiecairn. I dinna like the idea of untended lands next to mine."

"Hae ye ever met the Brodie of Killiecairn, m'lord?" Colin inquired. "He's a wicked old bugger, and verra canny. Still, he hae six sons and is always happy for good coin, or so I am told."

"Why hasna he given Brae to one of his lads?" the duke wondered.

"'Twas nae their mother who was the Gordon, m'lord. The Gordon was his second wife. He was much her senior. She died about ten years ago. Old Brodie must be well over eighty now. His lads are all older than ye are, m'lord, but his Gordon wife did birth him a daughter. I imagine Brae is her dower portion."

"The lass would be better off wi' a bag of gold coins than this old tumbled-down pile of stones and its lands," the duke observed. "Come on, then, and let's hae a wee look around at old Brae Castle."

They rode around the lake to where a rotting wooden bridge connected the small island to the mainland shore. Leaving the horses, for they deemed the bridge too chancy, Patrick Leslie and his men carefully picked their way across the rotting span to reach the island. It was a rocky place with few trees. The mists had finally lifted and were being blown away by a light breeze. A weak sun was trying to make itself seen through the leaden autumn skies.

The island was not particularly welcoming. There was no sandy shore of any kind, the shoreline being craggy. The land between the bridge and the castle was once an open field and had obviously been kept that way as a first line of defense. Now it was filled with trees. The castle itself was built of dark gray stone with several towers, both square and rounded. The peaked roof over the living quarters was of slate, and there were several chimneys. On closer inspection, the castle did not seem to be in irreclaimable condition. Still, Patrick Leslie thought, it was the lands belonging to Brae that interested him. Not this little castle.

"What the hell!" He jumped back suddenly as an arrow buried itself in the ground by his feet.

"Ye're trespassing, sir," a voice said. Then from the open door of the castle a young woman stepped forth, a longbow notched with another arrow at the ready in her hands.

"As are ye, I suspect," the duke said coldly, not in the least intimidated. His green-gold eyes swept over the girl. She was the tallest female he had ever seen, unsuitably garbed in boots and breeches. She wore a white shirt with a doeskin jerkin, a red, black, and yellow plaid slung carelessly over her shoulder, and a small, blue velvet cap upon her head with an eagle's feather jutting jauntily from it. But it was her hair that caused him and his men to stare. It was *red*. But a red such as he had never seen but once. Bright red-gold that tumbled about her shoulders and down her back in a great mass of curls. "Who are ye?" he finally asked her.

"Ye first, sir," she pertly answered him.

"Patrick Leslie, Duke of Glenkirk," he said, wondering as he spoke if her hair was soft. He made her a small bow.

"Flanna Brodie, heiress of Brae," she responded. She did not curtsy, but rather looked him over quite boldly. "What are ye doing on my lands, my lord? Ye hae nae the right to be here."

"*And ye do?*" She was an impertinent wench, he thought.

"These are my lands, my lord. I hae told ye that," Flanna Brodie answered him implacably.

"I want to buy them," he told her.

"Brae is nae for sale," she said quietly.

"Yer lands abut mine, lady. They are, if I am nae mistaken, yer dowry. Unless ye wed a landless man, which I am certain yer father and brothers would nae allow, Brae will be as useless to yer husband as it was to yer da. Gold, however, makes ye a far more desirable bride. Name yer price, and I will nae niggle wi' ye over it," the duke told her.

She stood, legs apart, glaring furiously at him. "I hae told ye, my lord, that Brae is nae for sale! I dinna intend to marry at all. I plan to make my home here. Now, take yer men and get off my lands! Ye are nae welcome here!"

Patrick Leslie stepped toward Flanna Brodie, who moving back a pace sent a second arrow into the ground at his feet then reached back into her quiver for a third. Before she could rearm herself, however, he leapt forward, pulling the bow from her hands and tossing it aside. Then, roughly shoving the girl beneath his arm, he smacked her bottom hard several times. "Ye hae bad manners, wench!" he growled at her. "I am surprised yer father hae nae taught ye better."

The duke's men howled with laughter as, outraged, Flanna squirmed from his grip. "Ye arrogant bastard," she roared, then hit him a blow that actually staggered him. "How dare ye lay yer filthy hands on me?" She hit him an even harder blow, reaching for her dirk as she took up a defensive position.

The laughter ceased. The duke's men stared, surprised, quite uncertain what to do. Then they decided to do nothing. The duke could defend himself.

"Why ye little she-devil!" he yelped, grabbing her wrists in a single hand, while disarming her with the other. Then he held her fast.

Flanna struggled wildly. "Ye hit me first," she yelled.

"Ye shot an arrow at me, nae once, but twice," he countered.

"Ye're trespassing, and ye won't go away!" Flanna shouted.

"*Enough!*" the duke said, and picking the girl up threw her over his shoulder. "I'm taking ye home to yer sire, wench, and I'll hae nae more nonsense from ye. If Brae be sold, 'tis his decision, nae yers. I'm willing to wager a gold piece he'll sell."

"Put me down at once, ye bastard!" She squirmed and kicked, trying to escape him, but from her very awkward position it was just about impossible. She was finally forced to remain quiet as he picked his way back across the rotting bridge. If she tumbled them into the loch, this man was apt to drown them both. His men were snickering behind him and in her clear view.

"Colly, bind her hands and her ankles," the duke ordered his man when they had reached the horses. "I'll carry her over my saddle before me as we go. How far is Killiecairn?"

" 'Tis about ten miles, my lord. We hae to go through Hay Glen; then around the other side of the ben is Brodie land. Ye surely dinna mean to carry the lassie head down the whole way? Let her ride before ye, my lord. I'll tie her ankles together beneath the horse so she canna make trouble. I dinna think old Brodie would look kindly on yer mistreating his lass."

The duke nodded, but added, "Then, he should teach the wench better manners, Colly. I hae never known such a wild wench."

Flanna's wrists were bound. She was put upon the duke's stallion. "They call her Flaming Flanna, my lord," Colin More-Leslie said as he bent to tie the girl's ankles underneath his master's horse, avoiding the kick she aimed at him.

Patrick Leslie swung himself into the saddle, the girl before him. His arms went about her as he gathered his reins into his hands. She attempted to avoid the contact only to back into his chest. She then sat very still, barely breathing as he kicked his stallion into a quick walk, the Glenkirk men and their dogs following behind.

Well, here was a fine bungle she had gotten herself into, Flanna thought, very irritated with herself. When was she going to learn to curb that damned temper of hers? All this bloody duke had to do was dangle a fat purse before her father and her half brothers. Then Brae would no longer be hers. She would have nothing, for the old man was as tight-fisted as they came. How often had she said she didn't want a husband? Now they would take her at her word and end up being richer for it. She, however, would probably end up with nothing. When the old devil finally died she would be forced to rely on her eldest brother, Aulay, for her very subsistence. Worse, there was nothing she could do about it. Even if she agreed to sell the land, her father would have to approve the sale, and he would still keep the gold.

"Why the hell do ye want my lands?" she suddenly burst out.

"I told ye," he replied. "They abut mine."

"Ye never wanted them before," Flanna noted.

"Glenkirk wasna mine until my father was killed at Dunbar," Patrick told her. "Wi' war in England, and all the trouble about religion here in Scotland, in England, and in Ireland, I want to make certain Glenkirk is kept safe from the madness of others," he explained. "All I want is to be left alone, lady. The best way I can think of to do that is to own as much land as I can acquire."

"I won't bother ye living at Brae," Flanna said hopefully. "All I ever wanted was to be left alone and in peace, too."

"But who knows what yer husband will want," the duke remarked.

"I hae nae husband," Flanna told him. "I hae nae betrothed. I want neither, my lord. I dinna find men particularly congenial, and I dinna like being ordered about by them. My father was past sixty when I was born. My mother died when I was ten. I have six older half brothers, all sons of my sire's first wife. They are practically old men themselves, being fifty-six to forty-eight years of age. Most of my nieces and nephews are older than I am. They all live at Killiecairn. A huge household of loud, boasting, noisy men, bullying and ordering their womenfolk about. I dinna like it. As I hae my own lands I decided to go and live at Brae."

"By yerself?" he asked her. "And yer father agreed?"

"I hae a maidservant, Aggie. She's actually my youngest brother's bastard daughter," Flanna said. "I took her into my service when she was scarcely more than a child, for my brother's wife was cruel to her. She was always looking for an excuse to beat Aggie."

"Two lasses in an isolated and tumbling-down castle?" Patrick Leslie's voice was scornful. "And yer father agreed?" he repeated.

Flanna swallowed back her sharp retort. She needed this man's good will if she was to deter him from his planned purpose to purchase Brae and thereby disenfranchise her. "I hae Angus," she said slowly. "He was my mother's servant. When Mama died he became mine. He stands almost seven feet tall and is a most fearsome warrior."

Patrick almost laughed aloud. Two lassies and a daft, old soldier-at-arms. This Angus would have to be daft to agree to Flanna's plan. He restrained his mirth. He was doing Flanna Brodie a kindness in buying Brae. It was nonsense, of course, her wish not to marry. His gold would gain her a very respectable husband. He would even be a little more generous than he had anticipated, for in a strange way he admired her spirit. Flaming Flanna, Colly had said they called her. She was certainly well named.

"Dinna fret, lass," he told her. "It will all turn out for the best, I promise ye."

God's nightshirt! Flanna swore silently. Did this damned duke have a hearing deficiency, or was he just plain stupid? Had he not heard her or understood what she had been saying to him. "Please, my lord," she said, swallowing her pride for the moment, "dinna offer to buy Brae. 'Tis all I hae. My da will keep yer gold. I shall nae see a bit of it."

"Nonsense, lassie," he attempted to soothe her. "Ye're yer father's only daughter. He'll want to do well by ye."

"Damnit!" Flanna burst out. "Do ye nae understand, my lord? Lachlann Brodie is a mean-spirited old man! He'll nae spend a groat unless forced to do so. Why do ye think my brothers and their families are all forced to live at Killiecairn? He would gie my brothers nothing. So the wives they finally managed to marry had little themselves. Nae one of them hae a bit of land to call her own that her husband might hae for himself. And they hate the old man for it, although none is bold enough to say so aloud. Offer to buy Brae, and he'll take yer gold, leaving me as penniless as my brothers. And when he is dead and gone, the heir, my eldest brother, Aulay, will be just like him. I will hae nothing!"

Her words had the ring of truth to them, but Patrick Leslie could not believe any man would deprive his only daughter of what was rightfully hers. Especially such a pretty wench, for she was, indeed, pretty. The lass was exaggerating because she didn't want her mother's ancestral lands sold off. He could understand, but he nonetheless meant to have Brae. The Duke of Glenkirk said nothing more as they rode along. Flanna Brodie was silent, too, her body slumped slightly as if in defeat. It was mid-afternoon when they reached the glen of Killiecairn where Lachlann Brodie's large stone house stood dark against the gray sky. As they drew abreast of the front entrance, a woman emerged shouting.

"There ye are, ye wicked little devil! Where hae ye been? Who are these men? Get off that horse at once! Yer sire has been readying himself all day to gie ye the beating ye deserve!" The woman's face was red with her anger.

"This is my eldest brother's wife, Una Brodie, my lord," Flanna said dryly. "Una, this is the Duke of Glenkirk. I caught him trespassing at Brae, and he hae captured me." Mockingly she held up her bound hands. "I am afraid I canna dismount until my ankles are unbound."

At the sight of her sister-in-law's plight, Una Brodie began to shriek so loudly that her extended family came running from all directions, surrounding the riders, open-mouthed.

The duke was certain he heard Flanna Brodie chuckle wickedly, but on reflection decided he had imagined it. "There is nae need to shout, madame," he told Una Brodie. "If I meant the Brodies of Killiecairn any harm, I should hae scarce come wi' just six men at my back." He untied Flanna's wrists, instructing Colin More-Leslie to undo the girl's leg shackles at the same time. "Ye may get down," he murmured to her.

"Oh, no, my lord," she said, almost gaily, obviously enjoying herself mightily. "The view from up here is far better than I should get on the ground. Besides, I hae never been on such a fine beast as this one is."

"We shall both get down," he said through gritted teeth, dismounting first, then lifting the girl to the ground after him.

"What the hell is going on here?" a man, fully as tall as the duke, said as he pushed his way forward. "Flanna? Where hae ye been?

The old man hae been frantic all day wi'out ye." His glance met the duke's green gaze. "And, who are ye, sir?"

"Patrick Leslie, Duke of Glenkirk," was the reply. "I hae business wi' yer sire, man." He held out his hand.

It was gripped in return. "Aulay Brodie, my lord. If ye will come wi' me. Ye and yer men are welcome in our hall. Una! Cease yer caterwauling, woman! 'Tis nae a raid. 'Tis a visit, damnit! We get few enough. Dinna drive our visitors away before we can offer them our hospitality."

The duke followed Aulay Brodie into his house, Flanna hurrying ahead of them, the others following behind. The little hall was soon full with all the family and servants. There was but one smoky fireplace at the far end of the room, and seated in a high-backed, blackened oak chair next to it was a white-haired old man. He had been a large man once, but now he was gnarled and bent, his most prominent feature being his large, hooked nose. His eyes, however, were sharp, watching carefully as his visitor approached him in the company of his son.

"This is Patrick Leslie, the Duke of Glenkirk, Da," Aulay Brodie said.

Patrick bowed politely to the old man. "Sir."

Lachlann Brodie waved the younger man to a seat opposite him. "Bring whiskey," he said curtly. His command was quickly obeyed. His gaze swung about to his only daughter. "Where were ye?" he demanded.

"At Brae," she said. "I intend taking Aggie and Angus so I may live there."

"Huumph!" her father grunted, and then his eyes moved back to Patrick Leslie. "They say ye brought my lass home, bound hand and foot upon yer saddle. Why?"

"She attacked me," the duke replied quietly. "Nae one arrow, but two, shot at my feet, nae to mention the dirk she waved about. I considered it a hostile action."

"She could hae killed ye if she so desired," Lachlann Brodie replied, chuckling. "When she was sixteen I saw her bring down a full-grown stag with one of those arrows. Straight through the beastie's heart she shot it. She could hae found her own way back to Killiecairn."

"I want to buy Brae," Patrick Leslie said bluntly.

"Why?" The old man's eyes were suddenly sparkling with interest.

"It abuts my lands. I want as much land between me and my neighbors as I can get," the duke answered him. "These are dangerous times between the king's war down in England and the religious fanatics all about us."

"Aye," Lachlann Brodie agreed.

"Ye canna sell Brae, Da," Flanna interrupted him. "*'Tis mine.* My dowry. 'Tis all I hae!"

"I'll gie ye a fair price for it," the duke continued as if Flanna had not even spoken. "A dower of gold is more valuable to a lass than Brae and its forested lands. They are all surrounded by Glenkirk lands, useless to anyone else but me."

"How much?" Lachlann Brodie asked.

"Two hundred and fifty gold crowns," came the answer.

The old man shook his head in the negative. "'Tis nae enough."

"Five hundred, then," the duke replied.

There was an audible hiss of breath in the hall at the very substantial offer.

"'Tis nae gold I'm wanting for Brae, my lord," Lachlann Brodie finally said. "There isna enough gold in the world for ye to buy Brae."

"Then, what do ye want, sir?" the duke inquired. "If it is in my power to gie it to ye, I will, for I mean to hae Brae."

"If ye want Brae, my lord, then ye must take its heiress as well," Lachlann Brodie said. "Marry Flanna, and Brae is yers."

"Damn me!" Aulay Brodie said aloud, as surprised as the rest of the audience in the hall. Gold was his father's God, yet here was the old man actually attempting to do well by his youngest child.

"I dinna want to marry anyone, least of all *him!*" Flanna exploded.

"Shut yer mouth, lass," her father said calmly. "I'm a hard man, and 'tis true I'm tight wi' a merk, but I loved yer mam. She was the joy of my old age. I promised her I'd see ye wed well, and the truth is, lass, ye're nae likely to hae a better chance ever again." He turned back to the duke. *"Well, my lord, how badly do ye want Brae?* She's nae a bad-looking wench, although a trifle big boned. She gets that, I fear, from me and nae her mother. She's young enough to be a good breeder, although at twenty-two she's almost past her prime. She's got a fierce temper, I'll nae lie to ye, but ye could nae hae a better wench at yer side in a fight. She's a virgin, I'll guarantee ye, for none can get near her, so ye may be certain yer heir is yer own blood. If ye want Brae, ye must take my daughter to be yer wife. Ye dinna hae a wife, do ye?"

He thought about lying to the old man, but it would be a lie easily discovered. "Nay, I hae nae wife," he answered.

"I will nae marry him!" Flanna shouted, but she was ignored. This business was between her father and the duke, it would seem.

"Hush, ye stupid little ninny," Una Brodie hissed at her. "Yer da is going to make ye a duchess if ye'll keep quiet."

"I'll nae have him!" Flanna attempted to make her wishes known once again.

Patrick Leslie looked at the girl. He needed a wife. The truth was he didn't care if he loved her or not. He needed a wife who could give him heirs, and Flanna looked strong enough. Love was an unpleasant complication, he had already decided. The girl was pretty enough. The dowry was something he badly wanted. He didn't need gold, for he was a wealthy man. His family wanted him wed. Who else was there? True, the Brodies were hardly equal to the Leslies of Glenkirk. They were rough and rude Highlanders, but it didn't matter. It was unlikely he would see them often once Flanna was at Glenkirk. Unless, of course, he needed their aid in a fight. Looking about at the hard-eyed Brodie men, he decided they would be an asset in a battle. In that moment he realized he had made his decision. "I'll take her," he said.

"Nay!" Flanna stamped her foot and looked about the hall for some small support. There was none.

"My lord, this decision is ill-advised," Colin More-Leslie murmured to his master. "Surely there is another way. Would yer father, may God assoil his good soul, approve? And what of yer princess mother?"

"I need a wife," the duke said implacably, "and I want Brae. It seems the perfect solution to me, Colly."

"Go down to the village and fetch the minister from the kirk," Lachlann Brodie commanded his eldest son.

"Ye want me to wed her here and now?" Patrick Leslie was very much taken aback, but then it didn't really matter, did it?

"Ye'll wed her, and ye'll bed her, my lord, so my sons and I may be certain ye canna repudiate her on the basis of nonconsummation, while keeping Brae for yerself. I dinna trust nae man."

"He's a canny old devil," Colin More-Leslie said softly.

"As ye will, Lachlann Brodie," the duke said. "Send Aulay for the minister. 'Tis as good a time as any for a wedding."

"And ye'll remain the night," came the veiled order.

"Aye, and breach the lass so all may see her innocence on the sheets come the morrow before I take her back to Glenkirk. *The deeds to Brae safely in my possession then, eh?"*

Lachlann Brodie nodded. "Agreed," he said, spitting in his palm and holding it out to the duke.

Patrick Leslie spit in his own palm, and then the two men shook hands. "Agreed," he responded.

"Nay," Flanna Brodie said softly, but no one was listening to her. She might as well have protested to the wind.

"Five hundred gold crowns lost, and ye're to be a duchess," her sister-in-law Ailis murmured enviously. "What luck!"

"Luck?" Flanna said bitterly. "I see nae luck. At least ye love my brother Simon, and he cares for ye. All this Leslie of Glenkirk wants of me is Brae. Whether he buys it, or weds it, it makes nae difference to him at all. What the hell do I know about being a duchess? I'll shame myself and my husband wi' my ignorance. There is nae luck here."

"Ye can surely learn how to be a duchess," Ailis said. "Besides, I doubt ye'll ever go to court. The English, I am told, hae already killed one royal Stuart. Ye know how to manage a household, for we've all struggled to teach ye the rudiments of housekeeping.

Despite yer stubbornness ye're quite clever. Whatever else there is, ye'll learn."

"Take my daughter to her chamber and see that she's properly prepared for her wedding," Lachlann Brodie ordered the women. Immediately her brothers' wives and their daughters gathered around Flanna and led her off. Her maidservant, Aggie, pressed near Flanna.

"Ye'll take me wi' ye, mistress, won't ye?" she said nervously.

"Aye, ye and Angus will come to Glenkirk wi' me," Flanna replied. She turned suddenly, speaking directly to the duke. "I may have Aggie and Angus, may I nae? I'll nae go wi'out them."

"Of course yer servants may come wi' ye," he assured her. She had given him a very determined look when she importuned him, although the truth was she had no authority in the matter. Still, it was little enough, and all the brides who came to Glenkirk had come with their own personal servants.

Flanna felt numb. She stood, unprotesting, as her sisters-in-law pulled her clothing off her and hustled her into a hot tub. "We'd best start wi' my hair," she said low to Aggie, who nodded in agreement.

"We'll pack yer things for ye," Una said, "though I doubt much of it will be good enough for Glenkirk Castle. Still, ye know how to sew. Ye and Aggie can make some pretty new gowns, I'm sure. The duke will nae be tight wi' a bride. Ask right away before he grows bored wi' ye, Flanna. I'm certain he'll gie ye the key to the storerooms where ye're certain to find silks and other fine stuffs."

"I want nothing from him," Flanna said coldly. "He will hae the only thing I ever truly wanted, and that is Brae."

"Dinna be a fool," Una said sharply.

"The old man should hae taken the five hundred crowns," Ailis said. "Imagine Flaming Flanna a duchess," she tittered.

"Shut yer mouth, ye mean shrew," Una snapped. "If old Lachlann had taken the gold, do ye think ye or any of us would hae seen any of it, Ailis? I'll remind ye that my Aulay is the old man's heir. Yer Simon is but the next to youngest son. The land belonged to Flanna, through her mam. The luck is hers, nae ours, although

I'm as surprised as any of ye that Lachlann Brodie passed up five hundred pieces of gold. Still, he loved Meg Gordon dearly, and she loved him despite the disparity in their ages."

The chamber grew quiet then. Una was the matriarch of the family. Though a hard woman with little patience for fools and a quick temper, she had a good heart. There was none, even her own father-in-law, who could say she was needlessly cruel, but she ruled the women of Lachlann Brodie's house with an iron hand, demanding instant obedience and chaste behavior. She swiftly punished any who flaunted her authority, even Flanna, for whom she had a small soft spot.

Una Brodie had lost her only daughter in the same winter epidemic that had killed Flanna's mother. While she had four sons, her daughter had been the child of her heart. She had been ill herself, and it was Meg Gordon who had nursed both her and her child, thereby contracting the contagion that killed her. Flanna, though nothing like Una's Mary, was a daughter without a mother; and Una, a mother without a daughter. Though nothing was ever said, she took the child over, raising her as best she could, for Flanna had never been easy, even from her birth, and Meg had spoiled her.

Properly scrubbed, Flanna stepped naked from the oaken tub to be dried. Her thick hair was toweled and then brushed by the fire until it was soft and shining. A snow-white linen shift was brought, and the bride dressed in it. A small wreath of heather and Michaelmas daisies was fashioned by her nieces for her head. It was all she would wear to her wedding, and she would be barefooted, her hair loose to signify her virgin state.

"Ye may be tall like yer da and yer brothers, and ye may hae their red hair," Una observed, "but ye hae yer mother's face, lassie. Meg was a beautiful woman, she was. Ye hae clear skin, fine eyes, and a mouth fashioned for kissing. The duke will nae be unhappy wi' ye.

"Now, listen to me, Flanna. When the time comes for yer husband to bed ye, lie quietly and let him do all the work. It will hurt ye a bit when he goes into ye the first time, but 'tis a momentary discomfort. Afterward, if he's good at what he does, ye may even gain some pleasure from it, but even if ye dinna, tell him ye did. All men like to believe they are peerless lovers, lassie. There's nae harm in letting them think they are."

"Are my brothers good lovers?" Flanna boldly asked her six sisters-in-law. Her gaze swept them. Then she laughed wickedly at their discomfort. Una looked very displeased with her. Flanna knew she was itching to smack her, but would not allow the others to believe she was annoyed. Ailis, Peggie, Eileen, Mona, and Sorcha were all red-faced.

"Behave yerself, ye little bitch," Una snapped. "Because ye're to be a duchess doesna mean ye can be rude to us. Aulay hae never disappointed me in our bedsport, and I'm certain his brothers hae done well by their wives," she defended the others. "Now, lassie, mind yer mouth, and down on yer knees, all of ye. We will pray for Flanna's happiness, and that she gies her husband a fine son in nine months' time."

"Gie over, Una," Flanna said pertly. "I am nae used to the idea of a husband yet, and ye're already speaking of bairns."

"A male heir will solidify yer position, lassie," her sister-in-law said sagely. "If ye're wise, Flanna Brodie, ye'll gie the duke a bairn as quickly as possible."

Chapter

3

Una sent one of the younger women back into the hall to see if the minister had arrived from the village. He had. So without further ado Flanna was led down the stairs and brought forward before the Reverend Master Forbes, the local Presbyterian cleric. Patrick Leslie came and stood beside her. He was slightly surprised by her dress until he remembered it was an old country custom for a bride to come to her husband barefooted and in her shift. It signified not just innocence, but obedience. He almost laughed, suspecting Flanna's lack of that virtue, but as long as she kept his house well, he didn't care.

The minister cleared his throat and then performed the simple ceremony with dispatch. Patrick Leslie's voice was clear and strong as he agreed to take Flanna Brodie for his wife. When Master Forbes, however, asked Flanna if she would have the duke for her husband to love, respect, honor, and obey, Flanna hesitated, then said, "I dinna love him, for I dinna know him. He must earn my respect. I will honor him, however, as my lord, but I'll nae stand before God and promise to obey him, for I canna be certain that I will."

The poor startled minister was not certain what to do in the face of the girl's blunt declaration. Lachlann Brodie looked as if he were going to explode with rage. His face was purple with his anger.

"I accept the lady's terms," Patrick Leslie said suddenly, breaking the deadlock. "'Tis only fair, considering that we hae just met a few hours ago. I appreciate both her candor and her honesty. It speaks well of her character."

"Verra well, then," Reverend Forbes said quickly, relief pouring through his very soul. "Then I pronounce that this couple are now husband and wife."

"If ye were still my responsibility, lass, I'd take a stick to ye," her father said, "and I advise yer husband to do so."

For once Flanna held her peace, not answering her father back.

"The meal is ready," Una announced, and they all sat down to eat.

The duke was surprised to see what a truly fine table his new father-in-law kept. Given Lachlann Brodie's reputation for parsimony, he would not have expected it. There was fish, freshly caught, both trout and salmon on beds of wild watercress. A half side of beef, roasted and dripping its juices; a large platter of ducks, their skins crisp, and stuffed with bread and apples; a rabbit stew in a fragrant brown gravy with carrots and leeks; fresh bread, butter, and a small wheel of cheese; and the best October ale Patrick Leslie had ever tasted. There was no wine, but there was fresh-pressed cider for those with a more delicate palate.

Flanna, whose appetite was usually quite good, found herself picking at her food. It was quickly dawning upon her that she would shortly be forced to get into bed with this dark stranger. She knew virtually nothing about what really transpired between men and women. She had never been particularly interested. As she had no female friends of her own age with whom to gossip, her scant knowledge had come from Una, who was quite loath to discuss such matters with a maiden. Una's few words before they had come into the hall had only confused Flanna further. *I shall look like a damned fool,* she thought to herself, suddenly just a little frightened.

Patrick Leslie watched his new wife surreptitiously and saw she was hardly eating. *Just how much of a virgin was she?* he wondered. The old man said she was untouched, but one could never tell with these Highland lasses. And was the reason for the hasty marriage as simple as it appeared? Or was the lass with another man's child?

Looking at Flanna, he discarded that suspicion. There had been nothing to indicate the lass was loose in her previous behavior. The canny old Brodie simply had seen a chance to wed his only daughter to a title, and he had taken it. But, the duke decided, he would, indeed, bed his bride tonight in her father's house. If she proved not to be a virgin, he would repudiate the marriage immediately. Brae, however, would still be his, a forfeit to the fraud.

The meal was finally cleared away. A piper came into the hall to play. The Brodie men arose by ones and twos to dance before the board. The air was beginning to become slightly blue with the smoke from the fireplace which was drawing badly. Patrick realized he had said nothing to Flanna since they had taken their vows before the minister. Neither, however, had she spoken to him. Holding out his hand to her, he arose from the table, drawing her up with him.

"Come, madame, and let us dance to celebrate our union." He led her forth into the middle of the floor, and the piper began to play the stately wedding dance. He was surprised to find she was extremely graceful despite her height. Holding up the skirt of her simple shift, she dipped and trod with a sure step. He twirled her, drawing her into the curve of his arm, and leaning back her head, she looked up at him for a brief moment. *Her eyes are silver gray.* He had not known it until now. He offered her a small smile of approval at her skill. "Ye dance well, madame," he said softly to her.

"Thank ye, my lord," she replied low.

"They make a handsome pair," Una Brodie whispered to her husband. "Yer da had the devil's own luck here today. I'd nae thought we would get her married off at all, let alone married off so well, *and* to the Duke of Glenkirk."

"Pray he gets her with bairn quickly and she delivers a healthy lad," Aulay Brodie answered his wife. "His family will nae be pleased when they learn of this marriage. I'm certain they would hae sought a far better match for their duke than a Brodie of Killiecairn. Da had the luck here today, Una, ye're right, but pray Flanna has that same luck in the months to come. I canna help but feel sad for my little sister. The duke doesna know her and wants only her dowry of Brae. I hope he will come to care for her, or at least be kind to her."

"Dinna fret about Flanna," Una said to her husband. "She's a strong lass. If she wants her duke to love her, he'll come to love her. 'Tis poor Patrick Leslie I feel sorry for, Aulay. He hae nae idea of how fierce a lass Flanna can be."

Aulay Brodie chuckled. "He'll learn soon enough, wife."

Lachlann Brodie leaned over and said to his daughter, "'Tis time for ye to leave the hall, lassie. We'll send yer husband to ye shortly. God bless ye, Flanna. Yer mother would be proud this day."

She arose and, bending down, kissed his worn cheek. "I know ye did it because ye thought it best for me, Da. Perhaps one day I'll thank ye. *Or curse ye.* Only time will tell. I want none of the women wi' me. I am capable of doing this by myself."

He nodded, and quietly bid the females in his household to remain seated as his daughter left the hall.

Flanna hurried upstairs to her small bedchamber. She was surprised to find two small trunks already out in the hallway packed with her belongings. Entering her room, she saw that almost all of her possessions were gone. The bed, which was just barely big enough for two people, was made up with fresh linens. On the table there was a copper ewer and, next to it, a pitcher of lukewarm water. A clean cloth lay next to the ewer. Flanna poured a small dollop of water into the ewer and washed her face and hands. Then she scrubbed her teeth with the cloth, finally emptying the basin out the small single window. Hearing footsteps in the hall outside her door, she turned quickly. The door opened, and the duke stepped into the chamber. Flanna's heart began to beat violently.

He closed the door behind him, turning to bar it. "Dinna look so frightened," he said. "I dinna intend harming ye, madame. Ye hae been strangely silent this evening. Ye were nae so silent earlier today." He sat down on the edge of the bed. "Help me off wi' my boots, madame," he said.

"What would ye hae me say, my lord?" she asked him, turning her back on him, taking a boot between her legs with her hands and drawing it off. She then swiftly removed the other boot and turned about to face him once again. "I did nae seek this union between our families. The truth is neither did ye. It was Brae ye wanted, and now ye hae it. Ye dinna want me."

"I also needed a wife," he told her honestly. He unbuttoned his jerkin and, removing it, handed it to her.

Flanna took the garment and laid it carefully on the room's single chair. "But had the opportunity nae presented itself," she replied, "ye would nae hae sought out a Brodie of Killiecairn, would ye?"

"I dinna know who I would hae sought out," he answered her candidly. "Before my mother went south, she advised me to take a wife, but the truth is I dinna know any respectable young women in the vicinity. I dinna expect to inherit so soon, for my father was in good health; but then I did inherit, and it became necessary that I find a wife. Ye'll do as well as any other, lass. As ye said, I wanted Brae."

"Do ye hae a mistress, then?" Flanna demanded to know.

Unexpectedly he grinned at her. "Would ye be jealous if I did?" he teased.

"Dinna flatter yerself, my lord," she said sharply. "I simply wish to know what to expect when I get to Glenkirk."

"I enjoy the lasses," he admitted, "and I hae three acknowledged bastards, two lads and a wee lass; but their mams were momentary diversions for me. Still, I do acknowledge my bairns and see them free of any want. I hae never kept a mistress at Glenkirk, however, or anywhere else, madame."

Flanna nodded. "What does a duchess do? I am nae well educated. I know how to manage a household. I can sign my name; but I am unschooled in refinements, and I canna speak in any foreign tongue. I dinna want to shame ye, my lord."

Patrick Leslie was strangely touched by Flanna's frankness. She was an uncomplicated and honest girl. Perhaps this hasty match would not prove to his disadvantage after all. He stood and began to unbutton his breeches. "Glenkirk is larger than yer father's house, of course," he began. "Since my mother's departure, there hae been no woman to manage the castle. Her personal servants, who had come wi' her when she married my father, ran the household.

Glenkirk badly needs a woman's touch, madame. Yer skills will be appreciated. Ye may choose whomever ye wish to serve ye from among our people, and ye'll hae yer Aggie and yer Angus wi' ye." He stepped out of the dark woolen breeches, then his linen drawers, again handing them to her.

Suddenly silent again, Flanna took the proffered garments, her eyes casting a quick look at his long legs that stuck out from beneath his almost knee-length shirt. The rounded tops of his knees were just visible from above his stockings. He bent to quickly roll them off, kicking them aside. Then he turned to face her once again. "Well, madame, we are ready to proceed now, I believe."

Flanna swallowed hard. "I certainly dinna know what to do," she said.

"Come here to me," he gently ordered her.

She moved the few steps to stand before him.

"Tell me exactly what you know, or have heard, about a husband and wife's private moments," he said quietly.

"Nothing, really," she admitted. "Before I came into the hall for our wedding vows, my sister-in-law told me to lay quiet when ye went into me, and if ye were skillful, I might gain some pleasure from ye; but, my lord, I havena the faintest idea what Una meant! I am sorry to be so ignorant, or to displease ye, but there it is."

Now it was Patrick Leslie's turn to swallow hard. If Flanna was to be believed, and he was certain she was, then she was a virgin with no knowledge at all, as opposed to a virgin with some education in the school of passion. *Had he ever had such a virgin? Had he ever taken any virgin?* He didn't believe so. "Hae ye ever let a lad kiss ye, Flanna?" he asked her. Suddenly addressing her as madame seemed inappropriate. "Or cuddle wi' ye?"

"Of course nae!" she answered him indignantly. "What do ye take me for, my lord? I'm nae some loose lightskirt, quick to duck into a dark corner or lay out in the heather wi' every lad."

He nodded. "I never thought otherwise, lassie, but a quick kiss or a cuddle is nae a crime. Still, if ye hae nae education in the school of love, then I must teach ye from the beginning. Yer da expects yer maidenhead sacrificed by the morrow, or he'll nae gie me the deeds to Brae. We hae much work to do, ye and I, before the dawn."

"Brae again!" she cried. "Ohhh, take it, and leave me in peace, my lord! I should sooner die a maid!" She turned her back on him.

Patrick laughed softly. Then reaching out, he drew her back so she stood against him, one arm loosely about her waist. Unable to help himself, he buried his face for a moment in her long, red-gold hair. It was fragrant with the scent of white heather. "Nah, nah, lassie," he said in a soothing voice, "'twould be a crime if ye died a maid, for ye're so verra fair." He pushed the thick mass of curls aside and placed a light kiss upon her nape. The skin beneath his lips was soft. She would easily engage his lust, he thought, pleased. He had lain with other women on shorter acquaintance.

Her breath caught in her throat. His arm gently, but now firmly pinioning her against his hard body, the warm touch of his mouth on the back of her neck was both startling and intriguing. "Do ye *really* think me fair?" she asked him shyly when her voice finally returned. What the hell was the matter with her? She was behaving like a perfect ninny.

"Aye," he answered, turning her about to look at him again. He tilted her oval face up to his, then bending his head kissed her gently.

To her mortification, Flanna almost swooned with the contact between their two lips. Her heart beat wildly, thundering within her chest cavity and echoing in her ears; her head swam dizzily. Her whole being was suffused with warmth as she swayed like a sapling in the wind. "*Ooohhh,*" was all she could manage to say when he finally lifted his mouth from hers.

His hands went out to steady her. She blushed, embarrassed, and hid her head in his shoulder. Her guilelessness charmed him. "I think ye may hae a talent for kissing, Flanna," he told her, smiling.

Now that her senses had ceased to reel, Flanna decided that she, too, had enjoyed their first kiss. She raised her eyes to him again, saying boldly, "We'll nae know unless we do it some more, my lord." Then her arms went about his neck, drawing him into her embrace.

He laughed softly, saying, "I am my lady wife's to command," and he began to kiss her again.

She melted against him, letting him lead her, quickly learning from his most expert tuition. At first their mouths were like twin butterflies, softly brushing against each other. Then the tenor of his tutelage began to subtly change. His mouth became harder, more demanding, against hers. Flanna felt her belly beginning to roil with a nervous excitement. His thumb and his forefinger were holding her head firmly. His tongue ran along her pouting lips, and surprised again, she gasped, allowing his tongue to plunge deep into the warm, moist cave of her mouth. Her instinct was to struggle, to escape, but he would not permit her. Instead the hot, probing digit sought out her retreating tongue, teasing at it, stroking it, taunting it into a slow and very sensuous dance. Unable to help herself, Flanna followed his lead.

And then she realized that his hand was no longer holding her head. She was a willing participant, and the hand was unlacing the ribbons of her shift. She tore her head from his and cried out, *"Nae!"* Her hands tried to pull his away.

"The kissing comes first," Patrick Leslie said thickly. "Then the touching, lassie. Trust me, Flanna. I'll nae hurt ye, but I need to touch ye now."

"Why?" she half whispered. Oh, God! His big hand was slipping between the halves of her shift's neckline to cup her breast. She shivered.

"Because I am nae a virgin, lassie, and ye hae, it would seem, managed to arouse my lust wi' yer kisses. I must take the edge off of that lust now, or I'll take ye before ye're ready," he told her frankly.

"Oh." Her voice was very small.

"How quickly yer little heart is beating," he murmured, and bending his head he kissed the very tip of her breast.

"'Twill beat far faster if ye continue to do that," she gasped. His hand was so warm, and her breast, it would seem, fit quite snugly into the curve of his palm. When he had kissed her nipple, it had been as if she had been struck by a bolt of lightning. The nipple had puckered and grown tight with a little ache.

"A woman's breasts are meant to be caressed," he told her.

"I am nae a woman yet," she quickly countered, her fingers threading themselves into his dark head and pulling it up.

He laughed. "I canna resist yer most bountiful charms, lassie," he informed her. "Ye're much too delicious."

"We dinna know one another," she protested. "Until this day I never laid eyes upon ye, Patrick Leslie. When I shot my arrows at ye, I but meant to drive ye off. I dinna think we should end the day man and wife."

"*Nor did I, Flanna,*" he replied quietly, "but we are man and wife, and I canna think of a better way to know one another than by making love. Many a lass hae been wed wi' a stranger and found herself none the worse for it. I will be a good husband to ye, lassie."

"I never thought to be a wife," she said low.

"But ye are. *Ye are my wife.*" He held her close. "I am trying to go slowly wi' ye," he said to her.

"I know," she acknowledged, thinking he smelled of soap and leather, horse and man. There was something comforting about it. One arm enfolded her tenderly. A hand caressed her silken hair. She realized she could feel his heart! It was beating steadily beneath his breastbone. *Thrum. Thrum. Thrum.* Drawing away from him slightly, she undid the laces of his linen shirt. Boldly she kissed his broad chest. It was smooth and warm. Daringly she touched one of his nipples with the very tip of her tongue; then unable to help herself, she began to lick it. How she had thought of such a thing astounded her, but he stood very, very still beneath the wet warmth of her tongue, enchanted by her boldness. Then suddenly she ceased her actions and pressed a hot cheek against his chest, confused.

"That was nice, lassie," he told her. He wanted to encourage her. "I think now," he said, "we might remove the last of our garments," and before she could protest, he drew her shift over her head and dropped it to the floor. " 'Tis yer turn," he told her.

"I've never seen a naked man," she told him.

"I hope ye'll nae be disappointed," he answered as she pushed back his shirt, allowing it to fall to the floor.

She squeezed her eyes shut as her hands pressed the fabric off him. She couldn't breathe. Patrick Leslie bit his lip hard, forcing back the chuckle that threatened to break forth from his throat. He stood perfectly still and silent as Flanna slowly opened first one eye and then the other to stare directly at his nose even as she drew a deep gulp of air. Reaching out, he gently drew her into his embrace.

"Do ye like my nose?" he teased her.

"Wh-what?" She had actually found her voice despite the fact she was standing stark naked and breast to chest with an equally naked man. "*Yer nose?*" She looked puzzled.

"Ye are staring quite hard at it, Flanna," he said.

"I dinna know where else to look, my lord," she replied candidly.

Unable to help himself, he burst out laughing.

"It is nae amusing, my lord," Flanna protested, attempting to draw away from him, but he would not allow it.

"Ah, lassie, I am only astounded to learn that ye are shy," he told her. "The wench who shot her arrows at me this afternoon and then went after me wi' her dirk is both bashful and reluctant. I am surprised and charmed by the knowledge." He took one of her thick curls between his thumb and his forefinger, rubbing it, marveling at the soft texture, then putting it to his lips a moment. "To make love is the most natural event between a man and a woman. Every maiden of good reputation must rely upon her bridegroom to show her the way. If yer da were nae so insistent that this marriage be consummated tonight, I would gie ye all the time ye wanted to learn to know me better; but he is emphatic in his demand. He fears I might leave ye a virgin and then claim nonconsummation as an excuse to hae the marriage annulled. If that happened, I would be allowed under the law to retain yer dowry. *Brae.*"

"Oh," she said, and looked anxiously into his eyes.

He brushed her cheek lightly with the back of his hand and continued. "I would nae do such a thing, Flanna. I am nae a dishonorable man, nor is my family dishonest. 'Tis truth that I took ye for yer lands at Brae, but every woman is chosen for the attractiveness of her dower. I am a rich man and hae no need of gold, or cattle, but I wanted Brae. The more lands I hold, the better my clan is protected. I should hae refused a king's daughter wi'out Brae. Do ye understand, lassie?" His knuckles grazed her cheekbone.

"Am I a fool, then, to want to be desired for myself and nae my lands, my lord?" she asked softly.

He shook his head. "Nay, Flanna, ye're not foolish. My own mother disobeyed a direct order from King James to wed wi' my father because the king's decision was based upon other factors than if they would suit, or if they loved one another. My father had to woo my mother before she would hae him."

"Did he win her heart, then, my lord?" she queried.

"Aye," Patrick Leslie replied, smiling. "He did, indeed, win her heart, so much so that when he was killed at Dunbar she left Glenkirk."

She was silent a moment, and then she said, "Do ye think we shall love one another one day, my lord?"

The question startled him. Love, it had been his observation, was a complex emotion. Many-sided, it offered both bitter and sweet. He had always been afraid of love, he now realized, in light of her innocent query. Passion was something he understood well, and lust, aye, but *love?* "I dinna know, Flanna," he told her honestly, "but ye're my wife now. I will honor ye wi' my body and respect ye, lassie. More, however, I canna, in truth, promise ye. Only time will tell."

She nodded, grateful for his candor and the integrity of his answer. It was more, she realized, knowing her brothers and father, than most men would have given her. "Well, then, my lord," she said, "we hae best get to this consummation that is so important to my da. What would ye hae me do? Remember, I am really quite ignorant. I apologize for my lack of knowledge; but my brother's wife dinna believe lassies should hae any learning in these matters until they went to their marriage beds. Most lasses, of course, know who they will wed. They walk out and cuddle in the corners wi' their man, but I wanted nae man. I wanted to be free."

"I will nae enslave ye, lassie," he promised her. "Keep my home well. Gie me heirs, dinna become involved in any scandal, and ye're free to go yer own way. Ye'll learn when ye meet my female relations that they are all independent women of spirit." His arm tightened about her waist. "We will hae nae love this night, Flanna, my wife, but I will teach ye passion, and pleasure, which will suffice for now, ye will find." Then, picking her up, he immediately set her in their bed and lay beside her. Side by side he noted how long her legs were next to his.

She struggled with herself to remain calm, but she could not hold back the tremor that shook her body. She was filled with a mixture of emotions. *Fear. Curiosity. Excitement.* She had still not looked upon his body. Now, though, she raised herself up upon an elbow, her gaze slowly moving down his great length. He watched her covertly so as not to intimidate or embarrass her in her careful inspection. Broad shoulders. A broad chest just lightly covered with a dark down that narrowed into a slim waist. His belly looked hard and was quite flat. Reaching out, she touched it. The skin was muscled, and warm beneath her fingers.

He had very long legs, and both his calves and thighs were corded with muscle. This was an active man, not one who sat by the fire all day long. And his feet! She had never seen such big feet. Long and narrow, quite unlike her father's and brothers', whose feet were broad and far shorter than longer. While she had perused his limbs, her hand had not left his belly. Turning back to that area of his body, she brushed the thick, dark thatch of curls covering the juncture between his stomach and his thighs from which his manhood sprang. It lay but half roused upon its bed of curls.

"This is yer manhood?" she asked matter-of-factly.

"Aye," he answered her, swallowing hard as she took it in her hand. "Ye must treat it gently, lassie."

" 'Tis nae verra big," she noted.

"It needs to be filled wi' lust to be big," he replied, his ego surprisingly bruised. Little did this untamed virgin comprehend how once his lust had risen, his manhood would grow not just in breadth, but length as well. She would more than likely be terrified.

"How do I engage yer lust?" she inquired bluntly, releasing him.

"Like this," he responded, rising up suddenly to roll her beneath him. Then his mouth found hers in a deep and fiery kiss as his arms wrapped tightly about her. To his surprise her lips parted easily beneath his, her tongue leaping forth to engage his in amorous combat. Her lithe, yet amazingly lush body molded itself against him. "Dinna be afraid, Flanna," he murmured against her lips.

"I'm nae," she half lied, but her heart was pounding madly.

"Ye hae such sweet breasts," he told her, his hand going to caress them. "They are like ripe apples at autumn's zenith. His head lowered, and he kissed her nipple. It had grown tight like a frosted flower bud. His mouth opened, and his tongue began to gently lick at the nipple, slowly encircling it again and again. Just when she thought she would scream, his lips closed over the nipple, and he began to suckle hard on her sensitive flesh.

"*Ohhhh, Jesu!*" she gasped. His insistent mouth was raising a corresponding tug somewhere deep between her legs. She squirmed slightly in her attempt to escape this new torture. His mouth continued to draw strongly upon her nipple, wreaking havoc with her unsuspecting body. "Oh, cease, my lord, I beg ye," she cried softly, but he didn't seem to hear her.

"Sweet! Sweet!" he murmured as his head raised, and he moved quickly to her other nipple, teasing it with the very tip of his tongue, licking it until she was afire, and then nursing upon it as he had the other breast.

Flanna watched him through half-closed eyes. Inside she was afire. Her belly felt tight and knotted with the tension of unfamiliar sensations. She reached out to touch his dark hair, which he kept closely cropped. It was soft for a man, and very thick. Her fingers tentatively touched the graceful back of his neck, and he sighed deeply, lifting his head to look into her eyes.

"Ye're beginning to catch my attention now, lassie," he said softly, a small smile touching his lips.

"Is this what they call making love?" she asked, a blush staining her cheeks.

" 'Tis a beginning, Flanna," he replied; then lowering his dark head again, he ran his tongue between her plump breasts. God's boots, she was delicious. He was hard already; but his virgin wife needed more time, and he had to give it to her. Go rough with her, and she would hate him. They had to live together till death parted them. He certainly didn't want her hating him. She was distressed enough about Brae as it was. He began to kiss her again. Her lips, her face, her eyelids, her slim throat. His mouth moved across her body, pressing warm kisses on her navel, her torso.

Flanna reveled in his kisses, although her breasts now felt quite deserted. They had grown rounded and tight, it seemed, with his kisses. Her nipples were tingling. They almost hurt. She jumped, startled, as resting upon an elbow he began to stroke her thighs, which were tightly clenched together. Looking down, she saw his manhood, no longer small and helpless in appearance, but long and thick. Her mouth made a small *O* of surprise. His fingers caressed her subtly, the long digits trailing down her thighs and then up again. Her legs began to open slightly, seemingly of their own accord. She shivered with anticipation.

Patrick Leslie smiled slowly. She was untried, but she was brave, he thought approvingly. He tenderly brushed over her Venus mons. It was covered in red curls, just slightly darker than her glorious red-gold hair. Leaning forward, he began to kiss her again, all the while stroking her. Her nether lips grew plump, and he was finally able to slide a single finger along her deep slit. She was already wet with her innocent arousal. His finger pushed a small ways between the folds of warm, moist flesh. She gasped, but he quickly reassured her with soothing sounds and little kisses.

Flanna's heart was beating wildly. He was awakening feelings in her that she had never known even existed. He bestirred her senses recklessly. She felt like a cauldron being brought to a fierce boil. There were so many questions she wanted to ask him, but somehow it didn't seem like the right time. *But there were things she needed to know!* Dear God, his finger was pressing forward to touch her so intimately that Flanna thought she would do the unthinkable and swoon. Instead she gasped again, drawing in a lungful of air to clear her head. The finger began to push within her. *"What are ye doing?"* she half sobbed, now a little frightened.

" 'Tis all right, lambkin," he attempted to reassure her. "I need to know how tightly yer maidenhead is lodged. I would hurt ye nae more than I must, Flanna. Lay quiet, sweeting." He kissed her lips, distracting her while his finger sought the answers to his questions. Finding them, he frowned. It would be no easy passage, for her maidenhead was tightly lodged, and she winced as he pressed his finger lightly against it. He had thought she might be easy to breach as she was used to riding, and that frequently loosened a maid's virginity.

Oh, God, Flanna thought, *what is going to happen? Do I want this? No matter! He will take me anyways, and all for Brae.* Tears began to slip from the corners of her eyes and down the sides of her head. His body was pinioning hers now as he covered her. She trembled and turned her head from him, biting her lip to keep from crying out in protest.

He saw the tears, and it almost broke his resolve. He wasn't a brute who forced women to his will. Passion brought pleasure, and he wanted to give that pleasure to his bride. Sitting back on his heels, he called to her, "Flanna, lassie, dinna fear me. Look at me now, and tell me what troubles ye. I dinna want to take ye yet fearing me."

She turned her head and looked up at him, her young bosom rising and falling with her emotions. "It means naught, my lord. I dinna want it to mean naught. I never thought to wed, but this shouldna be for naught. I know I make no sense!" And she began to sob.

"Ah, Flanna, my fierce wife," Patrick Leslie said gently, " 'tis nae for naught. Do ye nae know how I cherish and esteem the gift ye are about to gie me? Ye hae guarded yer prize yer whole life, and I am honored that I shall be the sole recipient of it. 'Tis nae for naught, lassie. No bride could bring her husband, be he shepherd or king, a more precious gift than that of her virginity. 'Tis nae for naught. I honor ye for it, Flanna Leslie."

"*And Brae?*" she demanded softly.

"Brae is yer dower, Flanna," he replied.

"Ye want it more than me," she said. "Ye would hae had it for gold but that my father wouldna sell it to ye."

"Aye," he agreed, "but I wanted it enough to want ye as well, lassie, and ye are about to gie me a bonus that is worth more gold than there is in the entire world."

"*Oh!*" His words touched her.

"I want ye, Flanna Leslie," he whispered, leaning over to nibble on her earlobe. "I want to join my body wi' yers and gie us pleasure. Ye hae never known the kind of pleasure I will gie ye." The tip of his tongue swept around the whorl of her ear.

"Ye're sly as a fox, and yer words are as smooth as the waters of the loch," she told him, regaining her courage as she spoke, a frisson of excitement running down her spine

"We must stay in this chamber until the deed is done, lassie," he told her. "Surely ye dinna want to remain here the rest of our lives. Ye'll love Glenkirk, Flanna. *And,* ye'll be free of yer da and brothers."

"Will ye let me refurbish yer castle so I may make it my own?" she boldly asked him.

He chuckled, a warm and rich sound. "'Tis ye, madame, I think, who is the sly one. Aye, ye may hae yer way wi' my coffers," he answered her. His manhood was hard as iron, and if he didn't plunge it into the hot velvet of her sheath soon, he would burst. She had, indeed, engaged his lust to the point where rapine was a possibility.

"Kiss me, then, my lord, in token of yer pledge," she whispered to him, sliding her arms about his neck and drawing him forward so that her full breasts were crushed against his chest. "I will try nae to be afraid, and ye will go gently wi' me."

His lips met hers in a scorching kiss, his mouth pressing hard against hers in an effort to divert her as his knee levered her thighs wide apart. They were both panting; he with desire, Flanna with her nervousness. She was not so deterred that she did not feel him position his manhood and push slowly, gently into her body. Her breath came faster as he filled her, and she remembered Una's words.

Lie quietly, and let him do all the work.

But she couldn't lie quietly. Her untutored body wanted to find his rhythm and move with him. When he stopped his forward movement, she was puzzled. "What is it?" she whispered to him.

"'Twill hurt," he said, and then before she might question him further, he drew back and then plunged deeply into her.

Flanna cried out. Una's voice rang in her head.

It will hurt ye a bit when he goes into ye the first time, but 'tis a momentary discomfort.

But this was no mere discomfort. She cried out again as he thrust once more, but this time he managed to break through whatever had been impeding his progress. Hot pain radiated up into her chest, making it almost impossible to draw a breath, and down into her thighs, making them seem leaden. He lay quietly now upon her, and gradually the hurt began to ease.

"Ye're a brave lass," he murmured into her ear, and then he began to move upon her.

She stiffened, bracing herself for further punishment, but to her surprise and relief there was none. Only the strong drive of his loins as he propelled his manhood within her hot sheath. She was suddenly caught up in the cadence of his rhythm. She began to move with him, and after a moment or two an odd heat began to infuse her body with such a honeyed sweetness she didn't think she could bear it. *"Ohh! Ahhh! Ahhhh,* 'tis lovely," she half sobbed.

He groaned so loudly that she thought him injured, but he ceased his movement, stiffening, then shuddering. She felt the hardness within her dissolve and cried out softly with the loss. There had been some small pleasure after the pain. Una had been right. He rolled off of her, parting, and lay silent upon his back for a time. Flanna lay beside him, a sudden feeling of loss overwhelming her. She began to weep softly, and Patrick Leslie, astounded by the passionate lust she had aroused in him, gathered his bride into his arms.

"There, lambkin, ye were braw, and ye gave me much pleasure. I gave ye pleasure, too, for ye told me so." He stroked her silken head. "Dinna greet now, lassie. 'Tis over and done wi'. I will nae hurt ye again, Flanna Leslie. Sleep now." He kissed the top of her head.

She was astounded by the comfort his arms about her and the small kiss gave her. Surprised she should be such a foolish creature and weep like every female she had always scorned. Still, she snuggled into his embrace, reveling in the masculine scent of him, and closed her eyes.

Patrick smiled in the darkness as he felt her relax against him and her breathing grow even as sleep overcame her. He had married her for her lands, but perhaps he had gotten more of a bargain than he anticipated.

Outside the bedchamber door, Lachlann Brodie smiled triumphantly at his eldest son, Aulay. "'Tis done," the old man said, satisfied. "He canna deny her now."

Chapter

4

"*Lady! Lady!*"
Her arm was being pulled insistently. Flanna slowly awoke, swimming up from the depths of a very deep sleep.

"*Lady!*" Aggie's young voice pleaded with her.

"What is it?" Flanna finally managed to say, but her eyes were still tightly shut. She burrowed back down into the featherbed.

"Yer husband says ye must arise. He would be gone as soon as possible, lady," Aggie said. "A storm is brewing and threatens to be a hard one. Angus and I are ready to leave. We only wait on ye. The old man wants the bedsheet, lady."

Her husband? *Her husband!* The events of the previous day and night crashed down upon her. "Bring me hot water," she said, rolling over, drawing the coverlet with her to cover her nakedness.

"I already hae," Aggie answered, "and I hae laid out clean clothing for ye, lady."

Flanna arose, and Aggie blushed at her mistress's nudity. Ignoring her, Flanna said, "Take the sheet to my father and tell him the marriage has been well and truly consummated. Then bring me something to eat. I'll nae go down into the hall to be leered at by the whole damned family. When I leave this chamber, I will leave Killiecairn. Tell my lord to eat while he can, Aggie."

Her eyes widened at the large, bloody stain on the bedsheet she had just removed from the bed, Aggie nodded silently and hurried off.

Flanna looked about the room. There was nothing to indicate Patrick Leslie had ever been there. *But he had.* She smiled to herself. The coupling was one part of marriage she was going to enjoy, particularly when she finally learned how to do her part to please him. He was a strange man, her husband. Proud to the point of arrogance, but kind. Flanna knew Patrick Leslie had, indeed, been kind to her last night. He might have put her on her back and taken her virginity coldly. Instead, he had tried to ease her fears and make the experience a pleasant one for her. She was grateful and would tell him so. She had never thought to be a wife. She hadn't really ever wanted to marry, but now she was wedded and bedded. Still, Patrick had promised not to enslave her like her brothers' wives.

"I must be a good wife," she said softly to herself. "Ailis is right. I know how to keep a house. At Glenkirk I'll have servants to do my bidding." She took the washrag Aggie had left for her, quickly washing her face and hands. She rinsed her mouth with water and turned to dress. It was then she saw the dried blood staining her thighs. She felt her cheeks redden and, taking the cloth from the basin, vigorously scrubbed the blood away. Her woman's place felt suddenly sore. She gently bathed it as well, staring half-horrified at the water in the basin, now turned brown.

She drew on a pair of knit stockings, her green wool breeches, a white cotton shirt, and finally her doeskin jerkin. After yanking on her worn boots, she walked back over to the basin where Aggie had left her hairbrush. Flanna vigorously brushed her long hair, then braided it into a single thick plait. She stuffed the brush into her pocket and taking up her blue cap put it on her head. She glanced about the little room that had been hers most of her life. Then without a backward look she departed it. Aggie had not returned with the food, which meant her father wanted to see her and suspected her plan to leave Killiecairn quickly. Annoyed, and not just a little hungry, she hurried into the hall.

It was even as she had suspected. They were all there. The

women smirked, certain that proud Flanna had now been tamed. The men would not meet her eyes, but for her father, who gave her a hard and assessing look. He nodded to her, indicating she seat herself on his left hand. Flanna sat down, letting her sisters-in-law serve her. A bowl of oat stirabout was placed before her. She reached for the pitcher of golden cream, spilled some on the porridge, and silently ate it down. She reached for the cottage loaf and tore off a piece, buttering it with her thumb. A piece of hard, yellow cheese was offered her on the end of a dirk. Her eyes met those of her husband, and he smiled faintly as she took the cheese and put it atop the bread and butter. Her goblet was filled with—she sipped at it—*wine*. Wine was not usually served with the morning meal. When she had finished her meal she sat silently.

Finally her father spoke. "Ye hae done well, lassie," Lachlann Brodie told his only daughter approvingly. "Yer husband says yer a braw lassie. I hae given him the deeds to Brae. They are now his, as are ye, Flanna. Ye're welcome in this hall whenever ye would come."

The duke arose and held out a gloved hand to his bride. "There is a storm brewing. We must leave now."

"I know," she said, putting her hand in his. She bent and kissed her father's withered cheek. "Farewell, Da."

"Farewell, daughter," he said. "Yer mam would be proud this day to see ye leave my hall a duchess."

"I thank ye for yer hospitality, Lachlann Brodie," Patrick Leslie said. "*And for yer daughter,*" he finished with a smile.

As they walked through the little hall, Una hurried up to them. "Ye're all right?" she asked.

Flanna stopped and bent to kiss her sister-in-law's leather cheek. "Aye," she said. "Ye were right. There was some pleasure."

"Good!" came the reply. "Now remember what I told ye. Gie yer husband an heir as quickly as ye can, lassie. God bless ye."

Flanna gave the older woman a quick smile and then moved off with her husband.

"She loves ye well," the duke said softly.

"She's a good woman," Flanna replied.

"Ye'll ride wi' me," he told her. "When we get to Glenkirk I will gie ye yer own horse."

"Of course," she said sharply. "The Brodies of Killiecairn dinna hae yer wealth, my lord, but we are comfortable."

As if to give substance to her words, her eldest brother, Aulay, now came from the stable leading a dappled gray mare with a black mane and tail. "She's yers," he said gruffly. "Ye'll nae leave Killiecairn wi'out being properly mounted."

"But ye've raised her from a colt," Flanna said protestingly. "I know ye meant her for yer granddaughter, Moire. 'Tis nae fair."

"Moire is but three, and too young for such a fine beastie as Glaise. I'll raise another mare for her, and next time she'll be ready for it. I was too enthusiastic as Moire was my first granddaughter," Aulay Brodie said with a faint smile. "Glaise is my wedding gift to ye, sister."

Flanna threw her arms about her brother and kissed him. "I accept yer gift, and I thank ye, Aulay," she told him.

He shook her off. "I'll help ye up, lassie," he said huskily. Then, bending, he cupped his two big hands, and when his sister put her foot into his grasp, he gently but firmly boosted her into her saddle. "Remember, she hae a soft mouth, Flanna. Dinna pull on it."

The new Duchess of Glenkirk leaned forward and patted her mare lovingly. "We're going to get on just fine, Glaise," she whispered to the creature.

Aulay Brodie now held out his hand to the duke. "Ye dinna mind, I hope," he said quietly.

Patrick shook his head. "Nay. She's beautiful," he replied.

"The horse, or the lass," Aulay Brodie said seriously.

"Both," came the reply, and then the duke mounted his own stallion. "Ye'll ride by my side," he said, turning to his new wife.

They rode away from Killiecairn. Flanna turned about but once to look back at the large stone house in which she had been raised. The air was very cold and still. She could feel the damp in it, pushing past her garments, chilling her to the bone. It would be almost a full day's ride back to Glenkirk Castle. She shivered and pulled her heavy wool cloak about her, but she held her head high. Her new husband said nothing to her as they made their way, but she could hear the murmur of the men behind her. She concentrated on her surroundings.

The sky above them was gray. The hills about them were dark with trees, either evergreen conifers or the trunks and bare branches of the trees that leafed throughout the summer only to drop those leaves in the autumn. The hooves of their mounts now trod upon a carpet of those leaves, encouraging the earthy scent of damp rot to arise faintly. The dogs with them scampered in, out, and ahead of them, occasionally flushing a rabbit or a bird, which was quickly killed and brought along to help fill the castle's larder. In late morning before they stopped to eat and rest, they took a red deer.

By early afternoon a light rain began to fall. It shortly turned to sleet. Flanna pulled up the hood on her cloak to protect herself. Silently the sleet began to turn to snow, almost obliterating the trail they followed. The duke called to his head huntsman, Colin More-Leslie, to come forward and make certain they were following the proper trail. The mare beneath her, however, was as surefooted as a goat. Flanna was grateful that all she had to do was sit her.

"Another hour," Patrick Leslie finally spoke to her. "I yet recognize the terrain despite the snow. Are ye all right, lassie?"

"Aye, my lord." Flanna nodded. In actuality she was freezing and could scarcely feel her toes right now, but he was undoubtedly just as cold. There was no need for complaint. They wouldn't be warm again until they reached the safety of the castle, she knew.

"Good lass," he replied, and then turned his attention ahead once more.

She might have been his horse or one of the dogs, Flanna thought, almost irritated by his tone. But then, why should he have any feelings for her? she reasoned. Even though he had lain with her, he didn't really know her. The possibility that Una might be right and she had best produce an heir quickly flitted through her mind. It wasn't that she had any particular feelings for her husband either, for Flanna had no more knowledge of Patrick Leslie than he did of her. But if he should ever take it into his head to divorce her because his family disapproved of a simple Brodie of Killiecairn, she would have nothing left. Brae now belonged to Glenkirk. The mother of Glenkirk's heir, however, would be a power to be reckoned with. Flanna smiled to herself.

She had never thought of herself as a mother, just as she had never thought of herself as a wife. In another time she would have been offered two choices. Marriage to a man or marriage to the church. Now there was but one choice, for the wicked practices of locking women up in convents to spend their lives in dark papist practices had been wiped out by the Covenanters. A woman married or she didn't; and those who didn't were dependent on their fathers or brothers unless they possessed their own wealth or land. Flanna realized with shock that she had nothing but that which Patrick Leslie would give her. It wasn't a position she found enviable, and she didn't like it at all; but what could she do about it?

The horses ploughed onward through the darkening day. The snow was now falling heavily. The trees and the hillsides were already well coated with a blanket of white, but fortunately there was no wind at all. Then finally she saw looming ahead of them a great dark hulk of stone, its towers piercing upward into the sky. She wished she could gain a clearer glimpse of her new home through the falling snow, but it was impossible. She heard the muffled sound of wood beneath the animals' hooves as they crossed the lowered drawbridge and passed beneath the portcullis into the courtyard where they came to a stop.

Patrick Leslie slid easily off his stallion and, going over to Flanna, lifted her from the mare's back. But he did not put her down, instead carrying her into the castle within the enclosure of his arms. "Welcome home, madame," he said as he finally set her on her feet.

Slightly disoriented, Flanna looked about her. "Where are we?" she asked him, her eyes taking in the silken banners hanging from the rafters, the two enormous fireplaces, and especially the two portraits hanging over those fireplaces.

"This is the Great Hall of Glenkirk Castle. That gentleman"— the duke's hand pointed toward one of the portraits—"is my namesake, the first Earl of Glenkirk. He served King James IV as ambassador to the Duchy of San Lorenzo. The lady above the opposite fireplace is his daughter, Lady Janet Leslie. Someday I shall tell ye her tale. Come by the fireplace, madame, and warm yerself."

Flanna gladly accepted his invitation, pulling off her gloves, which were frozen to her fingers, and holding her hands out to the blaze in the big fireplace. "'Tis surely a large hall, my lord," she told him. "I've nae seen bigger, but of course, I've nae been far from Killiecairn before. The hall at Brae is nae even half as large."

"Ye hae been in Brae Castle itself, lass?" He was genuinely interested. He moved to a sideboard where he poured them two drams of his own peat-flavored whiskey, handing her one. "'Twill warm ye," he said.

"Aye, I've been inside Brae," she told him. Then she swallowed the whiskey down in a quick gulp. "There is some damage to the roof beneath the eaves, but the castle itself is sound, if dusty."

"And so it will remain, for I hae no use for another castle. 'Tis the land I sought," he replied. Then he swallowed his own dram down and taking the two pewter cups set them aside.

"I want the castle," Flanna said. "The castle, and its island."

"Why?" he demanded, curious.

"Because I hae nothing to call my own now, my lord," she answered him. "Brae and its lands were all I possessed. Ye now hold them, but ye hae said ye hae no desire for the castle. Gie it to me. I do want it."

It was a ridiculous request, he thought, and was about to refuse her when she spoke again.

"Ye hae nae given me a wedding gift, my lord. I want Brae Castle and a bit of coin to repair its roof. Certainly yer own mother did nae come to yer father as penniless as I am."

"Nay," he admitted, "my mother was a princess and possessed great wealth when she wed wi' my father."

"And was yer grandmam also an heiress, my lord?"

His paternal grandmother, Cat Leslie, had been an amazing woman, Patrick remembered with a smile. He recalled the story of his own father's birth in Edinburgh. Part of his grandmother's dowry had been a small piece of property that actually belonged to her and not her father, yet he had included it in his daughter's dower portion. His grandmother had been furious and had refused to marry his grandfather until her bit of property had been returned to her possession. His grandfather had nonetheless managed to impregnate his betrothed wife, assuming she would have no other choice but to do her family's and his bidding and marry him. His grandmother, however, had run away. She would have her property back or his child would be a bastard. It had taken his grandfather months to find her, and desperate that his heir be born legitimate, he had, when he found her, returned Cat Leslie's small piece of property to her sole possession, marrying her but minutes before his son entered the world. His maternal grandmother had also been an heiress.

"Aye," the Duke of Glenkirk said in answer to his young wife's question. "My grandmother was well dowered, Flanna. Both of them were."

"Can ye understand, then, my lord, why I seek to hae my wee castle? My predecessors came to their husbands with monies, jewels, plate, lands, and linens. I come to ye wi' but my small bit of land and the clothing I own. The land is now yers, so I hae naught but my clothes. While they are suitable for a chief's daughter, I doubt they are what a duchess would wear. Please gie me Brae Castle as my bridal gift and let me restore it so I may hae something of my own." She tried hard to keep a pleading tone out of her voice, for she had her pride.

Looking at her, he could see the effort it took for her to ask him for anything. She was as proud as he was. The castle meant nothing to him, but it obviously meant a great deal to her. "Ye may repair the roof to keep the rest from tumbling down," he said to her. "Nothing more, however. 'Tis yers to do wi' as ye will. I will hae a deed of ownership drawn up for Brae Castle, madame, in yer name, and ye will keep it safe, eh?"

She flung herself at him, wrapping her arms about his neck and kissing him heartily. "Oh, thank ye, my lord! Ye hae made me so verra happy! I promise I will be frugal in the expense." Then she loosed her hold about his neck and blushed, realizing how bold she had been. Biting her lip, she stood before him, not knowing what to do next, but Patrick Leslie grinned mischievously at her.

"I can see, Flanna, that ye'll nae be a great expense to me. The castle cost me nothing, and ye've sworn to be careful wi' the repairs. Ye might hae asked me for jewels and a coach."

"What would I need jewels for, my lord?" she said honestly. "As for a coach, they are for old ladies. I hae a good mount and am capable of riding. 'Twould be a great waste of good coin, a coach."

He laughed, remembering his mother's magnificent coaches and his grandmother's as well. While each of those women rode very well, neither ever traveled a distance without all her comforts. Still, his wife was a practical wench, and the truth was that neither of them would be going anywhere distant. They would not require a coach. "I can see ye'll see I dinna waste my monies, Flanna," he told her.

"Do ye hae a lot of gold, my lord?" she asked.

"Aye, a great deal, but that knowledge is only for ye and me to know. In time, lass, when we know one another better, *and I am certain that I can trust ye*, then I will share such information wi' ye."

"Ye can trust me, my lord," Flanna said seriously. "I am yer wife now, and a Leslie. My allegiance is to ye and to Glenkirk. Where else would I place my loyalty."

He gave her a warm smile, touched by her speech. This Highland wench he had so hastily married was perhaps a bit more complex than he had thought her to be. "I believe I can trust ye, Flanna," he told her. "Now, however, is nae the time to discuss such matters as what I possess. Ye hae a great task ahead of ye, lass. Ye must make my castle a more livable place again. Since my mother left, and took Adali wi' her, there has been no one to direct the servants. They hae grown lax wi'out a strong guiding hand. Ye must provide that hand."

"Who was A . . . Adali?" she asked him, and sat in one of the two chairs by the blazing fire.

He sat opposite her. "Adali has been my mother's servant since her birth. When she came to Glenkirk as my father's wife, Adali became the castle's majordomo. When she left Glenkirk after my father's death, Adali, and the two other servants who hae been wi' Mother her whole life, departed with her. They hae been together so long they cannot be separated. It was Adali who managed the household, seeing that the servants did what they should, making certain we had what we needed to survive, purchasing what we dinna grow, make, barter, or hunt. Now 'tis yer task, Flanna. There is more to being a duchess than fetes and beautiful clothing," he finished.

She stared at him, astounded. "I hae nae been to a *fete* in my entire life, my lord, nor do I hae beautiful clothing. As for yer household, I will do my best, but I dinna hae the faintest idea of how to manage so large an establishment. I will learn, of course, but ye must be patient wi' me. This is nae Killiecairn. This is a great house Even yer own mam had servants to do her bidding. I am nae a servant, my lord. *I am yer wife.*"

"Lass, I dinna mean . . . Ye will hae all the servants ye want to help ye. If I hae offended ye, I apologize," Patrick Leslie said.

"My lord, ye wed me for the land," Flanna replied in matter-of-fact tones. "We both understand that. I know my duty. 'Tis to make yer home a place of comfort and to gie ye an heir as quickly as possible. Fortunately, I hae my servant Angus to help me wi' the first. Angus came to Killiecairn wi' my mother from Brae. He remembers how a fine establishment should be kept and will help me. As for my second task, 'tis up to ye and I to manage."

"I hae nae considered—" he began, but Flanna interrupted him.

"What month were ye born in, my lord?" she demanded of him.

"March," he answered her.

"And how old will ye be on yer next birthday?" she pressed.

He thought a moment, then replied, "Thirty-five, lass."

"I was born in August and was twenty-two this year, my lord. How old was yer mam when her first child was born?" Flanna asked.

Again he thought for a long moment. That had, after all, been before his time. His half sister, India, was the oldest of his siblings. "I think she was seventeen," he said. "Aye! She was seventeen."

"And how many bairns did she hae by the time she was my age?" Flanna queried him.

"Four," he said, seeing where her line of questioning was leading him, but still not at all certain he was ready for fatherhood. He wasn't even certain he was ready for marriage, though married he now was.

"Four," Flanna repeated. "Yer mam had four bairns by the time she was my age! I think, my lord, we hae much work ahead of us. How many bairns did she hae in all?"

Patrick Leslie swallowed hard. "Nine," he murmured, "but one of my sisters died before she was even a year old. Ye must understand, Flanna, that my mother had several husbands, and a lover, to father her great brood."

"*A lover?*" Flanna didn't know whether to be shocked or not.

"Prince Henry Stuart—he should hae been king after James— was the sire of my half brother, Charlie," the duke told his wife. "It was before she wed wi' my father, of course."

"What happened to *him?*" Flanna wanted to know.

"Who?" Patrick said.

"*The bastard.* Yer mam's bastard," Flanna responded.

Patrick Leslie burst out laughing. He had never considered Charlie in that manner. To his knowledge, no one had. "My half brother, Charles Frederick Stuart, the Duke of Lundy, has never been thought of in that light, Flanna. While we teasingly call him our *not-so-royal Stuart,* he was always considered just one of mother's bairns. Old King James and Queen Anne loved him dearly. He was their first grandchild. Sadly his father, the prince, died shortly after his birth. His uncle, our late King Charles, for whom Charlie was named, was very fond of him. One reason mother retired to England is to make certain Charlie doesna endanger himself by involving himself in this factional fighting over religion and Divine Right. Charlie is deeply loyal to his father's family."

"But he was born on the wrong side of the blanket," Flanna persisted. "How can he be anything other than a bastard?"

"Lass," the duke explained patiently, "the royal Stuarts hae always recognized their bairns nae matter the mother. 'Twas that way when they ruled here in Scotland, and 'tis that way now in England as well. They are a most loving family. My own blood is also mixed wi' theirs, as are many families here in Scotland."

Flanna shook her head. "I dinna understand," she said, "but if ye say 'tis all right, I will accept yer word."

Patrick laughed again. "Are ye hungry?" he asked her.

"I am, and I canna help but wonder why there is nae meal on the table, and the master in the house almost an hour now," she replied. She stood up. "Who did ye leave in charge, my lord?"

"Nae one has been in charge since my mother left," he said.

Flanna sighed. "Angus, to me," she called, and the giant man who was her servant stepped from the deep shadows of the hall. In his arms he carried Sultan, purring noisily as Angus stroked him rhythmically.

Patrick Leslie chuckled. "'Tis rare he takes to strangers, but I trust his judgment in men."

"He's a grand beastie, my lord," Angus replied. He was a man of indeterminate age, but he stood straight like a great oak, seven feet tall. His hair was dark brown with streaks of silver. He wore it pulled back and tied with a leather thong. His matching beard was full, but it was a small vanity of Angus's that he kept it well trimmed and neat. All who knew him knew he took great pride in his beard, as he did in his dress. Angus always wore his Gordon kilt.

"Put the creature down," Flanna said, "and see why there is nae supper on the table. Are the men supposed to starve after that long ride through the wet today? Tomorrow ye and I must see to putting the management of this house back properly." She turned to her husband. "Is the castle mine?"

He knew exactly what she meant. "Aye, madame," he replied.

Flanna turned back to her servant. "Ye're now the majordomo of Glenkirk Castle, Angus," she said. "Aggie, where is my chamber? I want a hot bath. I'm yet frozen through despite whiskey and the fire."

"There are so many rooms, mistress, I dinna know where to look first," Aggie said, coming forward in the company of an older woman. "She knows," she continued accusingly, "but she will nae tell me."

"Hae ye taken to bringing yer wantons into the castle now that yer mam is nae here, my lord?" the woman demanded. She was small and plump, with white hair, but a youngish face.

"*This is my wife,* Mary," the duke said. "I wed wi' her yesterday in her father's house at Killiecairn. She is yer new mistress. Ye will render her yer respect. Flanna, this is Mary More-Leslie."

"Can ye housekeep?" Flanna demanded fiercely of the woman.

"Aye," came the reply, and Mary More-Leslie looked Flanna over critically, recognizing a Highland wench when she saw one.

"Then, ye'll be the housekeeper here unless Angus says yer a slattern. Now show me to my chambers, Mary More-Leslie." Flanna knew enough from her sister-in-law, Una Brodie, to know she must exhibit immediate and firm authority over those who served her or lose control of her household. Her gaze never left that of the older woman.

Mary finally looked away and, turning, said, "This way, *my lady*. We were nae expecting a *bride*, and so 'twill nae be in readiness; but we'll manage tonight. Tomorrow is another day, eh?"

The Duke of Glenkirk looked on in surprise as Mary meekly led Flanna and her female servant away. He turned, and Angus was also gone. Sultan wreathed about his ankles. Patrick Leslie sat back down in his chair. The cat leapt into his lap and settled itself.

"Well, Sultan," he said, "what think ye of yer new mistress? I think, wi'out meaning to, I hae found me a verra fine wife." *A day.* He had known her only a day. He had learned she was brave and practical. She seemed to enjoy his lovemaking. She appeared honest and loyal. It was as good a basis as any to begin a marriage. Still, there was much, much more he had to learn about this young woman. He had done a very rash thing by marrying her, he knew.

Patrick Leslie smiled to himself. What would his mother think of this outspoken Highland girl of not particularly distinguished background? What would his siblings think? He numbered a duke and a marquis among his four brothers. Charlie and Henry led different lives than he led, although now with the difficulties in England, their lives must certainly be disrupted to some extent. Henry would know how to bend without breaking. He would survive with barely a wrinkle in his silken breeches, and his family as well. Henry was seven years his senior, and while he had been a kindly elder brother, he had had little time for Patrick Leslie.

His brother Charlie, however, was a different matter. The not-so-royal Stuart was only three and a half years older than Patrick Leslie. He had always had time for his little brother and, consequently, was closer to Patrick than even his two younger Leslie brothers, Adam and Duncan. What was happening to Charlie amid all the strife? He had always been devoted to his father's family. Had Prince Henry been permitted to wed with the widowed Marchioness of Westleigh as his mother was then titled, Charlie would have been England's king when old James had died. But Charlie didn't care if he was king or not. He had been as loyal to the royal Stuarts as any legitimately born son would have been. News filtered slowly into the eastern Highlands. They hadn't even known of the king's execution until late spring. Where was Charlie now? "God keep ye safe, brother," the duke whispered to himself.

"My lord." Angus was by his side. "The cook will hae the supper ready shortly. I hae spoken wi' him. Meals will be served on time in the future. Nae one was certain when ye would return, and hence the delay." He gave the duke a faint bow. "Shall I tell her ladyship, or will ye?"

Patrick Leslie stood up, placing Sultan on the floor as he did so. "I will tell her," he replied. "I am happy to hae my house in such safe hands now. Thank ye." He walked from the hall.

Angus now took a moment to look about him. Flanna had done well despite her best efforts to avoid the responsibility accorded her sex. She was wild like her mother that way, although only he could remember Meg Gordon's stubborn nature. Lachlann Brodie had been entranced with her and found her willfulness amusing. But the old Brodie had kept his promise to his dying wife, although how he would have done it but that the Duke of Glenkirk had fallen into their laps, Angus didn't know. Still, it was done now. Flanna was both a duchess and a countess with this marriage.

Angus knew a great deal more about the duke and his family than Patrick Leslie would have imagined. His own grandfather had been the duke's grandfather, the fourth Earl of Glenkirk, also a Patrick. This Patrick had spawned any number of bastards throughout the region. Angus's maternal grandmother, Bride Forbes, had caught the earl's eye and birthed a daughter, Jessie, in March of 1578. Jessie Forbes in her turn had caught the eye of Andrew Gordon, the Earl of Brae. She had died two days after giving birth to a son, named Angus after an ancestor, and who was recognized by his father as a Gordon and raised at Brae Castle. The young Countess of Brae, Anne Keith, had married her husband when Angus was three and given birth to her only child, a daughter, Margaret, when Angus was seven. She had treated her husband's bastard as her own child, the only difference being that he would not inherit either his father's title or his father's lands. Those would go to his legitimately born sister, Margaret.

When the Earl of Brae had died shortly after his daughter's twelfth birthday, it was Angus who had taken over management of Brae, protecting the widowed countess and her child from any and all who would make an attempt on either the heiress, her mother, or Brae. It was Angus who had seen Lachlann Brodie's interest Meg Gordon one summer at the games at Inverness; but Meg Gordon would not leave her mother, who was then ill and failing. Only two years later, when Anne had died and was buried, did Meg, at her half brother's urging, accept the suit of the Brodie of Killiecairn.

"Our blood is better," he told his half sister honestly, "but ye're far past yer prime, Meg. He doesna care if ye hae bairns, for he's got half a dozen lads by his first wife, God assoil her. He's old enough to be yer da, but he's in love wi' ye, any fool can see. Ye'll do nae better, for all ye hae is Brae and its lands. Ye hae nae cattle or coin. This is as good a match as ye'll get, and he'll be kind."

"What will happen to ye, Angus? I'll nae leave ye," Meg Gordon had told her half brother.

"Few away from Brae know I am our father's bastard," Angus replied. "I'll come wi' ye as yer personal servant. Brodie will nae deny ye yer servant, and anyone wi' eyes can see I'm useful."

So Meg had accepted the offer of marriage from Lachlann Brodie, a man thirty-three years her senior, and to her surprise her husband had, despite his years, proved a vigorous lover. He had also adored her and done everything he could to make her happy. And Angus Gordon had entered the household at Killiecairn, silently watching over his younger sibling and eventually her child, making himself as useful as possible so that none would complain that he didn't earn his keep. When Flanna's mother had been on her deathbed, she had confided to her only child that Angus was her half brother and Flanna's uncle. Flanna had continued to keep the secret.

Angus Gordon noted the portraits hanging over the two fireplaces. He saw the well-made furniture, the fine tapestries, the beautiful silk banners hanging from the rafters, the silver on the sideboard, the porcelain bowls, and the beeswax tapers in the candlesticks. The lamps burned pure, fragrant oil, and there was both wine and whiskey on the table. The place needed a good cleaning, but it had not been left for too long a time, it was obvious. This was the great hall of a wealthy man, and his niece was now that man's wife.

She had a great deal to learn, Angus thought to himself. Meg had loved her only child, but she hadn't taken the time to teach her how to manage a great house. His sister had probably never thought Flanna would do so well. When Meg had died, Una Brodie had done her best to teach Flanna the rudiments of housekeeping; but Flanna had never been very interested, and besides, Killiecairn wasn't an impressive establishment. His niece preferred the out-of-doors, riding and hunting from dawn to dusk. Meg had taught her daughter to sign her name; but other than that, Flanna could not write, nor could she read. The only language she knew was her own. Angus shook his head wearily. His niece was very badly prepared for her new high station. He wondered what the duke would think when he learned it. He shook his great head a third time. There was so much to do. The household, he could manage, but Flanna had to be educated enough so that she didn't shame her husband. Had he not heard Patrick Leslie tell his wife that his own mother was a princess? Certainly a princess knew how to read, and to write, and to converse in foreign tongues. Flanna spoke a brand of Highland English, and Scots Gaelic only a Highland Scot could understand.

He heard the servants begin entering the hall to set the high board and bring the food. He turned quickly and began directing them in an authoritative voice. The duke and Flanna entered the hall, and he escorted them to the high board, seating his niece at her husband's right hand. Then, with a flick of an eyebrow, he signaled the servants to bring the meal to the table. "'Tis a simple meal, my lord, for the cook was ill-prepared, I fear. It will be better tomorrow."

"I prefer a simple meal," Patrick Leslie replied, his eye taking in the broiled trout, the roast of beef, the game pie, the steamed artichokes, the bread, the butter, and the cheese. "'Tis an amazing repast for one so ill-prepared," he noted dryly.

"If ye are pleased, my lord, then I shall certainly tell Cook," Angus said, pouring the wine with a deft hand and then stepping back. "I regret, however, we hae only pear tartlet for a sweet. Wine or ale, my lady?" He bent by Flanna's side.

"Oh, wine!" she told him, turning to her husband. "We only had wine on special occasions at Killiecairn. Will we hae it at every meal, my lord?" She sipped at her cup greedily.

"If it pleases ye, madame," he replied.

She nodded vigorously. "I hae never tasted a wine so good," she enthused. "Where does it come from?"

"France," he said, half amused. "My mother hae family there."

"Is yer mam French?" Flanna asked him.

"Nay. My grandmother, who is the Countess of BrocCairn, and whom ye will meet, was English born. My mother's father was the ruler of a great empire in the East. The English call it India."

She nodded, and to Angus's relief asked no more questions of the duke. It would have only shown her appalling ignorance. Flanna knew only that England was to the south and there was a place called Ireland just across the sea off the western coast of Scotland. She knew France was across the water from England, but other than that, she was woefully ill informed.

The late Earl of Brae had educated his only son, and Angus had even spent two years at the university in Aberdeen. He had never thought to use his education again, but now he could see he was going to have to recall all he had been taught if he was to save his niece from eventual disaster. Once the Duke of Glenkirk had gotten an heir on his wife—once her charms wore off and his eye strayed to other women, which it surely would—Flanna would need her wits to survive. A man could only be held so long by a lush body.

Chapter

5

Flanna looked about the bedchamber that was now hers. It was the most beautiful room she had ever seen, and she wasn't certain she would ever be comfortable in it. Everything was so elegant, so rich. The walls were panels of warm golden wood. Every other panel had a colorful floral design upon it. The alternating panels were plain but for an edging of design. The ceiling was painted. Flanna had never seen such a ceiling as the one above her. It looked like a sky on one of those perfect September days, blue and filled with bright white clouds edged in apricot and pale gold. Little winged babies, voluptuous women, and beautiful men, some with their nakedness discreetly draped with diaphanous lengths of fabric, and others plainly nude, floated in that ceilinged sky. It was all quite amazing to her eye, and she blushed at the sensuousness of it. She hadn't seen this room earlier when old Mary had brought them upstairs. She had been too busy gawking at the equally magnificent dayroom that she would share with her husband, whose bedroom was next to hers, connected by a small door in the paneled wall.

Her eye now carefully scanned the furnishings in the room. The great oak bed had an eight-foot, linenfold paneled headboard. The pillars holding up the canopy were turned and carved with vines and leaves. Even the heavy wooden canopy was carved to match. Looking up, Flanna saw the inside of it was also painted, divided into panels with small designs of stars, moons, flowers, birds, and small animals. The bed was hung with wine-colored velvet and had a wine-and-gold coverlet.

The bed, the chests, the tables, and the chairs were all of warm golden oak. The chairs had rose-and-gold-tapestried backs and seats. Tall stone greyhounds flanked the large fireplace. There was a polished wooden clock upon the stone mantelpiece that chimed the hour. Upon the burnished wood floors were the most marvelous and colorful woolen coverings Flanna had ever seen. Turkey carpets, Mary had said, when they had been in the dayroom. There were silver candlesticks with beeswax tapers, and crystal and silver lamps burning scented oils, for light. The windows were hung with the same velvet wine-colored draperies as the bed. Flanna was open-mouthed with wonder at the beauty of the room.

"There's even a special chamber for yer clothing," Aggie said, equally awed, "and lady, a wee room for me, Mary says. She showed it to me, lady. I never had a place all to myself. This is a verra grand house."

"Perhaps too grand for me," Flanna said nervously. "Who lived in these rooms before me? I wonder."

"Mary says these hae always been the apartments of the master and the mistress of the castle. The duke's mother and father once inhabited these rooms, lady. And before them, his grandparents. Mary says the lady Jasmine was a verra fine lady, and that ye would nae know she came from a wild, foreign place. Mary says ye knew right away that she was of royal blood, and her servants were stately, especially Master Adali. Mary says the castle will nae be the same again now that she's gone."

"Mary says a great deal, although she is probably correct," Flanna noted dryly. "She will, I fear, hae to get used to a plain new mistress, and that mistress is me. I am nae royal, and ye are certainly nae stately, although Angus might be called so because of his great height. Now help me get ready for bed, Aggie. I am tired, and ye must be, too. We had a long day. Where is my husband?"

"I dinna know, lady. He was in the hall when we left it. I imagine he is still there, or in his own chamber. Shall I find Donal and ask him, lady?"

"Nay, nae yet. I want a bath. There was nae time before the meal. Go to Angus and see to it now, Aggie. The duke does nae sleep here, does he?

"His chamber is next to yers, lady," Aggie replied. "'Tis like that in fine houses, Mary says. Lord bless me, lady, we hae much to learn in, and about, this new place." Then she hurried off to find Angus.

Why had she asked Aggie such a foolish question? Had Mary not told them earlier that her husband had his own bedchamber? Flanna began to pace. She was tired. Worse, she was beginning to realize that her father, in his eagerness to catch her a fine husband, had not even begun to consider the consequences of a simple Highland Brodie marrying a duke. Did the old man even know? Probably not. He had never been farther than five miles from Killiecairn in his whole life but for two journeys to the summer games. All of Killiecairn could have fit into the Great Hall of Glenkirk. Her situation was impossible. A husband who didn't want her, and a castle she hadn't the faintest idea of how to manage.

There was a knock upon her chamber door, and she called out, "Come in." When she saw it was Angus, Flanna actually began to cry. *"What am I to do?"* she wailed, and he knew immediately what she was thinking.

"Cease yer greeting, my lady," he told her quietly, closing the door behind him. "I know how to govern a castle staff. Was I nae raised at Brae? All my instructions will appear to hae come from ye. Ye hae but to watch and learn from me, my lady. Ye must also master how to write more than just yer name, and know how to read. Yer mam could do both. I know ye hae nae patience for it, but ye *must* learn."

"I dinna want him to know how ignorant I am," she agreed nervously.

"I will teach ye myself," Angus reassured her. "Did nae yer grandfather educate me, though to what purpose I dinna know until now, my lady. Dinna fear. The winter is setting in, and few if any will come to Glenkirk. There is a library here, and once ye hae mastered the pursuit of reading, ye can begin to educate yerself. His mother, and those before her, were well-read women. There is nae shame in yer nae knowing foreign tongues, for yer naught but a Highland lassie; and few, if any, with whom ye will associate will speak in any tongue but our own. However, ye must learn how to speak proper English, lass, and reading and writing ye must know. There may be times when the duke must be away. He will correspond wi' ye, and ye wi' him. We will begin tomorrow, my lady."

Flanna sniffled and nodded. "Oh, Angus! What would I do wi'out ye? Ye hae always been there for me, uncle."

He gave her a quick hug, then set her back. "Hush, my lady. We dinna know how yer husband would feel about a Gordon bastard taking over the management of his household."

"He thinks little harm in bastards," Flanna replied, and then she told Angus about her husband's half brother, the Duke of Lundy.

"Ah," said Angus when she had finished, "but his brother is a prince's son, and but for an accident of birth might hae been a king. Remember my mam was plain Jessie Forbes, daughter of Bride Forbes."

"Who was yer mam's father, Angus?" Flanna asked him. "Did she ever know him? Why didna he wed wi' yer grandmam?"

"Aye, I know who he was, my lady. Like my own father, he was a nobleman. Old Fingal Forbes, my grandmam's father, always said the Forbes lasses could nae refuse a handsome lad who asked nicely." The big man chuckled. Then, changing the subject entirely, he said, "The water is being heated for yer bath and will be brought to ye shortly, my lady. His lordship says he will nae join ye tonight as he believes ye must be verra tired wi' yer journey today." Angus then bowed to her and withdrew from the chamber before Flanna might ask him any more questions.

Was she disappointed or relieved? Flanna wondered to herself as Aggie reappeared with several young men who lugged a large oaken tub into her chamber. She watched silently as the tub was filled. When the young men had gone, Aggie fussed at her to hurry and remove her garments. Flanna bathed herself silently as the serving girl pulled several bricks from the fireplace where they had been heating and wrapped them in flannel. Then she placed them in the big bed to warm it before helping her mistress to dry off, get into a nightgown, and into her bed. Finally Aggie hurried off, bidding her lady good night, but obviously very eager to gain the luxury of her own little chamber.

"It even hae its own wee window, lady," she had told Flanna before leaving her, *"and* a chest for my things!"

Flanna smiled in the dimness of her chamber. Aggie had little but a change of clothing and a pearwood comb for her nut brown hair. She was as lacking in material possessions as was her mistress, Flanna thought with a small chuckle. She snuggled down into her bed, enjoying the first real warmth she had felt all day. The soft light from the fireplace gave the room a faint golden glow. She felt more confident now than she had earlier felt, for she had complete confidence in Angus to help her overcome the deficiencies in her education and manners. Her uncle, for all his apparent lesser status, had been raised a gentleman.

Her thoughts moved on to her husband. She was sorry now that he was not joining her in her bed. She was quite revived after her bath and had enjoyed their coupling last night. If she was to give him an heir quickly, she could not allow him to avoid his husbandry duties again; but perhaps it was he who had really been tired after their daylong trek through the wet weather. He was, after all, some years her senior. Flanna rolled onto her side, pulling her legs up and curling about one of her pillows. This was a good place, and she would survive the challenges before her. She slept.

The snow had ceased by morning, having left at least half a foot of the cold, white stuff upon the ground. By the time Flanna entered the small family hall of the castle, she learned that her husband had gone out again with his huntsmen and would be gone for several days. The castle would need more than one deer to get it through the winter months. The cold larder, she learned as she made her first tour of inspection with Angus, could hang at least six fully dressed deer, and now there was but one. However, there was an abundance of game birds and wild foul hanging in neat rows.

"I would hae liked to hae gone wi' them," Flanna complained. "I'm as good a hunter as any man is. When did they leave? Mayhap I can catch up wi' them! Their tracks will be plain in the snow."

"Wi' the duke gone," Angus said quietly, "'twould be an excellent time for ye to begin yer lessons, my lady. I hae set up yer schoolroom in the duke's library. I will meet ye there shortly."

"But I want to go hunting!" Flanna protested to him.

"If ye wish, my lady, but what happens when yer husband learns how ignorant ye are? Ye hae nae really engaged his attention yet. A bridegroom who beds his bride on their wedding night, but nae the next, and then goes off hunting for several days?" Angus shook his big head very disapprovingly. "Tsk, tsk," he murmured.

"He wed me for the land," she said through gritted teeth.

"Aye," Angus agreed. "But now he hae the land, *and ye don't.* He'll need a good reason to keep ye around, and he doesna seem to hae that reason right now, *my lady.* Ye need a bairn or two."

"I'll hae them!" Flanna said fiercely.

"Nae if ye canna get him back in yer bed," her uncle said with perfect logic. "What is there about ye, Flanna lass, to interest and intrigue yer husband? Of course a man doesna want a wife far wiser than he, but he does enjoy one who can speak wi' him after the coupling. What will ye talk of to yer husband? Hunting? Housekeeping? What will ye say to him that will fascinate him and make him fall in love wi' ye, for, lassie, ye will find wi'out love the coupling will nae gie ye the pleasure it can wi' love. Lust is a grand emotion, but love is a better one. Shall I hae yer mare saddled, my lady?"

She was silent a moment. Finally she replied, "I will await ye in the duke's library, Angus." Then, with a swish of her skirts, she left him. His words had very much disturbed her.

Angus Gordon smiled as he watched her hurry off. His niece was an intelligent lass, although she didn't know how intelligent yet. He suspected she would learn quickly, and he was not disappointed in his judgment. Within two days Flanna had mastered the alphabet and was putting together small words, taking down books from the shelves and reading those words aloud, then copying them with a careful hand. To her uncle's surprise, the new Duchess of Glenkirk was also proficient in simple arithmetic.

"Mama taught me. She said I should know how to calculate so the merchants could nae cheat me. Sometimes I helped Una wi' her figures. Ye know how tight my father is wi' a merk," Flanna said.

"Aye," Angus replied, pleased his half sister had done something useful for her child.

The duke and his men returned five days later, bringing with them four fine deer to be dressed and hung in the cold larder of the castle's kitchens. Flanna was, by now, fairly familiar with the castle, having spent the time she was not at her lessons in the library exploring her new home with her uncle, the indomitable old Mary, and Aggie. She found the west tower, which had once been the domain of the lady whose picture hung over the fireplace, most interesting.

"Lady Jasmine's old grandmother used to stay there," Mary informed them. "The west tower were deserted for years until she began to visit. She liked it. Said it felt just right. She be dead and gone many years now, old Lady de Marisco. Killed a man, they say, and saved Lady Jasmine's life when she was an old woman."

"*Here?*" Flanna was fascinated.

"Nay, down in England at her home that now belongs to the Duke of Lundy," Mary said.

What kind of a family had she been married into? Flanna wondered. A mother-in-law who was a princess. A brother-in-law who was a royal bastard. So many lords and ladies if old Mary was to be believed, not to mention a murderess! "What happened to her?"

"Why, naught, my lady," Mary replied. "Lady de Marisco killed a wanted criminal who had already murdered four people. She was a verra braw old woman, God rest her!"

And now her husband was returned, Flanna decided, she must learn more about his family. She noted Patrick Leslie's look of approval as he strode into the Great Hall to see the furniture polished and the floors free of dust. The chimneys had been cleaned and burned smoke-free. The windows were shining. There were bowls of potpourri.

"Welcome home, my lord. Ye were successful, I believe, and we hae meat enough for the winter." She handed him a goblet of wine, then curtsied.

"Four stags, madame," he replied, and drank down his wine. "The weather is turning again, and so we must remain indoors; but I intend going out again as soon as we can. 'Twill be rain this time; but the snows will come again soon, and winter will set in. I hope to find at least one other deer and perhaps a wild boar for the larder."

"Ye will want a bath, of course," Flanna said. "I hae prepared it for ye." To his surprise, she took his hand and led him upstairs to their apartments. "Donal," she spoke to the duke's manservant, "take his lordship's clothing. The shirt, drawers, and stockings should go to the laundress. I will bathe my husband. Tell Angus we will eat in our dayroom this evening." She smiled, and Donal was dismissed.

Taking his master's garments, he hurried out.

Bemused, Patrick climbed into his tub. The water was hot, and as it pierced his flesh, he realized how sore his muscles were from several days of riding, the cold, and the dank weather. "Madame," he said to her, his green-gold eyes closing with enjoyment, "ye are proving to be the perfect wife. The hall was a joy to my eye, and now a bath."

"If ye're pleased, then I am content," she replied modestly.

He laughed. "How meek and mild ye hae become, lass," he teased.

"I can scarcely argue wi' ye if ye are satisfied wi' my conduct, my lord husband," Flanna answered him tartly. She took up a boar's bristle brush and, soaping it, began to brush his back and shoulders as she knelt upon the wooden steps of the tub. The brush moved swiftly and with purpose over the broad expanse of skin. Lifting an arm, she scoured it thoroughly. Then she did the other. Moving the steps about so that she faced him, she took up a foot and leg, washed it, then did its mate.

She had taken off her skirts when Donal had left the chamber, and now bathed him in her petticoats and blouse. It was the same skirt she had worn the day after their marriage. He realized suddenly that Flanna probably had few clothes, and certainly none that suited her station as his wife. He had been so intent upon making certain there was enough meat in the larder for the winter months, he had given no thought to this young woman who was now his wife. He would remedy that as quickly as possible. Still, she was quite fetching, her red head bent in concentration as she bathed him. The laces on her blouse had come undone, revealing to his eye her round, ivory bosoms. A wicked smile touched his lips. It was simply too tempting.

Flanna shrieked in surprise as he pulled her into the tub atop him. "Are ye mad, Patrick Leslie? Do ye think I hae clothing to spare that ye can make so free wi' me!" She struggled against him.

He ducked her blow, yanking the scrubbing brush from her hand, and kissed her mouth. She continued to struggle, pulling her head away from his, even as his hand slipped into her blouse to cup a breast. "Madame, ye canna show me yer wares and nae expect me to buy," he murmured in her ear, and then his tongue swept about the whorl of it.

"Ohhh, ye're a villain," she protested faintly. She bent her head, and her lips brushed over his softly. "Is this what they call *loveplay*, my lord?" Her silver-gray eyes were half closed and glittering as she settled herself facing him.

"Aye," he answered her, his tongue running over her lips. Removing his arm from about her supple waist, he slid his hand beneath her petticoats.

"Ye're wicked, ye are," she half whispered, but she shifted her position even as she spoke to facilitate the roving hand.

"Ye're a shameless hussy, madame," he said. "I knew it from the first when ye attacked me, but then, I am a man who likes shameless hussies, Flanna." His fingers teased at her nether lips, twining themselves amid the luxuriant curls adorning her Venus mons.

She sighed, and her face nuzzled into the curve between his neck and his shoulder. She did like this lovemaking, and tonight he would come into her bed again; but it would not be like their wedding night. Tonight she would be without fear and very anxious to learn how to please him. "Ohhhhhh!" she gasped, totally unprepared as he lifted her up to impale her upon his love rod.

"There now," he murmured, "that's better, eh, lass?" He pulled her forward, drawing her sopping blouse off and dropping it upon the floor. Her tight nipples brushed his lightly furred chest.

She could feel her cheeks burning. Her head was spinning dizzily. "Ohhhhhh!" His hands were cupping her buttocks as he began thrusting movements with his pelvis. The sensation of their two bodies locked in amorous conjunction was absolutely delicious, Flanna thought, as she mimicked his sensual movements. "Ohhh, aye!" she cried, surprising him with her enthusiasm.

God's boots, if she were skilled in the arts of love, she would be a truly dangerous woman, he considered, as he pistoned her. "Kiss me again, lass," he commanded her, and accepted her mouth with supreme pleasure.

Wonderful! Wonderful! Flanna reflected mistily as she experienced the pleasure his thick and probing lance gave her as he drove himself within her. She sensed she might offer him even greater delight if her sheath were tighter. She experimented in an attempt to squeeze him. When he groaned loudly, she knew she had been successful and tried again. Pulling her head away from his, she asked, "Does that please ye, my lord? Shall I do it again?"

"Aye, ye witch, ye gie me incredible enjoyment." He pushed himself deeper and harder into her, and the water in the tub sloshed violently.

Flanna shuddered, soared to heights she hadn't even known existed, and then collapsed against him, feeling quite distinctly his juices thundering into her body. "Ohhh, my lord, 'twas delicious," she whispered. "I do enjoy this coupling wi' ye verra much."

Patrick Leslie laughed weakly. "So do I, lass," he admitted.

The water about them was rapidly cooling. He had withdrawn from her and now stood, pulling her up. Flanna blushed at her naked breasts and stood in her sopping petticoats considering what to do. He solved the problem for her by loosening the tapes of the garments and pushing them off her body so that now she stood naked before him.

"Ye're lovely, Flanna, and hae nae reason to be shy wi' me. As yer husband 'tis my right to look upon ye, and admire yer beauty," he told her.

She blushed again, then said, "Step out of the tub, my lord, and I will dry ye. I set towels on the rack by the fire to warm."

"We'll dry one another," he told her, smiling, taking up a towel and beginning to rub her briskly. "Are ye hungry, madame? I certainly am. I wonder what Angus hae brought for us to eat."

"God's boots!" Flanna swore. "Do ye think he heard us?"

"'Tis possible, but I suspect yer Angus is a man of the world, lass, and 'twould nae be shocked to hear a man and his wife sporting."

When they were dry, he put on a fur-trimmed, green velvet dressing gown while Flanna slipped on a clean, soft linen shift. Barefooted they walked into the dayroom where they found the table laid with a platter of raw oysters, another of prawns in white wine, a roasted capon, a plate of lamb chops, a salad of lettuces, fresh bread, a crock of sweet butter, a wedge of hard cheese, and lastly, an apple tart. There were two pitchers, one holding October ale, and the other, wine.

"Allow me to serve ye, my lord," Flanna said.

"Gie me the oysters first," Patrick said. "If ye like the coupling so much, madame, I will need my strength returned swiftly." He sat down at the head of the table, looking at her expectantly.

"Do ye mean we can do it again tonight?" Flanna said, surprised.

Patrick Leslie laughed at her ingenuousness. "Aye, and probably more than just once, madame, if ye will allow me to rest between our bouts of passion. Does the thought please ye?"

"Aye," she said frankly. "I like it when ye make me fly like a bird, my lord. Una said I might know pleasure, and I surely do when ye go into me; but I would like to please ye as much as ye please me. Will ye nae tell me how I may do that?" She watched wide-eyed as he swallowed down the entire dozen oysters.

"Sit next to me, Flanna," he said, indicating the chair on his right.

For a moment he ignored her query. There would be time later to explain. Reaching for the platter of prawns, he told her, "We'll share them." Choosing a large crustacean by its tail, he began to enthusiastically devour it.

His appetite was prodigious. When the prawns had been eaten, Flanna filled him a plate with a large portion of chicken, several chops, and some of the lettuces. She pushed the loaf of bread between them, tearing off a hunk for herself and buttering it lavishly. Her own appetite was, she discovered, almost his equal. She felt ravenous and ate appreciatively until there was nothing left but the small tart, which they split between them. The pitcher of brown October ale was drunk.

"We'll keep the wine for later," he said with a grin.

"Is it proper," she asked him, "for a wife to enjoy her husband's attentions as much as I enjoy yers, my lord? Wi'out this love everyone talks about? We hae but known each other a week, and ye were away most of that time. Is it right that I like ye so much? I would be a good duchess and nae bring shame to the Leslies of Glenkirk."

He took her chin between his thumb and forefinger and looked into her silvery eyes. She was really quite beautiful, he considered on reflection. The small, straight nose, the oval-shaped eyes fringed in thick, sandy lashes and crowned with sandy brows. He brushed her cheek with his thumb. Her skin was like cream and soft to his touch. It had a translucent quality to it that only true redheads possessed. There was just the faintest smattering of golden freckles across the bridge of her nose. Patrick Leslie kissed the tip of that nose.

"Ye're an intelligent lass," he said. "I know ye can be a good duchess, Flanna, although our life at Glenkirk will nae be an exciting life. I will nae, like my father and mother, go to the king's court—if there even be a court now. I will nae become involved in politics or the religious infighting, or even wi' my neighbors unless I canna help it. There are those who would seek to destroy my family and steal our wealth because of the meanness in their wizened souls. I would be left in peace to live my life, to care for my people, to raise our children to be free of all prejudice, vanity, and envy. I canna do that if I allow the world and its noisy foolishness to intrude. Ye will nae entertain kings, Flanna, as my parents and my grandparents did. Ye will gie me bairns and oversee this castle, which will be yer kingdom. Do that for me, and ye will be a good duchess, and I will certainly honor ye. Can ye be happy wi' such a life? 'Tis all the life I can gie ye, Flanna, but I will nae ever leave ye to fight for the cause of any ruler, be it a king or a parliament."

"I can be content, my lord, wi' the life ye describe. 'Tis the life I hae known. I feared a different life to which I hae nae been bred. I did nae want to embarrass ye, Patrick Leslie, for ye are, it would seem, a good man."

"Come sit in my lap, Flanna," he said, releasing his tender hold upon her chin and drawing her up by the hand. She settled herself, and he cradled her in his embrace while the fireplace crackled noisily.

Laying her head against his shoulder, Flanna sighed, satisfied. She had not expected to come to so easy an arrangement with Patrick Leslie, nor so quickly. She hadn't imagined marriage would be like this at all. She couldn't see her brothers cuddling their wives. Her brothers were too busy ordering their women and children around for any show of kindness. She liked his tenderness as well as she liked his lovemaking. Perhaps her life wouldn't be so terrible after all. He had, after all, promised her her freedom if she did her duty well. Without thinking she rubbed her cheek against the velvet of his dressing gown, smiling to herself as he kissed the top of her head.

"What hair ye hae, madame," he remarked. " 'Tis the same redgold color as my ancestress whose picture hangs in the hall. I should like a wee lassie wi' hair like that." His hand slipped into her shift and cupped her breast, his thumb absently rubbing her nipple.

Her heart jumped in her chest. "First," she struggled to answer him, "we must hae a son or two for Glenkirk." She knew her duty. She would do it before his family discovered that the elegant, wealthy, and educated Duke of Glenkirk had wed with an ignorant Brodie of Killiecairn. "I am used to lads wi' all my brothers," she said.

"Yer brothers were long grown by the time ye were born," he replied, chuckling. "Aye, we'll need sons for Glenkirk, and we'll work hard ye and I to get them, but a lassie wi' her mam's flaming pate will nae displease me, Flanna . . ." He nuzzled her ear. She could surely rouse his lust, this hot-tempered, wide-eyed wife of his, he thought, his tongue dipping into the shell of her ear to tickle it wickedly.

This was ridiculous! She could feel the strength draining from her limbs as it did each time he touched her with passion. Did women always feel this way? Powerless and defenseless? It was delicious, but it was also extremely disquieting. "*Nay!*" she said, squirming away from the marauding digit.

"What is it, lassie?" He had ceased his actions the moment she had protested them.

"Dinna women make love to men, Patrick?" The silvery eyes met his green-gold ones in an honest query.

"Aye," he answered her slowly. What was this all about?

"*How?*"

"*How?*" He echoed her, looking puzzled.

"Well, certainly, my lord, all women dinna just become passive in a man's arms! Ye touch me, and I find it pleasant. Should I nae touch ye? Would ye find it as pleasurable if I did? Do two people nae participate in lovemaking, or is the woman just a *thing* to be used for her husband's gratification? Please tell me, Patrick," Flanna finished.

Patrick Leslie suddenly felt like a selfish fool. He had known from the beginning that Flanna was an innocent, but he had been so enjoying her delicious body, and her obvious delight in his prowess, that he had never considered anything else. "Mimic my actions, lass," he told her. "What pleasures ye will pleasure me. I forgot yer own unfamiliarity wi' passion in my delight of ye." He stroked her breasts gently and kissed the mouth she offered him. "Ye were a wee bit bolder on our wedding night, Flanna lass," he teased her.

"I dinna know what was to come then," she responded. Then she slid her hand beneath his dressing gown and caressed his hard chest, her fingers tangling gently in the soft down bedecking it. She burrowed her face into the curve between his neck and his shoulder, kissing it softly. Her hand reached up to draw his head to her, and she boldly tickled the inside of his ear with her tongue, blowing softly afterward. "Like this, my lord?" she murmured hotly.

"Aye," he drawled the word, and pinched her nipple tightly.

She squealed, rotating her bottom upon his lap, and nipped at his earlobe. Her hands pushed his gown from his shoulders, baring him to the waist, and she impudently began to trail kisses across his skin, twisting her body to facilitate her actions.

He was thoroughly enjoying her daring. Even more so when her shift rode up to bare her bottom to him. He sleeked his big hand over the tempting twin moons, causing her to gasp with surprise and attempt to rise from his embrace. Firmly he turned her about so that they faced each other again. He pulled the shift from her so that she was now quite naked in his arms. "Petting one's lover is much to be desired, Flanna lass. His mouth took hers in a fierce kiss. When he lifted his head from hers, she pulled him brazenly back, their lips meeting in a burning kiss.

"Ye're shameless," he groaned against her mouth.

"Ye dinna seem to like a shy lass as well," she pertly answered him as her tongue slid across his lips boldly.

Regaining control of the situation, Patrick buried his face between her breasts, causing her to squeak with surprise. For a long moment he was almost overwhelmed with the pure sweetness of her. Then, raising his head, he fastened his hands about her waist and lifted her up, settling her down again so that she sat upon his thighs facing him. Taking her face between his two hands, he kissed her again. His fingers tangled themselves in her red-gold hair.

Her hands were flat against his chest as if she meant to fend him off, but she didn't push him away. Instead, she threw her head back and sighed gustily when he kissed the long line of her throat. The heat from his body was overpowering, and she could now feel his manhood beneath her. "I want ye inside of me, Patrick Leslie," she husked. *"Now!"*

He said nothing, but lifting her, he impaled her on the long, hard length of him. Her eyes half closed as she felt him entering her, then opened to stare directly into his gaze. He was startled, but equal to the challenge. "I canna do all the work like this, Flanna lass," he told her. "Ye must ride me."

Her cheeks grew bright pink at his words, but she began to move upon him, slowly at first, then with a quicker rhythm. Her eyes never left his, and her boldness excited him even further. Reaching out, he grasped her breasts in his hands, fondling them strongly as her body slid up and down the length of him. The hard, probing love lance within her was wonderful, Flanna thought. He filled her. She squeezed his length, enjoying the sensations and his hiss of obvious pleasure.

Suddenly to her great amazement he stood, sliding his hands beneath her buttocks. Flanna wrapped her legs about his waist, clinging to him as he walked slowly from the dayroom and into his bedchamber, laying her at the foot of his bed. She felt the mattress give way beneath her weight. To her shock they were still joined, and he began to piston her fiercely, forcing her arms above her head as he looked down into her lovely face. His gaze was intense, and Flanna was unable to turn away, so mesmerized was she by her husband's great passion. He pushed hard into her, grinding himself against her, and she reveled in his almost savage demeanor, pushing her hips back up at his every downward thrust.

"*Aye! Aye!*" she encouraged him softly, her silvery eyes glittering.

"Oh, bitch, ye hae unmanned me!"

She shuddered beneath him, and he groaned deeply as his juices flooded her.

She soared once again, consumed by his fire, filled with a honey-eyed sweetness that was becoming more and more familiar, eagerly anticipated, and desperately necessary to her very existence. "Oh, Patrick," she sighed, "*I truly do like the coupling!*"

He had collapsed upon her, but now he drew away and, standing up, went to the head of the bed and pulled the coverlet back. Then he picked her up and tucked her beneath it, climbing in next to her. His arms went about her, and she rested her head upon his damp chest as his hand stroked her graceful back. "Madame, I dinna know what good fairy led me to Brae, and to ye, but I am mightily glad of it. No man could hae a better bed partner than ye are becoming."

"Is there more?" she asked him softly.

"Aye, there is love, Flanna lass," he told her.

"What is love?" she wondered aloud. "They say my father loved my mother, but I never understood what love was. Do ye know?"

He was silent for several long moments, and then he said, "I am nae certain either, Flanna. All I know is my parents seemed to be bound by some invisible cord even when they were nae together. Sometimes they spoke nae wi' words, but wi' a look. When my father was killed at Dunbar, my mother could nae longer remain where they had known so many years of happiness. She left Glenkirk. I dinna understand it, but I think that is love. Perhaps it comes in time, even as the passion between a husband and wife grows."

"Do ye think we will ever love one another, Patrick?" she said low.

"I dinna know, Flanna lass, but know that I am content wi' ye despite our short acquaintance." He rolled her beneath him, and kissed her slowly, deeply, on the mouth, then scattered kisses across her face and throat. "Verra content," he murmured against the pulse at the base of her throat.

"Ohhhh," Flanna replied ingenuously, "we're going to do it again, are nae we?" His kisses were so sweet.

"Aye, lass," he growled into her ear. "We're going to do it again. *And again. And yet again."*

Part Two

The
Do-Naught
Duchess

Chapter

6

Flanna shrieked as a hard hand smacked her bottom. She whirled angrily about to face a handsome man with shoulder-length auburn curls and laughing amber eyes.

"Come then, wench, and tell the duke his big brother, the not-so-royal Stuart, has arrived to see him. But first give us a kiss! Why, you're the prettiest lass I've seen in many a day." Reaching out, he pulled Flanna to him, kissing her mouth quite lustily.

Flanna pulled away, slapping the man with all her might. "Ye're a bold one, ye are! I'll thank ye to keep yer hands to yerself, my lord! How dare ye accost me?" she sputtered furiously.

Charles Frederick Stuart, the Duke of Lundy, rubbed his burning cheek. "You pack a mighty wallop, lassie. Don't you like to be kissed?"

"Only by my husband, my lord," Flanna said tartly, glaring at her antagonist.

"Is there trouble, my lady?" Angus materialized out of the shadows of the hall. He stood every inch of his seven feet, and the Englishman was mightily impressed, although not in the least taken aback.

"I am the duke's brother," he told Angus.

"Which one, my lord? The duke hae four brothers if I am nae

mistaken. From the sound of ye, ye're one of the English ones," Angus said, and deliberately looked down in an effort to intimidate the visitor.

The Duke of Lundy laughed. "I am the royal bastard," he replied with a grin. "And who might you be, my giant of a friend?"

"I am Angus, my lord, the majordomo of the castle," came the reply.

"And who is the wench with the quick hand?" He leered wickedly at Flanna, who glowered back fiercely.

"There is but one woman in the hall, my lord, and so I assume 'tis she to whom ye refer. She is nae wench, but the lady of the castle. I will tell yer brother that ye are here." He gave the Duke of Lundy a small bow and withdrew.

Charles Frederick Stuart stared hard at Flanna. *"The lady of the castle?"* His look was perplexed.

"I am yer brother's wife, ye randy devil!" Flanna snapped.

"Since when?" Charlie Stuart was having difficulty absorbing this.

"Almost two months," Flanna replied.

"Well, I'll be damned," came the laughing reply.

"Ye certainly will if ye continue in yer bad behavior," Flanna told him sharply. "Do ye always enter a house and grab at the women ye find there? Ye ought to be ashamed of yerself, sir!"

"Not all the women in the houses I enter are as tempting as you are, madame," he told her with a mischievous grin. "I did not know Patrick was planning to wed."

"He wasna and neither was I," Flanna said, "but circumstances intervened, and here we are."

"Does Mother know? I saw her several months ago, but of course she would not have known then. *Circumstances?* Are you with child, then, madame, that my brother decided to make an honest woman of you?"

"Ye're insulting, my lord," Flanna said. "I was nae wi' bairn when yer brother married me, but I hope I will be soon. Glenkirk needs an heir, and I intend to produce one as quickly as possible. I know my duty, my lord."

"Where did you come from, madame?"

"I am the only daughter of the Brodie of Killiecairn and the heiress of Brae, sir," Flanna told him proudly.

"God's blood!" the Duke of Lundy replied. "Killiecairn is a rustic backwater as I remember it from my days here at Glenkirk."

"We live simply at Killiecairn," Flanna said with understatement. "Are ye always this rude, my lord, or is it just because ye're English and think yerself superior to the Scots?"

"Madame, I surely did not mean to give offense," the Duke of Lundy began hastily.

"Then, ye are merely careless and thoughtless in yer speech?" she asked him sweetly.

"God's blood, madame, you are as prickly as a thistle," he responded. "I swear I did not mean to insult you. I am just very surprised to learn Patrick has taken a wife and none in the family know it. Why the need for secrecy if you are not with child?"

"There's nae secret about our marriage, my lord," Flanna said stiffly. "Perhaps ye noticed the snow as ye came our way? Today is the first time in weeks the sun hae shone. Besides, what difference should our marriage make to yer family?"

"*Charlie!*" Patrick Leslie came into the hall. "Welcome back to Glenkirk, big brother! What brings ye here at this terrible time of year? I see ye hae met my bride. Is she nae a beauty? Do ye note her hair? 'Tis the same color as my ancestress, Janet Leslie, who hangs over the fireplace. Look! Do ye see it?"

"Does Mother know? She did not seem to when I left England in November," Charles Frederick Stuart said by way of greeting to his brother.

"Nae yet. The weather has been too poor to send a messenger south. Besides, I dinna know the political situation and hesitate to risk the life of a Glenkirk man," Patrick answered. "When did ye leave Queen's Malvern? And more important, why? Mother went down into England for the express purpose of making certain none of her bairns involved themselves in the king's war, although now wi' poor King Charles dead, 'tis a moot point, is it nae?"

"King Charles II will be crowned at Scone on the first of January," the Duke of Lundy announced.

"*King of what?*" Patrick said scornfully.

"Scotland, first. Then England and Ireland," his brother replied. "He arrived in Scotland last summer."

"I know," Patrick said. "And then came Dunbar, Charlie. Father died at Dunbar. To what purpose, I ask ye? So the royal Stuart has a crown upon his head again. I dinna gie a damn, big brother! He'll nae be able to live much longer alongside his bigoted Covenanter masters, I guarantee ye. He'll bolt soon enough and leave Scotland to survive as best it can. As for England, to hell wi' the English as well!"

"God's blood, you're bitter, Patrick!" the Duke of Lundy said.

"Aye, I am. I miss Father, and I miss Mother as well. She would be here but for the Stuarts. They cause trouble for the Leslies of Glenkirk and always hae. But why are ye here, Charlie?"

"Wine, my lords?" Flanna had busied herself as the men spoke.

"Am I forgiven, madame?" Lundy asked as he took a goblet.

"I will consider it, my lord, but I suspect ye will take a bit of getting used to. Ye'll be staying the night, I assume."

"Aye, and my children, too," the Duke of Lundy said quietly.

Flanna looked startled, but before she might speak, Patrick said, "*Your children?* What has happened, Charlie?"

"Bess is dead. I had to find a safe place for my children, Patrick. They are no longer safe in England, I fear. For one thing, my wife's family are not Anglicans any longer. They would steal my sons and daughter from me, raising them to be as joyless and as narrow-minded as they are. I cannot allow that. It isn't that I care one way or the other as to how a man worships. Did not our Lord Christ say that there were many mansions in His father's house? Common sense would dictate that if there are many mansions, there are many roads leading to those mansions. Let each man follow his own conscience. I hate this bigotry over religion!"

"How did yer wife die, Charlie?" Patrick remembered his sister-in-law, Elizabeth Lightbody, the Earl of Welk's daughter. She had caught his brother's roving eye when she was but sixteen and Charlie twenty-six. While her family had looked askance at Charles Frederick Stuart's birth, they had also, with a more practical eye, noted his wealth, his estates, his title, and his closeness to the king, his uncle. They had managed to overcome their qualms and allow the marriage. It had been a very happy one.

"She was shot by one of Cromwell's troopers," the Duke of Lundy replied. "I was away for the day in Worcester. It was one of those raiding parties Cromwell uses to put fear into ordinary folk. Worcester is, of course, a royalist town. Cromwell's troopers occasionally raid the outlying estates and farms. They burst into the house and shot Smythe, my majordomo, who attempted to restrain them. When Bess ran forward to protest, they shot her, too. She died instantly, I am told. Autumn survived by remaining silent. She killed the trooper who shot Bess, but that's another story. They looted the house of what they could find, which was not a great deal. We had hidden and buried everything we could several years ago when all this began. We will regain it when this rebellion is settled. As they left, they torched the house."

"*They burned Queen's Malvern?*" Patrick was shocked. This had been his mother's home in England as a girl, his great-grandparents' house. He had spent many a happy summer there as a child.

"It's damaged, especially the east wing, but I will restore it one day when I can go home again. The servants I settled with their families upon the estate. They will watch over the house while I am away. My children I have brought to you, Patrick. Will you shelter them for me? They will not be much trouble, for they are good bairns."

"Of course we will take them," Flanna said before her husband might speak. "Where are they, my lord? Surely they hae nae been out in the cold all this time? Fetch them in at once!"

"Biddy," the Duke of Lundy called, "come into the hall and bring the children, please." He turned to his sister-in-law. "Biddy," he explained, "is the children's nurse. She was Bessie's nurse, too."

A small, plump woman of indeterminate years came forth now. With her were three children. The youngest she carried in her arms. The two others were a girl and a boy. They looked both tired and frightened.

Flanna's heart contracted. "Ah, the poor bairns," she said. "What a terrible time for them. Come by the fire my wee ones and warm yerselves."

Charles Frederick Stuart smiled softly. His brother's bride had a good heart. "These are my chicks," he said. "Sabrina is almost ten, Freddie is seven, and Willy is three. And, of course, this is our good Biddy, without whom none of us can survive." He smiled at them, then continued, "Children, this is my brother, your Uncle Patrick, and his bride, your Aunt Flanna. They will shelter you and look after you while I am gone away to help the king."

"But, Papa, we do not want you to go away," Sabrina Stuart said, with tears in her amber eyes. She clung to him.

"I shall not go until you are well settled, Brie. The king is not due in Aberdeen for another two weeks. By then Glenkirk will be as familiar to you as Queen's Malvern was," her father promised.

"We'll hae ponies for ye to ride, lassie," Patrick Leslie told his niece. "Ye like to ride, dinna ye?"

"Why do you speak so oddly?" Sabrina asked him.

"I'm a Scot, lassie, nae an Englishman. Ye're in Scotland now," he answered. "Ye'll get used to it shortly."

"I want my mother," Freddie Stuart said in a woeful tone.

"Mama's dead, you dunce! The wicked soldier shot her," his sister reminded him. "She has gone to heaven to live with Jesus."

"I don't want her to live in heaven with Jesus," Freddie now wailed. "I want her to live with us! Why won't she come home?"

"Because she won't," his sister told him grimly.

Flanna knelt so she might face the little boy. "Do ye know how to use a longbow, laddie?" she asked him.

Wordlessly, he shook his head.

"I do," Flanna said. "Would ye like me to teach ye?"

"Could you?" Freddie was intrigued with this red-haired lady with her appealing talent who smelled so good. Mama hadn't even let him have the little sword his cousin, Prince Henry, had sent him on his last birthday.

"I can," Flanna said. "Tomorrow if it doesna snow, or rain, we'll hae the butts set up in the courtyard and begin our lessons." She turned her head to Sabrina. "I'll teach ye, too, if ye like."

"I never knew a lady who could shoot a longbow," Brie said, equally fascinated with her new aunt.

"Well," Flanna told her with a chuckle, "I'm just learning to be a lady, lassie; but I'm nae one yet, and I shoot a longbow verra well." She stood up and chucked the baby beneath his chin. "And ye, wee Willie, we'll teach to sit a pony come the spring. Now, however, we must get these bairns fed and tucked into warm beds. Ye've come far." She turned her attention from the children, calling out, "Angus, where hae ye gotten to, man?"

"I am here, my lady," the majordomo said, coming forward. He bowed to the two gentlemen. "I hae already spoken wi' the house-keeper, my lady. We are preparing rooms in the east tower for the bairns. I'll take them to the kitchens to be fed wi' yer permission."

Flanna nodded, then turned to her guests. Biddy's eyes were enormous as she took in Angus, and the children looked frightened again. "Angus will nae harm ye, my bairns," Flanna said. "Like yer Biddy, Angus came wi' my mother when she wed wi' my da. He helped to raise me. Now he has come wi' me to Glenkirk. He is my friend as well as my servant. Ye must rely upon him for anything ye need. He will take good care of ye, I promise."

"Thank you, my lady," Biddy said, still looking somewhat doubt-ful rather than reassured.

Freddie, however, had regained his voice. He looked up at Angus and asked him, "How tall are you?"

"Seven feet high, laddie," came the reply.

"What is it like to be so big?" Freddie persisted.

Reaching down, Angus lifted the little boy up into his arms. "Like this, laddie. What do ye think?"

Freddie laughed. "I like it!" he shouted, laughing.

"Take me up, too," Sabrina cried, and shrieked gleefully as Angus complied with her command.

"Follow me, Mistress Biddy," Angus said. "We're off to find a good supper in the kitchens." And he marched out with his two new young friends, Biddy hurrying to keep up with him, Willie in her arms.

The Duke of Lundy turned to Flanna. "How can I thank you, madame? I can see my children will be happy and safe in your care."

"There is little to keeping bairns happy, my lord," Flanna told him. "Now, I must go and make certain the maidservants hae the children's apartment properly prepared." She curtsied and left them.

"Come, and sit down, Charlie," Patrick said. "I want all the news. Ye dinna come up to Scotland just for yer bairns, I'm certain."

The two men sat facing each other by one of the two large fireplaces in the Great Hall. Glenkirk refilled their goblets.

"How is Mother?" he asked. "When did ye see her last, and why did ye nae leave yer bairns at Cadby with Henry and his family?"

"Mama grieves deeply for Papa," Charlie answered his brother. Like all his mother's offspring by their various fathers, Charles Frederick Stuart, the not-so-royal Stuart who had never known his deceased sire, had called the late Jemmie Leslie Father, for in truth his mother's third husband was the only father he could remember. "She has taken Autumn to France along with her faithful quartet of servants, including your Glenkirk man, the one married to Toramalli. I do not think he misses this Highland lair of yours at all."

"Is there any danger of Cromwell's soldiers attacking Cadby as they did Queen's Malvern?" Patrick queried his elder sibling.

"Nay, I doubt it. That was why I brought my children to you, Patrick. Henry has been very careful in avoiding the appearance of favoring any faction at all. If I had brought my chicks to him, he could have become a target for the fanatics. Like all of us, Henry was disgusted at the old king's execution, but he saw the bigger picture. One day all the horror will be over, and the young king restored to his rightful place. If the Lindleys of Westleigh are to survive until that time, they must remain impartial. That is Henry's way, and I, too, espoused it despite my close ties to the royal family. I, however, was always suspect because of those blood ties. When Bessie was slaughtered, I knew I could not stand idly by any longer. I had to choose sides, and so I declared for the king. My children could make me vulnerable, Patrick. Here at Glenkirk they are safe, for there are few in England who know my extended family. You, brother Patrick, in your splendid isolation, will keep my children secure and unharmed. Mama knows where her Stuart grandchildren are and will not worry now."

Patrick nodded, sipping his wine slowly; then he spoke. "And ye will be doing what, Charlie, while I watch over yer young offspring? What rashness are ye planning? The Scots parliament keeps a tight rein on young Charles Rex. Did I nae hear ye tell yer daughter that the king would be in Aberdeen in two weeks? Why is he coming to Aberdeen?"

"We need to recruit an army, Patrick," Charlie replied. "If England is to be retaken from the rebels, we must have an army."

"Ye're mad! Did nae Father's death teach ye anything, Charlie?" the Duke of Glenkirk angrily shouted at his brother.

"The Scots would have never lost the battle of Dunbar if General Leslie hadn't, in his overwhelming pride, brought his troops down from the hills where he held the advantage and camped them directly in front of the English lines. Did it not occur to that pompous old trout that the English, being desperate, might attack first? England is in the grip of a monster. People have had enough. A strong army to retake it, and the king will be welcome home once again!"

"*A Scots army, ye bloody fool!*" Patrick said angrily. "Do ye really believe that an invading Scots army will rally the English to Charles Stuart's side? Two Stuart kings hae nae eased English fears of an invading Scots army! When they see all those men in their plaids, banners flying, bagpipes skirling, coming at them, the English will rise up to drive the Scots back, nae run out to greet them wi' hymns of joy and welcome. For two generations the Stuarts hae been thought of as foreigners by the English."

"That was because King James and the first Charles were born in Scotland. This Charles was born in St. James's Palace. He is English-born, and the people loved him when he was their prince. They have not changed, Patrick. They love him yet. They have had enough of Cromwell, his brutal soldiery, and the psalm singers who would purge our church of its liturgy, its bishops, and its worshipful joy," Charlie finished passionately.

"I dinna disagree wi' ye, Charlie," Patrick said, "but ye canna restore the young king to his English throne wi' a Scots army. The English will nae hae it. Ye may even hurt the king's cause."

"He wants to go home," Charlie said softly. "Bessie was killed in late September. I came north in mid-November. We have been with the court, if you can call it a court, ever since. The Scots parliament has virtually cut the king off from his true friends, banishing them from his court. Their clerics preach at him day and night. Do you know what they told him after Dunbar? That the Scots' loss was the fault of the royal Stuarts because they had not accepted the National Covenant sooner. Because they persisted in clinging to their Anglican church ways instead of leading the nation into the path of Presbyterianism! The only reason they brought him to Scotland and will go down into England with him is that they hope to bring their religion with them and enforce it on all the English."

Patrick shook his head wearily; then he said, "Do ye recall the stories Mama used to tell us of our grandfather, the Grande Mughal, Akbar? That he invited all faiths to his court and allowed them to speak freely. Catholics, Anglicans, Orthodox Greeks, Protestants, Jews, Muslims, Hindus, Buddhists, Jains, Zoroastrians. Any and all religions he encountered, he brought to his court at Fatehpur Sikri. For years he listened as they fought and argued wi' one another over whose faith was best, was the true faith. And in the end he founded his own religion which he practiced, having taken what was best from all the others. And he forced no one to accept his faith, nor did he forbid any their particular form of worship. When I see what is going on about us, Charlie, I can easily understand our grandfather's reasoning."

"So can I," Charlie agreed, "but I also know that the Grande Mughal would have never allowed a rebellion like this one, or let its rebels go unpunished. Queen Henriette lives in poverty and exile in her native France with her baby daughter, the Princess Henrietta-Anne. Prince James is with her now, although he moves back and forth between France, England, and Scotland. Prince Henry is held by Cromwell's people. The young Princess Elizabeth suffered greatly over her father's death. He brought her his prayer book before they executed him. It was the last time she saw him. She died several months ago in her prison, not yet fifteen. They said she would not be parted from that prayer book, Patrick. She was buried with it. The king holds his power *not* from the people, *but from God.* I believe that. I always will believe it. By murdering my Uncle Charles, Cromwell and his parliament rogues have attempted to thwart God's will. We must right this wrong and restore my uncle's son to his proper place upon the throne of Great Britain!"

"Cromwell believes God is on his side, too," Patrick Leslie said in reply to his brother's impassioned speech. "He and his adherents quote the Bible extensively wi' passages that would appear to prove their point. Those who use God as an excuse for their behavior are the most dangerous creatures on God's earth, Charlie. Belief in such a God allows them to murder, torture, and steal wi'out any qualms, because the deity is on *their* side alone. I dinna see how there can be a compromise in any of this, and particularly as long as the English hold Edinburgh and most of the Lowland south."

"Which is why the king is coming to Aberdeen from Scone to recruit his army from the men of the north," Charlie explained. "Patrick, you must raise a troop of Glenkirk men and ride with us. It is your duty as a loyal Scotsman, brother!"

"Nay," the Duke of Glenkirk told his sibling firmly. "My first loyalty is to my clansmen and to my immediate family. I will shelter and guard yer bairns, Charlie, but I will nae join wi' ye. The royal Stuarts are verra bad for the Leslies of Glenkirk. Our history hae proven that."

"Enough politics, my lords," Flanna said as she reentered the hall. "'Tis time for dinner. The bairns are in the kitchens having their supper. When, Charles Frederick Stuart, did ye last feed those poor mites? I hae never seen such prodigious appetites!"

"Food was scarce in England these past months," the Duke of Lundy said apologetically, "and what has been fed them here in Scotland has not been greatly to their liking, I fear. It has been peasants' fare for the most part. Brown bread, oat stirabout, boiled cabbage, salted fish. They have seen little meat, or vegetables, or sweets."

"Or a decent hot meal," the Duchess of Glenkirk said. "Cook put down barley and carrot soup made from the lamb bone of yesterday's roast, along wi' some fresh-baked slices of cottage loaf, well-buttered, and wi' a slice of good cheese each. Yer poor bairns fell on their food like young wolves. And their Biddy nae far behind them, although she tried to show more manners, poor woman. I've told Cook to gie them stewed pears, but I fear to gie them much more lest they sicken. Those poor bairns were starving!" she finished indignantly.

Charles Frederick Stuart rose up, and taking his sister-in-law's two hands in his, he raised them to his lips and kissed them. "Madame, whatever happens, I know my children will be well mothered by you. I can never repay you for such kindness."

Flanna pulled her hands away from his grasp, flushing at the compliment. "Come, sir, and sit again," she said, settling herself into her husband's lap. "Tell me about this king of yers," she said.

"He is your king, too, Flanna Leslie," came the reply. Then the Duke of Lundy said, "Well, his mother always said he was the ugliest child ever born, but the truth is he favors his Italian grandmother, Maria d'Medici, with his darkish skin, hair, and eyes. Those eyes sparkle wonderfully, though. Some call him the black boy for his coloring. His features are a mixture of both sides of the family. He had, after all, a French grandfather, an Italian grandmother, a Scots grandfather, and a Danish grandmother. He is tall, with a long face and a very sensuous mouth, or so the ladies say. He is learned, but not bookish as his grandfather and father were. He is a good soldier, if sometimes a bit reckless; but above all he has charm. *Great, great charm.*" The Duke of Lundy turned to his half brother. "You worry he cannot win over his Scots subjects, but he already has, Patrick. He already has!"

"He may hae won over the people," the Duke of Glenkirk said wisely, "but the people dinna control those men who now control the king, Charlie. He is nae an absolute ruler, and unless he can become one, there is nae hope of him regaining his English throne."

Flanna ignored the brothers' quarrel, and asked, "What is the court like?"

Charles Frederick Stuart laughed, almost bitterly. "There has been no true court in years, madame," he said. "Not that I was one for court, for I wasn't; but sometimes my uncle, the king, would invite me to join them. 'Twas usually on family occasions such as the time just before Christmas until just after Twelfth Night, for hunting in the late summer and autumn, at Eastertide, or my cousin Charles's birthday. In those days, as in the days of my grandfather, there were masques, and dancing, hunts and banquets. The women dressed in beautiful clothing and jewels, and the men were equally resplendent; not like today, with everyone in somber black, relieved only by starched white collars. It was a grand time, Flanna Leslie. Not like today." He grew silent for several long moments, and his handsome Stuart face was sad. Then the Duke of Lundy sighed deeply. "We must restore our rightful king," he said. "Great Britain and our people were not meant to live this joyless existence where even the celebration of Christmas is banned. Simple folk can no longer dance about their Maypoles on a warm spring night or bowl a game upon their village greens on an autumn day. Mother met Henry, India and Fortune's father, on May Day, you know. They say he fell in love at first sight. Do you remember how extraordinarily beautiful Mother was in her youth, Patrick?"

His younger brother nodded. "No one was ever as beautiful as our Mother, except perhaps Madame Skye," Patrick replied.

"Who was she?" Flanna asked.

"Our great-grandmother," Charlie answered. "There has never been anyone quite like her, nor, I expect, will there ever be again."

There was a deep silence again, and Flanna could see the two men were becoming maudlin with their memories, encouraged by the castle's good wine. She arose from her husband's lap. "My lords, the servants are bringing in the supper, and cook will be greatly offended if you dinna do justice to his fine meal." She led them to the high board and sat between them. "I will serve the gentlemen," she told the attending servant, and then she filled the pewter plates from the platters and dishes offered, handing the first to their guest, the second to her husband, and keeping a third plate for herself.

It was a simple meal with only a few dishes. There was broiled trout, a venison stew with a rich, winey gravy, slices of leek and carrots, a platter of roasted quails stuffed with dried fruits, a half ham, creamed onions, boiled beets, a bowl of tiny lettuces lightly braised in white wine, a large round loaf, still warm from the ovens, a crock of sweet butter, and a small wheel of hard cheese. The men ate heartily, and their goblets were kept well filled by Angus, who oversaw all. A fresh-baked apple tartlet with heavy cream completed the meal.

Charles Frederick Stuart pushed back his plate with a sigh of contentment. "Madame," he said to Flanna, "you are every bit as good a chatelaine as all the ladies who have come before you here at Glenkirk. 'Twas a very fine meal, indeed. The best I have eaten in many a month, I vow."

"I would imagine it stands well in comparison to boiled cabbage and salted fish," Flanna replied dryly. Then she arose. "I must go and see that the bairns are settled comfortably, my lords." Then she left them.

"She's not at all what I expected the next Duchess of Glenkirk to be," the Duke of Lundy told his brother. "Still, she is a good lass, I can tell, if a bit outspoken."

"Ye were too comfortable wi' yer sweet Bess," Patrick Leslie answered his brother. "Outspoken women are nae an oddity in this family, big brother. I think Flanna fits in quite well."

"Why did you wed her?" Charlie queried. "You could have done a helluva lot better than the Brodie of Killiecairn's red-haired daughter. You're a duke as well as an earl, Patrick. You could have had a great heiress for Glenkirk. You surely don't love her."

"When Mother left she said to take a wife to get heirs on for Glenkirk," Patrick Leslie explained to his elder sibling. "I dinna know any *suitable* women. Christ, Charlie, ye know I hae hardly ever left Glenkirk. When our parents were yet here it always seemed as if there was time. Endless time, and we would all go on forever wi'out changing. Then I was alone. I decided I wanted Brae lands for Glenkirk. The only way I could obtain them was to marry Flanna. Her old father would nae take gold, and believe me, I offered him an outrageous amount. I needed a wife, and Flanna was a virgin wi' a property I desired and could obtain only one way. Our marriage served a purpose, Charlie. It gave the old Brodie of Killiecairn what he wanted, and it gave me what I wanted. *Brae.*"

"And what did Flanna want, little brother?"

Patrick Leslie laughed. "To be left alone at Brae wi' her two servants, so she might run wild. Still, she is adapting well to life at Glenkirk, for all her rough upbringing. She is always eager to learn and desires nothing more now than to be a proper lady."

"And give you heirs," his brother said with a chuckle. "She told me that herself. Does she enjoy bedsport?"

Patrick Leslie actually blushed. "Aye," he mumbled.

"Enthusiastic, is she, then?" Charlie teased. "Ahh, you're a lucky man. A woman can be taught many things. To be a lady. To appreciate fine art and jewels. To dance and to keep the household accounts. But she cannot be taught to be enthusiastic in her passion. That must come naturally as you well know. Perhaps your Flanna will be a suitable, if unconventional, duchess, dear brother. She is certainly quite a beauty with that hair and skin. What color are her eyes?"

"Gray," Patrick Leslie said. "Sometimes like a storm cloud, and other times like silver. It depends on her mood."

Charlie chortled. "If you've noticed that, Patrick, then perhaps 'tis more than her lands that are of interest to you now."

"She is a pleasing lassie," came the reply. Patrick could feel his cheeks flushing again with his brother's remark.

Charlie laughed all the harder. "Could it be, Patrick Leslie, that you are falling in love? And for the first time, too! God's blood, how Henry will himself laugh when I see him again and tell him!"

"I'm nae in love wi' her," the Duke of Glenkirk denied. "I will nae ever love a woman. Loving but leads to pain, Charlie. Mother loved Father, but he would nae heed her warning and got himself killed needlessly. Ye loved yer Bess so much that her death hae made ye reckless, and yer foolish actions will probably end in yer death, too. India and Fortune loved, too; but India almost lost her firstborn because of her love; and Fortune's love hae cost her Maguire's Ford, and she is exiled from our family forever. Nay, I shall nae love, brother."

"Mother had many happy years with our father," Charlie retorted. "India did not lose her son and found her happiness with Deverall. Fortune loved Kieran Devers so much she was willing to leave Ireland and go to the New World with him. As for me, I am the son of a royal Stuart. That family welcomed me from my birth and always treated me with loving kindness. I could not sit on the fence forever in this matter between king and parliament, Patrick. Bess's death but forced me to my decision. A decision I would have made sooner or later. To love is a gift from God. I hope someday you will realize that and allow yourself to love. Flanna appears to be a warmhearted girl. I did not notice you objecting when she sat herself in your lap earlier."

"I am fond of her as I am of my dogs and cats," was the reply.

"Then, you're a fool, Patrick," his brother told him.

Flanna reentered the hall then, saying, "Yer bairns are settled, my lord, but they would verra much like it if ye would go and bid them good night. The lassie is fretting herself that ye will leave them wi'out saying farewell. Ye must reassure her that ye intend remaining at Glenkirk until ye must go down to Perth to meet the king. Surely ye and my husband hae argued yerselves out by now."

Charles Frederick Stuart arose from the high board with a lazy smile. "Aye, for tonight, we have, eh, Patrick? He's a great fool, madame, but I expect you already know that." Then, with a bow, the Duke of Lundy left the Great Hall of Glenkirk.

"What did he mean, ye're a great fool?" Flanna asked her husband.

"He believes I will endanger the family more by nae declaring for the king than by asserting my loyalty to the royal Stuarts. I hold that my neutrality serves us better. That is all, lassie," Patrick lied.

"Come by the fire," she invited. "I would sit wi' ye again, my lord, and perhaps seduce ye a wee bit." She smiled at him and held out her hand to him.

For a moment he felt guilty, remembering his words to his

brother that he would never love, but then he stood up and joined her. Flanna was his wife whether he loved her or not. Sitting down, he pulled her into his lap, kissing the ripe red mouth she offered him. She was so very tempting, and becoming more so as each day passed, it seemed to him. *But he was not in love with her.* She murmured and pressed against him, her lips softening beneath his, opening for him, her tongue, now outrageously skillful, wreaking merry havoc with his senses. He pulled his dark head away from her and ran his thumb along her mouth.

Flanna's eyes, glittering silver fire, but half opened. Gently she bit his thumb, then sucked it into her mouth with a purr.

"Ye're a shameless lass," he murmured as his other hand slid beneath her petticoats and began to stroke her thigh. True to her Highland upbringing, she wore no drawers. *A lady would hae worn drawers*, he thought, but he didn't want her to ever become that much of a lady. His fingers tangled themselves into the thatch of tight curls springing from her Venus mons. Her slit was moist with her rising ardor. "Shameless," he repeated, and he pushed two fingers past her nether lips, stroking her little jewel until she squirmed her bottom against his tightening crotch, sucking all the harder on his thumb before he pulled it away from her. His fingers slid into her wet sheath, moving back and forth with intense rhythm until she was gasping with her passion. Leaning over, he nipped her earlobe, and whispered to her, "Tell me ye want me, Flanna! Tell me ye want my cock deep inside of ye, gieing us both the pleasure we crave. *Tell me!*"

"Nay," she taunted him. *"Ye tell me!* I am content as we are, but I think ye're nae so content. Ahhhhh! I can feel yer naughty laddie struggling to escape the confines of yer trews, my lord. *Do ye want me, Patrick Leslie? Do ye?* Ohhhhhhhh! Dinna take them out!"

"Oh, bitch," he growled, struggling to undo the fastenings that kept his hot desire in check. Successful, he lifted Flanna a moment from his lap and then slowly lowered her onto his raging lover's lance, groaning as he encased himself in her throbbing warmth. His fingers tore at the laces of her gown, pulling them open, ripping her chemise to reveal her delicious breasts. He groaned again.

She laughed softly, slipping her arms about his neck and leaning back so he might avail himself of her bounty. "There, my lord. All for ye, and nae other. Ohh, aye! 'Tis lovely," she exclaimed as he began to lick at her nipples with long, sweeping strokes of his tongue. "Ummmmm," she sighed with delight as his touch sent waves of shivers down her spine. It was too delicious, and she was heedless that someone might come into the Great Hall so deep was her pleasure.

Charles Frederick Stuart stood in the shadows of the entry to the hall waiting until his sibling and the passionate Flanna had completed their little bout of Eros. He would not have come back at all except he had absolutely no idea where he was to sleep this night. Charlie smiled to himself, thinking that Patrick might not realize it, but he was already in love with his beautiful wife, and she with him. No two people could sustain lust like theirs for several months' time without feeling some tender emotion toward one another. He wondered if either of these innocents knew or understood that. Eventually one of them was going to realize what had happened, and then . . . He chuckled softly to himself. What a discovery it was going to be.

Flanna cried out softly with her crisis even as Patrick groaned as if he were in pain. She fell against him, and his arms closed about her. There they remained for several minutes until Flanna suddenly straightened up with a gasp.

"Ohh, Patrick! Yer brother doesna know where he is to sleep this night. He will surely be coming back into the hall!" She struggled to draw the torn halves of her chemise together, crying, "Oh, lace up my gown, my lord, before we are caught in such a state. Surely yer brother would be shocked by our impetuous behavior." She attempted to smooth her hair into a semblance of order.

Her husband laughed low, his skillful fingers doing up her gown as he spoke. "Charlie is a Stuart, lassie, and the Stuarts are given to deep and quick passions. More likely he will tease us if he catches us this way. There, lassie, ye're done. Would ye like to return the favor." He leered at her as she slipped from his embrace.

Flanna looked down at her husband's manhood, now limp and

shriveled with its recent exercise. Reaching out, she caressed him. Then she said, "Perhaps it would be best for ye to do it yerself, Patrick."

Charlie waited a few more moments until his brother's garb was neatened, and then he came loudly into the hall. "Well, the bairns are well settled, and I thank you both. Now, however, you must tell me where I am supposed to sleep, dear sister-in-law."

"Of course, my lord," Flanna answered him primly. "If ye will follow me, I will see ye settled comfortably." Her tone was the very model of the proper wife, not at all that of the lustful woman he had just observed.

Charlie reached out and caught at an errant tendril of Flanna's red-gold hair. "As comfortable as you had my brother settled but a few moments back, madame?" he teased her, simply unable to resist.

Flanna was at first shocked, then astounded by his words. She felt her cheeks burning, but looking at her mischievous brother-in-law directly in his dancing amber eyes, she said calmly, "Well, perhaps nae quite as comfortably, my lord, but ye will be verra cozy. We hae wonderful featherbeds and down comforters."

Charles Frederick Stuart burst out laughing, and turning, he winked broadly at his brother. "If she wasn't yours, Patrick, I could easily love this Duchess of Glenkirk," he said. "Remember what I told you earlier, and don't play the fool for too long. You could lose all if you do." Then he turned back to Flanna. "Lead on, madame. I long for this promised cozy bedding, although I will wager my bed will not be nearly as comfortable as my brother's tonight." Then, laughing, he followed her out of the hall.

Chapter

7

The Duke of Lundy remained with his brother until after Christmas. It was during that time that he told Flanna stories of their mother's family. How the mother-in-law Flanna had yet to meet, might never meet, was born an imperial Mughal princess in a land halfway around the world from Glenkirk in a place called India.

"Her name was Yasamin Kama Begum," Charlie told his wide-eyed sister-in-law. "Yasamin means Jasmine flower. Kama was her land's word for *love,* and Begum was a princess. Our grandmother, Velvet Gordon, the Countess of BrocCairn, believing her husband dead in a duel, had gone out to India to meet her parents, who were there in the interests of their trading company. She was kidnapped and given to India's ruler to be one of his wives." Charlie was deliberately keeping his story, which was a great deal more complicated, simple; because he knew that Flanna, unsophisticated and naïve to the world beyond her Highlands, would not otherwise understand.

"*One of his wives?*" Flanna was more curious than shocked. "How many did he hae?"

Charlie laughed. "Forty! Our imperial grandfather lived in a world where a man might have many wives. Most of them had been wed to him for political reasons. To end a conflict or to seal a treaty," he explained. Then he continued on with his tale. "Then our grandmother learned her husband had not been killed in his duel. But by then our princess mother had been born. Grandmama wanted to remain in India, but our grandfather would not do anything to bring dishonor upon his name. She was returned to England and to the Earl of BrocCairn. Our mother, however, remained with her father in India. No one but our great-grandparents even knew of mother's existence until she arrived in London in the winter of sixteen hundred and six. Her father was dead. Her first husband had been murdered. She was forced to flee her homeland. She came to our great-grandmother, Madame Skye, for safety."

"I hae heard mention of this Madame Skye since I came to Glenkirk," Flanna said. "Was she as fabulous as they say? Even now they speak of her. Yet she was an old woman when she visited, I am told."

"She was born in Ireland," Charlie began anew. "She lived through the reigns of two monarchs. She knew both the Great Elizabeth and our own King James. She sparred with Queen Bess and, I am told, got the best of her, although in the end the Queen's will prevailed, of course. She had six husbands, and she outlived them all. She bore eight children, seven of whom lived. She built a great trading empire that enriched us all and continues to do so today. She made it her duty to see to her family's happiness and safety until the day she died. In her old age she killed a man to protect our mother. Put a dagger right into his heart."

Flanna gasped. "She was an old fierce lady, was she nae? 'Tis good to know my bairns will hae such strong blood in their veins."

"Your husband's family had a matriarch every bit Madame Skye's equal," Charlie replied. "The portrait of the young girl above the fireplace here in the hall. She was the daughter of the first earl, and she went with her father to a little kingdom called San Lorenzo. The first Patrick Leslie was King James IV's ambassador to that city-state. Janet Leslie was wed to the heir of San Lorenzo, but she was kidnapped by Turkish pirates and somehow ended up in the Turkish sultan's harem."

"She was a *kadin*," Patrick took up the story his brother had begun. "That was the word they used for a favorite. When she gave this sultan his first son, she was elevated to the status of a *bas-kadin*, or favorite first wife. Her descendants rule in that place to this day. Her youngest son she sent back to Scotland to be raised, and then when her husband had died, she returned herself. It was she who obtained the Earldom of Sithean for that branch of the family, her direct descendants. We here at Glenkirk descend from Janet's brother, Adam."

"Imperial emperors and sultans!" Flanna exclaimed. "I hae never heard of such men before now. I am surprised ye would wed so humble a lass as a Brodie of Killiecairn, my lord."

"But ye hae Brae, lassie, and I wanted it," he replied bluntly.

It was a cruel remark. While Patrick didn't, Charlie did see the quick look of hurt that passed over Flanna's face. It was gone, however, as swiftly as it had appeared.

"Not all of our relations are royal or lordly," the Duke of Lundy said in an effort to smooth over the moment. "Madame Skye's two eldest sons were certainly not. One inherited the small bit of land his father had possessed in Ireland. The other was a sea captain out of Devon. Madame Skye's eldest daughter was the child of a Spanish merchant in Algiers. Her second daughter and youngest son were the children of the Irish Lord Burke, who was landless and certainly without any influence."

"But how did Madame Skye become a lady?" Flanna wondered.

"It was her third husband, the Earl of Lynmouth, who was responsible for elevating her into the ranks of lords and ladies. It was then she was introduced into the queen's glittering court. Her husband gave a masquerade each Twelfth Night that was the talk of London in its day. The queen always attended it, and not just for a few ceremonial moments, but for the entire night. To obtain an invitation to the Earl of Lynmouth's masque was considered quite a coup. You had arrived socially if you went."

"And their son continued the tradition," Patrick said. "Mother caused a scandal wi' Father at one of those masques."

"How?"

Patrick chuckled. "She was caught abed wi' him after the guests hae gone home. It was our Aunt Sybilla who found them and raised a merry hue and cry over it. Our aunt, ye see, hae been brought up at BrocCairn. She was my grandfather's bastard, whom he legitimized. Our grandmother hae raised Aunt Sybilla as her own. She was fiercely jealous of Mother when they first met and hae planned to ensnare our father for herself. She was furious to discover him wi' our mother and caused a great havoc."

"So it was then yer parents were wed," Flanna said.

Patrick chuckled again. "Nay. Mother would nae hae Father under such circumstances. Despite the fact the situation was compromising, she refused to be forced into marriage wi' him, or hae him forced to the altar. So, Madame Skye hae her wed to Rowan Lindley, the Marquis of Westleigh, who was already in love wi' Mother. When several years later he was killed in Ireland, Mother would allow nae one to make a match for her. Charlie's father became enamored of her, and she wi' him; but Prince Henry died shortly after Charlie's birth. It was then old King James and his queen, meaning well, ordered Mother to marry Father. Instead, she ran away to France wi' her bairns. And it was almost two years before Father caught up wi her, and they reconciled. It was then they were wed and came home to Glenkirk."

"But," added Charlie, "the old king had made a muddle of the whole situation and half promised Mother to another man as well. When Mother married Father that fellow was furious. He sought to destroy them. He did not, of course, but instead was sought for a murder he had committed and attempted to blame on the Leslies of Glenkirk. He disappeared, only to show up again and threaten Mother's life."

"And that was when yer Madame Skye killed him?" Flanna asked.

"Aye," the two brothers said in unison.

Flanna was amazed. What kind of a family had she married into? Great rulers and lordlings. Incredible wealth. Women who were beautiful, adored, clever, sought after, and fought over by powerful men. *And then there was Flanna Brodie.* A Highland lass of absolutely no import; her value only in a small piece of land called Brae. She had seen the portrait of Janet Leslie over the fireplace; and in the portrait gallery of the castle the portrait of Patrick's mother, the fabled Jasmine; and his beautiful grandmother, Cat Leslie, who had defied a king to be with the man she loved. Who was Flanna Brodie when compared to these wise and wonderful women? She wanted to make her own mark at Glenkirk so that one day her portrait would hang in the family gallery, and her successors would say, "Ah, yes, and this is Flanna Leslie, wife to the second duke, who . . . Who what?" Flanna sighed deeply. What could she possibly do to make her mark?

Over the next few days Flanna mothered her two little nephews and young niece. True to her word, she began to teach the elder children how to use a longbow. Sabrina Stuart was fascinated by the flame-haired woman who, she was discovering, was quite wonderful.

"I hit it! I hit it!" the little girl cried excitedly the first time her arrow found its mark in the straw butt set up in the castle's courtyard. Notching and letting fly another arrow, she once again found her target. "You have really taught me to do it," she said, raising shining eyes to Flanna.

"Now ye must teach me to be a real lady in return," Flanna replied, smiling down at the little girl. "Someday I might go to court, and I wouldna want to embarrass yer uncle wi' my rough manners."

"Your manners are quite good," Sabrina answered. "You speak with a funny accent, of course, but then you are not English. You are a Scot. The Lowlanders with cousin Charles have a little accent, but I understand them better. I do not like them, though. They are sourfaced and mean to the king. Still, King Charles is a gentleman, and he pretends not to notice." Sabrina was quite mature for a girl of nine. "Cousin Charles has beautiful manners," she continued. "I hae never seen him be unkind or rude to any, no matter their attitude to him. He does miss the ladies, though. There are few women with the court right now. Those that are there are dour and not at all to his taste. Cousin Charles likes me," she confided to Flanna. "Papa says it is a good thing I am just a little girl or the king might take it into his head to seduce me. Papa says I will be very beautiful one day."

"Pretty is only as pretty does," Flanna heard herself quoting her sister-in-law, Una, "but aye, I think ye'll be verra pretty when ye're a grown lady, Brie."

"How long are we to remain with you, Aunt Flanna?" the little girl asked. "Will we be here until the spring?"

"I dinna know, lassie," Flanna answered honestly, stamping her booted feet to get a bit of warmth back into them. "Glenkirk will be yer home as long as ye need it to be."

"I miss Mother, and I miss Queen's Malvern," Sabrina said pensively. "I know Mother is dead, and gone from me, but I want to go home!" Tears sprang into her amber eyes. She was really, for all her sophisticated chatter, a little girl.

Flanna knelt and put comforting arms about the girl. "The way I understand it, Brie, there is a civil war in England. Ye canna go home until it is settled. Then, too, yer home was damaged and must be repaired. It will take time, lassie." She stood again and, taking Sabrina's hand, led her back into the house, leaving Angus to watch over her nephew. "When the king goes home to England again, then ye can go home to England again, too." A servant took their cloaks as they entered the hall. "Hot mulled cider for my lady Stuart," the Duchess of Glenkirk ordered, "and wine for me."

"If only Uncle Patrick would send his men to help the king, it would all be all right," Brie said with perfect youthful logic. "Why won't he help the king, aunt?"

"Because the royal Stuarts seem to bring bad luck upon the Leslies of Glenkirk whenever they become involved wi' one another, or so ye uncle says," Flanna explained. "Besides, it would take more men than Glenkirk could supply to help the king regain his throne in England," she explained.

"I wish I were older," Lady Sabrina Stuart said passionately. "Then I should go and raise up men for my cousin Charles!"

It was as if Flanna had been struck with a lightning bolt. Brie might not be old enough to help the king, but Flanna Leslie certainly was! This nonsense that Patrick kept nattering about bad fortune was just silly! There was no curse between the royal Stuarts and the Leslies of Glenkirk. This would be how she could make her mark among the Leslie women. She would be the Glenkirk duchess who helped King Charles II regain his throne, by traveling among the Highland clans and encouraging them to join their king in his righteous quest. First, however, she must meet the king. She had to be certain that he was worthy of her efforts, and she needed his permission. *But how?*

Patrick would certainly not approve of her plans, Flanna knew, but this was something she knew she had to do. She was not some milk-and-water lass unable to act without her man's permission. Then the thought struck her. She could follow her brother-in-law, Charles Frederick Stuart, when he departed Glenkirk. That would be the easy part. Finding a way to cover her absence would be harder, but the trusting Aggie would unwittingly help her. Angus, she knew, would greatly disapprove. He might even attempt to stop her, but she would not be stopped.

She would trail the Duke of Lundy until he had reached Perth. Then she would reveal herself to him. Charlie would insist on sending her home, but she would refuse to go until she had met the king. After all, the Duke of Lundy could scarce bind his sister-in-law up hand and foot in order to control her. He wouldn't want to draw attention to her behavior. Yes! That was just what she would do. And if the king gave his permission, she would solicit men for him herself no matter her husband!

But the time of Christ's Mass was approaching. While the new church in Scotland did not favor undue celebration, if indeed one celebrated at all, Flanna knew here at Glenkirk the old traditions would be kept. And no complaint would be made to the distant authorities who were, after all, strangers. Each clansman, and his family, able to make the journey would be welcome at the castle. There would be gifts for everyone. Knives, honingstones, and arrows for the men. Ribbons, thread, and lace for the women. Sweets for all the children. Each family who came would receive a silver coin. Rents were forgiven the most ancient of the pensioners. There would be feasting in the Great Hall for everyone over the twelve days of festivities.

It would be an odd celebration, Angus knew, as he began the preparations. James Leslie was dead, and his wife, beloved by the clansmen and women, was gone from them to foreign places. Still, it would be his niece's first Christmas as mistress of Glenkirk. He wanted it to be a memorable one for her and a happy one for their guests. Angus had made a friend of Mary More-Leslie. It had not been easy for Mary had been devoted to the Duchess Jasmine and practically worshiped her servant, the legendary Adali. If the duke had been embittered by the events of the last few months, so, too, had Glenkirk's housekeeper. But Angus Gordon had charm, and he had manners. Mary realized immediately that he was a bit more than a mere servant.

Adali, Angus quickly learned, had overseen all the domestic arrangements at Glenkirk, ruling the servants with a firm, but kindly hand. Angus now did the same. Relieved to have a strong hand in charge again, the castle folk responded to his authoritative rule. Mary, pleased, was suddenly Angus's good right hand. The new duchess might be a bit rough and wild, Mary considered, but hopefully that would change as the lass felt secure. Glenkirk was alive again. There were children laughing and causing mischief. It was just like old times, Mary More-Leslie decided, content for the first time in months.

"There's the Yule log to find," she told Angus. "Perhaps her ladyship would like to take the children out into the forest to seek it. The duke and his brothers always went for the log."

"An excellent suggestion, Mistress Mary," Angus agreed.

"And the duke and his men must find a boar. I dinna care what these dour Presbyterians think. We celebrate the Lord's birth here at Glenkirk. Come Christmas Day the good Mr. Edie will be sitting next to Father Kenneth eating and drinking wi' the best of them, and ye'll hear nae complaint from him, I can assure ye."

"Ye know the castle folk verra well," Angus remarked with a chuckle, and he smiled at Mary.

"Oh, go on wi' ye, Angus Gordon," she said, laughing. "I'm already charmed by ye. Ye're a good man, and between us we'll manage verra well, I'm thinking."

He gave her an elegant bow. "Wi'out ye, Mary, I couldna do it, and ye know that's the truth of it."

"I wonder if we can get turkeys," Mary mused. "It's too far to the town. I suppose we can make do wi' capon, beef, and fish. Better we hae too much than nae enough," she decided. "I've baskets of apples in the cellars, so we'll hae tarts for the sweet. The bairns from the cottages dinna see sweets often. Wait till ye see how big their eyes get when we bring them in, Angus. It just does a body good." Then she wiped her eyes with her apron.

"Ye've a soft heart, Mistress Mary," he said softly.

"I suspect ye're nae better than I am, Angus Gordon," she replied sharply. "I've seen ye patiently working wi' her ladyship over her letters. Why on earth did the lass wait until now to learn? She hae to know that one day she would wed and hae to manage a home. She should hae been educated long since. Did her mam nae care?"

"I am my Gordon sire's bastard, and dinna look so innocent, Mary, for ye hae guessed it already even if the others dinna see it. My half sister died when Flanna was ten. Our father and Meg's mam, God assoil them, raised us together. My sister, being true born, was the heiress to Brae, but I was never treated as anything less than my father's son. When Meg wed Brodie, I went wi' her to Killiecairn. Flanna resisted her mother's efforts to teach her to read and to write. After Meg died, Flanna's sister-in-law tried to take charge of the child, but it was almost impossible, for all my niece wanted to do was run wild out-of-doors. I taught her to ride, to hunt, to fish, and to shoot. The women in her family, wi' difficulty, taught her how to sew, weave, and cook, but they are nae pursuits that she relishes. When she came to Glenkirk, she realized her error in refusing to be educated. She looks at the portraits of the previous ladies of Glenkirk, and she is intimidated. She longs to make her own mark, but knows she canna as she now is. Aye, I am patient wi' her, Mary. Meg would want me to be, although I will admit to ye there are times when I should like to turn the lass over my knee and smack her bottom."

Mary burst out laughing at the big man's acknowledgment. "I think," she said, "ye can leave that to the duke. He canna ignore her like her sire did. He doesna understand that he is already in love wi' her, *and she wi' him*. I've seen them looking at each other when they dinna think anyone notices. I'm looking forward to a new generation of Leslies, Angus. His mother would be verra happy."

"Even if Flanna is a bit wild?" the big man teased the housekeeper.

"Nae all Glenkirk's ladies can be born princesses, and most werena," Mary said calmly. "Ah, Angus, I hope that one day ye will meet her, our Duchess Jasmine, but she couldna remain here wi'out her Jemmie Leslie. Still, wi' them gone, there is a void at Glenkirk Duke Patrick and his wife will hae to fill." She sighed and wiped her eyes again with her apron. Then, straightening up, she said briskly, "Now, Angus Gordon, what else do we hae to do to make this a happy Christmas for us all?"

When Angus told his niece how helpful Mary More-Leslie had become, the young duchess was openly grateful to the older woman. She took her suggestion, and with the three young Stuarts in tow, and in the company of a group of clansmen, they rode into the forest surrounding the castle to find the perfect Yule log for their celebrations. The day was unusually sunny and mild for a December morning. There was no wind.

"We canna linger," Flanna told the children. "There will be a storm before tomorrow. Nor should we go too far from the castle."

"How do you know there will be a storm?" Brie asked her aunt. "I wish it would be like this all winter. I haven't seen the sun a great deal since we came north."

"It should nae be sunny now, nor should we hae the warmth," Flanna explained. "Then, too, there is nae wind, lassie. All this portends a coming storm." She sniffed. "Smell the air," she told the three children. "Can ye nae scent the snow? And while the air is soft, there is an underlying chill to it."

"How do you know all of that?" Freddie Stuart asked her.

"This land is where I was born and where I was bred," Flanna replied. "I hae nae been a prim lass to sit by my loom, Freddie. I was out wi' Angus learning how to hunt and track my quarry. Ye canna depend upon the weather to remain constant, so ye must learn how to understand the signs it gives ye."

"I want to learn," Freddie said.

"If ye stay wi' us long enough, Freddie, I'll teach ye," Flanna promised him. "And yer sister and wee brother." Then she kicked Glaise into a trot. "Come along now, bairns. Angus says Cook is making scones today. The sooner we find our Yule log, the sooner we'll be home to eat them. And Mary says there is plum conserves."

They searched through the forest for over an hour before they came across a great oak that had fallen only recently. The clansmen dismounted and, taking their saws, began to cut off the bottom of the trunk where the roots were still in evidence. When the stump had fallen away, they cut several great logs, each one destined to fill a fireplace in the Great Hall. The largest piece would serve as an official Yule log. Ropes were wrapped about it, and it was dragged back to Glenkirk in triumph and stored outside the hall until Christmas Eve when it would be brought in with much ceremony. Several parties of men returned to the forest to drag back the rest of the oak logs before the storm.

Flanna shepherded the children to the kitchens from where the scent of baking was coming. Seeing them enter, the assistant cook smiled and drew forth a tray of freshly baked scones from the brick oven next to a great fireplace. She set the tray upon the wooden table in the center of her domain. Then, carefully splitting three of the scones, she buttered them lavishly and spread plum conserves upon them. With much formality she handed each child a scone. The look on the three young faces caused her to chuckle.

"Thank ye, Cook," Flanna said to the woman. "The bairns are already looking healthier and plumper because of ye."

"And thanks to yer good mothering," the cook replied. "Puir Master Charlie to lose his wife and be left alone. I remember him when I was but a scullery maid in this kitchen, and he a wee lad like this angel." She ruffled Willy's hair, beaming down at the youngest Stuart, whose face was liberally smeared with purple jam.

"Everyone here hae history wi' it," Flanna said softly.

"And did ye nae at Killiecairn?" the cook replied.

"Aye, but 'twas different," Flanna responded.

"I should think so," the cook said. *"This is Glenkirk.* There is nae place like it, m'lady, on the face of the earth. And when 'tis gone one day, for all things fade eventually, there will nae be anything like it again."

In the next few days that followed, Flanna, the children, and several of the servants decorated the hall with greenery, boughs of pine, and bunches of holly. Flanna knew the Christmas customs that were to take place from Christmas Eve until Twelfth Night. The number twelve played an important part in the festival. Twelve candelabrums were set about the hall. Each bunch of holly was made up of twelve sprigs. Gifts, totaling twelve, would be exchanged over the twelve days of Christmas. There would be Yule dolls made of gingerbread. On the afternoon of December twenty-fourth, a green line was drawn about the hall. At the appointed hour, the guests would enter the Great Hall, being careful not to disturb the green line. No feasting would begin until the lucky bird stepped across that threshold.

"We do not have such a custom at Queen's Malvern," Brie told Flanna when her aunt explained.

"Is it a real bird?" Freddie wondered aloud.

"Ohhhh!" Little Willy cried, and pointed his fat finger toward the door.

There stood on auburn-haired man, dressed all in green clothing sewn with bells and wearing a bird's mask. With a great leap he crossed the threshold and began to dance about the hall to a tune played by reeds and drums and flute. Going first to the high board, he flourished a bow and tipped his cap. The duke gave him a silver coin. The lucky bird continued to dance about the hall, greeting all the guests and receiving pennies from each table. When he had visited everyone, he brought the purse of coins to Mr. Edie, the Presbyterian cleric, saying, "For the puir, guid sir," and then danced gaily from the hall.

"Papa missed the lucky bird," Brie said, disappointed.

"He had to guard the Yule log," Freddie replied.

"It can come into the hall now," the duke said. "Would ye three like to escort it since ye found it?"

The three children scrambled from their places and ran from the high board.

"Will Charlie hae time to change?" Flanna wondered.

"He hae done this before," Patrick explained to her. "When my brothers and I were small. I canna think of the lucky bird wi'out thinking of Charlie. Henry wanted to do it one year, but he canna dance like Charlie. Even now he leaps higher than any."

Flanna reached out and placed her hand over her husband's. "Ye miss them, I know, but we will make new memories, my lord."

His eyes met hers, and he smiled. "Aye, lass, we will," he promised her. "Now, tell me how it is ye're so damned intuitive, Flanna Leslie. I am nae certain I am comfortable wi' a wife who understands my deepest thoughts so well." He took her hand up and kissed it.

"Christmas was always a special time at Brae," she said. "My mother and Angus told me all about it. It wasna so special at Killiecairn, and I know that she missed it. She never complained, but I could see it in her eyes. She loved my father, but Killiecairn was never really home for her. Perhaps that is why I love Brae and want to restore it to its former glory."

"And what will ye do wi' it when 'tis habitable again?" he asked her with a small smile.

"It shall be there for me should ye become impossible to live wi', my lord," she told him pertly. "Glenkirk is yers; but Brae will be mine, and one day one of our bairns will hae it. Ye may own the land now, but the castle is mine alone."

"Ye would leave me, lass?" His look was amused.

"If we dinna get on, I would, indeed," she responded.

"Ye're an independent woman, Flanna Leslie," he said, chuckling.

"Look, my lord, here is the Yule log," Flanna answered him, neatly changing the subject. She had no intention of getting into a discussion with him about Brae. He had returned it to her and said she might make it habitable again. It would be from there that she would marshal men for King Charles Stuart. Patrick did not want

Glenkirk or his Leslies involved, and she would respect that as he had respected her love for Brae.

The guests began to cheer the passage of the great Yule log as it was dragged into the hall to the fireplace above which hung the portrait of the first Patrick Leslie. The three Stuart children sat atop the log as it was brought along, singing an ancient Christmas song in Latin that traditionally accompanied the Yule log. They jumped off the huge timber as it reached the great hearth and helped push it into place. Then Lady Sabrina Stuart took the flame handed to her by Angus and lit the kindling beneath the log. A great shout went up from those present in the Great Hall of Glenkirk.

"Well done, daughter!" Charlie said, and he picked Sabrina up and carried her about the hall, laughing before depositing her once more at the high board with the rest of the family.

"Papa, you missed the lucky bird," Sabrina said. "He was quite wonderful in his green and his bells, and he jumped every bit as high as you do when he danced."

"*Did he?*" Charlie pretended surprise. "I thought that no one could leap as I do. 'Tis a Stuart trait, or so I am told. My father, Prince Henry, was a fine dancer with a nicely turned leg, my mother has said. Your Uncle Henry would remember, as would your Aunt India."

"I miss the family," Sabrina said wistfully. "I wish you didn't have to go away, Papa, but I know that cousin Charles needs you."

"I hae been given to understand that the gentlemen who came wi' the king from France were nae welcome any longer. They are said to be ungodly, Lady Sabrina," Mr. Edie ventured, and he looked toward the Duke of Lundy. "Is it so, sir?"

"There are those who are not pleased with the king's lifelong companions, it is true, Mr. Edie," the duke replied, "but they cannot expect the king, who is a loyal and good man, to send away those who have supported him faithfully. Many have grown up with my cousin. I believe it is up to the kirk to lead these men into the ways of righteousness rather than flinging them out into the darkness of their continuing sins. Would you not agree?"

There was a gleam of humor in Mr. Edie's eye as he answered the duke. "I am a simple country parson, my lord. I cannot judge my betters, nor can I instruct them in their behavior."

"You are a wise man, sir," the duke replied with a chuckle.

"We live in difficult times," the minister said quietly, "but here at Glenkirk we are isolated from evil, and we follow the laws of our land. That is all, I believe, God requires of us."

Around them, and below the high board, the guests ate heartily of the beef, and capon, and salmon that was served up. There was venison, and game pies, and platters of roasted rabbits passed around. Each table had breads, crocks of creamy butter, and small wheels of cheese. The high board had bowls of carrots and peas, and a platter of artichokes that had been steamed in wine. There was wine, ale, and cider aplenty. Then the apple tarts were brought in along with bowls of clotted cream. As Mary had predicted, the children were delirious with their delight at this special treat. And when the food was cleared away, Patrick and Flanna stood before the high board, and distributed the presents to the clansmen, the clanswomen, and the children.

More ale and wine was drunk. A piper began to play. The men began to dance. At first the dances were careful and studied, but then they grew wilder and more passionate. Finally Patrick and Charlie arose. Swords were placed upon the stone floor of the hall. The two brothers began to dance. Patrick was the taller by an inch. His black hair was cropped close. His green-gold eyes glittered as, wrapped in his green kilt with its narrow red and white stripes, he danced amid the crossed swords. A sardonic smile upon his equally handsome face, Charlie Stuart, his dark auburn hair tied back, his amber eyes sparkling, danced with his younger brother wrapped in his red Stuart plaid. The music grew fiercer as the brothers danced in concert until with a final shriek the pipes stopped as suddenly as they had begun. The siblings fell into each other's arms, laughing as the hall erupted into cheers of congratulations, and the clansmen spilled out onto the floor to clap the two men on their backs and shake their hands.

Promptly at midnight the feasting ended, and the hall emptied as the inhabitants of Glenkirk made their way to the village church where Mr. Edie was prepared to preside over the first service of the day.

"Pray God he doesna sermonize long tonight," the duke murmured to his wife, patting her on her bottom through her skirts. "'Tis cold, and I've a fancy to bed ye, Flanna Leslie."

"'Tis hardly a godly thought, my lord," she whispered back.

"But is it ungodly, wife?" he asked her.

"Hush!" she scolded him. "Mr. Edie is about to begin."

To their surprise the minister spoke but briefly. The sacrament was dispensed, and they were once again outside in the night. It had begun to snow.

"Aunt Flanna said it would," Sabrina said smugly.

"That was three days ago," Freddie said half scornfully.

"Ah, laddie, it takes time for the snow to come on the wind from the north," Flanna told them. "'Tis right on time."

"Thank you for my pearwood comb," Sabrina said as they reentered the castle. "I love the red deer carved on it. I have never seen a comb like it."

"That is because I made it for ye," Flanna told the child. "Angus taught me to carve years ago when I was yer age."

Patrick listened with interest. Here was something he wouldn't have imagined about Flanna. That she could carve and was artistic. When they lay together abed afterward he asked her about it.

"What made ye want to learn such a common skill?" he wondered.

"My mother had died," she replied. "I couldna stop thinking about it, or believing it would nae hae happened if she had nae nursed her niece who died, and from whom she had caught the contagion. I believe I was slowly going mad. Angus saw it, and he took me in hand. My mother had carved little figures of birds and animals. He said she had always hoped I would learn her skill. So I began to learn. I had to concentrate so hard upon what I was doing that I could nae longer think about my mother, or how she had died. It was very clever of Angus, dinna ye think?"

"He is yer blood, isna he?" Patrick said.

"He was my grandfather Andrew Gordon's bastard," Flanna said. "My grandmother Gordon raised him. He was seven when my mother was born. I never knew until Mama was about to die. She told me then because she said she didna want me to be alone. My grandfather educated him as if he were his heir. My mother, of course, was his only legitimate offspring. She and my uncle loved each other dearly."

Patrick nodded. "The More-Leslies descend from a bastard line," he said. "They hae always been loyal to us. Yer uncle is a good man."

"Aye, he is," Flanna said. Then she burrowed into his shoulder. "Ye dinna gie me my present yet," she said to him.

"Is the deed to Brae nae enough for ye?" he teased her.

"Ye would gie me what was already mine, my lord? I canna believe ye're a pinchpenny. Fie!" She hit him a light blow to the shoulder.

He chortled. "Get up, madame, and remove yer night garment," he instructed her.

"What, sir, is this ye demand of me?" she asked him.

"If ye want yer giftie, lass, ye'll obey yer man, or must I beat ye into obedience?" he said, a smile touching the corners of his lips.

Curious now, Flanna arose from their warm bed and pulled off her simple white night garment.

"Now unbraid yer hair," he commanded her. "I want to see that fiery mass spilling over yer shoulders and down yer back."

Even more fascinated, Flanna complied, her fingers unweaving her thick plait, combing through her tresses until her long hair flowed all about her. "Well, my lord?" she queried him.

Patrick Leslie climbed from their bed and, reaching beneath the pillows, drew forth a long strand of black pearls which he looped over her head. Then, setting her back, he stared, pleased, at the round ebony beads upon her milky white skin, its pureness broken only by the brilliant red-gold of her hair. He felt himself hardening, his lust fully engaged at the seductive picture she made, naked, with those pearls.

Flanna had never before seen black pearls, but from the look of them, she realized whatever they were they were valuable. They were smooth to the touch and slid through her fingers like liquid silk as she examined them. "What are they called?" she asked as her eyes met his.

"Pearls," he said. *He wanted her!*

"I hae a wee strand of pearls that were Mam's," Flanna said, "but they are white." She could see his manhood poking out beneath his nightshirt. "These are magnificent, my lord, thank ye," she told him, and slipping her arms about his neck, she kissed him.

He pulled her hard against him—so hard that the pearls bit into her tender flesh—and she cried out, surprised. His mouth was fierce and demanding. His tongue fenced with hers. His lips moved from her mouth and began to travel over her face, her throat, her shoulders. He knelt before her and kissed her breasts. She murmured softly. His tongue licked slowly over her nipple. His mouth closed upon it, and he began to suckle her. One of his hands held her by a buttock. The fingers of his other hand began to push into her sheath, and finding her already wet, he thrust hard even as his teeth came down upon the nipple.

Flanna felt herself going weak with the pleasure he gave her. She pushed herself against him, encouraging him. Her hands pulled at his dark hair. She moaned as his mouth moved to her other breast, his fingers relentlessly thrusting, thrusting. Her love juices spilled forth as she reached her first peak. He groaned and, pulling his hand away from her, sucked his fingers hungrily as she sagged half fainting against him. "Ye're a wicked man, Patrick Leslie," she said low, and then bending down, she began to tease at his ear with her tongue.

His breath hissed from between his lips. Then he pulled her down roughly onto the floor by their bed, and covering her body with his own, he entered her in a sharp, swift thrust. Flanna wrapped her legs about her husband's torso. Her fingers dug deeply into the muscles of his shoulders and back. As he began to move rhythmically upon her, she clawed at his flesh.

"Ahh, the cat will scratch, will she?" he husked, thrusting harder and harder against her. "Ye're a wicked little wanton, wife, but by God I hae nae ever wanted a woman before the way I want ye, Flanna!"

His words sent her heart racing furiously. It was the closest he had come in their brief acquaintance to saying that he cared at all for her. She wanted him to love her. She didn't understand what love was all about, but she knew that she wanted it. She cared for him. She didn't know how such a thing had happened, for he was a very aggravating man, but Flanna knew she cared for Patrick. *Was it love?* She didn't know, and if it was, would she know? But she did know she wanted him to care for her.

"I never knew until ye wed me how it could be between a man and a woman," she admitted. "Dinna stop loving me, Patrick! *Dinna stop!* Ye make me feel as I hae never felt before, and I like it."

He laughed, and it was a joyous sound. "Shut yer mouth, woman, and let me love ye, then. I canna, it surprises me, get enough of ye."

Their bodies moved together, finding a passionate cadence that pleased them both as they writhed and strove to seek perfection. Their limbs were intertwined. Their hearts raced. Their mouths were dry with a surfeit of lust, yet their bodies were wet with their exertions. He knew what he strove for. She didn't. Her ignorance was exciting, and he worked to bring her to a little death such as she had never before known. His mouth found hers again.

She was almost unconscious with the immense font of pleasure welling up in her body. It was like an enormous wave that threatened to overwhelm her, and suddenly Flanna, feeling out of control, began to panic; but Patrick calmed her, murmuring softly against her mouth.

"Nah, nah, lassie, let it happen. 'Twill be the greatest pleasure ye hae ever known. Trust me, lovey."

And she did, and was quickly swept up and away in a rush of such incredible enjoyment that she believed she was dying, and to her astonishment she didn't care. Warmth suffused her body. She felt weightless. She soared while about her her world exploded with delight. And then as suddenly as it had begun, it was over. She felt herself falling into a darkness that reached up to enfold her tenderly.

His own pleasure mushroomed with hers, erupted, and then burst forth in a flood of his love juices even as she cried out and fainted in his arms. He collapsed atop her, gasping with their exertions. Then, coming to himself, he rolled away, cradling her in his arms as he did so. His big hand caressed the tangled mass of her red-gold hair. It was soft and fragrant. Even now it sent his senses reeling. *Jesu,* he thought to himself. *I love her! I love this impossible, wild girl I took to wife only for her property, but I can't say it to her. What if she didn't believe me? How can this have happened?*

Flanna slowly opened her eyes. Her heart was still beating a bit quickly. Her cheek lay against his damp chest, and she could smell the now familiar scent of him. "Are we alive yet?" she ventured.

"Aye," he replied with a chuckle.

"Can it be *that* way again, Patrick?" she wondered.

"Nae every time, lass. That's what makes it so special," he told her softly.

"Did ye . . ."she began, not quite knowing how to ask, but Patrick Leslie understood.

"Aye, it was . . . splendiferous!"

"What kind of a word is that?" she demanded, propping herself up on an elbow to look into his handsome face.

"A fancy one, lassie. It means glorious, magnificent, splendid!"

She thought a moment, and then she said. "Aye, Patrick, it was indeed splendiferous!"

"Ye hae better don clothing the next time ye wear yer pearls," he said, fingering them with a grin.

"We're fortunate they dinna break all over the floor," she noted with a mischievous twinkle.

Reaching up, he gathered the strand in his hand against the base of her throat and pulled her down to him. "Come, and kiss me, wife," he said softly to her. "I believe I am regaining my longing for ye, Flanna Leslie. Ye could tempt the angels." Their lips met once again in a torrid touch.

As their mouths separated, she said with a little smile, "We hae several hours until the dawn, Patrick. The pearls were my Christmas Eve gift. What hae ye got for me for my Christmas gift?"

"More, madame, than ye can imagine," the Duke of Glenkirk told his beautiful wife. "Much, much more!"

Chapter

8

Charlie announced on Christmas Day that he would be leaving Glenkirk on the twenty-seventh of December for Perth, where the king would be crowned on January first. His children cried their protest, but Charlie explained to them that it was a long ride to Perth, and he had little time as it was to get there. His royal cousin would desperately need some friendly faces about him on that most auspicious day. Sabrina, Freddie, and Willy were the king's own blood. Now that he had explained it to them, Charlie said, his children certainly must understand their duty, which was to see their father off with good cheer and to send along their prayers for the king's success. Reluctantly the trio of Stuart children agreed.

Flanna thanked providence that her brother-in-law had made his announcement early. She sought out a young man-at-arms she had seen looking at her admiringly on several occasions. "Ian, is it nae?"

"Aye, my lady," the young soldier replied, his cheeks reddening, amazed that the duchess should know his Christian name.

"I need ye to perform a small service for me," Flanna said. "Will ye take a message to my brother, Aulay Brodie, at Killiecairn?"

"Aye, my lady!" he replied eagerly.

Flanna smiled a brilliant smile at him. Then she hung her head and shuffled her feet slightly. "And ye must nae tell my husband," she almost whispered. "I would nae hae the duke know how much I miss my family. I want my wee nephew to come and visit wi' me. The duke will welcome him, I know. Will ye help me, Ian?"

"Aye, my lady!" Ian responded, delighted he might be of service to the beautiful duchess he so admired.

"Go now, and say to Aulay Brodie that the Duchess of Glenkirk, yer mistress, would hae his son, Fingal, return wi' ye this same day. The Brodies will offer ye hospitality, but thank them and say the duchess is anxious to see her nephew. Do ye understand me? Ye must return wi' my nephew today. The weather is dry again, and I sense nae storm approaching."

"I'll leave at once, my lady," the soldier said.

"Take an extra horse from the stables for the lad, but dinna let anyone see ye go," she instructed him.

"I understand," Ian answered her, and giving her a quick bow, he turned and hurried off.

At Killiecairn he was met with much questioning by Aulay Brodie. Ian repeated his mistress's request, adding politely that he thought his mistress, while obviously happy with her lot, nonetheless missed her family; and that the duke would welcome this nephew by his marriage to Flanna Brodie.

"'Tis a grand opportunity for our Fingal," Una said, pleased. "If he pleases the duke, he's apt to be educated and hae a better chance in life than to be just one of our sons, one of the many Brodies here at Killiecairn. Flanna always hae a soft spot for Fingal. He was the only bairn I gave ye after our Mary died. Remember how Flanna used to lug him about and watch over him for me? 'Tis her way, I'm certain, of thanking us for our care of her after her mama died and yer da lost interest in his daughter."

"What could he aspire to at Glenkirk that he could nae hae here?" her husband demanded.

"Well, he might learn to read and write," Una said. "He could study to become a minister of the kirk."

"*Fingal?*" Aulay Brodie laughed heartily. "He's as rough and determined as Flanna herself. We beat him more than any of our bairns. He is as wild as they come."

"Well, and no wonder," she replied, "being the youngest of our sons and, indeed, many of his cousins. If he were nae rough and wild, they would hae killed him long ago. I want Fingal to go to Glenkirk, Aulay. I want him to hae a chance at a better life. Besides, yer sister has sent for him. Would ye insult the Duchess of Glenkirk? Flanna is nae longer just yer wee sister. She is a great lady. Besides, what do ye need our laddie here for, husband?"

"Oh, verra well, woman, hush yer nagging. The lad may go to my sister at Glenkirk." He turned to the messenger. "Ye'll remain the night and eat wi' us?"

Ian bowed deferentially. "I should like to, sir, but my mistress hae instructed me to bring the lad back immediately. She even sent a horse for him to ride. The king's cousin is at Glenkirk, and I think she would hae him see the royal," Ian answered, thinking quickly.

"*What king?*" Aulay Brodie demanded.

"Why, King Charles Stuart, sir, the last King Jamee's grandson. He be driven out of England, 'tis true, but he hae been welcomed home to our fair Scotland and will be crowned next week at Scone, as God intended," Ian explained to the Brodies.

"I'll fetch my son at once," Una said, excitedly. "Aulay, our Fingal is to meet wi' a royal prince!" She ran out of the hall.

"Nae a prince," Ian quickly amended, "just the king's cousin, sir. He is the Duke of Lundy and also called Charles Stuart."

"Glenkirk's bastard brother?" Aulay asked bluntly.

"Aye, sir," Ian said, instinctively knowing that honesty was the best policy with Aulay Brodie, who obviously knew more than he was ready to admit to any other. "They call him the *not-so-royal Stuart*. He is a widower and has brought his three bairns to Glenkirk to shelter."

Aulay Brodie nodded. "'Twas wise, and wi' my sister there, those bairns will be well taken care of, I'm thinking. Now I understand why she wants Fingal wi' her. This duke has lads, eh?"

"Two, and a daughter," Ian answered him.

Aulay Brodie smiled. "Aye, Flanna wants a lad to help wi' those lads, and though he be wild, my Fingal can be trusted. Is my sister breeding yet?"

Ian blushed red to the roots of his nut brown hair. "*Sir!*" he sputtered. "I would nae know such a private thing. I am just a man-at-arms, one of many who serve the duke."

"Humph," Aulay grunted. "Dinna fret, laddie. I just thought ye might hae heard a rumor, or two, and be willing to share them wi' yer mistress's older brother."

"To my knowledge, which is nae great, sir, there is nae yet hope of an heir for Glenkirk," Ian responded.

"She hae been wed two months now," Aulay Brodie grumbled almost to himself. "What is taking the lass so long?" He looked up at the Glenkirk messenger again. "She and yer duke are on good terms?"

"Oh, aye, sir," Ian enthused. "The duke is mad for her. 'Tis all the talk among my mates, meaning no disrespect, of course, to either the duke, or yer good sister."

"None taken, lad. I'm glad it worked out so well for the both of them. 'Tis nae easy to be wed, I can tell ye. Come now, while my wife is getting our lad, and tell my father what ye hae told me. He loves his lass, and I know he misses her."

By the time Ian returned to Glenkirk with Fingal Brodie in tow, it was almost dark. Leaving the horses in the stable, he brought the boy to his aunt. Wide-eyed, Fingal Brodie couldn't stop looking all about him, for he had never been anywhere in his whole life other than his own home. Seeing Flanna, he ran to her, and she hugged him.

"Remember, Ian, ye know nothing of this lad," she said softly.

He bowed and was gone without another word.

"Thank ye," she called after him. Then, turning to her nephew, she said, "Listen to me, laddie. My husband is to believe ye were sent here by yer da in order to bring me back to Killiecairn for my da is not well and wishes to see me. Do ye understand?"

"What mischief are ye up to, Flanna?" he asked cheekily, and he grinned at her, his blue eyes dancing wickedly. "My mother said me fortune was made by yer calling me to Glenkirk."

"If ye like it here, ye can stay wi' me, laddie," she replied, and she ruffled his chestnut brown hair. "I'll nae send ye back."

"If ye want me to help ye, then tell me what ye're doing," he repeated. "I'm quick, Flanna, but I canna help if I dinna know what it is ye want of me."

She explained, and when she had finished, he said, "Ye're daft, Flanna Brodie, to even consider such a thing."

"Flanna *Leslie*," she said. "Ye dinna know what life is like away from yer backwoods, Fingal. I do. I'll take ye to the gallery where hang all the paintings of the ladies of Glenkirk who came before me. Great ladies, every one of them, I tell ye. And here come I, wi' only Brae to recommend me. I dinna want to be known in the future as the duchess who did naught, Fingal. I want to be like those women before me, nephew. I dinna hae great wealth, but I can be a woman of action as they were. The king needs an army. We are his subjects. Where can he go but to the Highlands for help? Those Scots in the south are more English than Scots, and the English are the ones who drove him out of his realm and murdered his father. He must be revenged! And who but his blood to do it?"

"Verra well, aunt, but what do ye want of me?" Fingal asked.

"The day after tomorrow the Duke of Lundy, my brother-in-law, the king's cousin, leaves Glenkirk for Scone. We're going to follow him, but Patrick, Angus, and the rest will think we hae gone to Killiecairn."

"They'll send ye back," Fingal predicted gloomily.

"Aye, they will, but nae before I've met the king, and pledged myself to his cause, and received his permission to raise troops for him, Fingal," she said. "That is the whole purpose of this deception."

"And why not just go wi' yer husband?" the boy demanded.

"Patrick has some foolish notion that the royal Stuarts bring ill fortune to the Leslies of Glenkirk. His mother told him that, but she was only distraught over losing her husband at Dunbar. Ohh, Fingal, I do want to help the king! And a hundred years from now, I want it said of me when they see my portrait hanging on the wall here: *'Oh, that's the Duchess Flanna. She raised fighting men and helped put King Charles II back on his throne.'* Willna that be grand, Fingal?"

"I still think ye're daft," the boy replied, "but I'll go wi' ye, auntie, because 'tis an adventure, and 'tis away from Killiecairn and all our family. But when we get back, I want ye to get yer Angus to teach me to read and write. I dinna want to be a dunce like my brothers and my cousins at Killiecairn. I'll nae live my life there, marry some local wench like the others, and add more unwashed bairns to the family. I want to go to Edinburgh."

"The English hold Edinburgh," Flanna told him. "Tell me, Fingal, what do ye want to be?"

"I dinna know," he answered her honestly. "How can I when my whole life has been spent at Killiecairn? But I do know, Flanna, that there is more than eating, drinking, brawling, hunting, wenching, and the like. Whatever it is, I want it!"

"Help me, and I'll help ye find yer dreams," she promised him. "Now, remember to say yer da sent ye when my husband comes into the hall. And remember to beware of Angus. He can see a lie. And dinna confide in Aggie. She gossips wi' everyone."

He nodded. Then he gave her a wink. "Speak of the devil!"

"Fingal Brodie!" Angus had entered the hall, seen the boy, and now came over to where he sat with Flanna.

"Aulay has sent him," Flanna quickly said.

"*Why?*" Angus demanded suspiciously.

"Grandsire has been low ever since our Flanna wed and left Killiecairn. Da thought she might come and visit. He dinna sense any storms, and 'tis but a few hours' ride," Fingal said smoothly.

"Hae ye asked yer husband, lady?" Angus said.

"Fingal only arrived a short while ago," Flanna told Angus.

"Ye rode?"

"I walked, and it took me two whole days," the lad said indignantly. "I'm hoping to gain the loan of a mount to go back wi' my aunt."

"If 'tis all right wi' Patrick, we'll go in another day," Flanna said quietly. "God forbid the old man die! I should feel guilty, but I'll nae leave while my husband's brother is our guest."

"Yer da will live to be a hundred," Angus said dourly, and Fingal laughed aloud. "I'll go wi' ye, then."

"Dinna be silly," Flanna countered easily. "Ye're needed here, especially wi' Charlie gone. The children will need cheering. Fingal will ride wi' me. We'll be on Glenkirk lands almost all the way, and then on Brodie lands. There are no robbers hereabouts except our own," she finished with a small smile. Then she added, "Besides, Angus, ye know I fight as well as any man. I am not some delicate flower needing protection from the wicked world."

"I'd be happier if ye had men-at-arms wi' ye," he said stubbornly.

"Oh, verra well, I'll choose one to accompany me, but only one, Angus. I dinna want to look like some little ninny who canna take care of herself. Besides, a troop of galloping men would certainly attract attention if, indeed, there were robbers about. I'll move faster and safer wi' just Fingal and another."

"Is there anyone ye favor, my lady?"

"I'll take Ian. He's old enough to hae experience, but young enough nae to behave like some old woman. And, of course, the duke must approve my little venture, Angus."

"Aye," her uncle agreed.

Fingal Brodie hid a smirk. No one could dissemble like his aunt.

Flanna told Aggie, "Fingal Brodie has arrived. My da is nae well, and I'll go in another day to see him."

"What time should I be ready?" Aggie asked promptly.

"Ye needna come," Flanna said. "I need ye here, and Angus, too, to look after the children. Dinna forget that my brother-in-law is going. Old Biddy will hae her hands full. I want it to be as easy for the bairns as we can make it. Remember, they hae just lost their mam, and now their da is going off to fight for the king."

Aggie nodded. "I'll stay," she said. "How long will ye be gone? What shall I pack for ye?"

"I dinna know, a few days, maybe more," Flanna told her. "I'll pack for myself. I dinna want much, and whatever I need can be found at Killiecairn."

The hardest part was telling her husband. Lying had never bothered Flanna. She rarely did it except in unusual circumstances, but she felt guilty prevaricating to Patrick. Still, she knew if she was truthful, he would forbid her going, and then she would have to disobey him, and their difficulties would be even harder to overcome. He might not be pleased with her when she returned home to

Glenkirk, but if she had seen the king, and obtained his permission to raise troops, Patrick couldn't forbid her then. He was too honorable to defy his king. Flanna smiled to herself. Her plan was really quite foolproof.

She spoke with him as they sat in the Great Hall eating their evening meal. "I must go to Killiecairn," Flanna began. "Fingal Brodie, where are ye? Come here to me."

Her nephew came from his place below the salt and bowed.

"This is Aulay's youngest son. He was born the year after my mother died. He came to tell me that da isna well and misses me. My brother wants me to come home for a short visit. Wi' ye permission, my lord, I will go to Killiecairn. I should nae be gone long, and I'll nae leave till Charlie does." She put her hand on Patrick's. "Ye'll let me go, won't ye?"

He nodded. "How old are ye, laddie?" he asked Fingal.

"Eleven, my lord," the boy responded.

"And what do ye think of Glenkirk?"

"I should like to live here, my lord," Fingal said promptly. "'Tis a grand place."

"So ye would be one of my soldiers one day, eh?"

"Nay, my lord! I want to learn to read and to write, and to be someone important," Fingal said bluntly.

Both Patrick and Charlie burst out laughing.

"By God, laddie," the Duke of Glenkirk said, "I like yer ambition! When my wife returns home, come wi' her. I'll educate ye along wi' my nephews and my niece. If ye hae a knack for learning, perhaps one day I'll send ye to the university in Aberdeen."

"Thank ye, my lord," Fingal Brodie said, and he bowed again.

"Come up here, laddie, and join us. Ye're my wife's kin and are welcome at my board." And when the boy came, Patrick drew him near and said, "This is my brother, the not-so-royal Stuart. He has the same name as the king, Charlie."

"Why are ye nae so royal, my lord?" Fingal asked, and then looked nervously about at the silence that had descended on the hall.

But Charlie wasn't in the least offended. It was a fair question from an innocent boy. "My father was Prince Henry Stuart, laddie. I was born on the wrong side of the blanket. Had he and my mother been wed, I should be your king." And Charlie gave Fingal a friendly wink.

Fingal Brodie turned to his aunt. "This be a strange but grand house into which ye hae wed, Flanna," he said.

Flanna took a sweetmeat off her plate and, kissing the boy's cheek, pushed it into his mouth. "Go and get some sleep, Fingal. Ye've had a long and busy day. Angus will show ye where to put yer head."

"He can share my room," Freddie said eagerly.

"That would be lovely," Flanna said to the boy. "When we return, I will gie ye and Fingal yer own chamber. Willy is still a bairn and should be in a nursery."

"Aye!" Freddie agreed enthusiastically.

"And while I am gone," Flanna continued, "ye must look wi' Angus to see which chamber ye think will suit two boys."

"What am I to do while you are gone?" Brie demanded irritably. Freddie was getting all the attention, along with that rough-looking boy.

"Did ye hae an herb garden in England?" Flanna asked.

"Aye, the gardens at Queen's Malvern were famous," Brie answered.

"Then, I want ye to decide what we need to grow here at Glenkirk come summer. A good mistress cares for her people, and there is nae a good supply of medicines that I can find. Ye and I must begin at the beginning, Brie."

"Mama had a fine herb garden. She made all kinds of potions and salves. I helped her."

"Then, I must rely upon ye, Brie, for I am nae skilled in such pursuits," Flanna told her niece.

"But can we get the root stock that we'll need?" Brie was suddenly all involved.

"Mary More-Leslie should be able to help ye while I'm gone,"

Flanna replied. "She would know what the Duchess Jasmine, yer grandmam, had in the gardens."

Brie nodded.

"You are a very clever woman," Charlie said quietly. "I believe my brother has made a far better match than he anticipated when he first decided he wanted Brae. I know you will care well for my children."

"I will," she promised him. Then she arose from the high board and curtsied to them. "I must go and pack the few things I will need so I may depart early on the twenty-seventh. I will nae go before ye, Charlie."

"I'm leaving at first light," he said.

"Of course," she agreed. "Yer journey is a long one, and I shall leave directly after ye." She smiled at the two men. "Good night, my lords." And with another quick curtsy she hurried from the hall. In her chamber she found Aggie had laid out the small pack she would carry on her saddle. Flanna stuffed in two clean shirts, some knit stockings, her hairbrush, and the little boar's bristle brush she used to clean her teeth. She thought a moment, then added a sash of Leslie plaid and a little bag of coins. The maidservant took the saddle pack to the stables for her mistress.

Aggie woke her before the dawn on the twenty-seventh. Flanna saw her husband had slept in his own room. The chamber was cold and damp. She prayed as she carefully dressed herself that there would be no heavy rain or snow. She drew on a pair of heavy knitted stockings over which she pulled a pair of wool breeches, carefully tucking her chemise into the waistband and down over her buttocks. Next she added a long-sleeved shirt that tied at the neckline and was also tucked into her breeches. A lamb's-wool-lined leather jerkin with bone buttons followed along with her leather boots. Her hooded cloak was dark green wool and lined in beaver as were her leather gloves. Fully dressed, Flanna departed her apartment.

She found Fingal in the hall stuffing his face with hot porridge. She joined him. Shortly Charlie and Patrick arrived, each looking slightly under the weather.

"Ye got drunk," she accused.

They nodded sheepishly, wincing slightly at the sound of her voice.

"Shame on ye both," she scolded. "'Twill nae be a pleasant ride for ye today, Charlie."

"Don't remind me, Flanna," he pleaded with her.

"Eat!" she instructed him firmly. "Angus, see that Lord Stuart has some good hot porridge and cream."

Charlie paled.

"Ye'll travel better wi' something in yer belly, and 'twill help yer head, I promise," she assured him. Then she returned to her own meal of porridge, bread, butter, cheese, and ham.

Charlie ate slowly, almost hesitantly, but shortly he had to admit that he did, indeed, feel better. His color began to return.

Flanna handed him a small goblet of wine. "Hair of the dog, my da would say," she explained.

He sipped carefully, but the wine seemed to make him feel even better. Finally he arose. "I'm ready," he said.

Patrick rose, too, and the men gripped hands, then embraced. "Dinna be a fool and get yerself killed," the Duke of Glenkirk advised his eldest brother. "Mama wouldna like that at all."

"You and Henry will be cautious for us all," Charlie teased. "As for the young Leslies in Ireland, they will have their hands full just surviving both Cromwell and the Irish. I don't envy them."

"Old Rory will keep Maguire's Ford safe if they listen to him," Patrick told him.

"Jesu, is Rory still alive?" Charlie asked.

"Aye," Patrick said with a grin. "He's over seventy but still, I am assured by my brothers, active. Cullen Butler died last year, though, just after his eightieth birthday. There's nae priest in Maguire's Ford now, nor will there be."

Charlie nodded, and then embraced his brother a final time. "The sun is just about up," he said. "I had best be on my way, and Flanna, too, if she expects to reach her father's house in good time." He turned to his sister-in-law and taking her hand up, kissed it. "I leave you with more decorum, Flanna Leslie, than I greeted you," he said with a mischievous grin.

"Ye'll nae get off that easily, Charlie," she told him, and hugging him, Flanna kissed his cheek soundly. "Travel safely, my nae-so-royal Stuart brother," she said.

He bowed to her and then with a wave left the hall.

"The children!" Flanna cried suddenly, realizing that they had not been here.

"He made his farewells last night," Patrick explained. "He thought it better that way."

"I agree," she replied. Then she said, "I had best go now myself. I'll be back as quickly as I can, my lord."

"See that ye are, wife, for I find the thought of spending any time away from ye most disturbing." He pulled her into his arms and kissed her soundly, his lips soft, then fierce.

"Ohhh," Flanna sighed, and for a moment she wondered why she was bothering to follow this scheme of hers; but then she remembered she was the do-naught duchess, and she didn't want to be. With a sigh she drew away from him, calling to her nephew, "Fingal Brodie, come!"

Outside in the courtyard she found Ian waiting, holding the horses for them. She cursed softly beneath her breath. She had meant to tell the young man-at-arms that he could visit his parents for his service to her. Now, with Angus standing there, she dared not.

"Dinna stay long," her uncle said quietly so only she might hear him. "Ye hae a duty to Glenkirk ye hae nae fulfilled, lassie."

"I'll tell my da that ye send yer regards," Flanna sassed him as she mounted Glaise.

Angus laughed. "Do that," he teased back. Then he turned and boosted Fingal Brodie into his saddle. "And ye, laddie, hae nae ye fallen into a nice pot of honey wi' our duke. Ye're lucky."

"I hope I am," Fingal Brodie replied.

Now what did he mean by that? Angus wondered as he watched the trio ride off. Then he shook his head. The Brodies were always wont to look at good fortune askance. It was their way.

Flanna's horse clumped slowly across the heavy wooden drawbridge that exited from Glenkirk's courtyard. Her mind worked out the difficulty of telling Ian More that they were not going to Killiecairn, but to Scone. She didn't want him racing back to the castle and exposing her careful plans. Fingal caught her eye questioningly, but she shook her head at him. Still, by the time they reached the bend in the forest road, she would have to make her decision. Two roads revealed themselves at that bend. One leading north to her father's lands, and the other southwest to Scone. What was she to do? The bend was in sight. She had no more time in which to consider.

"Are ye loyal to me, Ian More?" she asked him bluntly, stopping her mount at the fork in the road.

"Ye're my duchess, lady," he answered simply.

"I am Glenkirk's duchess, Ian More. I know that ye're loyal to Glenkirk, but are ye loyal to me?" Flanna repeated.

"I dinna understand, my lady."

How old was he? Seventeen? Young enough to be idealistic like she was? Or merely loyal to Glenkirk? Flanna had no choice but to pursue her problem further. "I hae lied to the duke," she said, almost laughing at the look of surprise on his plain, honest face. "I am nae going to Killiecairn. I am following the Duke of Lundy to Scone."

"But why, my lady?" His look of confusion was evident.

"Let us ride on, Ian More, and I will tell ye," Flanna said. She moved Glaise forward in an easy walk. "Ye hae heard in the hall the tale of the Stuart kings," she began, and he nodded.

God's boots, she was clever, Fingal thought as they rode along. Each step their horses took moved them farther away from the castle and along the path his aunt wished to follow. Fingal moved his mount ahead in order to make certain they did not catch up with the Duke of Lundy. They just needed to keep him barely in sight while keeping their own presence hidden until Flanna deemed it otherwise. He could hear the drone of her voice as she made her case. Fingal wondered if the young man-at-arms could be seduced into letting his aunt have her way, or if he would turn about and ride back to Glenkirk.

"I want to help our king," Flanna explained to Ian earnestly. "I want to raise troops for him and bring honor to the Leslies of Glenkirk. My husband, however, mourns his father deeply and holds the king—well, nae exactly the king himself, but the king's situation—responsible for his da's death. Now, Mary has told me that the Duchess Jasmine begged the old duke nae to go, but he wouldna listen to her. The king's problems are nae responsible for Duke Jemmie's death. His decision to ignore all the good advice he was given, and go nonetheless, caused his death."

"They do say, my lady," Ian said, "that the Stuarts bring bad fortune to the Leslies of Glenkirk."

"'Tis nonsense!" Flanna declared. "The Leslies of Glenkirk were simple lairds until a Stuart king made them earls. And another Stuart king gave them the dukedom. Would they hae been luckier if they had remained lairds?"

"I dinna know," he answered her, feeling a bit confused.

Flanna laughed. "Nor do I," she said. "Ian, ye must know I would bring nae dishonor upon my husband, but I want to help our king. What right hae the Sassenachs to kill old King Charles? He was a king of Scotland as well as England. He was born in Scotland, yet they murdered him wi'out so much as a by yer leave," Flanna pleaded her case. "The duke of Lundy can gie me an introduction to the king. I will ask his permission to raise troops, and if he says nae, then I won't. We'll travel together until 'tis too late for Charlie to send me right back. Then we'll reveal ourselves. As soon as I meet the king, I'll come home. I swear it on my honor as a Duchess of Glenkirk! Hae ye ever seen the portraits of the past ladies of Glenkirk? They were all women of strength and purpose. I dinna want to shame my husband by being known to my descendants as the do-naught duchess. I want to do my part, and if ye help me, yer name will go down wi' mine."

"Angus will kill me," Ian said nervously, but Flanna could tell she was convincing him.

"Angus is an old dear. He's like all loyal dogs; he growls at what he perceives to be a threat to his mistress. He will nae growl at ye, I promise, for 'tis ye who will keep me safe. Did I nae choose ye myself to be my guardian?" She gave him a small smile of encouragement.

Ahead of them Fingal Brodie heard it all and almost laughed aloud. He had known Flanna his whole life, and did his mother not always say the wench was the most devious she had ever known when she wanted something she should not have. He chuckled to himself. He had been concerned that the duke would hold him responsible for Flanna's behavior, but if Flanna would protect the likes of simple Ian More from Angus, Fingal Brodie would have no fear of the Duke of Glenkirk. He would take a leaf from his auntie's book and play the innocent. And he would make use of the opportunities given him, and one day he would be someone.

Ian did not agree to his mistress's adventure, but neither did he return to expose her. He wasn't quite certain she was really doing the right thing, but he also didn't believe he could stop her. She was a very determined young woman, and he could lose his place at the castle if he angered her. That she would protect him if he cooperated with her, he had absolutely no doubt. He could see his duchess was far more formidable than his duke. Better he remain with her and protect her from any dangers she might encounter along their way.

The day was cold; but it was dry, and no wind blew to add to their general discomfort. They plodded along through forest and field, keeping the Duke of Lundy and his party just barely in sight. They didn't want to appear that they were following Charlie Stuart. Finally it began to grow dark, and Flanna wondered if they would have to overnight in the open. They had stopped briefly only once since leaving Glenkirk, and the horses were tired. They lost sight of their quarry as Charlie and his men went over a hill. Flanna sent her nephew on ahead to scout.

When Fingal returned, he told his aunt, "There is a small inn up a ways. 'Tis too small for both parties, and besides, 'tis too soon for yer brother-in-law to know ye're following him. I dinna know what we will do, Flanna. We canna remain in the open, and the horses need shelter and to be fed."

Flanna turned to Ian. "Would the Duke of Lundy know ye?" she asked, and when he shook his head in the negative, she said, "Take off yer badge of service to the Leslies and hide it in yer pocket. Ye can ask for shelter in the stables for us and our horses. Nae one will see I'm a woman, for I am dressed like a lad, and I shall nae come into the inn. Just tell the innkeeper that ye and yer brothers are traveling south and need shelter for the night. Gie him these few coppers. He'll agree. Then remain to obtain our supper. Fingal will help me wi' the horses."

They reached the rustic inn and dismounted. Flanna led the three mounts into the stables while Ian went into the inn. The stables were clean and warm. The stalls were well swept and filled with fresh hay. Charlie Stuart's horses were already settled for the night. Flanna led each of the animals into an empty stall at the rear of the building, leaving one empty stall for them to use for themselves. She and Fingal unsaddled the beasts and, fetching the water bucket, gave them each a small drink. Too much and the horses would bloat, but a little would not hurt them. Then she filled the mangers with feed. Fingal helped her, brushing the horses down and checking their hooves for stones. By the time they had finished, Ian More returned with their supper.

"Innkeeper was happy we were willing to shelter in the stables," he said. "Yer brother-in-law and his party hae filled his wee inn to overflowing. His wife and daughters are cooking for more than they ever hae." He chuckled. "I've fresh bread, rabbit, cheese, and a draught of cider for us." He set it all out upon a narrow bench.

They ate quickly before their food cooled, and then set a schedule of watch for the night. Flanna would watch first, then Fingal, and finally Ian, who would awaken them when the duke's men came to get their own horses to depart. Her two companions wrapped themselves in their cloaks and were quickly snoring. Flanna sat, her back against the stall, considering that the day had gone very well. Patrick would think she was at her father's. Ian had not betrayed her, and Charlie had not realized he was being followed.

She could see the moon shining through the stable window. She had never before attempted such an adventure. Strangely she was not afraid. Rather, she felt exhilarated and excited by the prospect of meeting the king. Would he think her foolish, a woman, offering to raise troops for his restoration? She hoped not. Patrick was going to be very angry with her as it was, but if the king laughed at her, it would be awful.

She tensed as the door to the stable opened, and two of Charlie's escorts entered, but they had only come to check the horses. They didn't bother to even come to the back of the stables where Flanna and her party lay. They probably didn't even consider the other travelers, for which she was grateful. She could see by their badges that both men were Glenkirk men. She learned from them, however, that it was just about midnight. When they departed the stables, she awakened Fingal, telling him, "When the moon shines through the other window, awaken Ian."

"Aye," the boy said, stumbling to his feet.

Flanna pulled her cloak around her and settled down into a pile of sweet-smelling hay to sleep as best she could. It seemed as if she hadn't slept at all when Fingal was shaking her awake. Outside the sky was still dark, and the moon not yet set. She looked questioningly at her nephew.

"Ian says the inn is up. He has gone to fetch us something to eat. He says he's certain the others will be ready to leave shortly."

Flanna stretched, and then with a sigh sat up. "Go watch," she told him. "I hae to pee." Fingal went to stand by the stable doors while Flanna lowered her breeches and relieved herself in the straw in a corner of the stall. She was just readjusting her garments when Ian returned.

"I hae porridge," he said by way of greeting her. Then he handed her a small trencher of bread filled with the cereal and a wood spoon. "I hae cheese, too, and cider."

"The duke is awake and preparing to leave?" she asked him.

"Aye, they are eating now, my lady," Ian told her.

"Then, we hae best hurry ourselves," Flanna said. "If they come to the stables to get the horses, keep yer back to them, and dinna speak unless spoken to, else they recognize ye. I shall duck down where I canna be seen."

"The Glenkirk men wi' the duke are nae men who would know me," Ian assured his mistress.

They ate, and when the duke's men came to fetch their own animals, they but nodded to Ian and Fingal as they saddled their mounts and led them outside into the cold morning air. When they had closed the doors to the stables, Flanna and her party quickly prepared their own horses, then watched by the doors for the duke's party to leave. After they had, the trio from Glenkirk carefully followed, keeping just from sight as they had the previous day.

They trailed their quarry in this manner for the next four days, grateful that the weather remained dry, noting that each night as they grew closer to Perth, the inns grew larger and the number of people upon the road more. It seemed that quite a few Scotsmen and women were going to see the king crowned. Finally in midafternoon of the fifth day, they reached the fair city of Perth.

Standing on Kinnoul Hill, Flanna stared below in amazement at the first town she had ever seen. Her two companions were equally openmouthed. There on the plain below, set on the banks of the Tay, was Perth with its clustered streets, houses, and churches. The river wound like a silver ribbon in the afternoon sunlight as it moved beneath the town's stone bridges, across the snowy fields on the town's edge, and into the thick woods beyond. All around them they could see through the winter haze the hills and mountains beyond. A Highland wind blew its gentle icy breath across the landscape.

"We must nae linger, lady," Ian warned. "We'll lose the duke in this gathering, and ye need to know where he means to lay his head tonight, do ye nae?" He tugged at her horse's bridle to urge it forward.

"Aye," she agreed. "I should nae like to be lost in this place. I dinna know how we would ever find Charlie here."

They followed the Duke of Lundy and his companions down into the town and through the narrow, twisting streets until they came to a large inn. Outside hung a colorful sign, a purple thistle topped with a gold crown, indicating that the inn's name was the Crown and Thistle. Flanna could see her brother-in-law quite clearly, and as he dismounted, she quickly moved her horse up next to him. Looking down upon him, she said, "Good day to ye, then, Charlie, the nae-so-royal Stuart."

The voice was familiar, but of course it couldn't be. Charlie looked up. His jaw dropped first with surprise, and then with shock. "Jesu, Flanna!" he said. "What the hell are you doing here, and where is your husband?"

Chapter

9

Flanna smiled nervously at her brother-in-law. "At Glenkirk, I expect," she answered him as she slid from her horse to stand before him. "I came alone wi' my nephew, Fingal, and my man-at-arms, Ian More."

"How did you get here?" he demanded. What the hell was happening? Patrick must be frantic.

"We followed ye," Flanna said as if the whole thing were really quite obvious. "We've been following ye since ye left Glenkirk."

"*Why?*" Charlie could feel the blood pounding in his head. She had followed them. She made it sound so damned simple.

"I want to help the king," Flanna said earnestly. "Ye said, Charlie, that he needs men to fight. I want to help raise a levy for yer cousin. Patrick is just being silly when he natters about curses and bad fortune. If my husband willna bring new glory to the Leslies of Glenkirk, then I will!"

I need a drink, Charlie considered. *Whiskey. Strong and smoky. Lots of whiskey!* His brother was going to kill him when he learned that Charlie's loyalty to his Stuart family had inspired this adorable and naïve sister-in-law of his to a burst of patriotic fervor. "We had best go inside, Flanna," he said. "Your companions can remain with my escort. Half of them are Glenkirk men. They can escort you home when they return." He took her firmly by the arm and led her inside.

The landlord greeted them effusively. "I hae yer rooms set aside, my lord," he said, bowing and bobbing.

"My sister-in-law, the Duchess of Glenkirk, has joined me unexpectedly," Charlie explained to his host. "Can you accommodate her?"

"Ohh, my lord, I am sorry, but wi' the king's crowning tomorrow, we are filled to the brim wi' guests. Ye're apartments hae a wee room for a servant off the dayroom. Her Grace will hae to share wi' ye, I fear."

Charlie nodded graciously. "I understand," he said. "Will you bring us supper as soon as you can? Her ladyship has not eaten since early this morning," Charlie remarked dryly.

"More than anything," Flanna spoke up, "I should like a hot bath. I hae been cold for five days. Is such a thing possible?"

"Of course, my lady," the innkeeper said. "I'll hae the tub and water brought immediately. Annie!" he called to his daughter. "Take the duke and her ladyship to their apartments at once."

The innkeeper's daughter bobbed a curtsy to Charlie and Flanna and then hurried off as they followed. She led them down a narrow hallway and at its end flung open a heavy oak door. "There's a dayroom, and through here a bedchamber," she said, "and we hae a small room for yer ladyship's maid." She curtsied again and then moved across the room to light the fire that had been laid in the fireplace, then departed.

Charlie looked into the tiny chamber. There was a cloth-covered straw pallet and nothing else. He grimaced, but it would have to do.

"I'll sleep there," Flanna offered.

Charlie sighed. "Nay. I can hear my mother if I took you up on your offer, which I really ought to considering your behavior," he said. "But nay, sister, you will have the bedchamber until I send you back to your husband."

"Ohh, Charlie," Flanna begged him, "dinna be angry wi' me, and dinna make me go back until I hae met the king. And certainly nae on the morrow, for is he nae to be crowned tomorrow?"

"Patrick is going to be furious," he began.

"He probably hae nae missed me yet," she told him with a small smile. "I'll be halfway back to Glenkirk before he does. Ohh, Charlie! Hae ye nae seen the portraits at Glenkirk? The Duchess Jasmine and all the others? Who am I beside them? They were women of family and wealth. I want to make my mark as they did."

"Come sit by the fire," he invited her. "You still look chilled."

"I never knew it could be so cold," she admitted.

"You never rode five days in winter weather. Praise God it didn't snow or rain on us." Charlie chuckled. "Now tell me, Flanna, what this is all about? What does your behavior have to do with my mother and the women who came before her?"

"They were wealthy," Flanna began. "Heiresses! They came from great families. They were women of action who brought luster to the Leslies of Glenkirk."

"And one day you will, too, in your own way, even as did they," he reassured her.

"I was nae rich," she said.

"You had Brae, and Patrick wanted it. It was a fair bargain, and many marriages have been made for less," Charlie said.

"My family is nae a great one. Yer mam was a princess."

"And my great-grandmother a Grey of Greyhaven. They were a simple family without great wealth, Flanna. Just like the Brodies of Killiecairn. And remember, your mother was a Gordon of Brae. There is nothing wrong with either your pedigree or your dower portion."

"I will nae be known as the do-naught duchess," she said.

Charlie laughed. "You have been wed to my brother for only a few months, Flanna. Can you not wait a while before you set out to conquer the world for Glenkirk?"

"How can ye understand?" she said despairingly. "'Tis true ye're bastard-born, but ye're a royal bastard. And yer mam was born a princess. Ye've been surrounded by power, wealth, and privilege yer whole life. I hae nae been. What seems ordinary to ye is nae to me. I see the things yer mam and the others accomplished. They brought nae just wealth to the Leslies of Glenkirk, but accomplishments that added luster to the family. How can I compete, especially in this time and place? If I dinna take the chance to do something now, I will nae hae a chance again. I will go back to Glenkirk and wi' God's blessing produce another generation for Glenkirk, but do nae else."

"Are the bairns not enough?" Charlie asked her softly, reaching out to take her hand in his.

Flanna shook her head sadly. "Nae, Charlie, not for me. Any bitch can breed up a litter. I would be more!"

"I don't believe my brother will let you raise up a levy for the king," Charlie said, and he kissed his sister-in-law's hand. "But I know that my royal cousin would appreciate the sentiment, Flanna."

"I can do it, Charlie! I can!" Flanna said. "Just dinna send me away before I meet the king."

"I have to send you back, Flanna," he said. "I love my brother, and I would have no cause for dissension between us. Now that I know you have followed me, I must return you as quickly as possible, but it is too late for you to go today. And tomorrow the king will be crowned, and I will have no time to see you safely off. So, little sister, you will have a wee bit of time here in Perth amid the celebration of the king's crowning. That will be something to tell your bairns one day, eh?" He smiled at her, releasing her hand.

"I want to meet the king, Charlie," Flanna said. "I will nae go home until I do. If ye try to force me, I shall only run away, and then what will ye tell Patrick?"

"Flanna, understand that those who are the king's keepers here in Scotland have done their best to drive away his English friends and supporters. They believe we are a bad influence upon him, and to be truthful with you, some are. These Scots are hard, narrow-minded men whose lust for power is every bit as much as the king's English adherents'. Even I, who have avoided politics my entire life, am considered suspect."

"But why?" she asked him.

"There was a time here in Scotland when being a royal bastard was not considered shameful. To bear a royal Stuart on either side of the blanket was thought an accomplishment by many families. It is not so now here in Scotland. I am Prince Henry Stuart's bastard; but not only that, my mother is deemed a foreigner whose legitimate birth is believed suspect, too. That I am the Duke of Lundy, a widower with children who has never dabbled in the government, but rather kept to his own affairs, is not accounted. I am a bastard Stuart, an Englishman, and therefore a bad influence."

"But ye can still get to the king," Flanna insisted. "Ye are his cousin, and he loves ye."

"I will go to Scone tomorrow, and stand in the church there, and hope to catch his eye like so many others so he will know he is not alone and without his friends," Charlie replied. "I will go to the banquet afterward, and if I am lucky I will be able to get past his keepers for a moment to speak to him; but that is the best that even I can hope for, Flanna."

"Nay," she said firmly. "Ye are his cousin, and ye're clever, Charlie, and I know ye can do more. Take me to Scone and introduce me to the king so I may swear my fealty to him! You shall nae get me to go home until I do!"

God's boots! Charlie thought to himself. She was surely the most stubborn woman he had ever met in all his life. His mother was determined, too, but she could be reasoned with. Flanna could not. However, before he might argue with her further, there was a knock at the door, and Annie reappeared.

"Here's the lady's bath, my lord," she said, struggling into the room with a round wooden tub, followed by several young men carrying buckets of steaming water. She set the oak container by the now warm fire and directed the serving men to empty their buckets. After several trips the tub was full. "Shall I remain and help ye?" she asked Flanna.

"Aye, remain and help her ladyship," Charlie quickly answered for his sister-in-law. "Flanna, I shall be in the taproom. Have your bath, and then we shall eat here. Annie will come and fetch me." He quickly followed the serving men from the room.

"Coward!" Flanna called offer him.

Charlie laughed. "'Tis a wise man who knows when to give up the battle, lassie," he called over his shoulder.

The door was firmly closed behind him. "Is he yer husband, then?" Annie asked Flanna.

"He is my brother-in-law," Flanna said.

"Is he yer lover?" the innkeeper's daughter queried, curious.

"*Nay!*" Flanna denied. "What kind of thought is that for a decent lass to hae?" She looked so genuinely shocked that Annie believed her.

"Begging yer pardon, my lady. I meant no offense," the girl quickly apologized. "Dinna tell my father I asked."

"My husband recently lost his father in defense of the king's da. While he respects the king, he will nae offer him any aid. I followed my brother-in-law in order to promise the king that I will raise a levy in his honor."

"Oh," said Annie, who really didn't understand the ways of the gentry. "Hae ye scent for the bath?" she asked Flanna.

Flanna gave a short bark of laughter. "I hae a change of clothing and nae more than that," she said. "My husband dinna know that I was coming to Perth."

"He would hae forbid ye, then," Annie said, and then she nodded. "Ye were wise nae to tell him, lady. Sometimes 'tis better that way. I know my mother doesna always tell Da what she is about. Here, and I'll help ye off wi' yer boots." She knelt.

Flanna was quickly divested of her footwear and her garments by the industrious Annie, who clucked with distress over the condition of the lady's clothing. "I'll take yer boots to be cleaned, and if ye can wash yerself, I'll take the rest to be laundered."

"Just brush my breeches," Flanna instructed. "If ye wash them, they'll take a week to dry in this weather. I hae to return home in a day or two, Annie. I thank ye for the rest."

Annie curtsied and gathered up the boots and clothing. Then she bustled out the door, shutting it firmly behind her. Flanna sighed with pleasure as the heat from the water permeated her bones. She had seriously never thought to be warm again. She undid her thick plait and pinned it atop her head. The serving girl had left a tiny sliver of soap on the tub's rim. Reaching for it, Flanna dipped it in the water and lathered it between her hands. The faint, elusive fragrance of heather touched her nostrils, and she smiled as taking up the small flannel cloth Annie had left her she began to wash. The water felt good upon her face as she cleaned the grime of the road away. Then her neck and ears. Her arms, her chest. Leaning back, she raised a leg from the water, sweeping the soapy cloth over it and her foot. Rinsing, she lifted her other leg and was busily repeating her previous actions when the door to the room banged open.

Flanna gasped, her leg splashing back into the tub. She clutched the wet cloth to her chest, eyes wide at the tall, dark-haired man with the equally surprised look upon his face.

" 'sblood!" the gentleman exclaimed, and then he smiled. "By God, sweetheart, you are surely a sight for these eyes of mine!"

Flanna began to shriek at the top of her lungs at the intruder. *"Get out! Get out!"*

"Oh, my lady, I am so sorry!" Annie was there. "It was that dolt-headed boy in the kitchen!" She turned to the intruder. "Sir, if ye will come this way. The Duke of Lundy is in the taproom."

"But these are his rooms?" the gentleman inquired.

"Aye, sir," Annie said. "Please to follow me, and I will take ye to him."

"And who are you, my beauty?" the gentleman asked Flanna, his amber eyes sweeping admiringly over the tantalizing bits of her he could see.

"Get out!" Flanna said, but she had lowered her tone now, realizing that the intruder had been seeking Charlie and had not meant to presume upon her.

Instead, the gentleman pushed Annie from the room and, closing the door, walked over to the tub where Flanna sat. "You are obviously Lord Stuart's friend, m'dear, though where he found you in this benighted land I have no idea. However, I consider it insulting that he should withhold such charming company from me, especially knowing what trials I have suffered and will surely continue to suffer."

"Ye assume, sir, and ye're wrong," Flanna said. "Now leave this room at once. Annie will hae gone for the duke."

"Since I came to see him, that will suit me quite well, sweetheart," came the calm reply. "I don't suppose you would consider giving me a wee kiss?" He smiled roguishly at her, leaning forward.

"Oh, ye're a bold one, ye are!" Flanna sputtered angrily. "If ye hae nae caught me at such a disadvantage, I should gie ye a smack!"

The gentleman burst out laughing, genuinely amused. "You have a true redhead's temper, I can see, sweetheart. I can only imagine that you are a wildcat in bed."

"*Ohhhh!*" Flanna cried, flinging her wet cloth at him, and then realizing she had in her temper lost her barricade between those prying amber-gold eyes and her ample bosom. "Villain!" she snarled through her gritted teeth. "Hae ye nay manners than to spy on a lady in her bath, sir? What would ye mam think?"

"That I was incorrigible, as she has always suspected, sweetheart," came the chortled reply. "Come, lovey, stand up and let me see your treasures. I'm sure that your duke would not mind." He attempted a winning smile, revealing his white teeth in his swarthy complexion.

"Ah, sir, but my duke would be most out of sorts should I do such a thing," Flanna assured him. "Ye hae nae idea how angry he would be, will be, when I tell him of this invasion. Now, get out before I scream the inn down!"

Again the door to the chamber opened, but this time it was Charlie Stuart who entered. Immediately he bowed low to the gentleman. "Your Majesty," he said.

"Cousin," came the reply. "The gossip I manage to get said you were here, but I did not know that you had so charming a companion with you." He grinned. "Your lady has been entertaining me."

"She is not *mine*, sir, but rather my brother's wife. Sire, this is Lady Flanna Leslie, the Duchess of Glenkirk." Then Charlie turned to his sister-in-law. "Well, Flanna," he said, "you said you would not go home until you met the king. *This is he.*"

Flanna looked from Charlie to the intruder. Both had dark hair, although the king's was black. Both had amber eyes. Charlie's nose was not quite as prominent, and his skin was lighter in tone; but the two men were alike. As the shock of it hit her, she burst into tears, confounding both of her companions. *"How could you?"* she sobbed. *"Ohhh, how could you?"*

"Have you any idea what she is wailing about?" the king asked the Duke of Lundy.

"None whatsoever," Charlie replied. "I suggest we repair to the taproom for a mug of ale. The landlord has a rather excellent supply of it, I've already discovered."

"I have escaped my keepers for a short while," the king responded. "I don't want to be seen in public lest my presence cause a stir. We will step outside, sweetheart, and give you time to recover yourself and put some clothing on. Then I shall return with Charlie, and we'll all have a nice goblet of something. I shall apologize for my wicked behavior, you will forgive me, and we shall be friends, eh?"

Flanna looked up at him and nodded. Then she sneezed.

"I'll send the serving wench to you, sweetheart," the king said in kindly tones.

"Th-thank ye," Flanna sniffled.

The two men exited the room, and Annie hurried back into it. As Flanna stood up, the innkeeper's daughter wrapped her in a towel that had been warming by the fire, drying her with another. Then she pulled out the clean chemise that Flanna had in her saddlebag and slipped it over her head.

"Now, lady, into bed wi' ye," Annie said, and drew Flanna into the bedchamber where another little fire burned brightly. The bed had been warmed with a warming pan, and there was a flannel-wrapped brick at its foot. "I'll tell the two gentlemen that ye are ready to receive them, and I'll go to the taproom to bring back some hot mulled wine for ye," Annie said. "What a bold fellow that one is!"

"Thank ye," Flanna replied.

Annie hurried out, and a few moments later Charlie and the king came back into the chamber.

"Charlie, gie me my brush," Flanna said softly. " 'Tis in my pack on the stool."

The Duke of Lundy pulled the item from the leather bag, but to his surprise the king took it from him. Then the monarch sat next to Flanna on the edge of the bed and, reaching up, pulled the pins from her hair. He began to brush her hair, drawing the boar's bristles slowly and carefully through Flanna's thick red-gold mane.

"I liked to brush my sister Mary's hair before she went away to be married," he explained. "She had fine hair, but yours, sweetheart, surpasses anything I have ever before seen. Its color is magnificent."

Both Flanna and Charlie were speechless.

"My cousin tells me your husband does not approve of me," the king said quietly.

"Nay, sire! Patrick is as loyal a subject as Yer Majesty could hae," Flanna defended her duke, "but he says that every time the Stuarts become entwined wi' the Leslies of Glenkirk, misfortunes occur to his family. His father was killed at Dunbar. His mother hae left Glenkirk to go to France wi' his youngest sister. He hae never before been alone, and he doesna like it. He wed me for my lands; but I canna make up for the loss of his family, sire, and for that he holds the royal Stuarts responsible."

"You may tell your husband when you return home, sweetheart, that I, too, have lost my family. My father was murdered, executed. My mother lives in poverty in France with my youngest sister. My brothers are I know not where at this time. My sister Elizabeth has died in her captivity. My sister Mary struggles in a foreign land to aid me and my cause. Your husband and I have more in common than he acknowledges, including his half brother, my favorite cousin, the not-so-royal Stuart," the king said with a small smile. "I will, however, in the end prevail over my enemies, but I shall not hold it against Patrick Leslie that he does not aid me in my hour of need. I understand. The Leslies of Glenkirk have always been loyal to the house of Stuart. Patrick Leslie mourns his father deeply as I mourn mine." The brush slicked down her tresses rhythmically.

"Patrick may nae aid ye, Yer Majesty, but I will!" Flanna burst out. "I will go into the Highlands and raise troops for ye, if ye will gie me yer approval."

The brush stopped. Then the king took Flanna's chin in his hand

and smiled into her silvery eyes. "Why, sweetheart, you surely have my approval for such a generous offer, but I would not cause any breach between you and your husband." Then he leaned forward and kissed her on the lips.

Flanna was thunderstruck. His lips were warm and, to her great surprise, very inviting. She sighed, and her mouth melted against the king's.

And then Charlie's voice broke into her enchantment. "Ahh, here is Annie with your wine, Flanna. Shall I have her bring you a bit of supper here in your bed? I think that would be best."

For a moment she was totally confused, but then she managed to say, "Aye, Charlie, 'twould be good to stay where I am warm. I can still feel the chill from my ride."

The king chuckled at the bemused look she gave him. *What a delicious little duchess,* he thought, *and very ripe for seduction.* Perhaps Scotland would prove to be an entertaining place after all as long as he was forced to remain here. "Your offer of aid is not only accepted, sweetheart, but most welcome," he told her, his amber eyes attempting to pierce the delicate fabric of her chemise. *What an adorable creature with her red-gold hair, her silvery eyes with their thick lashes, and her delightfully pouty mouth.* He reached over and gave her a final quick kiss upon those lips. Then, laying her hairbrush aside, he arose and bowed to Flanna.

"Can you eat with me, cousin?" Charlie said calmly, but he was feeling far from calm. He had seen that particular look in his royal cousin's eyes before. The king was even now contemplating how he was going to seduce Flanna, who had the same charming earthiness as the king's previous mistress, Lucy Walters. Lucy, however, had had no husband to be offended, but Flanna certainly did.

"I'll take a cup of wine with you, Charlie," the king answered. "I cannot elude my keepers for too long a time, and it costs me a fortune in bribes each time I wish to escape for even a short while." He turned back to Flanna. "Good night, sweetheart. Sleep well, and if you dream, I hope it will be of me." Then, blowing her a kiss from his fingertips, the king turned and left the room.

"Stay in that bed, and do not leave this room until I come back to speak with you," Charlie said sternly.

Annie was wide-eyed. "Be that . . . *the king?*" she asked softly. Flanna nodded.

"And he came to see ye?"

"He is my brother-in-law's first cousin," Flanna said. "The duke's father was Prince Henry Stuart, who died long before either ye or I were born." She took the goblet of mulled wine from Annie's hand and sipped it. It was hot and strong, and she somehow felt she needed it.

"I'll go fetch yer supper," Annie said.

"Dinna speak of who ye hae seen here," Flanna cautioned. "Those who keep the king would be angry to learn he has slipped away from them to be wi' his cousin. Please."

"The old men in the Kirk Party, always preaching at a body, and constantly at the king, 'tis said. I'll nae tell a soul, even me da, that I have seen the dark lad," Annie promised.

"*The dark lad?*"

" 'Tis what they call him because his skin is darker and more French than 'tis fair like we Scots," Annie explained. Then she hurried out, and Flanna heard her giggling for a brief moment before the dayroom door was shut tight.

She could hear the low murmur of voices in the room beyond her, but she was unable to make out the words. Propped upon her pillows in the warm, comfortable bed, she sipped her mulled wine and contemplated the past hour. *She had met the king!* He had given her not one, but two kisses! Flanna Brodie, Leslie, she corrected herself, had been kissed by her king. And he had brushed her hair. She sighed. *I would do anything for him,* she thought silently to herself. *I will go to Killiecairn, and beyond, and raise up troops for King Charles. Maybe one day we will meet again.* She set her goblet aside and slipped into a light doze.

The king prepared to take his leave of his cousin. He peeped into the bedchamber and saw Flanna asleep. "What a beauty," he murmured softly as he closed the door again.

"She is my brother's wife, cousin, and not to be seduced," Charlie said quietly. "As it is Patrick is going to be furious when he learns she is here and that she aspires to raise troops for Your Majesty." He chuckled. "Patrick met her, wed her, and breached her virginity in the space of a day because he wanted her land to add to his and could have it no other way. She has only learned to read and write and can hardly be called sophisticated; but he has fallen in love with her, although I think he knows it not."

"And does she love him?" the king asked.

"Aye, I believe she does. She wants to make him proud of her. She seeks to raise troops for Your Majesty so she will not be remembered as the *do-naught duchess* as she has styled herself. You will remember my mother, of course. My stepfather's mother was also a proper hellion, not to mention the most remembered ancestress of all the Leslies who was called Janet. As legend goes, she was stolen away as a young girl, became the wife of a Turkish Sultan, and in her old age returned home to Scotland. I do not know how true this all is, but she is spoken of with reverence at Glenkirk. I suppose it's not more unreal than my mother coming from India almost fifty years ago."

"And the fair Flanna seeks to be the equal of these ladies," the king said. "She is naïve, Charlie, but not unintelligent, I suspect. She will make her mark, I am certain. As for seducing her, ahh, would that I might. I can see she would prove a delicious armful, but I was fortunate enough to escape my keepers that I might see you. Do not let them drive you away, Charlie, as they have attempted to drive the other of my friends and family away. They surround me with their Kirk Party members, and I am preached at nonstop by their ministers day and night. Every evil that has ever befallen Scotland is attributed to the godlessness of my family. I have accepted the Covenants for the sake of gaining my throne back, but—" He stopped as Charlie held up his hand in warning.

"We cannot know who is listening on us, cousin," Charlie said in low tones. "I understand, and I will not desert you until you have come into your own again. Only then will I return to Queen's Malvern with my children. Our fathers were brothers. We are cousins. Our blood is the same blood. *I will not leave you.* You are my king." Then Charlie, the not-so-royal Stuart, knelt before his monarch.

The king felt tears prickling at his eyes. He blinked them back and raised Charlie up so they were once again facing each other. "I know the sacrifice you make for me, cousin, for you are not a man of politics or a man who seeks power. You desire nothing but your family and a simple, quiet life. You have to my regret lost your wife in this war, and for that I am right sorrowful; but one day, cousin, we will go home again to England." He embraced the Duke of Lundy, and then he turned without another word and was gone from the chamber.

Would they? Charlie wondered. Would they one day go home to England? Would he repair the damage done his home and live in that wonderful house, so filled with memories, again? He hoped that the king was correct. The door to his apartment opened up again, and Annie came in, struggling beneath the weight of a large tray. Charlie jumped to his feet to help her, taking the tray and placing it on a table.

"Shall I fill a plate for her ladyship, my lord?" she asked.

"Aye, and fill it full. My sister-in-law has a prodigious appetite, for a woman." Charlie chuckled, his nose twitching at the delectable aromas arising from the covered dishes on the tray.

Annie had brought them a roast of beef, a platter with several thick slices of ham, a capon stuffed with apples, bread, and raisins, a dish of prawns that had been steamed in white wine and were being served with a mustard sauce, a second platter containing a broiled trout, a small dish of carrots, another of braised lettuces, a hot cottage loaf, a crock of sweet butter, a half wheel of hard yellow cheese, a slice of French Brie, and a dish of baked apples with clotted cream.

The bedchamber door opened, and Flanna, wrapped in a quilt, came out, sniffing. "I'm ravenous!" she declared.

"Annie will bring you something," he suggested.

"Nay, Charlie, I'll eat wi' ye. We can sit by the fire. Annie, bring that other wee table and put it between us. Then run along, for I am capable of serving his lordship, and yer da will need ye wi' the inn so busy tonight."

Annie did as she had been instructed, then curtsied and departed.

"You have recovered from your long ride, I see," Charlie said dryly. "You looked so frail and worn I thought surely you would but nibble and sleep the night. The king looked in on you before he went."

"He is a striking man," Flanna noted. "Nae handsome like my Patrick, but the lasses would nae neglect him if he were nae a king." She handed a plate, heaped with food, to her brother-in-law. Then she began to fill the second plate for herself.

"He was touched by your loyalty," Charlie said, and began to eat.

"I was nae flattering him," she replied. "I mean to raise men for the king. I'll go to Killiecairn first. The Brodies love a good fight, and there are so many of us it would take a burden off of my father if I took a few away. Besides, it will bring honor on my kin as well as the Leslies of Glenkirk." She dipped a prawn into the mustard sauce and bit into it.

"Patrick will not allow it, Flanna. Your first duty to Glenkirk is to produce an heir for my brother," Charlie reminded her.

"There is time," Flanna replied easily.

"At twenty-two you are hardly in the first flush of your youth," Charlie said bluntly. "I was the fourth of my mother's children, and I was born when she was twenty-two."

"I dinna intend haeing so many bairns as yer mam," Flanna replied. "How will they survive? Glenkirk would end up like Killiecairn, overflowing with bairns, and eventually their bairns. Nay, I think nae."

"At Glenkirk there is wealth enough to pave any child's way," he explained to her. "The two youngest of the Leslie sons share an estate in Ireland. Only Patrick was left home. Your husband is a rich man, Flanna. Didn't you know that?"

She shook her head. "I know he has lands aplenty and the castle is in good repair. Is there more?"

Charlie nodded. "Ask Patrick. He will tell you."

"Are we going to the coronation tomorrow?" she asked him.

The not-so-royal Stuart thought a moment. He was going, but

Flanna? Then he laughed. "Aye, we are going," he said, "but we shall have to find you a gown, lassie, for you cannot go into the kirk at Scone in your trews. When Annie comes to get the tray, I'll ask her."

The innkeeper's daughter was delighted to be of help to the Duchess of Glenkirk. "I can loan ye the gown I wear to the kirk," she said proudly. " 'Tis very fine, and my da says much too fancy for a lass like me. It has a linen collar edged in lace. Let me take the tray away, and I'll fetch it for ye, m'lady."

Annie's garment was, to Charlie's surprise, quite acceptable, if plain. Both the bodice and the skirt were made from black silk. While Flanna's bosom was a trifle more ample than Annie's, the rest of the gown fit perfectly. It was a modest gown, and his sister-in-law would not attract any undue attention in it, Charlie thought, relieved. Both he and Flanna thanked the girl, Flanna promising to be very careful with Annie's best.

The first of January dawned gray and cold. Charlie and Flanna arose, ate their porridge, and then joined the crowds riding across the river to the cathedral at Scone. While called a cathedral, it was in reality no more than a small church. The Scots nobles did their best to keep the English nobles from the coronation ceremony. Neither side particularly cared for the other, and each jealously coveted the king for themselves. Then, too, there was the matter of religion dividing the two sides. The Scot kirk abhorred the Anglican communion with its more Catholic rites and rituals. They particularly disliked the bishops. Bishops had been excluded from the kirk in Scotland.

Charlie, however, found himself in a rather interesting position, for he was liked and accepted by both sides. He had been among the first of the English nobles to make his penance in sackcloth and ashes within the Scots kirk. An Anglican, he was willing for the sake of his royal cousin to give up his church as long as it was necessary. No one, after all, was asking him to give up the Lord Jesus. He remembered his great-grandmother who was so fond of quoting the great Elizabeth. *There is but one Lord Jesus Christ. The rest is all trifles.* The logic made perfect sense and allowed Charlie to do what he had to do so he might be there for Royal Charles.

Charles Frederick Stuart looked like his father, and there were many within the crowd who remembered Prince Henry. His not-so-royal son, however, had lived a good deal longer than Henry Stuart. Still, the amber eyes, the facial features and his stance were all recognizable as Stuart. The only difference between Charlie and his father was the color of their hair. Prince Henry had been blond like his Danish mother. Charlie's hair was the traditional deep Stuart auburn.

Arriving at the little church, they dismounted. The crowds parted for the not-so-royal Stuart and the lady he was escorting. The common folk murmured among themselves that this man might have been their king but for an accident of birth. Some reached out to touch him. Charlie smiled warmly and nodded, stretching out his hands to clasp the hands offered him.

"God bless, Yer Worship!" an old woman said, kissing his hand.

"God bless our King Charles, grandmother," Charlie replied, and the crowd within the sound of his voice cheered.

They entered the small church, standing in the back, for it would have been impossible to move forward, and Charlie had no part in the ceremony. A platform some six feet in height had been constructed so all might see the crowning of the king upon his throne. The rituals to be performed were set within the context of the new kirk and had been approved by the Assembly of the kirk. The royal procession entered the small church, and Charlie managed to catch his kingly cousin's eye briefly. The royal nodded just imperceptibly. The crown of pearls, the gilt spurs, and the sword of the state were all carried by nobles strongly associated with the Covenanters' cause. Only the Earl Marischal, a royalist, was allowed to perform a long-time family duty of escorting the king.

Once more Charles II enthusiastically endorsed the principle of the Covenants and declared them sacred. Those gathered to see him crowned were impressed by his zeal. Charlie, however, smiled to himself. The kirk did not have quite the hold on the government as they had previously had. His royal cousin was doing what he needed to do in order to be crowned. It would be quite a different thing when the king finally gained firm control of his government.

In the meantime he played his part, a talent at which the Stuarts were particularly good. Finally the crown was placed upon His Majesty's dark head. Cheers erupted.

Flanna had been openmouthed and wide-eyed through it all. She had never when she followed after her brother-in-law anticipated seeing the coronation itself. What a tale she would have to tell her children and her grandchildren one day. She could not wait to share this day with Patrick. *Oh, if only he were not so obdurate about the king.*

"I'm taking you back to the inn," Charlie murmured to her as they exited the church at Scone. "You begin your return journey tomorrow, and you are still, I can see, exhausted from the first trip, Flanna. I will send a note to my brother explaining everything, and accepting the blame for you following after me."

"Why should ye accept culpability for my actions?" Flanna asked him. "I did what I did because I wanted to do it, Charlie."

"I know," Charlie chuckled as he boosted her into Glaise's saddle, "but knowing my brother better than you do, I suspect that it is best he not realize quite yet how headstrong you can be." He mounted his own beast.

"If Patrick persists in believing there is some bad fortune between his family and the king's, I canna dissuade him," Flanna said. "But I dinna hae to behave as foolishly as he does. I hae given my word to the king that I will raise a levy for him. 'Tis nae my habit to gie a promise lightly, or to break it if I do."

Charlie said nothing more. It was, he knew, useless. He would warn his brother to be wary of Flanna's motives and actions. Then it was up to Patrick to control his wife. He returned Flanna to the Crown and Thistle, saying as he lifted her from her mount, "I must return to the king now. I will see you either later this evening or come the morning before you begin your journey back to Glenkirk. Try to behave, Flanna. Remember that your first loyalty is to your husband, and to Glenkirk, which needs an heir, lassie."

He did not see her stick out her tongue at him as he rode off again.

Chapter

10

Flanna returned the gown to Annie, asking, "Hae ye seen my nephew about? The lad I rode in wi' yesterday."

"He was wi' the duke's men, m'lady," Annie replied. "Do ye want me to fetch him to ye?"

"Nay," Flanna said. "I just wanted to know where he was. My brother would be angry wi' me if the lad were harmed or got into mischief. Worse, Fingal's mam would hae the hide off of me."

Annie chuckled. "I understand. Me mam is fierce where her lads are concerned. Shall I bring ye something to eat, m'lady?"

Flanna nodded. "There were nae women asked to the king's feast," she explained.

"Was the coronation grand?" Annie asked, curious.

Flanna nodded. "And verra long," she told the innkeeper's daughter. "The preacher chosen to speak went on and on and on. He didna think highly of the Royal Stuarts, for he said terrible things about them. He called them godless and fornicators. From all he said, and if it were true, I'm surprised they let our king back into Scotland at all," Flanna observed.

Annie giggled. "Me da says they're a bunch of sour old psalm singers who would squeeze all the joy out of life if they could. But dinna say I said it, for we could get in trouble." She curtsied. "I'll fetch ye something nice, m'lady." Then she hurried out with her gown.

When she returned, she carried a tray containing a breast of capon, a small loaf of fresh bread, a crock of butter, a dish of cherry jam, and a generous wedge of hard yellow cheese. She set the tray down.

"Will ye hae wine or ale, m'lady?" she asked Flanna.

"Ale," Flanna told her.

"I'll fetch a pitcher," Annie responded, and was gone again to return a few minutes later. She set the container on a sideboard.

"Just shout out if you need me again, m'lady," Annie said, and she curtsied again before disappearing out the door.

Flanna sat down and devoured the food the girl had brought. In the streets outside, and in the inn itself, she could hear the celebration for the king's crowning going on despite the cold winter weather. She sat by the fire, full and warm, and was suddenly aware of how tired she really was. She had never undertaken such a journey as the one to Perth. She had been concerned the entire way that Charlie would catch her and send her right back. She had not slept well in the stables in which they had sheltered. The food had not agreed with her. And all the time she had fretted that Patrick might realize she had not gone to Killiecairn and come after her before she could attain her goal.

But she had achieved her objective. She had met the king, and she had received his kind blessing to raise troops. And raise a levy she would! She would be Flanna Leslie of Glenkirk who had done her duty in grand style for Charles Stuart, the second king of his name. Her portrait would be painted to hang in the family gallery, and future generations would speak reverently of her as they did of Janet Leslie, and Catriona Leslie, and Jasmine Leslie. And the king would reward the Leslies of Glenkirk, and Patrick would see that all his mother's nonsense about misfortunes between the two families was nothing but foolishness. She drew the quilt she was using for a house gown about her shoulders. Her eyes were growing heavy with her exhaustion and her full belly. Flanna fell asleep in her chair, the soothing crackle of the fire her lullaby.

The night came, and she slumbered on comfortably in place by the warm hearth. She did not hear the door to the chamber open or the footsteps as they came across the floor. The king stood quietly looking down at the sleeping woman. She was beautiful, he thought again. One of the loveliest women he had ever seen. What a pity what passed for a royal Scottish court today had no room for such delicious armfuls as the luscious Duchess of Glenkirk. Removing his plumed hat and his fur-lined cape, the king set them aside.

The banquet celebrating his coronation was over, and his sour-faced keepers lay in their beds. He had been allowed to remain with his friends, an unusual privilege on the part of his Scottish keepers, who considered the king's English friends a very bad influence. They were, after all, Anglicans and Roman Catholics, who were, of course, to be avoided at all costs. The king smiled to himself. His keepers were not very clever, however, and many of his compatriots had donned sackcloth and ashes, accepted the Covenants, and done their public penance in order to remain with Charles Stuart. Some of the greatest names in England had humbled themselves for their king.

He had left them drinking and talking together. Planning his eventual return to England. But the king had decided to celebrate his ascension to Scotland's throne in a different manner. He gazed down at Flanna Leslie. It had been some time since he had indulged himself in a delicious seduction, and the Duchess of Glenkirk was ripe for it. Patriotic. Naïve. And utterly adorable. His tongue swept over his fleshy lips in anticipation. Charlie had said he was sending her home tomorrow, but the king had other plans for the lovely young woman.

Bending, he quickly picked her up in his arms and then resettled himself in the chair by the fire. She murmured softly and slowly opened her silver eyes. The beautiful eyes focused, then widened with shock as she recognized the king. She struggled to sit up, but he held her firmly in his embrace. "You are the fairest thing I have seen in Scotland so far, Flanna Leslie. I doubt there is anyone, or anything, to compare with you," he murmured in his rich, musical voice. The amber eyes were devouring her face.

"Yer Majesty!" Flanna's voice squeaked, and she attempted again to rise from his lap.

"Let me hold you, sweetheart," he pleaded prettily with her. "It has been so long since I have known any tenderness. I have spent months and months running from my enemies. I have been poor and seen my mother, a French princess, struggling to survive, to care for my wee sister, Henriette. My entire family has suffered, Flanna Leslie. Now, today, I am King of Scotland, but I am a lonely king. Do not forbid me your company, sweetheart, I beg you!"

"I am pleased to offer ye my company, Yer Majesty," Flanna said, "but such close proximity to a man other than my husband is nae right, nor is it proper, and Yer Majesty well knows it. I am a country lass, but I am nae a fool."

The king laughed, genuinely amused. This was not going to be as simple as he had anticipated. "I want to make love to you," he said candidly to her. "Surely you will not deny your king, Flanna Leslie."

Flanna squirmed to escape his embrace. "I am a married woman, Yer Majesty," she told him firmly. "I dinna choose to betray my husband or bring shame upon Glenkirk wi' wanton behavior. Please let me go!"

"Very well," he said, his voice sounding most regretful, "but will you not give me a wee kiss first?" He smiled winningly at her. "A kiss of peace between us to show me you are not offended that I am besotted by your beauty and was driven to rash actions."

"One kiss?" she queried him, looking closely at him.

He nodded. What a delightful innocent. She obviously did not know how one kiss could lead to far more pleasant pleasures.

"Verra well. One kiss," she told him, and closing her eyes, she pursed her lips at him.

The king's mouth closed over hers. He kissed her deeply, setting her senses to reeling as his lips teased, and taunted, and tempted her onward. His mouth never left hers, but his hands began to caress her beneath her quilt, finding the opening to her chemise and sliding through to brush across her silken skin. He fondled her breast, his fingers pinching the nipple. His lips never released her even as she now struggled in his arms. She was fragrant with the scent of some elusive perfume he could not quite identify. He felt his manhood tightening in his breeches, and his hand slipped downward over her belly to brush at the tangle of curls at the junction where her tightly closed thighs met. A single finger slipped along the cleft of her mons even as she attempted to cry out against his mouth. He could not remember having been so quickly aroused in his entire life.

Flanna finally managed to tear her lips away from his. She was furious and gasped for breath as she squirmed to escape the embrace, her fists beating against him. *"Yer Majesty!* Shame! Ye're a villain! Let me go this instant! Ohhh!"

"I'm mad for you, sweetheart!" the king cried, attempting to avoid her angry blows. *"Ouch!"*

Flanna yanked at his black curls. "Let me go!" she shouted. "Ohhh, I canna believe that ye would be so dishonorable, sir!"

"There is no dishonor meant, Flanna Leslie," he insisted. "Many would consider it an honor to be approached by their king." He loosened his grip on her.

Flanna struggled to her feet, drawing her quilt about her. "I am a country woman, Yer Majesty. I am married to an honorable man. I respect ye as my king, but I will nae behave like some wanton tavern wench." She clutched the quilt to her slender frame and mustered her dignity. "I must ask Yer Majesty to leave at once," she said.

"You must give me a moment, or two," he said.

"And face more of yer tricks?" she demanded.

"I fear, sweetheart, I am at a disadvantage," he said, and his eyes went to the very discernable bulge in his breeches.

"Ohh, shame!" she cried.

"The shame," he said wryly, "is that I cannot do with it what should be done with it." Then he gave her a weak grin.

Flanna laughed. She couldn't help it. "If ye're haeing difficulty, Yer Majesty, 'tis yer own fault and nae one else's," she scolded.

"Am I forgiven, then?" he said, making an attempt at looking remorseful.

"Ye're a wicked lad," Flanna said, "but if ye can promise me that ye will behave yerself, then aye, I will forgie ye, Yer Majesty."

He sighed deeply. "I must retire defeated, madame, by your goodness and strong sense of honor. Will you still raise a levy for me, sweetheart?"

"Hae I nae given ye my word?" she replied. "I dinna break my word, Yer Majesty, once offered."

"You make me almost ashamed, Flanna Leslie," he responded.

"*Almost?*" Her silvery eyes were twinkling. "Did yer mam nae explain about yer conscience to ye, sir?"

"She did," he said, "but alas, my hot blood seems a stronger influence upon me. Not only am I a Stuart, but my mother's French family had quite a number of lusty kings in its line of descent. We cannot, it seems, resist a beautiful face, and yours is very beautiful, sweetheart."

"Sir, ye promised to behave!" Flanna scolded him further.

He sighed again. "And I will," he said, finally standing up. Then he took her hand in his, raising it to his lips to kiss; and at that exact moment, the door to the chamber flew open to reveal the Duke of Glenkirk.

"So, madame," he snarled at her, "I find ye at last! And who is this fellow who makes so bold wi' ye?" He drew his sword.

"Put up your weapon, Patrick!" the Duke of Lundy said, coming up behind his brother. "*This is the king!*"

Patrick Leslie sheathed his sword, but as he did, he said scathingly, "Am I to be honored, then, that 'tis a royal Stuart making free wi' my wife and not some common fellow?" His look was cold.

Kissing Flanna's hand, the king released his hold, and then drawled, "So this is the Leslie of Glenkirk? I have heard much about you, my lord, from your brother." His look was almost dismissive.

"Then, Charlie has explained to ye that while I respect Yer Majesty, I will nae send my clansmen to be cannon fodder for ye. Ye hae nae passion for Scotland. Ye seek to return to England, and many will die in the attempt to put ye back upon yer throne there; but they will nae be Leslies of Glenkirk. We lost much at Dunbar, and before that at Solway Moss, and other battles fought in the

Stuart cause. We canna afford to lose any more of our people." He looked directly at the king as he spoke.

"I will raise a levy for the king!" Flanna unwisely cried out.

The Duke of Lundy groaned audibly at her words. Didn't his sister-in-law know enough to be silent in this situation? The answer was obviously she did not.

"Ye will do nae such thing!" Patrick Leslie said angrily.

"*I will!*" Flanna insisted.

"Yer duty is to me, to Glenkirk," he snapped. "Ye must gie me an heir, Flanna. Damnit, lass, that is yer obligation first."

"Am I a brood mare, then? Some bitch whose value lies in her abilities to breed up bairns?" Flanna demanded.

"*Aye, ye are!*" he said with devastating effect.

She grabbed the nearest object, a pewter goblet, and flung it at his head. "*I hate ye, Patrick Leslie!*"

He ducked, and in that moment both Charlie and the king withdrew quickly into the hallway.

"She has a fine temper on her, doesn't she?" the king remarked drolly as he and his cousin swiftly departed the inn.

"My brother has taken on far more than he anticipated," Charlie returned, and then he burst out laughing. "Flanna is a complicated lass, and Patrick has absolutely no experience with women. Oh, he's been bedding them since he was barely out of boyhood, but no lass has ever engaged his heart until he met Flanna Brodie."

"I thought they wed because he wanted her lands," the king said.

"That's how it began," Charlie agreed, "but he has fallen in love with her, and I believe she with him, although both of them are too stubborn and angry right now to understand what has happened." The Duke of Lundy chuckled. "I am most envious of him and the happiness that lies ahead for them both."

"You miss your Bess, don't you?" the king said quietly.

"I do, cousin, I do," Charlie admitted.

"She shall be avenged one day, I promise you," the king vowed.

"I thank Your Majesty," Charlie said, "but it will not bring her back to me, nor will my bairns ever know their mother again. At least I know they will be safe during this conflict, however long it may last. Bess's Puritan parents have no idea where they are. I spirited them out of England just in time. They will have a happy childhood at Glenkirk."

"Then, they shall survive, for my siblings and I had a most happy childhood until this damned parliamentary war," the king noted.

"Cousin," Charlie said as they walked the darkened street, "will you forgive my brother, Patrick, for his harsh words? Despite his years, he was not ready to take on the responsibilities of his station. My mother and my stepfather spoiled him, and cocooned him here in Scotland for his entire life. Mostly at Glenkirk. The sudden shock of the world intruding upon his life has been difficult for him. His precipitous marriage has actually proven to be a good thing, I believe. However angry he may be right now, he is a loyal and devoted servant of Your Majesty."

The king chuckled. "Cousin," he said, "you have the silver tongue of the Stuarts. I hold no grudge against Glenkirk. Indeed, I understand better than Patrick Leslie would imagine, for I, too, have lost my father to this violence. And I agree with you that his wife will be the making of him. My mother had a hot temper, too, and more often than not wheedled my father to her way of thinking by using it . . . and her more seductive charms. One day I will return to England, and when I do, the Leslies of Glenkirk will always be welcomed at court even as you are, cousin."

"Your Majesty is gracious," Charlie said. "When we have gained your lodging, I will return to the Crown and Thistle, for I suspect I shall need to mediate between my brother and his wife. They will leave tomorrow for Glenkirk."

"Of course," the king agreed. "I hope she will not have killed him before your return. Her aim was quite excellent. I wonder we should not put her behind a cannon." He laughed, and Charlie laughed with him.

By the time the Duke of Lundy had returned to the inn, however, the battle between his brother and sister-in-law had temporarily ceased. Flanna had gone to bed, her door firmly barred to her husband. Patrick sat nursing a tankard of ale in the taproom of the inn, which was now, by virtue of the hour, empty and quiet. Charlie joined his brother.

"Have you made peace with Flanna?" he asked, knowing the answer even as he inquired.

"She is impossible," Patrick said dourly. "I dinna ever remember Mama being so difficult."

Charlie laughed heartily. "Then, your memory is either faulty or quite short, little brother," he said. "Our mother has always been a woman to have and get her own way. We great-grandsons of Skye O'Malley seem to like strong women. If you would blame anyone for what has happened, blame me, Patrick. If I hadn't been so damned enthusiastic about the king, and his cause—if Flanna hadn't felt so damned intimidated by the portraits of Mama, our grandmother Leslie, and the great Janet Leslie—this might not have happened. Do you know what your wife told me? That she didn't want to be known as the *do-naught duchess.* That one day, when her descendants looked at her portrait, she wanted them to admire her accomplishments of having raised a levy for King Charles II, of having helped him regain his rightful place upon his throne. She is a charming innocent, your Flanna. And, extremely resourceful. She followed me from Glenkirk to Perth, and I never knew it until she accosted me outside of this inn." He chuckled. "It was a feat worthy of a Leslie duchess. Not only Mama, but Cat Leslie and Madame Skye would have lauded her little adventure."

"She is the most disobedient lass I hae ever known," Patrick grumbled.

"So were our sisters, India and Fortune," Charlie said, "but then, you were just a lad when they committed their offenses, driving both Mama and our da to distraction. I, however, remember it well."

"I am thirty-five, Charlie. I need a wife who will gie me an heir," Patrick said. "I dinna want a wife dabbling in the politics of a government she doesna understand. Flanna is naïve, and while I know her heart is good, her first loyalty must be to me, and to Glenkirk. Nae to the royal Stuarts. Whatever she may think, that family brings misfortune to mine."

"Break her gently, Patrick," his older and wiser brother advised.

"Now, tell me how you came here so quickly. Flanna believed you would not catch her in her little deception before she was well on her way back."

The Duke of Glenkirk allowed a small smile to crease his handsome face. "I hae to admit to ye, Charlie, 'twas well thought out, and I would nae hae caught her but for Una Brodie. She sent her husband, Aulay, Fingal's father, to Glenkirk. He arrived late the same day as Flanna had departed, bringing wi' him certain garments for their son. The lad had simply gone off with my man-at-arms, and Una Brodie sent Aulay with the clothing. She is a proud woman and did nae want me to think the Brodies could nae provide decently for their own. He was verra surprised to learn his son was nae at Glenkirk, *and I was verra surprised to find my wife was nae at Killiecairn.* Then Angus Gordon joined the discussion, and we pieced the puzzle together. It was Angus who realized where Flanna had gone. The next day I sent Aulay Brodie home, first gaining his promise to remain silent as to his sister's escapade. The day after, I began my own journey to Perth. My men and I rode, stopping only at nightfall when it became too dark to travel further. We slept wherever we stopped and carried our own provisions wi' us. That is how we got to Perth so quickly," he concluded.

"So there is no harm done," Charlie soothed. "Flanna is safe, and you will take her back on the morrow."

"Nae harm done?" Patrick said, now angry again. "I arrive to find my wife in her shift wi' a stranger all over her!"

"The king enjoys a pretty face, Patrick. It is his way. He met Flanna yesterday, and couldn't resist attempting seduction today. You have no idea how difficult his life is with these Scots Covenanters and Kirk Party lordlings. They have made my cousin a virtual prisoner, although sometimes he manages to escape their vigilant eye. But I know your wife, little brother. She is an honorable woman, and while you must ask her to satisfy your own needs, I assure you that there was no seduction of the Duchess of Glenkirk. Don't you realize it yet, Patrick? Flanna is falling in love with you. *And you with her.*"

"I am nae in love wi' the disobedient wench," the duke said.

"Then, why are you so angry?" Charlie wanted to know.

Patrick Leslie slammed his tankard down on the oak table. "I dinna know," he said to be honest, "but I am nae in love, Charlie!"

"Aye, you are," Charlie said with perfect logic. "And you're a lucky man. She'll give you fine strong children . . . in her own time."

"That is what I fear," Patrick said. *"In her own time.* I am nae a lad, Charlie."

"No, you're not," Charlie agreed, "but she is yet young enough."

"What if something should happen to me as it did to our father?" Patrick fretted. "Glenkirk would nae hae an heir."

"Nothing is going to happen to you, little brother. When Jemmie Leslie died, he was over seventy and had sired five sons and three daughters on two wives. He was older than you when he got you on our mother, followed by your two brothers and your two sisters. Besides, since you refuse to involve yourself in the king's war, you should be safe enough at Glenkirk," Charlie concluded. Then he thought a moment more, and said, "And should anything happen to you, and there be no heirs of your body, you do have two younger Leslie brothers. Adam would come home from Ireland to take his place."

"Ye fill me wi' comfort," Patrick remarked dryly.

Charlie chuckled. "You Leslies live to ripe old ages unless you fight for the Stuarts. Since you will not, I foresee you reaching an ancient and ripe epoch. Your sons will be legion as will your grandsons before you leave this earth, Patrick. And Flanna will be right there with you, a delicious little thorn in your side."

Patrick Leslie laughed. "Ye foresee a happy future for me in an unhappy time, Charlie." Then he grew sober. "But what of ye?"

Now it was the not-so-royal Stuart who grew serious. "I will do whatever I can to aid my cousin, the king," he said. "I am not a man of politics, nor have I ever been, nor do I want to be. My value to my cousin is being there to be his friend, to comfort and to encourage him in these troubled times. I have made my public penance as the real rulers of this place have required in order that I can remain by the king's side. I will follow him wherever he goes."

"He will go back to England," Patrick said.

"Aye, he will," Charlie agreed, "but how quickly he can regain his throne is another matter. I say nothing, for it is not my position to advise the king, but I think it will be some time, though how long, I do not know, before Charles II sits upon his throne again in England. And unless he can gain the upper hand here in Scotland, I cannot say how long he will remain here. He has been patient so far in order to obtain his first crown, but you know the royal Stuarts. They are firm believers in Divine Right. He will bear this trial without complaint for just so long, and then his patience will come to an end. He is far more clever than his father, my uncle, was. He can be convinced to compromise, although not easily, and he certainly does not like it."

The Duke of Glenkirk nodded. "Aye," he agreed, "but I dinna see the Kirk Party letting the king march into England, Charlie."

"Ahh, but they are losing their grip on the government, little brother. It is a slow process, but you know that the Stuarts, for all their faults, have always been popular with the people. This king is young and magnetic. His charm and gracious attitude have won him many adherents among the people. They will come when he calls them."

"Then, they are fools," Patrick said. "As our mother pointed out, the English will nae welcome our kilt-wearing, pipe-skirling armies. More times than nae we hae swarmed over the borders separating our two lands to war and to pillage. Those on both sides of the border hae long memories. If it were my decision, I would look for a way to assassinate the leaders of this so-called Commonwealth."

"Ahh," Charlie replied, "there speaks the Mughal in you."

"Well, creating a vacuum in the power structure in England would make it possible for the king's return to fill that vacuum," the Duke of Glenkirk said. "It seems a better way to me."

"But how would we do it, little brother? And how many would we kill? And if we began such a course of action, how would we pick off all the men of importance at the same time in order to avoid the lesser members of Cromwell's party filling that vacuum?"

"How many will die fighting the king's war?" Patrick countered, and then added ironically, "But then, they are the *people* and of nae importance to the royal Stuart's world, eh, Charlie?"

"Jesu!" the Duke of Lundy swore softly, "you have become a cynic, little brother. I am not certain it becomes you, or that our parents would approve. Of course it matters that good men die in wars, but wars must be fought to maintain the right."

"But who decides what is right, Charlie? And what gives those who decide the authority to make those decisions? We all, each of us, look at things differently, but does that make it wrong that ye and I dinna see eye to eye on everything? Look at the difficulty religion has caused. Do ye really think God favors one faith over another? Yet men will fight over popes, and bishops, and whether they are necessary or nae necessary. And each side believes that committing murder and mayhem in God's name allows them the right to spread their violence, and worse, they believe God favors them for their stand. What misery they hae wrought, and how the angels must weep, brother! Ye say the Stuarts dinna cause bad fortune, but I say they do. Hae nae Scotland always been at war wi' itself, king against earl, clan against clan? How many Stuart kings died young of murder, or in a factional battle? Yet to our south, England remained strong and prosperous. We hae nae ever had such abundance, nor has our land thrived. We hae fought against one another, and against our churches. Old King James could hardly wait to inherit Bess's throne. And how many of our nobility followed him south? And how bitterly hae the English resented the Stuarts and their ilk? We brought wi' us the dissension that has flourished in Scotland for centuries. And now the English hae murdered a Stuart king, and driven another out of their land, and sought to set up something called a Commonwealth."

"It will be destroyed, and so will those who executed the king," Charlie replied firmly.

"And how long will it take to accomplish all this, and how many will be killed, Charlie?" the Duke of Glenkirk asked quietly.

"I don't know," came the equally quiet reply.

Patrick nodded. "Nor do any," he said. "So, Charlie, I shall take my impetuous young wife and return home to Glenkirk. I hae sworn to the Covenants months ago. A minister of the kirk, an inoffensive fellow, preaches gently and wi'out rancor in the Glenkirk church. I obey the law of the land and dinna feud wi' my neighbors. I shall nae ask my men to lay down their lives for Charles II. We will respect his kingship, but we will nae fight for him; nor will we march down into England, for mark my words, that is where this is going. By year's end this king will force the bloody hand of Cromwell's government. The loss at Dunbar brought the English to Edinburgh where they yet remain. Pray God yer kingly cousin's next move does nae destroy Scotland entirely."

"I will not let this cause a breach between us," Charlie said.

"Why would it?" Patrick replied. "I understand yer loyalties, Charlie. I respect them, but as ye're loyal to yer Stuart family, so must I be loyal to my Leslies of Glenkirk. But those loyalties dinna change the fact that ye are my big brother and that I love ye."

Charlie's eyes grew moist, but he managed a small grin. "I forget that we are grown sometimes," he said low.

Patrick nodded. "Aye," he agreed. "We had a grand youth, Charlie. I can still remember how ye taught me to fish for salmon in the wee river near Glenkirk. I think I was eight, and ye were twelve."

"Remember the day we brought home six fish and gave them to Cook? And they brought them to the high board that night, and we were so damned proud! And then Duncan and Adam wanted to learn to fish, too," Charlie chuckled, "and we were forever sneaking off to escape them."

"Aye, Duncan was such a greeting bairn in those days," Patrick recalled. "Now both he and Adam are men grown. Except for our little sister, Autumn, ye all hae bairns but me. I want my own bairns, Charlie."

"Flanna will give you the children you want," Charlie said. "She's a good lass, and she knows her duty to Glenkirk."

"Her heart, I fear, is wi' the king now," Patrick said.

"You're a fool, little brother, that you cannot see Flanna has fallen in love with you. Be tender with her, and you will quickly win her back to your side. 'Twas a grand gesture she made, but even my cousin knows it will come to naught. He treated her passion for his cause the way he always does. With charm and fair words. Tell your wife that you love her, Patrick. 'Tis all you need do to win her."

"Why do ye keep saying that I love the impossible wench?" Patrick demanded irritably.

Charlie laughed. "If you didn't love her, little brother, then her actions would not annoy you so greatly. Nor would you have come so quickly after her. You care. Why will you not admit to it?"

"And gie the wench any more power over me than she already has?" he demanded. "Ye say she loves me, yet she hae nae said it."

"Nor will she until you do, and don't ask me why. I cannot explain it, but it seems to be the way of women. They refuse to admit the truth of their hearts until their men do. My Bess, God rest her, kept her own counsel until I fell helpless at her feet. Only then would she confess to her love for me." He shrugged. "Even today there are many things I do not understand about women. How Mama would laugh if she heard me saying it," he finished with a chuckle.

"Perhaps, when we get home," Patrick responded, "I will try and wheedle her wi' my admission. For now my problem is where I will sleep this night. Flanna hae barred the bedroom door on me, and I will nae beg admittance in a public place."

"There is a small chamber off the dayroom with a pallet in it. 'Tis where I have been sleeping. I'll beg a place at the king's residence. My Stuart charm has stood me in good stead with the kirk."

"Was the penance hard?" the Duke of Glenkirk asked.

" 'Twas nae so difficult as long as I remembered that my goal was to be able to remain near my cousin to be of comfort to him. The kirk was most impressed with my sincerity," he finished, grinning.

"Will I see ye on the morrow?" Patrick said.

"I'll come before you depart," the Duke of Lundy promised, rising and stretching his long limbs. "Good night, Patrick," he said, and then he left the taproom.

The Duke of Glenkirk took himself down the narrow hallway to the apartment where his wife slept. Entering it, he walked across the room and tried the door hopefully. It was still barred to him. Oh, she had a fine temper, his disobedient Flanna, he considered, almost laughing now. What a wench she was. Had her brother not come to Glenkirk, she very well might have gotten away with her little adventure, and he none the wiser. But there could not be any secrets between them from now on, he decided. Picking up his cloak, he went into the tiny chamber and, taking the pallet, brought it out to place in front of the fireplace. The fire still burned, and he added more fuel to it. Then, lying down, he pulled his fur-lined cloak over himself and slept.

The sound of the bedchamber door opening awakened him. Flanna stepped out of the room and was surprised to find her husband there.

"Good morrow, wife," Patrick said, arising from the pallet.

"When are we leaving?" she asked him, eyeing him a trifle nervously.

"After a good breakfast, and when we hae bid our farewells to Charlie," he replied. "Will that suit ye?"

"Aye," she said. "Do the men know ye're here?"

"They do, and they'll be ready, including yer two dupes." He chuckled. He had decided to treat the entire matter lightly to win back her favor. "Once we've returned to Glenkirk that nephew of yers will take his lessons wi' Freddie and Sabrina. As for young Ian More, he is verra chastened and will no more be cajoled by his naughty duchess."

"I'll nae hae him punished for obeying my orders," she said. "What else was he to do, Patrick? I am his mistress, and he is loyal to Glenkirk. He dinna realize what I was about."

"I know," the duke replied quietly. "That is why, now that I hae spoken wi' him, he will nae obey any but me or his superior officer ever again, Flanna. I am pleased, however, to see ye accept blame for this misadventure. I doubt yer father will be pleased."

"Aye, Aulay would hae hurried back to tell him," Flanna said. "The old man would beat me for it if he could."

"I should beat ye for it," Patrick said softly.

She looked startled. "Ye wouldna!" she cried.

"Nae this time, lassie, though I should," he responded. "But I find I am developing a tenderness toward ye."

Again she looked startled, and she actually blushed. *"Oh!"* was all she said. Then, "I had best get dressed." She disappeared back into the bedchamber, closing the door behind her. She did not lock the door this time.

God's boots, he swore silently to himself. Was Charlie correct? Was it possible that she was as in love with him as he was with her? If he admitted to it, would she? Patrick Leslie was suddenly forced to face the fact that while he knew how to *make* love to a woman, he knew absolutely nothing about being in love with a woman. It was obviously not a learned skill. He smiled to himself. They would learn it together, he decided. He went to the bedchamber door and knocked before opening it.

"Hae ye water I can wash myself wi'?" he asked her.

"Come in," she said. "I hae already used it, but I was nae really dirty." She pointed to the basin on the nearby table. Then she continued dressing herself.

He had several days' growth of beard on him, but until they returned to Glenkirk, he would be unable to shave. He washed his face and his hands thoroughly. "I must look rough," he said.

"Aye," she agreed. "I dinna like it."

"Nor I," he agreed.

"Good morning, my lady," they heard Annie call. "I've brought ye yer breakfast. Oh!" Her eyes widened at the sight of the duke.

"This is my husband, the Duke of Glenkirk, Annie," Flanna said. "He has come to escort me home. Ye had best go back to the kitchens and bring us more food. The duke likes a good breakfast, lass."

Annie set her tray down upon the table and curtsied. "I'll go at once, m'lady," she said, and ran from the room.

Patrick Leslie chuckled. "She'll probably tell the cook that there is a wild Highlander hungry for his food wi' her ladyship," he said.

"Ye look like a wild Highlander," Flanna observed. "Ye look like my brothers, and as I told ye, I dinna like it. I prefer ye smooth-faced. Ye're a handsome man, but nae one could tell it this morning."

"So ye think I'm handsome, wife?" His green-gold eyes scanned her face for some sign of softening, and to his amazement he saw it.

"Aye, ye're handsome, and dinna tell me ye hae never been told it before," Flanna said sharply.

Patrick Leslie reached out to pull his wife close. "Aye, I hae been told it, but I hae never been told it by my beautiful wife." His lips brushed her forehead.

"Well, now ye hae," she said softly. "Are ye still vexed wi' me, Patrick?" she asked him.

"Aye, I am," he told her, but his look was not that of an angry man. "Ye're a bad lass, Flanna Leslie, but I am of a mind to forgie ye if ye promise to never keep secrets from me again."

Her heart was suddenly beating very quickly. He had never before looked at her in quite that way. Was it possible that he cared for her? Could he love her for more than Brae? "I will try to be good, my lord," she said softly.

"Charlie told me how ye felt when ye looked on the portraits of the other Leslie women," Patrick told her. "I will call a painter from Aberdeen to come and paint yer portrait, and do ye know what our descendants will say about ye? They will say, '*And this is Flanna Leslie, the second duchess.* She was the most beautiful of all the Leslie women, and her husband loved her and prized her above all others.' That is what they will say, Flanna."

"*They will say her husband loved her?*" Flanna's eyes were wide with her surprise at his words.

"Aye," he said, wondering how big a fool he had made of himself.

"Oh, Patrick!" she sighed, melting into his embrace, a look upon her face such as he had never seen. She absolutely glowed. "And is it true?"

"Aye," he said, seeing her sudden happiness, realizing that his brother had been correct. "I love ye, lass."

"And I love ye!" she cried, putting her arms about his neck and kissing him. "Oh, how I love ye!"

He grinned, overwhelmed with his own burgeoning happiness. "Ye're the damnest woman, Flanna Leslie!" he told her.

"Aye," she agreed, nodding, "I am," and they laughed together.

Part Three

Flaming Flanna

Chapter

11

The flat surface of his tongue blazed a hot trail down her creamy torso. Outside of Glenkirk Castle, the wind howled mournfully as a mixture of rain, icy pellets, and even some snow beat against the windows; but the fire in the bedchamber hearth burned high, warming the room and illuminating the couple entwined upon the large bed.

The Duchess of Glenkirk sighed with contentment as her husband tasted each and every inch of her skin. He licked across the sole of her foot, pushing suggestively between each toe. He drew his tongue over the curve of her calf. Then he kissed her kneecap. Her breasts were tingling with his earlier attentions, the nipples puckered and hard. He mouthed the soft flesh of her belly, nuzzling, savoring the silkiness of her. Flanna drew a sharp breath when he began to burrow his face against her furred mons.

"*Do it!*" she husked at him, even though she knew that she couldn't stop him. *Did not want to stop him.*

He lifted his dark head up, and his green-gold eyes were glittering dangerously. "We will do it together," he told her.

"*Together?*" She was confused.

His big hand cupped her mons, and squeezed hard, causing her to shudder. "Ye like it when I touch ye there wi' my mouth. Ye like it when my tongue teases ye. Ye like it when I suck upon yer naughty little love bud, Flanna. But I need to be teased and played wi' too." He suddenly shifted his body around in such a manner that his head lay between her thighs, but his manhood pressed against her mouth.

As startled as she was, Flanna was no coward when it came to passion. "What do ye want me to do?" she asked him.

"Use yer tongue, but nae yer teeth, lass. Take as much of me between yer sweet lips as ye can and suckle. We'll see how ye get on, and afterward, if ye like, we'll add a few more refinements." He opened her nether lips to his view and began to lick at her.

Shivering with her own instant pleasure, Flanna hesitantly parted her lips, her tongue slipping out to lick at his manhood, timidly at first, then with increasing enthusiasm. Boldly now she took him into her mouth and drew hard upon the rod of flesh that began to swell and to grow even harder, caught in her sensual embrace. She reached out to hold him, her hand cupping his twin jewels as she worked her lips over and her tongue about his length. Her excitement was burgeoning with the knowledge that she had a power over him, even as he had power over her. There was something so deliciously wicked about his mouth upon her most secret parts while she suckled upon his. His tongue probed her intimately, sending shudders of enjoyment throughout her entire body. She sucked him harder and harder until he cried out to her to cease her torture. She released her hold on him, but not before licking a small pearl of liquid seeping from his manhood's Cyclops eye. It was salty.

He turned himself quickly about, and pinioning her beneath him, he thrust hard and deep into her, groaning with his delight as he did so. She was warm and wet, enclosing him tightly in her hot sheath. Her silvery eyes were closed as she slid into the endless ocean of her pleasure. He filled her full with his throbbing length. His rhythm sent her tumbling into an abyss of delight. She dug her fingers into his muscled shoulders, then raked them fiercely down his long back.

"*Bitch!*" he growled, his mouth taking hers in a fierce kiss.

Flanna soared. She was nothing now. *Nothing but sensation.* She screamed with her pleasure, but the noise was all in her head. The only sounds in the bedchamber were her fevered moaning and his howl of utter satisfaction as together they reached nirvana. Then all was pillowy darkness and deep silence. When she finally came to herself, she was cradled in his arms, the steady beat of his heart beneath her ear. *"Wonderful,"* was all she could say.

He chuckled. "Aye, lass, wonderful it was," he agreed.

"Patrick, we hae to get some rest," she said, smiling at him. "It has been like this every night since we came home from Perth. I can hardly rise to oversee my duties in the morning or direct the bairns' day," Flanna told him. "We hae responsibilities, my darling."

"The first of which is to get an heir or two," he chuckled.

"The bairns will come in time," she assured him. And the truth was that she was very possibly with child now, but until she could be absolutely certain, Flanna reasoned to herself, she would say naught. She certainly knew enough about the subject from growing up in her father's house. One or another of her sisters-in-law was always with child. There was yet time, for she had not yet begun to show. Besides, despite the weather outside of Glenkirk this night, spring was coming. It was already March. Soon the days would be fair enough for her to begin her travels to recruit men for King Charles.

She intended to go to her own family first, for as she had told both Charlie and Patrick, there were more than enough Brodies to spare. And then she would visit the Gordons. They had once been allied through marriage with the Leslies of Glenkirk and were her own distant kinsmen. But if she told Patrick she was with child, it would spoil all her plans. He would do everything in his power to keep her at Glenkirk. Flanna knew she couldn't allow him to do that. She had given the king her word. She knew her husband had still not come to terms with his wife's open support of King Charles. He did not have to as long as he did not hinder her, she decided.

She was happier, however, than she had ever been in all her life. To love this man—to know that he loved her—had opened a world to Flanna that she had never imagined existed. Now, at last, she finally understood her mother's relationship to her father. *A love match,* people had described the marriage of the beautiful Meg Gordon and the much older Lachlann Brodie. It had been said scornfully by some and wonderingly by others who never saw what her mother saw in the laird of Killiecairn. But Flanna now knew exactly what it meant. She would make certain her children understood so that one day they would marry for love alone.

It was a matter of honor for her to keep her word to the king, but she knew now what mattered the most to her was having a family of her very own. The more she learned of Glenkirk's history, and of the Leslies themselves, the more she understood that hers was a great responsibility. To be the mother of the next duke, and of other sons and daughters, was her destiny. Why else had Patrick Leslie appeared so unexpectedly at Brae that autumn afternoon when they met? It had been fate, indeed. And, she would make certain that her second son was given the title that had belonged to her mother's family. He would be the Earl of Brae.

When the king was restored to his throne, that would be the reward she would ask of him for her service to the crown. She would name the boy Angus Gordon Leslie. The first earl had been Angus, as was her uncle, Brae's last direct male descendant. She would not be known as the do-naught duchess after all. She would be Flanna, second Duchess of Glenkirk, who had helped to return a rightful king to his throne; *and,* who had brought a third earldom to the descendants of the first Earl of Glenkirk. As that earl's daughter, the fabled Janet, had won the earldom of Sithean for her direct family, so Flanna Leslie would win Brae for hers.

The goal clear in her head now, Flanna began to plan her escape from Glenkirk once the weather turned from cold and wet, so she might ride out without catching an ague. And again fate seemed to be lending her a hand. Her eldest brother, Aulay, appeared at Glenkirk one late March morning. Brought into the hall where the family was assembled, he hurried to his brother-in-law, bowing low.

"My sire is dying," he announced.

Flanna gave a small cry, her hand flying to her mouth to still the noise of it.

"He wants to see his lass. I'll take Fingal, too," Aulay said.

"Of course," Patrick Leslie immediately answered him. "Send to me when she is to return, and I'll come to escort her back home. Yer lad is welcome back, too. He and my nephew hae become great friends. He's an intelligent laddie, and we already hae plans for him."

"My wife will be pleased to know that, my lord," Aulay said, a small smile touching his stern features. "He's our youngest, and she has always doted on him."

"Ye'll gie her my felicitations, Aulay Brodie."

"I thank yer lordship," was the respectful answer.

"Come, and eat wi' me while my wife goes to fetch what she will need for her journey," the duke invited his brother-in-law.

Flanna stood up and ran from the hall. Her da was dying! She had thought the old man would live forever. He would be buried between his two wives, she knew, for it had been decided upon long ago. Aggie was already packing when she reached her apartment.

"Fingal," she said in answer to her mistress's unspoken query.

"Ye're to remain here wi' the bairns," Flanna told her. "Biddy will need yer help."

Aggie nodded. "Suits me. If I never see Killiecairn again, 'twill be too soon. I hae no love for the place, or for the Brodies."

"Ye're a Brodie," Flanna said softly. "And Lachlann is yer grandsire, too, Aggie."

"Nay, the old man never even looked at me. I was but one of his lad's *get* upon a servant lass who died birthing me. If it werena for yer mam, of blessed memory, I would nae be alive today to serve ye, my lady. It was she who found a wet nurse to feed me, and until she died, I was almost safe from my sire's wife, who was always beating me, and for nae reason but that I was her man's wood's colt. The wicked bitch! Nay, I hae nae love for the Brodies, or for Killiecairn. I hae found more kindness here at Glenkirk in yer service. I'm glad to remain behind. Now, I'll tell ye a secret. Aulay Brodie is his da's heir, but the old man has a small velvet bag that was yer mam's. 'Tis hidden in the bedchamber he shared wi' her. There is a loose stone in the floor of the hearth there. I thought he would gie it to ye when ye were wed, but he dinna. There's jewels in that bag, and they were yer mam's that she brought wi' her from Brae. I dinna know if the old devil forgot or means for it to remain wi' the Brodies, but 'tis nae their property. Yer mam always meant for ye to hae it. 'Twas she who told me about it as she lay dying. She would nae tell Una for fear she would covet that bag. Say naught to any, but when he is dead, take yer mam's property back. Angus can tell ye I speak the truth."

"I dinna hae to ask him," Flanna said. "When did ye nae speak the truth to me, Aggie?" She picked up her hairbrush and handed it to her maidservant. "So the old man kept me mam's jewelry," she mused. "Wicked devil! He damned well remembered he had it. When did Lachlann Brodie ever misplace a groat?" She laughed almost bitterly. "But I'll wait to see if on his deathbed he *remembers*."

In the hall her husband sat with her brother. The servants had brought meat, cheese, bread, and ale to the table. Angus sent word to the kitchens to send up a tray to the duchess. He could trust that Aggie would see Flanna ate before she departed. He found he was relieved to hear the duke speaking with Aulay Brodie about Flanna's desire to recruit men for Charles II.

"She is fascinated by my brother's cousin," Patrick told his brother-in-law. "And the king does hae charm. All the damned Stuarts do, but they are a dangerous lot nonetheless. The king will want this army he seeks to recruit to help him back into England. There will be many lives lost before he regains his throne there. Why should they be *our* clansmen, Aulay Brodie?"

The older man nodded. "Aye," he agreed with the duke. "We dinna know this king. They ask men like us to fight their wars, but when those wars are over, we are forgotten," Aulay remarked sagely.

Angus brought a tray holding two packed clay pipes. He offered them to the duke and to Aulay Brodie. Each man took one, and another servant lighted the pipes with a small brand from the fireplace. The blue smoke wreathed about their heads as they drew upon the pipes.

"Ahhh," Aulay Brodie said, a rare smile lighting his face. "'Tis a good pipe, my lord. I hae never tasted such fine tobacco."

"My sister, Fortune, lives in the New World. Each spring she sends us tobacco from her plantation in Mary's Land. Actually, she sent it for our father, but now I hope she will send it to me. She will hae already received word of his death last September, but perhaps she will continue to remember her brother here at Glenkirk. If she doesna, then I will remind her," he chuckled. "I hae grown used to her fine leaf."

"I'm certain that I could, too," Aulay Brodie concurred as he smoked the clay pipe, inhaling the sweet smoke.

Flanna hurried into the hall in her riding clothes and cape. She was obviously ready to leave and looked impatiently at her brother contentedly smoking his pipe.

"Hae ye eaten?" Angus demanded of her.

"I hae nae time," she replied.

"Sit down," he said firmly, and then he began filling a plate for her. "Lachlann Brodie can wait another few moments while his son finishes his pipe and his daughter fills her belly. Ye need yer food, especially now," he told her meaningfully.

"What's *that* supposed to mean?" Flanna said low.

"Am I a fool, then, niece?" he replied.

"I am nae certain," she said softly.

"*I am,*" he responded, "and if ye are nae, Flanna Leslie, it is because ye plan some mischief yet and dinna wish to acknowledge yer condition. Tell yer husband when ye return, or I shall tell him."

Flanna looked contrite. "When I return I will be certain in my own mind, Angus, and I will, indeed, tell my husband then." *When I return*, she thought, *but I shall not return until I hae recruited men for the king.*

He nodded, satisfied, unaware of her deception. "Eat," he said, setting the plate in front of her.

"Ye'll make certain my Patrick is well served in my absence?" Flanna said. "And be sure that Aggie helps out Biddy wi' the bairns, and that they keep to the schedule I hae set for them." She began to eat, surprised to learn that she was very hungry.

"The only thing that will be missing from Glenkirk will be its fair mistress," Angus said quietly. "Dinna remain after the old man is buried. He will nae need ye to mourn for him. His sons and their women should do it, though I wonder if they will. Tell Aulay to establish his authority firmly even before the old man dies, and hae his father confirm it to the others else all hell break loose after Lachlann

Brodie has gone to meet his maker. His sons will quarrel amongst themselves nonetheless; but if Aulay keeps a tight rein on them, all will be well at Killiecairn, and naught will change but the voice of authority," Angus Gordon finished.

"I'll speak wi' him as we ride, but ye know as well as I know that my sister-in-law, Una, will nae let any of my other brothers usurp her man's dominion over Killiecairn. She has waited years for Aulay to come into his own," Flanna observed wisely.

Angus smiled grimly. "Aye, lassie, and that be a truth!"

Aulay Brodie had finished his pipe, and now he laid it down, standing up as he did so. "Are ye ready, sister?" he asked her.

"Aye," Flanna replied, shoving a final piece of cheese into her pocket to eat along the way. She arose and, turning to her husband, said, "I thank ye, my lord, for allowing me to go to my father now. I will return after he is buried, but nae before, wi' yer permission."

"Ye hae it," Patrick said, and then he tipped her face up to his. "I wish yer da nae a minute less than God has given him, Flanna, but I hope ye will be back wi' me soon. I'll come for ye myself." Then he kissed her lips softly. "I already miss ye." His warm look caused her to blush, and he laughed softly as he released her. "Think of me each night," he told her wickedly.

"Oh, I will, my lord, and ye, I am certain, will think of me . . ." and then she added, *"and my black pearls."*

"Vixen," he chuckled, and turned her about, smacking her bottom lightly. "Go," Patrick Leslie told his wife.

Her lilting laughter seemed to echo in the hall even after she had departed it. Patrick Leslie climbed to the north tower of Glenkirk to watch her ride off with her elder brother and Fingal Brodie.

She could feel his eyes on them as they rode out, but she did not look back to wave a final farewell. It was too difficult, she suddenly realized, and she was torn. Her love for her father had never been great, for Lachlann Brodie's passion had been only for her mother. The little attention he had given the daughter they had made had been offered in her mother's lifetime to please his Meg. Once her mother had gone, Lachlann Brodie hardly remembered he had a daughter. Flanna had been practically lost in the crowd of her clan-folk, but for Una and her uncle, Angus Gordon.

That she now rode from Glenkirk, and the man she had come to love with all of her being, was but a filial duty to the dying laird. She was Lachlann Brodie's only daughter. It was her obligation if not for his sake, but for the love she had borne her mother, to return to Killiecairn and be by his side in his final hours. She didn't want to leave Patrick now. But she had to as a dutiful daughter to her father.

At least the weather held, she considered, as they rode along. Fingal couldn't seem to stop talking as he told his father of life at Glenkirk, of how different it was from Killiecairn, of the lessons he was learning along with Lady Sabrina and young Lord Frederick. "Brie is as braw as any lad," he told his father. "Flanna taught her to shoot wi' the longbow. She is nae as good as Flanna, but she can hit the target, Da, and is getting better."

Aulay nodded. "Ye're a fortunate lad," he told his son. "Dinna lose the opportunity ye hae been given." He turned to his sister. "The duke is pleased wi' him?"

"Patrick is kind to him, but Fingal is nae his responsibility, brother. He is mine as my kinsman. As long as Patrick is nae displeased wi' him, and he continues to behave himself, he will do well at Glenkirk. My husband has said if he learns more than his tutor can teach him, then Fingal can go to university at Aberdeen."

"Who teaches the bairns?" Aulay asked.

"The old Anglican priest. The Leslies will nae send him off, and while we follow Scotland's church now, the priest is an educated man. He obeys the law also, so there is none to complain of his presence."

Her brother grunted his satisfaction, and they rode on toward Killiecairn. She wanted to speak to Aulay as Angus had advised, but it was obvious to her that now was not the time. As they moved around Loch Brae, the sun came from behind the clouds to shine on the castle there. A smile touched Flanna's lips. She would begin Brae's restoration when she returned home. She intended using it to marshal her levy for the king. That way Glenkirk and the Leslies need not be involved at all. Her smile broadened. Everything was going exactly as she wanted it to go. Everything was perfect.

They reached Killiecairn late in the afternoon. Flanna gazed on her childhood home dispassionately. It looked strange to her now, and so very small. Smoke rose from the gray stone chimneys, but it was oddly quiet as the clan kept their deathwatch for Lachlann Brodie. Aulay's wife, Una, was awaiting them as they came into the hall. Had she always looked so worn? Flanna asked herself.

"He's still alive," she told them, "and he's waiting for ye," she said to Flanna. Then her brown eyes went to her son, and she smiled.

"I'll go right up," Flanna said, and hurried from the hall.

Entering her father's bedchamber, she saw her sister-in-law Ailis sitting by his bed. "Good day, Ailis," she said.

"So ye're finally home," came the sour reply.

"As quickly as Aulay could bring me," Flanna said.

"Lassie!" her father's voice croaked from the bed.

"I'm here, Da," Flanna told him, coming to his side.

"Get out!" he said fiercely to Ailis, who looked outraged, and as if she was going to break into one of her tirades.

"I think he would speak wi' me alone, Ailis," Flanna quickly said. "I know ye dinna mind and could probably use some rest yerself. I can only imagine how ye hae all looked after him. He's nae easy, is he?" She gave her sister-in-law a friendly little smile and put a hand upon Ailis's arm and squeezed.

To her surprise, Ailis smiled back. "Nay," she agreed. "He isna easy, and I could use some food."

"I'll stay wi' him until someone returns," Flanna promised.

"Thank ye," Ailis replied, rising from her place and exiting the bedchamber.

"Ye've softened," her father said.

"Nay, but I hae learned how to manage others, especially those below my station," Flanna told him bluntly. "Are ye really dying, Da, or was it just an excuse to make them all jump to yer satisfaction?"

The old man cackled, but then he grew serious. "I'm dying," he responded in answer to her question. "I would nae hae sent Aulay to ye otherwise. We hae some unfinished business, ye and I."

"Is it the matter of Meg Gordon's property?" she asked him candidly.

He nodded. "I couldna face yer mam if I did nae gie ye her wee bag. As much as I would like to believe it now Brodie property, I know 'tis nae. 'Tis yers, Flanna."

"Is it still beneath the stone in the hearth?" she inquired.

"Who told ye? Angus, of course," he said, answering his own question.

Flanna shook her head. "Aggie told me. Mam spoke to her before she died so I would know one day."

"Did Aggie come wi' ye?" he wondered.

"Nay."

"She is my granddaughter," he remarked pensively.

"Aye, she is, but she said ye never cared so why should she?" Flanna said frankly.

He nodded his white head. "She's right," he agreed, "but 'tis more a Brodie attitude than she would want, I'm thinking." He cackled again, but then he began to cough.

Flanna set her arm about the old man, raising him up, and with her other hand put a small pewter cup to his lips. "Drink it," she ordered him, and he did, gulping the liquid eagerly. She smelled the scent of whiskey on his breath as the cough subsided.

"Get the bag," he ordered her as he fell back against his pillows. "And secret it lass, so *they* dinna see it."

Flanna went over to the hearth where a fire now burned and, with her father's direction, found the loose stone on the edge of the flame. Carefully she pried it up and, reaching into the cavity, pulled the velvet bag out before replacing the stone. Opening the bag, she looked inside and saw a jumble of jewelry. She pulled the strings of the soft pouch shut and stuffed it into the pocket of her breeches.

"My conscience is clear now," Lachlann Brodie said quietly.

"Dinna tell me that's all that ye hae on yer conscience, Da," Flanna teased him wickedly.

He cackled again, and his eyes danced for a moment.

"Ye hae to confirm Aulay in yer place," she told him.

"He's the eldest," her father replied.

" 'Tis nae enough," Flanna said. "If ye dinna bring them all in here, sons, and wives, and grandchildren, and tell them outright that Aulay is now the Brodie of Killiecairn, they will quarrel amongst themselves, even though they know better. Dinna gie Aulay that burden to carry, Da. He has been a good son to ye, and Una has run yer household ever since my mam died. Make certain Aulay is recognized by the others. Make them gie ye their words to accept him. He's a fair and decent man and will bring nae shame upon yer name."

"I never thought I would see the day when ye would speak up for Aulay," her father noted.

"I hae learned at Glenkirk the importance of rightful authority," Flanna admitted to him.

"Tell them to come in, then, lassie," Lachlann Brodie said.

"*Now?*" She was surprised.

"Aye, now, for I will nae last the night, Flanna. I waited for ye, lassie, for when I meet yer mam again, I wanted to be able to tell her that ye're happy. Are ye?"

"Aye," she told him. "I am verra happy, Da."

"But ye hae nae given Leslie a bairn yet," he fretted.

"By late summer," she told him. "Ye're the first to know, and dinna tell the others, or my husband will come roaring across the hills from Glenkirk, and I'll be wrapped up in cotton wool. I am a strong lass and will gie Patrick Leslie strong bairns, but I dinna want to be shut away."

"Then, I'll go to my grave wi' this wonderful secret, but I'll tell yer mam, lassie. She'll be happy for ye," Lachlann Brodie said. "Now go, and tell them all I want to see them now."

What on earth had made her tell her father the secret that until now she hadn't even admitted to herself? Flanna wondered. Then she went out and down into the hall to announce, "He wants to see us all. Sons, and wives, and grandchildren. Ye'll nae all be able to get into his chamber, so sons and wives first," she told them, and she led the way herself, returning back up the narrow staircase.

They grouped themselves about his oaken bedstead. The linen and velvet bed hangings were grubby and worn, Flanna suddenly noted. Her brothers also seemed worn with their hard life. They were not young men. Aulay, the eldest at fifty-nine, bordered on old age himself. He was followed by Callum, who was fifty-eight; Gillies, fifty-six; Ranald, fifty-four; Simon, fifty-two; and Bhaltair, who was fifty. Together her six brothers had fathered thirty-seven children, who were now giving the family another generation. As only seven of her brothers' children were girls, and long wed, there were over one hundred people living at Killiecairn. Her nieces were gone to their husbands' families. Coming from such a large family of males, the girls had been prized as wives, and their modest dowries overlooked. They had all married well and already proved their worth to their husbands' families by birthing sons.

Lachlann Brodie opened his eyes and gazed at his assembled progeny with a fierce look. "I'll die tonight," he began.

They were all silent, knowing better than to interrupt him until he had finished speaking. He might be dying; but the wicked thorn cane he had carried in his later years lay by his side, and the old man was perfectly capable of lashing out at them with it. They waited respectfully to hear his next words. Outside the narrow windows of the bedchamber, they could hear the wind beginning to rise and the first patter of raindrops against the glass. The fire in the hearth crackled as a gust of air rushed down the chimney and caused the candle by the old man's bedside to flicker ominously.

"Hear my words, and obey my last request. Aulay, my first born, is now the Brodie of Killiecairn. In all the history of our family, the firstborn has followed the firstborn. So I follow our family's traditions, as will ye all, or my curse will reach ye from beyond the grave into which ye will lay my mortal remains. Now, what hae each of ye to say to me?"

Flanna quickly spoke up. "I recognize my eldest brother, Aulay, as the new Brodie of Killiecairn, and so will my husband, the Duke of Glenkirk, and all his clan. I hae his permission to speak for him in this matter. The Leslies of Glenkirk accept the last will and testament of Lachlann Brodie. So be it done according to his wishes."

Reaching out, Flanna lifted up her father's withered hand and kissed it before laying it gently back upon his coverlet. Then she turned and gave her eldest sibling the kiss of peace on both his cheeks.

Lachlann Brodie struggled to pull the ring of his authority from his finger. When he had succeeded, he grasped Aulay's hand and pushed it onto his eldest son's finger. It was a heavy gold band set with a deep green agate. Upon the round stone was a small gold hand clutching a sheaf of arrows, and beneath it, a single word. *United.*

Aulay Brodie stared at his hand. He had never remembered a time when the ring now adorning his finger had not been on his father's finger. He had always expected to succeed Lachlann Brodie, but to be suddenly faced with the reality of it all was somewhat overwhelming, even for a man his age. His father had seemed so strong to them all. They had expected him to go on forever. Now he understood his brother-in-law of Glenkirk better. Accepting the responsibility for a clan was no easy or simple thing.

Lachlann Brodie cackled sharply, startling them all. "Now, ye see it, do ye nae, Aulay?" he said to his eldest son.

"Aye, Da, I do," Aulay responded slowly. "I already feel the weight of it."

"And it will nae leave ye till the day yer eldest son wears the ring," Lachlann Brodie responded grimly. His look again glared about the chamber. "Yer sister has accepted my will and properly recognized her brother as the new Brodie of Killiecairn. What of the rest of ye? If ye dinna swear to support Aulay, then ye may take what little belongings ye hae that are nae mine and go from Killiecairn."

"Go where, Da?" his next eldest son, Callum, said.

"To the devil for all I care!" the old man snapped. "I'll nae hae the occasion of my death an excuse for my sons to quarrel wi' one another over a matter that is my right to settle, and which I hae already determined." He fell back against his pillows, and began to cough once more as he had earlier.

Flanna brought the cup of whiskey to his lips again, and the rack-ing cough was eased and died away. She glared at her brothers. Her look was very plain, and she was suddenly almost a stranger to them. They remembered a stubborn girl so much younger than they that she had seemed more one of their bairns and not their sibling. This, however, was a woman of wealth, power, and obvious authority. The five younger sons of Lachlann Brodie shuffled their feet almost in unison.

"*Well?*" Flanna demanded of them. "Is our sire to go to his grave discontent? 'Tis my recollection that a discontent spirit haunts those who caused his going to be an unhappy experience." She glowered at them, and the look was so like Lachlann Brodie's that they shivered as it touched them.

Callum Brodie quickly took up his eldest brother's hand to kiss his ring of clan authority. "I, Callum Brodie, secondborn son of Lachlann Brodie, laird of Killiecairn, accept his dying will and take for my new laird, my brother, Aulay, firstborn son of our sire," he declared. Callum was followed by his four younger siblings, who each swore the oath of loyalty to their eldest brother. And as they finished, they turned and departed the bedchamber, even as their wives, and their children, and grandchildren came forth to give their oath to the new Brodie of Killiecairn and to bid farewell to the old patriarch of their clan. Finally it was finished. Only Aulay and Flanna remained in the room with Lachlann Brodie.

The new laird turned to his sister. "Thank ye," he said.

"For what?" she asked him. "I only did what needed to be done so our sire might die at peace, brother."

"Ye put the might of Glenkirk behind me, Flanna," he said, a small smile causing the corners of his mouth to twitch. "Did ye really hae yer man's permission to speak for him?"

"I would hae had I thought to ask before we left this morning," she said, smiling. "By saying I did, I saved ye a good deal of difficulty, Aulay, and Da can pass into the next world content that Killiecairn will continue as he wished it. Our brother, Callum, has always coveted yer place. Ye're but ten months apart in age. For whatever reason, Callum has always felt cheated, and he has never cared who knew it. Now, if ye're to keep the peace here, ye must win him to yer side lest he cause trouble. The others can be led, but Callum is difficult. Watch him, and watch his sons, carefully."

"Ye've grown suddenly wise, little sister," he told her. And the truth of it was that she had surprised him with her shrewd analysis. Her swift words had turned the tide and made a hard situation easier.

"I'm learning to be a Duchess of Glenkirk, Aulay. The women who hae come before me were nae sit-by-the-fire mates to their husbands. I must make my mark so that I stand equal to them, so that a hundred years from now when my descendants see my portrait in the gallery at Glenkirk, I am remembered well, and the family of my birth is honored, too."

"And just how will ye do that?" he asked her.

"This is nae the time," she told him, and it was said with such authority that he did not question her further. "Stay wi' Da for a bit while I seek some food, for I hae nae eaten since this morning. When I am refreshed, I will sit the night wi' him. 'Tis my duty, for he saw me into this world. So I will see him out of it," Flanna told her brother.

"Go on, then," he said, and she left the room.

Lachlann Brodie opened his eyes. "She is like her mam," he said quietly. "She has the Gordon breeding."

"And the Brodie strength," Aulay replied.

"The Gordons of Brae are strong stock as well," Lachlann said. "Ye owe her now, ye know. She did ye a great service this day."

"Aye, I know," Aulay said. "I would hae never thought to be in my wee sister's debt one day, but it would seem I am, Da."

The old man cackled. "She be a clever lass. Glenkirk will hae met his match in our Flanna. Does he care for her?"

Aulay snorted with laughter. "He be a fool over her, Da. He's mad wi' love for her, and she for him. There'll be bairns soon enough from those two, or I miss my guess."

"Good. Good," Lachlann Brodie said, hugging his secret to himself and closing his eyes. "I'll rest a bit now," he said.

Flanna had gone down into the hall where the Brodies were now assembled eating. She walked directly up to the high board where her brothers and their wives sat. Una Brodie immediately arose and snapped at the others, "Make a place for yer sister, the Duchess of Glenkirk, ye ill-bred knaves!"

Flanna sat down next to her foster mother. Her brother Callum was on her right.

"Ye've become verra grand, Flanna Brodie," he said sourly.

"*Flanna Leslie,*" she corrected him quietly. "Did ye expect me to remain a hoyden forever, brother? If ye could but see the portraits in the gallery at Glenkirk of my predecessors, perhaps ye would understand better. I would make my husband proud."

"And will he be haeing a portrait done of ye?" her sister-in-law Ailis sneered. " 'Twill nae be easy painting yer flaming pate." And then she giggled nastily.

"If I had scant hair the color of mouse dung, Ailis, I'd be jealous, too," Flanna answered sweetly. "The first Earl of Glenkirk had a daughter wi' hair the same color as mine. Her portrait hangs in the Great Hall of *my* castle. They say I am even more beautiful than she was, but I try nae to listen to such flattery." She picked up the small joint that Una slapped upon her plate and began to tear the meat from it with her small white teeth.

Ailis began to sputter with her anger, but her husband snarled at her, "Shut yer mouth, woman!" Ailis grew silent, but her hazel eyes shot daggers at Flanna, who seemed not to notice at all.

Una chuckled softly, not displeased at all to see Ailis put down so firmly. Callum's wife, like her jealous husband, was a troublesome woman. Her brother-in-law may have promised to support his eldest brother as the new laird, but Una knew he was not content with the situation. Still, Callum had no real choice in the matter when it came right down to it. Unless he was bold enough to attempt to divide loyalties among the Brodie clansmen.

"Killiecairn is too small now for all of ye," Flanna said softly. "Until I left here I dinna realize it. Some will hae to go, Una, before ye kill each other." She tore off a chunk of bread from the loaf and buttered it with her thumb.

"The Brodies seem to breed well, and quickly. There are two new bairns since I left, and at least three new bellies."

Una nodded. "Something must be done," she agreed, "but we'll manage somehow as we always hae. Aulay said ye ran off to Perth."

"I saw the king, Una! I met him, and I even spoke wi' him. I saw him crowned. Patrick came after me. He is verra jealous, and he doesna like the Stuarts, but for his brother, Charlie. Patrick says they bring bad fortune to the Leslies of Glenkirk."

"And ye disagree," Una observed wisely with a knowing smile.

" 'Tis some silliness put into Patrick's head by his mother, Duchess Jasmine, before she departed Glenkirk."

"Her husband died at Dunbar, and nae one could ever say that Jemmie Leslie was a political man," Una noted. "If I were she, I would be bitter, too."

"I'm going to raise a levy for the king," Flanna confided to her sister-in-law. "He needs an army to take back what Cromwell and his ilk stole from him."

"Lassie, lassie," her sister-in-law said, "are ye mad? Hae we nae had enough of wars in Scotland? Are nae the English in our dear Edinburgh and likely to remain there? Scotland has crowned this Stuart. Let it be enough for him! Let him get married and breed up a new generation of princes for us, instead of seeking to destroy our sons in some new and futile war."

"Ye dinna understand," Flanna said. "If ye had met Charles Stuart and looked into his eyes, ye would see!"

"Ye're daft, Flanna Leslie," Una said. "When we hae buried old Lachlann, ye're to go home to Glenkirk and wait for yer bairn to be born, and dinna tell me it isna so. I know a breeding lass when I see one, and ye're breeding."

"Dinna say it aloud," Flanna pleaded. "I hae nae yet told my husband, although Angus saw it. And Da knows; I thought it would please him."

"And I'm certain it did," Una responded with a smile. "Now he can pass content that all is right wi' his wee world."

Chapter

12

Lachlann Brodie died just after four o'clock in the morning. It was the twenty-fifth of March in the year sixteen hundred and fifty-one. Flanna was sitting by his side, half dozing, when his hand on hers brought her to her senses. His old eyes looked lovingly on her as she could never remember them having done in her entire life. His fingers tightened about hers briefly. He gave her a small smile as he whispered, "Ye're a good lass, daughter." Then, the smile remaining upon his lips, he breathed his last.

She pulled her hand from his even as the other hand went to her mouth to stifle the cry. He had loved her, she realized now, although he had never said the words. *Ye're a good lass, daughter,* was the closest he could ever get. His greatest love had been reserved for her mother. Not the woman who had given him six sons nor those who had roused his youthful lust, but Meg Gordon of Brae, who had awakened his heart and quickened the passions of his later life. And she had been the child of that passion. As much as Flanna had missed her mother, she now realized that her father had missed Meg Gordon even more.

"God speed, Da," she told him, and then rising, she straightened the bedclothes about him and went to tell her brother, Aulay, and the others that an era had ended.

By the time the sun began to creep over the mountains, the elder women at Killiecairn had washed the old man's body and sewn him into his shroud. His sons had gone out with torches even before first light and opened up a grave for Lachlann Brodie between his two deceased wives, Giorsal Airlie and Margaret Gordon. In the kitchens the younger women were busy cooking the funeral feast, and Aulay Brodie's eldest son had ridden out to bring a minister to Killiecairn to say the final words over Lachlann Brodie.

As soon as the Presbyterian pastor arrived, the patriarch's body was put in his grave, the words approved by the kirk spoken over him. To the right of the grave the sons of Giorsal Airlie and Lachlann Brodie stood like so many steps in a row, their weathered faces worn, their red, black, and yellow plaids blowing in the raw March wind. To the left of the grave the daughter of Margaret Gordon and Lachlann Brodie stood alone, a shawl of green Leslie plaid wrapped about her shoulders. She found herself oddly saddened by the old man's passing.

He had hardly been a good father to her, yet at the last he had, in his own way, admitted his love for her. It would not make up for all the years of neglect, but it was a good last memory to have. And he had certainly seen that she had made a good marriage, cleverly snapping up an opportunity none of them would have ever imagined would come Flanna Brodie's way. A small smile touched her lips. *"Thank you, Da,"* she whispered so softly that none of them even saw her lips moving.

The grave was filled in by Lachlann Brodie's seven offspring and his many descendants, each taking a turn shoveling the dirt onto his shroud-wrapped body as the weak spring sun gave way to a gray overcast, and an icy rain began to fall. Her brother Simon was the family piper. When the dirt was finally mounded over the grave, he began to play a traditional Highland lament for a fallen chieftain. The shrill, yet mellowed squeal and screech of the music was strangely comforting to them all, and still playing, Simon led them back to the hall to partake of the feast that had been cooked in Lachlann Brodie's honor. Afterward they toasted the old man's memory in the October ale the Brodies were so adept at making each autumn.

They ate, and they drank. The men danced. They shared their stories and their memories as the day slid into night outside the rain-streaked windows of the little hall. Finally when they had finished retelling of their own misdeeds, they spoke of their sister's.

"Willful from the moment she was born," Aulay said.

"How would ye know?" Flanna demanded, "and how could an innocent bairn be governed wi'out reason?"

"I was there, lass," Aulay said. "*I know.*"

"Ye're daft," Flanna mocked him.

"Nay," Una replied, "he isna. Ye were so determined to come into this world, Flanna Leslie, that ye would nae wait to do it properly. Ye leapt forth from yer mam's womb feet first when everyone knows a bairn peeks forth politely wi' its head first, modestly shielding its wee self from prying eyes. But nae ye, lassie! Ye showed us who ye were before we were ready to know. 'Twas a hard birth and why yer mam could never hae any other bairns, nae that yer da minded. Six sons, he said, were enough for him. Yer mam, he said, had given him the most precious giftie of all, a daughter. He carried ye about the hall all wrapped in swaddling clothes, and ye glared at us all wi' those fiery eyes of yers, nae one bit afraid."

"I never heard that tale before," Flanna said.

"'Twas nae time to tell it until now," Una replied with perfect logic. "We were all quite jealous of ye at first. Yer brothers were grown men wi' bairns of their own. There were even granddaughters for Lachlann by then. He had never been particularly excited over them, but ye were different. Whenever yer mam would find ye missing from yer cradle, she would look for yer da, and there ye would be, curled in the crook of his arm while he went about his business."

"I never knew that," Flanna replied. "All I can remember of my childhood was that after Mam died, he seemed nae to care whether I lived or I died. 'Tis all I recall of him."

Una nodded. "Aye," she agreed, "he almost forgot completely about ye in his grief. He mourned her until his own death, I believe. It was harder for him that ye reminded him of yer mam, although ye hae yer da's silvery eyes and the same look in them when ye grow angry."

"I hae my father's eyes?" Flanna was amazed. No one had ever said that to her before either.

"Aye," Una said. "Same color and look." She laughed. "I can still remember once when ye and Lachlann quarreled over something or other; I dinna even remember what. Ye were nae more than seven or eight. Ye stood toe to toe glaring at one another, and the expression on both of ye was exactly the same."

Flanna's brothers laughed at Una's tale. They all well remembered the look to which she referred.

"But he loved ye, lassie, despite his apparent disregard." Aulay, her eldest brother, broke into his wife's thoughts. "I thought him mad when he turned down Patrick Leslie's offer of gold for Brae. I didna see what he saw, but he was right. Ye're happy, Flanna, even I can see that. Ye're married to a good man, a wealthy man, a man whose brother is kin to the king himself! Yer son will be the next Duke of Glenkirk, Flanna! A bairn wi' Brodie blood in his veins! We will profit eventually by this connection, and 'tis due to ye, sister."

She took the opportunity offered at that moment. "I hae been to Perth," she began. "And I hae met the king. I hae his permission to raise a levy of fighting men for him so he may take back all that is his and avenge his own da's death at the hands of their enemies."

The hall grew suddenly very quiet.

"I knew ye had run away," Aulay said.

"I dinna run away!" Flanna replied indignantly. "Patrick's da, an old man, and obviously a foolish one, went to Dunbar despite his wife's pleadings. He died in defense of king and country. The Duchess Jasmine was verra angry. She left Glenkirk, went down into England, and from there to France wi' her youngest child, a daughter. Before she left she told Patrick that the royal Stuarts bring misfortune to the Leslies of Glenkirk. That he was to hae naught to do wi' them. 'Tis, of course, nonsense, and I dinna believe it for a moment."

"But yer husband does," Aulay said, "and ye are honor bound, sister, to obey his wishes in this matter."

"My first loyalty, of all loyalties, should be to our king," Flanna replied.

"Yer first loyalty, Lady Leslie, should be to God," Mr. Dundas, the Presbyterian minister, said. "Ye do hold wi' the Covenants, do ye nae?"

"I do," Flanna responded quickly, and without any hesitation, "and so does the king, sir! I saw him crowned wi' my brother-in-law, Lord Stuart. He swore wi' such fervor to the Covenants that even the harshest of his critics wept that morning. It was grand!"

"And ye met him?" Her brother Ranald sounded skeptical.

"Before his coronation and afterward," she bragged.

"How?" Aulay queried her.

"He came to the inn where Lord Stuart and I were lodging, and Charlie introduced us. Then, because he knew I must return home quickly, he came after the feasting was over to bid me farewell and thank me for my loyalty. It was then I requested, and received, his permission to raise a levy of men to fight for him," Flanna told them, not daring to explain in detail her meetings with Charles II. Her brothers would have been, and rightfully so, shocked.

"Ye were in the king's presence *alone?*" Aulay asked her.

"Of course I was nae!" Flanna said, sounding offended. "What do ye think of me that ye would consider such a possibility? The first time Lord Stuart was wi' us, and the second, my own husband was there. I am shocked, Aulay, that ye would think me so foolish, or ill-bred, that I would behave like a hoyden before the king and disgrace both of our families." She pursed her lips and shook her head with her obvious disapproval.

"I beg yer pardon, sister," the new laird said.

"Ye're forgiven, of course," she told him with a small smile. "Now, since I am here, I invite any braw lad who seeks to better himself, and perhaps even find his fortune, to join the king's troops. There will be some looting, but only in the towns that are disloyal to the Stuarts," Flanna said knowledgeably. "What is there for most of ye here at Killiecairn? Ye hae nae property, for it belongs to Aulay. Ye hae nae cattle or sheep, for they, too, belong to Aulay. Ye live or die at his discretion; and while my brother is a good man, 'tis still he who is laird now at Killiecairn, and when he is gone, his eldest son will be laird. Ye hae nae opportunity to advance yerselves, nor will ye if ye remain here." She paused, and her gaze swept the hall, her glance touching those of her younger nephews' and her grand-nephews'. "Come now, laddies, when was it said that a Brodie did nae enjoy a good scrap? This family has always been loyal to our kings. There has never been the taint of treason spoken of the Brodies of Killiecairn. They say the war will be short, for the people want their king back and are shamed that they hae murdered the first Charles Stuart, who was their king."

One of her younger nephews spoke up. "If the English want the royal Stuart back, Flanna, then, why doesna he simply go home to them? He be the grandson of our last Jamie Stuart, but he was nae born in Scotland. He has the name, but they say he dinna look like a Stuart. He is nae a Scot. He is English."

"He is *first* the King of Scotland," Flanna said. "If ye could but hae seen him and talked wi' him like I did, Ian, ye would under-stand. They say my husband's brother looks like his da, Prince Henry Stuart, and I tell ye truly that the king does nae share a re-semblance wi' Charlie. But what difference does it make what he looks like? *He is the king!* He needs our help!"

"Why should we help him to leave us, sister?" Aulay asked her. "These Stuarts are soft men. They now prefer the pleasures and grand living in England to Scotland. If Charles Stuart would be king of Scotland, then let him be, but I'll nae help him to go back to England."

"The English murdered his da!" Flanna shouted. "Even the as-sembly of the kirk has condemned it. Are we Scots to sit idly by and nae revenge ourselves on those wicked men?"

"We are isolated, Flanna," her brother roared back, "but nae so isolated that we dinna hear the news. Cromwell and his ilk still oc-cupy Edinburgh. The king came to Aberdeen last month to raise troops and could nae do it. Do ye nae understand, sister, or are ye so foolish that yer eyes are blinded by his silken manner and a silkier tongue. The Stuarts were always the best liars in Christendom, and even more so when it came to the lasses. Why, there was a time when most of the families in Scotland had spawned a Stuart bastard or two. They are charmers to be certain, and I think, little sister, that ye hae been charmed. I suspect 'twas a damned good thing yer husband caught up wi' ye, or ye might hae been seduced yerself," he chuckled.

The hall erupted with good-natured laughter at Aulay's observation.

Flanna felt her temper rising. Aulay could not know how close he had come to the truth, but she was not going to allow him to spoil her plans to aid the king, to gain the earldom of Brae back for her family. She waited until the mirth had died, and then she said scathingly, "I never thought the day would come when a Brodie of Killiecairn would cry coward, Aulay. Thank God our da is in his grave this night."

Aulay Brodie's face darkened with his anger. *"Flanna,"* he said in a tight voice, "if ye were a man . . ."

"Ye would call me out?" she mocked him. *"Do it!* Ye were never any good wi' a sword, Aulay. I could beat ye wi' one hand tied behind my back. I could beat all of ye! Now, who among ye are brave enough to come to Brae wi' me, where I will assemble my levy for the king?" She turned her back on the laird of Killiecairn, who was now almost apoplectic with his fury. "Will ye remain here and be naught, hae naught?"

Her nephew Ian spoke up again. "We're nae cowards, Flanna, but we be tired of wars that hae naught to do wi' us. If we went wi' ye, and managed to come home again one day, what would we hae accomplished? We might be minus a limb, or an eye, for few escape battle unscathed. Perhaps we would return wi' some small cache of plunder we had managed to conceal from others, but it would be small and would gain us naught. We would still be at the mercy of our laird wi'out land, wi'out livestock. But there is a way for those of us who want to leave Killiecairn and seek a new life. We can go to the New World. There is opportunity there for men who are willing to work hard. There is land to be had and fortunes to be made! I will nae gie up my life for some dispossessed English king wi' a Scots name, Flanna; but I will dare to cross the sea, and I will welcome any who would go wi' me!"

There was a stunned silence in the hall, and then Flanna's nephews began shouting, almost as one, "I'll go wi' ye, Ian Brodie!"

"Now see what ye hae done, ye troublesome wench!" her sister-in-law Una said angrily. "How many mothers' hearts will be broken because of what ye hae begun here this night?"

"Dinna vent yer wrath on me!" Flanna protested heatedly. "I want them to remain in Scotland and fight for the king. 'Tis Ian Brodie who speaks of leaving."

"He would nae hae the courage to speak up had ye not offered the laddies a choice of death in the king's service, remaining here wi' naught, or leaving to make their fortunes," Una snapped back.

"If they will nae fight for their king, they had best be gone," Flanna responded. "If they prefer to serve themselves rather than their king, than Scotland, then let them depart and take their disgrace wi' them! My father would be shamed to see the Brodies of Killiecairn behave thusly!"

"If ye believe that, sister," Aulay said angrily, "then ye dinna know our da at all. Survival was his motto, even as 'tis the Leslies' of Glenkirk. A clan canna outlive its enemies if it sends its men to every war the king would fight. Charles Stuart has naught to do wi' me, or mine, but if there are those in the hall tonight who wish to join my sister's levy I'll nae stay them, nor will I stop those of ye who, like Ian Brodie, desire to go adventuring in the New World. We are a large family, and the truth is there is nae enough for all of our children and grandchildren. Perhaps 'tis time now for some to go. I will do what I can to help ye, Ian, and those who would follow ye, but ye must gie me yer word that ye will help any who would follow after ye once ye hae found yer place and hae settled it."

"Ye hae my word, uncle," Ian Brodie said, a pleased grin upon his face. "Gie us five years, and we will send for any who would follow us, and for wives as well. I would travel only wi' lads, for 'twill nae be an easy way we take."

"And who will follow the king?" Flanna demanded, still determined.

The hall grew silent.

"Ye're craven dastards, all of ye!" she finally shouted at them.

Callum Brodie jumped up from his place and shouted at his sister, "Dinna dare accuse us, Flanna Leslie! The Brodies hae always done their duty to their clan and to country. Ye, however, hae nae done yer duty to yer man yet. Go home and hae bairns like a respectable woman should! What right hae ye to demand that we send our sons and grandsons to be cannon fodder for this Sassenach king!"

"He is a royal Stuart king," she cried.

"An *English* king," Callum replied, and there were murmurs of assent in the hall.

"Then, tomorrow I will go to the Gordons," Flanna told them. "And after that I importune the Campbells, the Hays, and any others who will hear me. I gave my word to the king, and I will keep it!"

"Tomorrow," Aulay Brodie told his youngest sibling, "ye'll go back to Glenkirk. I'll take ye myself."

"I'll nae go!" she cried defiantly.

"For God's sake, lass, ye're wi' bairn!" Aulay replied, frustrated.

"I . . . ye dinna know what ye're saying!" Flanna responded, flushing.

"Well, I do!" Una Brodie interrupted the argument. "I know when a lass is ripening wi' her bairn as I already told ye, and ye surely are, Flanna Leslie! What's more, ye know ye are, and sly vixen ye are, yer man doesna know it yet, for ye're so determined to hae yer way in this foolishness. Well, I'll travel to Glenkirk wi' ye tomorrow, too, and if ye dinna tell Patrick Leslie the truth of the matter, then I will tell him even as I told my husband from whom I hae borne nae secrets. Now sit down and shut yer mouth!"

A ripple of laughter ran through the hall. Flanna glared furiously at her large assembled family, but then she sat down. "I'm nae a child," she muttered to Una.

"Then, behave like the duchess ye are," Una said low. "Ye'll sleep wi' me tonight. I'm nae of a mind to awake in the morning and find ye hae bolted off. I'll nae hae Aulay in difficulties wi' yer husband."

"But, Una, I promised the king," Flanna almost wailed.

"I dinna think a king, even a king of Scotland, would take the promise of a country lass verra seriously," Una replied scathingly. "'Tis as Aulay said. The Stuarts are noted for their charm, Flanna, and the king was being polite. I'm certain he was verra touched wi' yer offer, for it shows yer loyalty and duty to country; but nae for a moment do I think he believed ye could raise a levy for him. And ye hae the perfect excuse now. Ye can plead yer belly. 'Twould nae be expected that a woman, full wi' her bairn, could ride about the countryside raising soldiers for the king." She patted Flanna's hand comfortingly. "Ye're worn, Flanna, for the early months are difficult, especially so the first time; and ye hae done yer duty by yer da admirably. Come, and I'll put ye to bed, lassie." Una arose, and held out her hand to Flanna.

Sighing, Flanna stood up and took the offered hand. "I am tired," she admitted.

"That's my good lass," Una said soothingly as they left the hall. "'Tis confusing, the first time ye're wi' bairn. 'Tis the best time, and 'tis the worst time. At least that is how I felt. Yer man is going to be verra pleased wi' ye, Flanna, especially if 'tis a laddie."

"The bairn will be what God wills it to be," Flanna replied. God's boots, she was tired all of a sudden, but she was also confused. What was the matter with the men in her family? She had thought that they would leap at the chance to defend their king. Instead, they had refused, and now the younger men spoke openly about leaving Killiecairn, of leaving Scotland to find their fortunes in the New World. They would not have dared voice such thoughts while her father was alive, Flanna considered.

"Ye're too quiet," her sister-in-law said as they removed their outer garments and prepared for bed. "What do ye think about?"

Flanna finished peeing in the chamber pot and climbed into the bed she would share with Una. "I dinna understand," she said.

Una climbed into bed next to the younger woman. "Understand what, lassie?" she inquired.

"I dinna understand why the men will nae fight for the king. The Brodies hae always answered a call to arms and been brave." Flanna sighed. "Why will they nae be now, Una?"

Una sighed, too, and then she began. "For centuries the clans hae warred against one another. There isna a foot of clan land in Scotland that hae nae been watered wi' blood. Like Glenkirk, Killiecairn has been protected from the worst of it because of our isolation. Our most immediate neighbors, the Gordons and the Leslies, are more powerful, and we were nae considered a threat by them. Once, Flanna, the Hays held land here, but they are long gone, and their lands disbursed by marriage, by conquest. The year I was born, the old queen down in England died, and our King James inherited her throne. He could scarce wait to leave Scotland. It was never a peaceful place, nor are we an easy people. More Stuart kings hae died of violence than in their beds. King James was a peaceful man, and so he hurried down into England wi' his queen and his bairns. I dinna know if he ever came back again, but while Scotland has belonged to the Stuart kings, since the days of that particular king, we hae nae had a king in residence.

"And if the powerful men who made the Stuarts' lives miserable were difficult before they departed, they hae been more difficult after he left us wi' no king, or court, to amuse them, to command their attention. The English, 'tis said, despised our King Jamie, for he was a Scot, but they had no choice but to accept him. He was the legitimate successor to their old queen. But he was enjoying himself so much in that peaceful land, he dinna pay a great deal of attention to what the English thought. And when he died, his son, the first Charles, inherited. While still considered a Scot, for he was born here, this king fared a wee bit better, for he had lived most of his life in England, but then the troubles began. Ye see, 'twas an elder brother who was supposed to follow King Jamie, but he died young. They say he was greatly loved by the English."

"That would be the not-so-royal Stuart's sire," Flanna said.

"Aye," Una responded. "But, instead, the younger brother inherited, and he was nae a good king, or so 'tis said of him. I dinna really understand what this English war is all about, but it cost that Stuart king his life. Now his son, English-born, hae been crowned at Scone, and ye, yerself, saw it, Flanna. But he is nae satisfied to remain here and rule us. He would go back to England and leave us. But to do so he must raise an army and fight his way back to London.

"There is nothing moral about war, Flanna. There is naught just about it. Land is ravaged. Crops destroyed. Innocent women, bairns, and old folk are slaughtered. Our history is filled wi' war, and frankly we hae had enough of it. 'Tis as the men told ye earlier; we dinna know this king. While we will respect the laws of the land, we feel nae obligation to go to war wi' him. We are tired. Can ye understand?"

"But there are so many here now at Killiecairn," Flanna said. "Our young men canna wed because there is nae place for them to bring wives. If they dinna wed, the clan will die out. If they go wi' the king, they can make their fortunes, Una."

"If they survive," she responded grimly.

"But ye heard Ian tonight, Una. He will leave Killiecairn and take others wi' him. At least those who fight for the king will come home one day. Will Brodie sons return from the New World, or will they remain to make their lives there?"

"I dinna know," Una said, "but Ian and many of the younger ones will go. The truth is they hae been speaking secretly on it for months now. When ye spoke up so boldly tonight, they took the opportunity to speak up, too. 'Tis the sensible solution. There is land to be hae in this New World, and many Scots are going now. We will help them where we can."

"I didna know," Flanna said softly.

"They could nae speak on it while the old man lived," Una said with a chuckle. "Lachlann Brodie would nae want to lose a single clansman. He believed our strength was in our numbers, but we are well protected now by Glenkirk. To quarrel wi' us is to quarrel wi' the Leslies. Besides, we hae naught but our lands and cattle. 'Tis nae a great fortune. Certainly nae enough to start a feud over."

"Will the Leslies eventually suffer the fate of the Brodies?" Flanna wondered aloud.

"The Leslies hae managed in each generation to see that all the lord's sons and daughters were given something. If this king ye admire is yer friend, Flanna, then one day ye may regain the title that belonged to yer mam's family and gie it to a son. There is usually a way to do anything ye want to do, lassie, but we Brodies of Killiecairn are nae wealthy or powerful enough for such maneuverings."

"I hae certainly considered regaining the Earldom of Brae for a second son," Flanna said.

"Ye see, lassie," her sister-in-law said. "Ye're thinking like the Duchess of Glenkirk, though ye be wed only a short time. Now, enough of yer chatter. Let us get some sleep."

Una Brodie was quickly snoring, but Flanna lay awake for a while. She was very disappointed that she would not be able to raise a levy for the king, but perhaps her plan had been just a trifle ambitious. She was a country lass as Una had suggested so pointedly. She had been wed to Patrick for only a short time. There would be other ways of making her mark so that she would not be remembered as the do-naught duchess. Laying upon her back, she folded her hands over her belly. It was still flat, but beneath her palms she knew her child was growing.

Suddenly she could barely wait to return home to Glenkirk. Patrick was going to be so excited over the impending birth of his heir. She might not be able to fight for her king, or give him the troops he so desperately needed, but she was doing her duty by the Leslies of Glenkirk. By the end of the year, her child would be born. At peace with herself, Flanna fell asleep now, wondering as she did if the coming child meant that she and Patrick could no longer enjoy their pleasures. She would have to ask Una about it in the morning, and she did.

"Ye'll enjoy each other for a while longer, but ye must be careful now," Una told her as they prepared to depart Killiecairn. "And ye must nae be disturbed if he eases himself on some clanswoman when ye're too big to mount. Men will do that, but it means naught to them."

"I'll nae hae it!" Flanna said quickly.

Una laughed. "If he knows ye feel that way, then 'tis likely ye'll never know it, lassie; but men are only big lads."

"I'm glad ye're coming wi' me," Flanna said to her sister-in-law.

"I'm curious about this Glenkirk Castle," Una admitted. "'Tis said to be verra grand."

"I thought so when I first came there. I suppose 'tis, but to me 'tis just home now," Flanna replied. "It hae a grand history. I am amazed to realize that it will be my son who will be the next duke."

Una chortled. "So am I, Flanna. Never, when I was helping to raise ye, did I imagine ye would one day be a duchess."

They departed Killiecairn. Flanna's six brothers had all decided to accompany her back to Glenkirk. There was something about their only and much younger sister that worried them. She was far too outspoken and independent for a woman. They wanted to reassure the duke that the brothers of Flanna Leslie would side with him in any dispute between him and their sister. The Duke of Glenkirk was a powerful friend to have. Their sister, on the other hand, was still a troublesome vixen. Her words in the family hall the previous night had startled them. Marriage had not settled her at all, and she was as bold as she had ever been.

As they rode away, Flanna glanced toward the family burial ground on the nearby hillside. Her father's new grave was visible, and she said a silent prayer to herself as she rode away. A weak sun shone down on them as they traveled the miles between the Brodie enclave and Glenkirk. As they rode around Loch Brae, Flanna finally spoke.

"My husband hae given me Brae Castle to restore. One day I shall gie it to my second son. 'Tis Leslie custom to provide for all their sons."

"Does yer husband nae hae two younger brothers?" Aulay asked.

"Aye. Their mam hae a great estate in Ireland. She divided it between her youngest lads and managed to get titles for them."

"Then, yer mother-in-law is Irish?" Aulay continued.

"Nay. She comes from a land far, far away. Patrick says 'tis called India. Her da was a great king."

"What would the daughter of a great king be doing married to a Scot and living at Glenkirk?" her second brother, Callum, demanded scornfully. "Who told ye such a tale?"

"My husband," Flanna replied. "His family is verra unusual, brothers. His grandmam, the old Countess of BrocCairn, was told her husband was killed in a duel. Heartbroken, she went with an elder brother to India where her own mam and da were at the time. She was kidnapped and given to this great king to be his fortieth wife."

"*His fortieth wife?*" her brother Simon exclaimed. "God hae mercy on the poor man, for one wife is more than enough for me!"

The others laughed at Simon's outburst. "Yer husband is flummoxing ye wi' such a tale," Callum said.

"Nay, 'tis all true. Patrick says most of his grandfather's wives were political marriages to seal treaties, or stop wars, though there were some he loved. He loved the lady Velvet. Patrick says he called her his English rose. Shortly after she had borne the king a daughter, word came from England that her husband, the Earl of BrocCairn, was nae dead. Her family wanted her returned. The king, an honorable man, sent her away, but he kept his wee bairn, who grew up to be the Duchess Jasmine.

"Her first husband was a prince. He was murdered by her brother, and as her da lay dying, the princess fled to England and her grandparents. She was made welcome. Her second husband, the Marquis of Westleigh, gie her three bairns. It was he who gained the great estate in Ireland for her from King James. He was murdered there, and she left it. She met Prince Henry Stuart at court, and he gie her a son. Then he died, and she vowed nae to wed again, for she believed that she brought misfortune to the men who loved her."

They rode along, and Flanna's brothers were now all captivated by the story she was telling them. The content of the tale was beyond anything that any of them could have ever imagined. Flanna went on to explain how King James had ordered the marriage between the Duke of Glenkirk, who was a widower, and the Marchioness of Westleigh, who was a widow. The king wanted to protect his little grandson, and he wanted the lad raised by a good man. The king trusted the Duke of Glenkirk as he trusted few others. He remembered what it had been like being raised by strangers, and he didn't want his first grandchild to suffer the same fate that he had suffered.

"But," Flanna told her now fascinated brothers, "the lady did nae want to wed again. She knew Glenkirk, and she liked him; but she dinna want to be told she must wed again. She gathered up her four bairns and went to France. It took Glenkirk two years to find her, but he finally did wi' Madame Skye's help."

"Who is Madame Skye?" Aulay asked.

"The Lady Jasmine's grandmam, and that's another story altogether! I can hardly believe all that I hear about these women," Flanna told her brothers. "That is why 'tis so important that I nae be a do-naught duchess. By helping the king, I would hae made my mark. But let me finish my tale. The lady Jasmine and Jemmie Leslie were wed. They hae three sons and two daughters. One daughter died as a bairn. The other one is now in France wi' her mama. She is the youngest, and came into the world when the duchess thought she would hae nae more bairns. Patrick says they were all verra surprised when his sister, Lady Autumn, was born. And she was born in Ireland where they had gone to marry off one of his other sisters, and that, too, is another story. There seem to be a lot of fascinating histories at Glenkirk," she finished, laughing.

"Well," Una said, "I can see why ye're so anxious, lassie, but perhaps Patrick Leslie is perfectly content to hae a wife who is nae running off and getting herself into mischief. He seemed a quiet man to me."

"All the Leslie women hae been adventurous," Flanna admitted. "He speaks of them lovingly, but ye may be right, Una. He also says his sisters were troublesome hoydens who fretted his parents greatly."

"There, ye see!" Una crowed. "Yer man is a simple chieftain, for all his wealth and powerful titles. Ye can be the perfect wife to him if ye will put all this foolishness out of yer head. Ye'll keep his home well and gie him a family of healthy bairns ye'll nurture to become good men and women. When yer descendants look at yer portrait in the hall, Flanna, they will nae call ye the do-naught duchess. They will say of ye that the second duchess made her husband happier than any of the lords of Glenkirk who hae come before him. That he loved her wi'out ceasing and never wanted to be from her side."

"Why, Una," Flanna said, surprised by the older woman's words. She had never suspected that her sister-in-law was so romantic.

"Well, 'tis surely a better history than to be known as the naïve duchess who went gallivanting about the Highlands seeking to raise cannon fodder for a disposed king who deserted Scotland when he regained what he hae lost," Una said sharply. "Ye've got a good man, Flanna. Dinna drive him away by going against him. If Patrick Leslie believes that the king's family brings him misfortune, then ye must respect his sentiments, even if ye think them foolish. That is what a good wife does. She praises her husband's accomplishments, and she overlooks his errors in judgment—*most of the time.*"

"So, that's how ye've managed to live so peaceably wi' my brother all these years," Flanna teased her sister-in-law.

Una reached out to swat the younger woman; but it was done with affection, and she was laughing.

They had left in mid-morning from Killiecairn, and by late afternoon the towers of Glenkirk came into view. Flanna felt a wave of pleasure at the sight of her home. In the months she had been wed to her husband, she had come to love Glenkirk. Fingal moved his horse up next to hers now and grinned at her.

"I'll be glad to be back," he said. "I've actually missed the Stuart bairns, even wee Willy, who howls all the time."

"Ye behave yerself," his mother warned him. "I'll nae hae ye being sent home, Fingal Brodie. This is a great opportunity that has been given ye. I dinna want to lose ye to the New World like so many of the others will lose their bairns."

"I like it here," Fingal admitted to Una. "And I like the lessons we are given each day. Lady Sabrina studies wi' her brother and me. The Leslies feel a lass should be as educated as any lad. Even Flanna has finally learned to read and to write."

"Ye hae?" Una was astounded.

"I canna be the Duchess of Glenkirk and nae know how to read or write. I hae my duties. Angus taught me," Flanna said.

"And what does he do besides teach ye?" Una asked curiously.

"Angus runs the household. When the Duchess Jasmine lived here, she hae a man who hae been her servant since her birth. 'Twas he who ran the household. But when she departed, he left wi' her," Flanna explained. "We hae a housekeeper, but the staff need a majordomo to guide them in their duties. They all like Angus. Did ye know he was my uncle? My mam's brother, born on the wrong side of the blanket."

"I knew," Una said. "He's fortunate his sister—and now his niece—loved him enough to include him in her life. And how does Aggie thrive?"

"She's happy wi' me here," Flanna said. "And since there is nae a great deal to do for me, she helps wi' the Stuart bairns. They hae their own nursie who came wi' them from England. She and Aggie get on verra well, and as she is old, she is glad for the help."

As they neared Glenkirk, a rider came over the drawbridge toward them. Flanna moved her mount ahead and rode to meet her husband.

"Lachlann Brodie is dead?" Patrick said as they met on the road.

"Buried yesterday," Flanna answered. "I hae brought my brothers and Aulay's wife wi' me. I knew they would be welcome." She lowered her voice. "They were all dying of curiosity," she admitted, smiling.

The duke nodded imperceptibly at his wife; then he stopped his horse and, smiling broadly, said, "The sons of Lachlann Brodie, and brothers of my wife, Flanna, are welcome to Glenkirk. And ye also, Mistress Una. Come, for ye hae had a long ride this day." Then, turning about, he led them across the drawbridge and into the courtyard of Glenkirk.

They struggled not to gawk, but none of them had ever been in a castle. Glenkirk, while not large, was impressive with its four dark stone towers, and its heavy oaken doors, and its great iron portcullis. Their eyes widened at the many stablemen who hurried forth to take their mounts as they climbed down from their horses. Each of them dusted himself free of the road, suddenly very aware that they were about to enter a great house. They were startled by their younger sister's air of ease with all of this. She spoke with gentle authority to the lad holding her horse as she dismounted it.

"Be certain that Glaise is well brushed and has an extra measure of oats tonight, Robbie," she told him. Then, turning about, she smiled at her Brodie relations. "Welcome to Glenkirk, brothers. Welcome to Glenkirk, Una. Come, we'll go into the hall."

"I dinna know, Flanna." Callum was suddenly reticent.

"Ye'll surely stay at least one night," she insisted softly. "'Tis too late to return today. Come!" And she led them from the courtyard.

Angus met them as they entered the castle. "Welcome back, my lady," he said, bowing respectfully as he ushered them into the hall.

Servants seemed to appear from nowhere offering silver tankards of October ale to the weary travelers. The men took them up eagerly, if for no other reason than to calm their beating hearts as they looked about the Great Hall with its two massive fireplaces, its colorful banners that hung down from the carved rafters, and the two impressive portraits that hung over the fireplaces. Except for Aulay, they had never been in such a grand house in all of their lives and were not just a little intimidated by it all.

"I felt the same way the first time I entered this hall," Flanna said quietly to them. Then she called to Angus. "See that sleeping places are prepared for my brothers and for Mistress Una," she told him.

Angus Gordon bowed again. "At once, my lady," he replied.

"And tell Cook we hae guests."

He nodded.

Three children now ran into the hall crying Flanna's name. She knelt and enfolded them into her embrace. "Ahh, here are our bairns," she said. "Did ye miss me?"

"Did you bring us any gifties?" the little girl asked boldly.

"I went to bury my da, Brie. 'Twas nae a pleasure trip," Flanna explained. "And here are my brothers come back wi' me, and Una, of whom I hae told ye." She arose. "Brothers, Una, may I present to ye the bairns of the not-so-royal Stuart. Lady Sabrina Stuart and her brothers, Lord Frederick and Lord William. Bairns, here is my brother Aulay, the laird of Killiecairn, and his good wife, Una; and my other five brothers, Callum, Gillies, Ranald, Simon, and Bhaltair."

Sabrina curtsied politely as her brothers bowed. The sons of Lachlann Brodie bowed back, following Aulay's lead as Una poked him and then curtsied to the three children.

"Well, now that the introductions are over," Patrick Leslie said, realizing that his wife's family was just slightly uncomfortable, "let us seat ourselves at the high board and wait for the meal to be served. Ye're surely hungry after yer ride. The spring is still nae quite wi' us, although I hae felt a slight warmth in the air these past few days. I'm glad for the longer days. The dark months are hard." He brought his brothers-in-law to the table.

"When are ye going to tell him?" Una whispered to Flanna.

"Let me do it when we are alone tonight," Flanna said. "I think such news, especially delivered to a man for the first time, should be told in private."

Una chuckled. "Ye just want to couple wi' him before he knows," she said. "Ye like the bedsport, eh?"

"*I do!*" Flanna admitted.

"Then, ye're a fortunate lass to hae a husband who is skilled wi' his weapon, for there are many who are nae."

"Wi' all the bairns at Killiecairn, I would guess 'tis nae a complaint the Brodie wives are known to make," Flanna returned pertly.

Una laughed aloud. "Nay, Flanna, it has always been their greatest talent, as yer own mam would hae attested. Do ye love him, or is it just the pleasures ye enjoy?"

"Nay, I believe that I love him, though he can be fearfully stubborn at times, Una. Still, so can I, so I would suspect we are both well matched in this marriage we made," Flanna concluded.

"But ye'll tell him," Una persisted.

"He'll come to the hall on the morrow wi' a great smile on his handsome face, I promise ye," Flanna told her sister-in-law. "What ye said on the road today made a great deal of sense to me. I hae been so concerned wi' being like my predecessors that I forgot I am nae like them. Princesses, and sultan's wives! I am a plain Highland lass. My strength surely lies in making Patrick and the bairns I bear him happy. If there is more, it will come when it comes."

Una nodded. "Ye hae set my heart at ease, Flanna," she said.

"When my mam died, ye took me to raise. We hae nae always seen eye to eye in the past, and we may nae see eye to eye in the future, Una, but ye hae always been a good example to me. I am nae so foolish that I dinna realize it." Then Flanna hugged Una Brodie, even as she asked her, "Do ye think 'tis a lad or a lass I'll bear?"

Chapter

13

He had taught her to mount him, and he loved it when she did. His big hands fondled her pretty breasts as she sat atop him, smiling. Buried deep inside her, his eyes closed, he allowed the pleasure to wash over him, filling him until he felt ready to explode with the pure enjoyment of it. He groaned as she tightened the muscles of her love sheath about his lance. "Ye'll kill me yet, wench," he told her, his voice thick with emotion.

"Ye like it," she responded saucily, and she laughed.

"So do ye," he shot back. Then he turned her swiftly onto her back so that it was now he who was dominant. His green-gold eyes glittered dangerously as he took her mouth in a burning kiss that sent her senses reeling with confusion. "Such a naughty vixen ye are, Flanna Leslie," he said, moving deliberately on her now.

The rhythmic stroking of his manhood began to have the desired effect. She moaned a sound of distinct delight. "Oh, God, Patrick, that is *so* good. Dinna stop! Dinna ever stop!"

He laughed aloud. From the very first moment they had come together as man and wife, she had relished it. There had never been any doubt in his mind once he had taken her that first time that she was a virgin. He was the only man who had ever had her, but Flanna was a woman who naturally enjoyed her bedsport. He hadn't ever had to coax her. Once introduced to passion's pleasures, she had embraced them eagerly. And she still did. *But so did he.* He knew that no other woman would ever again satisfy him the way his beautiful wife did. And he would kill any man who even looked at her askance. His love for Flanna was totally irrational as he had discovered when he had found her with the young king. He couldn't ever recall having been so murderously angry in his entire life, but he knew enough to conceal it in the royal presence, *after he had sheathed his sword.*

Flanna writhed beneath her husband as her enjoyment rose and rose to fill her entire being. "Aye!" she sobbed. "Aye! Aye!"

He felt her beginning to reach her peak, and with a gasp of relief, he released his own lust into her welcoming body and then fell away from her as the satisfaction overwhelmed them both

Finally they came to themselves, and he drew her into his arms again. "I missed ye when ye were gone from me. I dinna like it when ye are gone from me, Flanna. Glenkirk is too empty."

"Wi' Charlie's bairns running about?" she teased him.

"They will be gone from us one day," he said.

"But we will hae our own bairns by then," she told him.

He sighed deeply.

"In *August*," she told him. "Ten months after our wedding, which should even be soon enough for my family, God help us!"

His arms tightened about her. "Ye're having a bairn?"

"Aye," she said.

"Why didna ye tell me sooner?" he demanded, sitting up and looking down at her. His gaze swept over her naked form. Her breasts had, indeed, grown lusher, and was that not a faint rounding of her belly?

"I dinna tell ye because I was nae certain at first. I hae never had a bairn, Patrick. My da saw it, and Una confirmed it for me. 'Tis she who hae convinced me nae to raise a levy for the king, but to hae yer bairns and be a good wife to ye," Flanna told him honestly.

"Ye went to Killiecairn to raise a levy?" His tone was angry.

"I went to Killiecairn to be wi' my dying sire," she responded. "But, aye, after we buried him, I tried to arouse my kin to arms, and I intended going to Huntley next to speak wi' the Gordons, for they are my kin through my mother's family. The Brodies mocked me, and my brothers threatened me for endangering my marriage to a good man."

His look was now stony. "Yer brothers hae more sense than ye do," he said angrily.

"I gave my word to the king, and now I must plead my belly in order to break it," Flanna said, her tone suddenly cold.

"Do ye really believe the king thought ye could raise a regiment for him?" Patrick asked her scornfully.

"Whether he did or nae," Flanna responded, "he made me believe I could. Ye all tell me that he has charm, and that is surely so. Yer view of the king is skewed by yer mother and the fact that yer da died at Dunbar. I know only the man I met in Perth. A trifler of hearts, perhaps, but an anointed king nonetheless. Mayhap I hae stars in my eyes, Patrick, but it hae never been said of Flanna Leslie that she was a fool. I am told I am naïve, and maybe I am, if 'tis naïve to believe in yer king."

"Whose bairn is this that ye carry?" he demanded furiously of her.

"What?" She had surely not heard him right.

"Do ye carry my bairn or the king's, Flanna? The question is plain and requires but a plain answer," her told her harshly.

"'Tis yer bairn, of course," she promptly answered him. "Why would ye even consider that I would dishonor myself, or ye, by wanton behavior?"

"I found ye alone wi' the king, did I nae?" he replied.

"If ye had found yer sisters alone wi' him, would ye hae asked such a question of them, Patrick?" Her anger was becoming dangerous.

"I know my sisters," he answered her icily.

"Get out!" she told him.

"What?"

"Get out of my bedchamber!" she shouted at him. "I dinna want ye here!" And she hit him a blow on his shoulder. *"Get out!"*

He caught her hands in his and held them fast. "Breeding women are nae supposed to distress themselves, Flanna," he told her.

"Why do ye care?" she shrieked. "Ye dinna think the bairn is

yers! Do ye know how much I hate ye at this verra minute, Patrick?
I will nae forgie ye for this insult! How can I! Ye think me a wanton
to sport wi' another man, and ye say ye dinna know me enough to
believe me when I tell ye it isna so!" She pulled herself from his
grip as she leapt from her bed. *"Get out!"* she repeated a third time.

"Ye're being irrational, Flanna," he told her, rising from the tangle of the bedclothes.

"I'm irrational, naïve, and a wanton. Are there any other insults
ye care to hurl at me tonight, my lord?" she queried him caustically.

"If ye endanger this bairn wi' yer bad temper," he began, but she
stopped him, raising her hand as she did so.

"Ye doubt the bairn's paternity, Patrick, or perhaps ye dinna now.
Why? *Ye dinna know me.* I am but the lass ye wed to gain a piece of
land. But when the bairn is born, and ye look into its wee face, and
ye see yerself, will ye believe me then? But if it favors me, will ye
still harbor yer wicked doubts? The king may be a seducer of naïve
lasses, but he did nae seduce me. The bairn I carry is yer bairn,
Patrick Leslie. This is the truth of the matter. The Brodies of
Killiecairn hae nae the wealth or the prestige of the Leslies of
Glenkirk, but we are honorable people. Now, please leave me."

She drew herself up to her full height, and despite her nakedness, he was reminded of the lass he had first met that autumn day
at Brae. He straightened himself up and, as naked as she, bowed formally before turning about to go through the hidden door that separated their bedchambers. As the door clicked shut behind him,
Patrick Leslie knew he was a great fool. He was jealous. That was
the plain truth of the matter. She spoke of King Charles as if he were
her hero. Patrick Leslie was jealous to hear his wife speak of another
man in such tones, but it surely did not give him the right to question her fidelity to him.

She was breeding with his child! He was suddenly very excited by
the knowledge. His son! By summer's end he would hold his heir in
his arms. How pleased his mother would be. *His mother!* In the
months since he had met and wed his wife, he hadn't even thought
to write to his mother. But even if he did, would a letter manage to
get through to her in France? He wasn't certain what he should do.

He pulled a nightshirt from the chest at the foot of his bed, and drawing it over his long body, he climbed into his own bed, falling into a troubled sleep.

When he arrived in the hall the next morning, he found his brothers-in-law and his sister-in-law with Flanna. They congratulated him, clapping him on the back and raising their tankards of ale in a toast to the next heir of Glenkirk. They grinned broadly with pleasure that their sister had done her duty in so timely a manner.

"I thought ye would nae mind, my lord, if I shared our happy news wi' my brothers," Flanna said sweetly, but her silver eyes were cold.

"Flanna pleases me right well," Patrick said to the Brodies. "Yer da, God rest him, did us both a good turn the day he said that I must wed yer sister to gain Brae."

Her brothers guffawed, reassured, but Una murmured to Flanna, *"What hae he done?"*

"He questioned the bairn's lineage," Flanna murmured back softly. "He asked me if it was the king's."

Una paled. *"How could he?"* she gasped.

"He asked it because he is a jealous fool," Flanna told her sister-in-law. "I was wi' the king, alone, when he arrived in Perth. I hae now learned the folly of keeping secrets, Una. If I hae told him when I first considered myself wi' bairn, this would nae hae happened. But I really wasna sure myself, and I dinna want to disappoint him." She sighed. "Dinna tell my brothers. They will be furious, and I want nae feuding between the Leslies and the Brodies. Patrick knows now he was wrong, but I will punish him so he never mistrusts me again."

"What do ye mean to do?" Una asked, her look a worried one.

"I'll nae tell ye. Yer heart is too soft, Una, and if I am to teach my husband a lesson, then what I do must be between us." She chuckled. "I'm taking a path set out by another duchess. Nay, I am in error. She was a Countess of Glenkirk, and her man was just as difficult. She brought him to heel just as I will bring my Patrick to heel."

"Ye're sure ye will nae drive a wedge between ye and yer husband?" Una fretted.

"Nay, I willna. Promise ye will keep my secret, Una?" Flanna's silvery eyes were dancing with such sudden amusement that Una was reassured.

"Verra well, lassie, but dinna break the man's spirit," she chuckled. "I like him, Flanna. He's a good man."

"I love him, and aye, he is a good man," Flanna agreed.

The Brodies departed Glenkirk Castle at midday for Killiecairn. The duke had asked them to remain longer, but Aulay believed, with his father dead, the new laird would be needed to restore clan confidence.

Patrick reluctantly agreed. "Tell yer people that I will finance their venture in exchange for certain considerations. Hae the leader of the group come to see me as soon as he can. If they are going to go this year, they must depart soon. They'll hae to find land and build themselves shelter before the winter comes. 'Twill take them several weeks to cross the sea to the New World. As ye know, my second sister lives in Mary's Land wi' her husband. I hear, however, that the lands to the south of them are ripe for settling."

"Thank ye!" Aulay Brodie said, clasping his brother-in-law's hand in friendship. "I appreciate yer help, my lord."

Patrick nodded, then stood with his wife at his side as the Brodies of Killiecairn departed the courtyard at Glenkirk Castle. When they had disappeared across the drawbridge, Flanna shook his arm from about her shoulders and walked away from him back into the castle. That night he found the door between them locked. Gritting his teeth, he climbed into his empty bed. He would let her sulk for a time. She would surely come to her senses shortly.

What she needed to do, she knew she couldn't do without help. But who would she trust with her plan? Angus? Or would he think her silly and refuse to help her. Aggie? Or perhaps Ian More, who had shown an interest in Aggie of late? Flanna knew she must consider very carefully before revealing her plan, and then the solution came to her. She would not hide from Patrick at all as his grandmother had hidden from his grandfather long ago in some equally ridiculous dispute. But, instead, she would leave Glenkirk Castle with his permission. He could not refuse her, for he had given her his word in the matter. Flanna called for her horse, but the servant returned saying Angus had forbidden it.

Flanna sought out her uncle. "Why hae ye told the servants that I canna hae my horse?" she asked him irritably.

"The duke, yer husband, doesna wish for ye to ride now that ye are wi' bairn," Angus answered her. His blue eyes were dancing with his amusement, for he knew this order would not sit well with his niece. To his great surprise, however, Flanna didn't burst into a tirade. Instead, she smiled and sighed deeply.

"How verra like a man, uncle. Was my father as overprotective of my mam when she carried me in her belly?"

"Nay, he wasna but then he hae already fathered six sons," Angus answered her. "Yer husband is naturally fearful that ye will miscarry of the bairn."

"Then, we must convince him otherwise, uncle," Flanna told him. "Patrick hae promised me that I may restore Brae, and this is the perfect time for such an enterprise. I am nae a woman to sit by her fire, or her loom, as ye know. My activities must, by the very nature of my growing belly, be restricted, but if the duke wishes me to hae more than one bairn, then he must allow me to find less dangerous pursuits than those I usually follow. There is naught for me to do here at Glenkirk. Ye and Mary keep the household in order. I must be allowed to choose my own amusement, and I choose to go to Brae."

"What mischief are ye up to?" Angus asked astutely.

"I would remove myself from Patrick Leslie's company for a time, uncle. If I dinna, I may kill him," Flanna answered him candidly.

This was serious. Angus Gordon took his niece's hand and said, "What hae he done, lass, that ye are so angered wi' him?"

"He asked me if the king was my bairn's sire," Flanna replied in low tones.

"*Jesu!*" The word exploded from the older man's mouth.

"He is a jealous fool," Flanna said.

"Why would he ask ye such a thing?" her uncle demanded to know.

"When he arrived in Perth, I was alone wi' the king. He was verra angry, uncle, but there was naught to it. Then, I kept the secret of this bairn from him. I wanted to keep my word to the king to raise a levy for him, but Una hae shown me that my first loyalty lies wi' my husband. I understand that now. While I am saddened that I canna help the king, my child is more important. However, I dinna tell my husband of our child until I returned home from Killiecairn. And then he insulted me wi' his question. He knows better, of course, but I am nae ready quite yet to forget his slander."

Angus nodded slowly. He understood completely. His niece was a proud young woman. "So ye wish to punish him by removing yerself from his presence for a time, eh?"

"Precisely, uncle. This is a lesson that Patrick Leslie must learn well, lest he be foolish enough to repeat the error. If I canna convince my husband that I am a loyal and faithful wife to him, there is little hope of our haeing a happy union. I canna think of anything worse than spending the rest of our lives suspicious of each other. *And,* Patrick's grandmother hae an equally thorny problem she solved in as strong a fashion."

"How?" Angus asked.

"Her da made the error of turning over a piece of property belonging to her alone to her betrothed husband. She would nae wed her Glenkirk until he returned the property to her keeping. He thought to force her to the altar by gieing her a bairn in her belly. He thought she would weaken, but she ran away from him. The earl realized that his heir was in danger of being born on the wrong side of the blanket. But their differences were solved only when he returned her property. They were wed as she labored to bring forth her bairn. I canna do that, for I am already wed to my husband, but I know, uncle, that he has come to love me. He will suffer the loss of my company, and that is just what I want him to do.

"I will go to Brae on the pretext of restoring it, but I will find excuses to remain there. I will nae return until he apologizes to me for his terrible words. I canna hae him looking sideways at his firstborn, that nasty suspicion still lingering wi'in his heart and mind. Only when he is ready to tell me he is sorry for mistrusting me will I know my bairn is safe, that Patrick and I may live together in peace. I might hae run off, uncle, as my husband's grandmam did once, but Patrick will know where I am. He will just nae be able to leave Glenkirk and be wi' me. Only when he comes to me and apologizes will I come home," Flanna finished.

"Ye'll take Aggie, of course," Angus answered her.

"And Ian More, too. He's young, but there should be a man in charge to speak for me to the workers," Flanna said.

"And if yer husband comes to drag ye back to Glenkirk?" Angus asked her. "He hae the right, ye know."

"There are hidey holes at Brae that even ye dinna know about, uncle," Flanna said with a wicked smile. "'Tis better that way," she chuckled. "Ye canna get into difficulties wi' my lord, *or wi me.*"

"When will ye go?" he queried her.

"I must choose my time carefully," Flanna said.

"Aye," he agreed, "and I will hae to play the innocent after ye hae gone. Why, my lord, did ye nae promise her ladyship that she might renovate and refurbish Brae? Why, everyone at Glenkirk knew of it, for yer generosity hae made her so happy. And ye do want her happy now that she carries the heir to Glenkirk, do ye nae?" Angus chortled.

"Verra good, uncle," Flanna said, laughing. Then she grew serious again. "Ye hae nae asked me the question my husband did."

"I dinna hae to, lass. I know ye, and ye're an honorable woman," Angus Gordon said.

Flanna hugged the big man, feeling wonderfully safe as he wrapped his arms about her and hugged back. It had always been that way since her childhood. Angus Gordon had always been a tower of strength, first for his beloved younger sister and, after her death, for his niece. "I love ye, uncle," she told him.

He kissed the top of her head and replied, "Now, dinna get all soft on me, lass. Why, yer mam was the same when she carried ye." But he was smiling, pleased, as he said the words.

"Now, may I hae my horse?" Flanna demanded.

"Tomorrow," he promised her. "I'll want to go to Brae myself this morning and make certain 'tis habitable for ye, Flanna. And I'll see what needs doing so I can send the right men and supplies."

"Verra well, uncle," she agreed. "Today I'll sit by the fire, but only today."

He chuckled as he departed the hall and went to the stables. There had been a time when his niece would have followed that earlier Glenkirk lady's path. Flaming Flanna would not have hesitated for a moment to cause her husband distress. This Flanna was different. She was more thoughtful. *Clever.* Willing to bide her time. He was grateful for it. Under normal circumstances, he would not have helped her in such a scheme, but he was outraged that Patrick Leslie had asked her if the child she carried was his or the king's. True, they had not been married for very long, but surely the duke had learned by now that his wife was a woman of honor. By inferring she was not, he had insulted not just the Brodies of Killiecairn, but the Gordons of Brae as well.

Taking his horse, Angus Gordon rode out of the courtyard at Glenkirk, across the drawbridge, and into the forest beyond. The day was clear, and the air had a distinct spring warmth to it after the long winter. Finally reaching Loch Brae, he stopped his mount and stood gazing out across the waters at the old castle which had been built during the reign of John Balliol in the year 1295. Brae Castle was set upon an island within the small loch, connected to the shore by a wooden bridge. The bridge had a legend. The Gordon laird who had constructed Brae had also planned to build a fine stone bridge that would join the island with the mainland. His wife, however, had pointed out that a stone bridge would allow their enemies to march right up to the castle door. A wooden bridge could be burned in the event of an impending attack and restored afterward. So the then Gordon laird of Brae had taken his wife's counsel and built his bridge of wood.

Originally the area between the bridge and the castle had been kept in field so intruders could be easily spotted. But it had been well over twenty years since the castle had been inhabited. In what had long ago been an open terrain, dark green pines and graceful aspens now grew. The rocky shoreline of the island had once had a landing on its south side, but it was gone. But for an accident of birth, Brae would have been his, and he, its earl, Angus Gordon thought. But it was not, and he was not. Some men might have been bitter about such a twist of fate, but he was not. He had a good life and always had.

Riding around the loch, he finally stopped and, dismounting, tied his horse to a tree. Then he carefully picked his way across the rotting timbers of the span to the island. He considered whether the trees now dotting the field should be removed. Perhaps some of them, not all, but he would suggest to Flanna that she have four separate structures built, one at each corner of the island, to serve as watch towers. Angus walked through the great, open, ironbound oak doors into the castle courtyard. He peered at the hinges on the doors. They were still sound, but perhaps could use resetting.

The wooden stables had collapsed into a heap of rotting timbers. They would have to be rebuilt first. Angus climbed up the stone steps into the castle itself. Reaching behind a small stone cornice above the door he pulled down the iron key and, fitting it into the entry lock, turned it to open the door. Stepping inside, he stood for a moment remembering his childhood in the house. All was silence, but he could swear that he felt the shades of his ancestors wafting about Brae. He laughed to himself and then began his inspection. It was as he had suspected. Brae, built of stone, standing alone for over twenty years, had survived amazingly well. It was dusty and full of cobwebs, but it was intact.

Examining the structure to its attics, he found damage to the slate roof that would need to be repaired. The cellars were filthy and filled with all manner of stuff. They would have to be cleaned out. The hangings were salvageable, but would require beating to be free of dust. The furniture wanted polish. The floors needed to be washed and swept. The windows were black with grime, and the wooden shutters belonging to them, hanging in many cases.

He moved on to the kitchens. Bending down, he looked up the chimney. It, along with every chimney in the house, was going to need sweeping. Generations of birds and rodents had made their nests within those chimneys. He wondered if perhaps it was not too much work for Flanna to take on, but then, his niece was a strong girl. Having Brae to concern her would help to take away the sting of Patrick Leslie's ill-advised suspicions. A span of days away from his wife would undoubtedly give the Duke of Glenkirk time to consider his poorly chosen words. Angus Gordon returned to Glenkirk Castle to report to his niece on what he had found.

"Now," he told her, "'tis up to ye to convince yer man that ye should go to Brae. It will nae be easy, Flanna."

"I know," she admitted. "I am still angry wi' him."

"Then, wait a bit until yer anger hae cooled," Angus advised.

"Nay," she said.

Patrick Leslie came to his table that evening. His wife nodded coolly to him, but said nothing. The servants brought forth the meal. There was roasted venison, sliced salmon on a bed of fresh green watercress, a duck that had been roasted crisp, set in a pond of plum sauce, a rabbit stew with carrots, and leeks in a rich wine gravy. There was a dish of new green peas, fresh bread still warm from the ovens, two cheeses, cherry conserves and sweet butter. There was nothing served him that wasn't one of his favorites. Pears stewed in sweet wine, along with tiny sugar wafers, completed the meal. The duke ate with gusto, and when he had finally finished, his mood was mellow.

"Ye're still angry wi' me," he noted, turning to Flanna.

"Aye," she agreed calmly.

"Yet ye served me a fine dinner," he noted.

"I dinna want to starve ye, and besides, I want a favor from ye, Patrick," she told him boldly.

The duke cocked a thick black eyebrow at his wife.

"Ye promised me I might renovate Brae," she began. "I want to go and do it before my bairn is born. I hae never before held my anger so in check, Patrick. If I am to cool that ire, I must be away from ye. Not for long, mind ye. I dinna intend following the example of yer grandmother Leslie, but I need to be by myself for a short time. Can ye understand that, Patrick?"

"My mam never left my da," he complained.

"I am nae yer mam," she said hotly, "and as I remember it, yer mam went all the way to France to escape yer da when he pressed her too closely. Can ye nae recall yer own family's history? I hae committed it to memory. The women in yer family were none of them weak. They were proud and gallant. There is nae one of them who would have suffered the insult that ye hae hurled at me, my lord."

"Verra well," he told her contritely. "If ye wish to go to Brae, then ye may go, Flanna."

"Thank ye. I will take Aggie and Ian More wi' me. Angus felt it would be good to hae him wi' us. The bairns will remain here wi' ye so ye will nae be lonely. I dinna want their lives disrupted further, and they need their lessons, ye will agree. I am sure," Flanna said.

"When will ye go?" he asked her. He didn't want her to go. He had been such a fool to accuse her of perfidy, but he had been angry that she had kept her news from him. The words had streamed from his mouth before he could contain them. Even as he said them, he had regretted them. He had no cause to suspect her of deceiving him.

"In a day or two," she said quietly. *Damn him!* Why could he not apologize to her? Would his pride destroy their marriage? Their child could not come into this world safely until he admitted his fault. But there was time, Flanna told herself. The child would come sometime in August according to the calculations she and Una had made.

"Ye'll need workers," the duke noted.

"Aye," she agreed. "Angus says the roof requires work, and a new stable will need to be built. The old one hae collapsed. The castle is filthy, but 'tis nae a big place like Glenkirk. Once the men do the heavy work, Aggie and I can make it habitable again."

"Why? I thought ye but meant to repair it so it does nae fall down," Patrick said.

"Brae is for our second son, my lord, provided we hae a second son. If nae, then for a daughter, one day. I hae always wanted to live at Brae. Once our bairn is born, I canna. Glenkirk's heir must grow up at Glenkirk," Flanna told him. "So, wi' yer permission, I will restore my mother's home and remain there for a little while." She gave him a quick, brief smile.

"I dinna like being parted from ye, lady," he grumbled.

"When ye accused me of deceit, my lord, ye separated us," she responded sharply. "I need time from ye to cool my ire. My choler canna be good for the bairn, Patrick."

He nodded reluctantly. "Aye," he agreed. Reaching out, he took a stray lock of her hair between his fingers a moment and fondled it. *God's boots, she is so beautiful,* he thought. He wanted her now as he had never wanted her before, but Patrick Leslie knew he had turned his wife's passion to fury. *Flaming Flanna,* her family had warned him that she was called. Her anger against him was hot, but it burned a cold heat. Reluctantly he released the silky tress.

Flanna arose from the high board. "I am tired," she said. "Good night, my lord. God grant ye a good rest." Curtsying to him formally, she then turned and left the hall.

Patrick reached for his goblet and drank deep. Would she ever forgive him? Sultan, the cat, leapt into his lap and began to purr as he settled himself. "Hae ye come to comfort me, old friend?" the duke inquired of the orange feline.

Sultan dug his well-honed claws into the duke's thigh, kneading vigorously as his rumbling purr increased in resonance.

Patrick Leslie laughed softly. And that was all the comfort he was going to get for the interim, he realized. His hand caressed the big cat affectionately. "Well," he said, "we managed before her, and I imagine we can manage for a while wi'out her, although I dinna like it. I suppose, sooner than later, I'll hae to apologize, although 'tis she who ran off and was a disobedient wife. I may be guilty of foolish words, but is she nae guilty of bad behavior?"

Sultan looked up at the duke as if to say, *"Dinna be a fool, my lord. Apologize."* The look was so clear Patrick would have sworn he heard an impatient voice speaking the words. Then the cat put its head down on the duke's lap and went to sleep.

Patrick chuckled softly and continued stroking Sultan. The orange beast was good company. His gaze swept the Great Hall, and he found its familiarity comforting. His father had left Glenkirk long ago after the tragic death of his first family. He had gone down into England and quietly served King James. As a boy he had visited the court of the Great Elizabeth. While James Leslie had liked his home, he had not had the passion for it that his eldest son did. Patrick realized that he never wanted to live anywhere else but Glenkirk. Whatever happened with the king, the Duke of Glenkirk would not go to court. His little sister, Autumn, had called him old before his time. She had always been eager to travel, to see new places, but not he.

He considered his brother Charlie, whom he had always thought much like him. But Charlie had left his home at Queen's Malvern and joined with the king after his wife had been murdered by Cromwell's men. Would he leave Glenkirk under similar circumstances? Patrick wondered. Nay. He would not. He thought about his mother's estate manager in Ireland, Rory Maguire. His mother had spoken often, and fondly, of the Irishman who had been the son of the former lord of Maguire's Ford. Rory's family had gone into exile in France rather than submit to the English, but not Rory. He loved his land and felt an obligation to it and its people. *As I do for Glenkirk*, Patrick considered.

"More wine, my lord?" Angus was at his side.

"Aye. Get a goblet and join me," the duke said.

Angus Gordon poured two goblets of wine and, handing one to Patrick, sat opposite him. "To the heir!" he said, raising his goblet.

"Aye, to my heir!" the duke agreed. He took a draught of the rich ruby-colored liquid, then said, "She's leaving me, Angus."

"Only for a little time so she may work off her temper, my lord. Ye hurt her grievously wi' yer words."

The duke flushed. "She told ye, then?"

"Aye, she did, my lord. Ye know that Flanna and I are kin. I am her mam's elder brother, but, my lord, I am yer kin as well," Angus said. "The grandfather for who ye are named, the fourth Earl of Glenkirk, Patrick Leslie who was the husband of Catriona Hay, sired a daughter named Jessie on a lass called Bride Forbes. When she was twenty, my mother died giving birth to me. As ye see, I am a big man, and they say I was a large bairn. Andrew Gordon, the Earl of Brae, was my father. I was born just before he married Anne Keith, who was my sister Maggie's mam. So, my lord, as ye see, we share a Leslie grandfather and are cousins. I am a man who feels strongly about his family. I love my niece, but I hae come to love ye, too, my lord. If ye will trust me as Flanna trusts me, I will guard yer interests as I do hers."

"I never knew my grandfather Leslie," the duke said. He was surprised, but not greatly so by Angus Gordon's revelation. "Hae ye seen his portrait in the family gallery? Ye hae his look about ye, and now that I know yer lineage, I understand why ye hae seemed so damned familiar to me since ye came to Glenkirk. How many years do ye hae?"

"Fifty-three come Lammas this year," was the answer.

The duke nodded. "Ye're a good man, Angus Gordon, and aye, ye hae my trust." He sighed. "What am I to do, Angus?"

"Ye're nae ready yet, my lord," came the amused reply. "Ye know what must be done, but ye're nae ready to do it."

"I must apologize," Patrick said.

"Aye, ye must," Angus agreed.

"But 'twas she who ran off," Patrick complained, a hand brushing through his dark hair fretfully.

"Aye, she did," Angus concurred, drinking down some of his wine.

"She dinna apologize to me for her conduct," Patrick said.

"Nor will she," Angus told him. "Ye must understand, my lord, that Flanna is a verra independent woman. After her mam died, there was nae one to care about her but for Una Brodie. That poor woman had her hands full wi' her own bairns and keeping Killiecairn just like old Lachlann expected it to be kept. None of her sisters-in-law would gie her much help, for they knew Aulay Brodie was his father's heir, and Una was, therefore, the next lady of the house. Una had scarcely a moment for herself, let alone a wild lass who rarely listened to anyone but herself. I did what I could for Flanna, but I am nae a nursemaid.

"My niece has always done as she pleased. Becoming yer wife was nae bound to turn her into a model of deportment. She's too

damned old to change, my lord. Her mam, now, was clever. Meg
knew how to get her own way while appearing to do exactly what ye
wanted." He chuckled with the memory. "Unfortunately she died
before she might pass on that talent to Flanna. But the lass is nae
stupid. She will learn in time how to manage us all wi'out butting
heads wi' us. And in the meantime, we will hae to be patient because we love her."

He smiled at the younger man. "She will go to Brae and make it
beautiful the way she has always wanted to do. And when 'tis finished she will play at being the lady of Brae. And by that time her
temper will hae cooled, my lord. I'll put it into her head to invite ye
to see what she has accomplished. I hope by then ye'll be ready to
apologize to her for yer words. If ye do, I expect ye'll both come
back to Glenkirk together while I remain behind to close up Brae. It
must nae be allowed to fall into disrepair again, my lord. Flanna
means to hae the earldom back for her second son one day, and his
home must be ready for him."

"I agree," the duke said, and then he grinned at Angus Gordon.
"Ye scheme like a Leslie, my friend." Then he stood up. "I'm for
bed."

Angus Gordon arose, too. "And I must see that all is locked and
the candles are out before I seek my own rest." He bowed to the
duke. "Good night, my lord," he said.

"Good night, *cousin*," Patrick Leslie said, and left the hall.

For a moment the unshakeable Angus Gordon was startled, but
then he smiled to himself and went about his duties as always.

Flanna did not depart Glenkirk for several days after that, for she
was secure in the knowledge that she might go unimpeded. With
her uncle's aid, she gathered the workmen she would need.
Supplies were dispatched along with a party of clansmen who would
erect a shelter for the workers and sweep out the hall so their lady
might reside there temporarily. The Stuart children were disappointed that they were not to go with Flanna, for they had grown
close to their aunt.

"When Brae is restored and ready for visitors, ye shall be the first
that I welcome," Flanna promised them.

"Is Brae to be a hunting lodge?" Freddie wanted to know.

"Brae was my mother's family home. The earls of Brae hae lived there since the time of the first King James, and before that the lairds of Brae were the lords there. If God wills it, Freddie, I will gie yer uncle several sons. Brae is to be for the second of them. I dinna want to wait until he is born." She smiled.

"I shall be the Duke of Lundy one day," Freddie told her. "I am my father's heir. Willy is only Lord Stuart. I don't know what he shall have but his good name."

"Papa will provide for him," Brie spoke up. "It is a family tradition to provide for all the sons and daughters. I shall marry well, of course." She sighed dramatically. "If this horrid war is ever over and done with, and I can go home to take my place in society."

"You are too young right now for society," Freddie said wisely. "We all are. However, I want to go home, too, so we must pray for our king to be restored to his throne so Papa will come and get us."

"Are ye nae happy here?" Flanna asked them. Until now, they had not expressed a great desire to return to England. Did it have something to do with her leaving Glenkirk? They had lost their mother, and now she was leaving them as well.

"You are most kind and very hospitable to us all," Brie spoke up, "but we miss our mother, and we miss Queen's Malvern."

"Yer mam is dead, Brie," Flanna said gently.

"I know," Brie replied, "but it would give me comfort to sit by her grave so I might talk with her again."

"Ye may talk wi' her wherever ye are, Brie," Flanna responded. "Yer mam is wi' God in heaven. Only her bones rest at Queen's Malvern."

"Do you think she would hear me here at Glenkirk?" Brie asked. "She never came to Glenkirk, you know."

"Yer mam knows just where ye are," Flanna assured her niece. "Ye can see the whole wide world from heaven, I hae been told."

"*You can?*" Sabrina Stuart's young face was suddenly lit with a smile. "And our mother can see Papa, too?"

"Of course," Flanna said.

"Will there be a war, Flanna?" the girl asked.

"Aye, there will be a war," Flanna said, "but we should be verra safe here at Glenkirk. War rarely comes to us. We must march from our Highlands to meet war in this case, Brie."

"And Papa will be with the king, won't he?" Brie queried.

"Yer papa is a Stuart, Brie. Aye, his loyalty will be wi' King Charles II. All of our loyalties should be wi' the king."

"Then, why is Uncle Patrick not with them?" Freddie demanded to know.

"Yer uncle is as loyal as any to his king," Flanna said, "but this war the king will fight is nae about Scotland, bairns. 'Tis about England. Yer uncle will nae fight for England, nor will he send his clansmen to fight for England. Yer da, however, is English. 'Tis his duty to fight for king and country," Flanna explained. "Yer uncle is an honorable man, and he will remain here to keep Glenkirk and his clan safe, for wars hae a tendency of spilling over into places that they should nae go. If the king's war came to Scotland, then yer uncle would fight, and so would his clansmen."

Both Brie and her brother nodded their understanding of Flanna's explanation.

Hidden in the shadows, Patrick Leslie had listened to his wife and the children. He was touched that despite their differences Flanna would not criticize him. More and more he was realizing that despite her less-than-elegant upbringing, this young woman was the perfect duchess for Glenkirk in this particular time. *And he loved her.*

Chapter

14

On July twenty-third, Henry Lindley, Marquis of Westleigh, rode into the courtyard of Glenkirk Castle. He was tired, wet, and chilled; *and* he finally understood the desire his grandmother Gordon and his own mother had for an English summer each year. Only September and October were tolerable in Scotland, he recalled. The marquis dismounted his horse stiffly. He had been riding north for several long days, coming from his own estates at Cadby in England's midlands. Having spent some of his youth at Glenkirk, Lord Lindley knew his way and went directly into the Great Hall.

Angus Gordon immediately came forward to greet the guest, wondering who he was. The man looked weary and worn. "Welcome to Glenkirk, sir," Angus said.

"I am Henry Lindley, Marquis of Westleigh. Fetch my brother, the duke, immediately," was the answer.

"At once, my lord," Angus said low, and he signaled a serving wench to bring their guest wine. Then he hurried from the hall.

"Uncle Henry?" A small figure rose from a chair by one of the fireplaces. *"Uncle Henry!"* Sabrina Stuart threw down her embroidery frame and ran across the hall to fling herself into Henry Lindley's welcoming arms.

"Sabrina, my dear child." The marquis hugged the young girl.

Then he set her back from him, and said, "Why, Brie, I believe you have grown since I last saw you. You shall be a great beauty one day."

Sabrina giggled, pleased, for she did love flattery. Then she said, "Uncle, what are you doing here?"

"I have come to see my brother," he said with a smile at her.

"All the way from England, and during hostilities?" Brie queried him closely. She was young, but she was not foolish. "Is my father all right, uncle? Tell me my father is safe!"

"I have not heard from your father since you departed England last year, my child," the marquis answered her honestly. "You would know more, my dear, than I would."

"We have not seen Papa since Christmas. He left almost immediately afterward to go to Perth to be with the king when he was crowned," Sabrina explained. "He must be very busy, for he has not been back."

"You and your brothers are happy here?" Henry asked her. Had it been safe, he would have offered his niece and his two nephews a home at Cadby; but Charlie's in-laws were sour-faced Puritans who wanted to take his three children to raise themselves, and his brother could not allow it. His late sister-in-law's parents were not aware of Glenkirk.

"We love it here," Brie said, "but we miss Queen's Malvern. Of course, since Aunt Flanna has been at Brae, it hasn't been as much fun as when she is here; but she wants to have Brae for her second son, and it needed to be refurbished," Brie explained.

"Who is your Aunt Flanna?" Henry Lindley asked his niece, puzzled.

"Why, she is Uncle Patrick's wife, and she's having a baby in a few more weeks," Sabrina informed him. "She's very fair, and she is the best archer I have ever seen. She has taught me to use the longbow, but I am not nearly as good at it as she is. I don't think I will ever be," Sabrina sighed.

Henry Lindley sought a chair and sat down heavily. He surely hadn't heard the young girl correctly. When had Patrick found himself a wife? And why had their mother not mentioned it in her letters to him from France? It was all very confusing, and then his younger brother entered the hall. The marquis immediately arose.

"Henry! Welcome to Glenkirk, and what the hell are ye doing here?" Patrick greeted his eldest brother. The two men embraced.

"Send Brie from the hall," Henry Lindley said softly. "We need to talk, and I would not frighten her." Then he sat down again.

"Brie, go and find yer brothers," the duke told his niece. "And make certain they come into the hall looking respectable, nae wi' torn garments and dirt on their faces." He chuckled. "We dinna want yer uncle to think they hae gone wild in my care, eh?"

"Aye, uncle, I'll see them washed up and properly garbed," Brie promised. She bustled from the hall to do his bidding.

The duke turned to Henry Lindley, sitting down opposite him as a servant offered them each a goblet of Archambault wine. "To our mam," Patrick said, raising his goblet.

"To Mam," Henry agreed, and raised his goblet in toast.

"Now," the duke said, "why are ye here, Henry? It canna hae been an easy trip. Is Mam all right?"

"She is fine," Henry assured his brother. "And, aye, it was not an easy trip. You have no idea what it is like in England now, Patrick. There is an air of fear that permeates everything and everyone. You can trust no one any longer, even your own servants. Every word must be carefully thought over before it is spoken lest someone misconstrue its meaning. There is no decent society any longer, for we all fear to meet. We keep to ourselves, pay our taxes, and make a public show of prayer in church each week. Our dress and demeanor have to be modest, and we speak of nothing of any consequence but for the weather, our health, and the farming. Those who have been foolish enough to speak out against Cromwell and his ilk have found their estates confiscated, their families thrown out of their homes and set to wander upon the high road, shunned by friends and relations alike, all of whom are afraid of the same fate.

"In order to come to Glenkirk, I had to go to the local authorities. I told them our mother was very ill in France, that I must notify you and feared to send a messenger lest he be stopped by the Scots rebels once he crossed the border. They understood that only a gentleman of my rank, with a half brother in Scotland, could avoid such a situation. So, I was finally given the proper documents, which I have had to show a dozen times daily as I rode north." Henry Lindley ran his hand through his dark hair, now showing silver threads here and there, and he sighed deeply.

"If Mam is all right, then why are ye here?" Patrick asked him.

"Mama is very worried about Charlie. Half of all she writes concerns her fears for him," Henry said. "She understands his loyalty to his Stuart family. From the moment of his birth he was treated as one of them, despite coming into this world on the wrong side of the blanket. Both old King James and his queen doted on Charlie and made no secret of it. I have always thought if they might have made him their heir, they would have. But Charlie has always avoided politics, never pushing himself forward. Even the late king's French queen adores him for his deferential manners. And had Bess not been murdered by Cromwell's people, Charlie would have done what I am doing. He would have kept his lips sealed and his head low, waiting for better times to come again to England. But mama is now afraid for our brother. While she knows he cannot return home to Queen's Malvern, she wants him to remain at Glenkirk with you and his children until this chaos is over and done with and reasonable men rule once again."

"Charlie is wi' the king, Henry," Patrick said.

"I know, Brie told me," the marquis answered. "You have to go and fetch him back, make him understand that he cannot throw his life away in this civil strife. God only knows if this particular Stuart will ever again sit on England's throne, but our brother must not throw away his life in this struggle, Patrick!"

"Why do ye ask me to go?" Patrick demanded of his elder. "Why can ye nae fetch him back to Cadby?"

"If I am found to have visited this king, I will be considered a traitor to Cromwell's regime. Most people do not even know that my half brother is Prince Henry Stuart's only child. If they did, it would be even worse for my family than it is now, Patrick. Mama is frightened that Charlie will be killed, or worse, that he will not be killed, but captured and made an example as a traitor to Cromwell's government. I have not a doubt that our brother would go gallantly to his death as other Stuarts before him have, but do we really want that?"

"I hae other responsibilities now, Henry," Patrick said. "I hae a wife, and we will soon hae a bairn. And I hae Charlie's bairns to shelter and protect."

"Brie told me that you wed. Who is she? I did not think you would ever marry, little brother," Henry chuckled.

"Her name is Flanna. She was a Brodie of Killiecairn. They are simple Highlanders. Flanna had something that I wanted. I offered Lachlann Brodie double its value. But the old laird, her father, would only gie it to me if I took her to wife. So I did! Our mother advised me to marry before she left England for France. She said I had a duty to Glenkirk." He grinned. "Flanna's uncle, the great fellow who welcomed ye, is Angus Gordon. His da was the last Earl of Brae. He was, of course, born on the wrong side of the blanket like Charlie," Patrick explained. "And to make things even more interesting, Henry, Angus's grandfather, was my grandfather Leslie. The Patrick for whom I am named. Angus was a part of my wife's dowry." The duke chuckled.

"When do I get to meet your wife?" Henry asked, quite curious.

"Tomorrow, when ye're rested, we'll go to Brae. Ye can meet her then," Patrick promised.

"Why is she at Brae?" Henry queried.

"The lands that belong to Brae were what Flanna possessed that I so desired. She has always wanted to restore the castle. She has been at Brae since late April doing just that. She wants it for a second son one day. But she is rightly angry wi' me. I shall soon hae to apologize to her if my heir is to be born at Glenkirk where he should be born," Patrick explained.

"What did you do?" Henry wondered.

"'Tis between us, brother," Patrick responded, "but I shall hae to make it right wi' her verra soon. So, ye can certainly see, I canna go after Charlie."

"*You must,*" Henry Lindley said. "You can get through the lines because you are a Scot. You have to do this for Mama, Patrick."

"Charlie will go down into England wi' the king, and all will be well, Henry. Ye worry too much," Patrick gently mocked his brother. "And the English royalists will join wi' their king as he marches south. There is little danger that I can see, and Charlie will hae put the king in his debt for the future by his loyalty."

"You don't understand," Henry said grimly. "Few, if any, will join the king, Patrick. The Scots do not now have a big enough army, and the English lords, like me, do not want to endanger what they still retain to fight for Charles II. There is also, and you well know it, a prejudice against the Scots. The English have never liked the Stuarts, but they had no other choice but to accept them. As for your countrymen, Patrick, they have lost too many battles of late despite the fact they had the superior odds. This time it is Cromwell who has the greater force. You must believe me, Patrick, the English will not rise up for the king! He is on his own, may God have mercy on him and all who foolishly follow him right now."

"Are the Stuarts finished in England, then?" Patrick queried.

"I don't know," Henry answered his sibling. "I honestly don't know. If the king won a great victory, then perhaps some would flock to him. And if he then won a second victory, the momentum would grow. Then perhaps he might retake his kingdom, and the royalists would rise up once again and crowd to his banner, but not now. He must prove himself worthy first, and he has not the forces to do so. You have to find Charlie and make him see reason. If he will only return to Glenkirk, I can deal with him myself, but I cannot be seen anywhere near the king and his forces, Patrick. And let me assure you that there are spies everywhere these days."

"I dinna know, Henry. Wi' Flanna so near her time, I hesitate to leave her," the duke said. "We will resolve our dispute when I take ye to meet her. Then she will come home, and our first child will be born here, which is as it should be. I am nae even certain that I know where the king's forces are right now."

"They are massing at the border," Henry said. "Cromwell's forces have outflanked the king's people to the east, keeping them in the west. They must go south now. There is no other choice. The Scots have not exactly rallied to the Stuart banner either, so they can't go north. I don't know when the king plans to advance, but surely if you travel alone, you can reach Charlie before he ruins himself. Then bring him back, and you will be in time for the birth of your child. Patrick, I did not come this far to fail. We must do this for Charlie, for his children, *for Mama.*"

"Uncle Henry!" The marquis's nephews ran into the hall.

"We will discuss this again when we are alone," the duke said. "I dinna want the bairns frightened. Say ye came to bring them news from Mam. They need nae know how difficult things are in England now."

Henry Lindley nodded in agreement and then, reaching out, enfolded his two nephews in a bear hug. "Bless my soul, lads, you have grown. Willy! You are out of skirts, eh? And what has happened to your curls?"

Lord William Stuart grinned proudly at his uncle. "Gone!" he said triumphantly. He did not mention to his Uncle Henry that he had cut them off himself for they kept getting tangled in the brambles. Nor did he mention how his old nurse, Biddy, cried when she discovered what he had done.

"Why, you are a wee manikin now," the marquis remarked with a smile. "And, Freddie, how are you, my boy? Keeping up with your lessons, I hope."

"Aye, uncle. The Anglican priest teaches us each day but Sunday. And we hae a Scots boy, Fingal Brodie, who learns with us," Freddie told his English uncle. "He is Aunt Flanna's nephew and would read the law one day. Uncle Patrick says he will send him to university in Aberdeen when he is old enough. He is a grand fellow!"

"Indeed," the marquis said. "Well, it is never a bad thing to have a barrister in one's family."

"Why are you here, Uncle Henry?" Sabrina, who had just returned to join them, asked.

"I have come to bring you news from your grandmother Leslie, my dears," the marquis replied smoothly.

"Oh, yes!" the children chorused, and they settled themselves on the floor in the space between the duke and the marquis.

"Your grandmother and Lady Autumn reached France safely,"

Henry began. "They were made most welcome by our French relations and settled themselves at Belle Fleurs. That is a charming little chateau that your grandmother possesses. When young King Louis came to a nearby chateau, your grandmother and Aunt Autumn went to meet him."

"Oh," Sabrina exclaimed. "Autumn is so fortunate!"

"Why, Brie," the duke said. "You have met a king."

"But not a French king," Sabrina replied. "Besides, King Charles is not much of a king these days, Uncle Henry."

Her two uncles laughed, and Henry continued on with his recitation.

"Three noble gentlemen have courted your Aunt Autumn. A duke, a count, and a marquis. Now she is to be married, my dears!" he told them all. "Your grandmother writes that at the end of September, Autumn will wed with the Marquis d'Auriville. She is very pleased."

"So," Patrick mused, "the bairn of the family will be a wife. Damn, I wish we could all be there, Henry! And I wish she did nae hae to wed wi' a foreigner. We'll nae see her again. At least Mam will return home to Glenkirk now."

"Mama intends remaining in France with Autumn and her husband," Henry informed his younger brother. "I do not expect we will see her back in England, or Scotland, until this civil disturbance is concluded."

"We live in peace here at Glenkirk," Patrick replied stubbornly.

"Only by virtue of your isolation, brother, but one day you may not have that security," Henry advised his sibling. "If war engulfed Scotland as completely as it has done in England, you could not even hide here at Glenkirk."

"May it never come to that," Patrick Leslie said.

"Amen!" his brother responded.

In the morning, the duke sent a messenger to his wife at Brae, telling her that his brother had arrived from England, and they would come to visit with her permission. The messenger returned in late afternoon to say the duchess would welcome her husband

and his brother on the following day, and the children must come along, too.

"She likes the youngsters," Henry observed to his brother as they sat late that night alone in the hall.

"Aye, she loves Charlie's bairns and hae been a good foster mam to them since they arrived here late last year," the duke said.

"Do you love her?" the marquis asked frankly.

Patrick smiled softly. "Aye, I hae come to love her for all she is a stubborn and hot-tempered wench. I hae never known such an independent and difficult creature as my wife, but aye, Henry, I do love her."

"Does she love you?" was the next query.

Again the duke chuckled. "Aye, she does, despite the fact that I vex her sorely," he told his brother.

"Tell me now, what has caused this rift between you?" Henry coaxed quietly.

"When Charlie was here, he filled her full of nonsense about the king and his noble quest to regain his throne," Patrick finally began. "Flanna is unsophisticated and ingenuous. I doubt she ever ventured far from Brae or Killiecairn in all her life. I certainly dinna know of her existence. She was intimidated by all the stories our housekeeper, Mary More-Leslie, told her of previous ladies of Glenkirk, so when Charlie departed Glenkirk, my wife followed after him. She wanted to make her mark so, as she so charmingly put it, she wouldnae be remembered as the do-naught duchess."

"Damn me, the wench must be clever," the Marquis of Westleigh noted admiringly. "Why did Charlie not return her?"

"He dinna know she was on his trail," Patrick admitted. "She sent to her family for her nephew, a lad wi' a talent for mischief himself. Then she gained the aid of one of my men-at-arms, a guileless lad who admires her. Together they followed after Charlie, having convinced me that her nephew came from Killiecairn by himself to bring her back for a visit to her da. It wasna until Charlie arrived in Perth that she revealed herself and her purpose to him. Flanna had come to meet the king and to pledge her loyalty to him. She wanted to raise a levy for him, she said."

Henry chortled. "It sounds just like something Mama or Madame Skye would have done," he said. "Well, continue on, little brother, and tell me what happened. You obviously quickly discovered the deception, but how?"

"My brother-in-law, the eldest of six of them, came to Glenkirk. It was his son who was wi' my wife," Patrick explained. "It was then I realized where she had really gone."

"She bloody well might have succeeded if you hadn't had that piece of good fortune," Henry noted. "Continue on."

"I immediately went after her, of course. By the time I reached Perth, the king was crowned, and Flanna had met him not once, but twice. When I arrived, she was alone wi' him, in her shift, a blanket wrapped about her. I dinna know who the man was, and I drew my weapon. Only Charlie's timely intervention saved us all," Patrick said.

"*My God!* You drew your sword on the king?" Henry Lindley was absolutely horrified. Such an action was a treasonable offense.

"Calm yourself, brother. I was forgiven my ignorance, but what would ye hae done if ye found yer wife in such a situation?" Patrick demanded. "*In her shift?*"

"Where were they?" Henry said. "And what were they doing?"

"In the dayroom, and both were on their feet, and he was kissing her hand," Patrick replied.

"Did your wife seem as if she had been assaulted or tumbled willingly?" Henry inquired.

"Nay," Patrick answered his elder sibling. "She was like a young queen, I tell ye, wi' her hand being kissed. She stood tall, and elegant, that blanket wrapped about her, holding it to her modestly wi' one hand while he kissed the other."

"And you asked your wife afterward what had happened?" Henry was beginning to understand, he thought.

"Nay, we fought, but then we finally made it up. Our difficulties stem from the fact that when Flanna told me she was expecting our bairn, I asked her if it was mine or the king's," Patrick admitted.

Henry Lindley's mouth fell open with his shock. "*You didn't!*" he gasped, horrified. "My God, Patrick, you are a great fool!"

"I was jealous," the duke admitted.

"Worse! A jealous fool," his brother said. "Well, now I understand your situation. It is nothing at all what I anticipated. If you had no reason to suspect your wife of being unfaithful, Patrick, other than the facts as you have recited them to me, why on earth did you ask such a question?"

"She was still attempting to raise a levy for the king," Patrick admitted, shamefaced. "Her father was ill unto death, and her eldest brother came for her. She went to Killiecairn wi' him and intended to begin her recruitment there. Then she said she would go on to Huntley." He sighed. "Her family laughed at her for her pretensions and refused to hae any part in her plans. They also decided to bring her back to me before she could run off. Only when she returned to Glenkirk did she tell me she was wi' bairn, and I, fool I am, asked that awful question."

" 'Tis a wonder she didn't kill you," Henry said, shaking his head. "You know, of course, what you must do to heal this unfortunate rift."

The duke nodded. "Aye, I must apologize to my wife and beg her forgiveness. Even then I wonder if I can ever heal the breach."

"If she loves you, she will forgive you," Henry said wisely. "That she left you for a time tells me that. Rather than remain here to let your words fester each time she saw you, she went to Brae and has occupied herself ever since in the restoration of her mother's home. God's blood, Patrick, your wife was a respectable girl from a good family. She had no reputation for deceit. I do not have to tell you what our mother would have done if Jemmie Leslie had asked her such a question."

"Flanna is nae our mother," Patrick said irritably. He knew he had done the wrong thing, and having Henry carry on about it so was like his brother rubbing salt into his raw wound.

"Nay, she isn't our mother, but any decent woman would have been offended by such a query." Then Henry Lindley smiled. "Now I am even more curious to meet your wife, little brother. That she didn't kill you speaks well of her character and her patience."

"They call her Flaming Flanna, and nae just for her red hair," Patrick told his elder sibling.

Henry laughed heartily. "Well," he said, "we shall see whether that temper has been calmed when we go to Brae tomorrow. Have you seen her since she left you?"

Patrick shook his head. "She said I was nae to come. I took her at her word, for Flanna is a woman who speaks plainly."

"So you have not seen your wife in over three months, Patrick?" Henry laughed again. "This is, indeed, a formidable woman that you have married, brother, that you obey her will so easily."

"I dinna want to harm the bairn," the duke answered.

"Ahhh," Henry said, "so there is no doubt in your mind that it is your child?"

"Nay, there isna, Henry," his brother admitted. "She was a virgin when I married her, and a woman of firm principles. I love her, but when I saw her wi' another man, my jealousy simply overcame me. I know Flanna would nae betray me."

"You had best tell her that immediately when we reach Brae tomorrow, then," Henry advised.

"I intend to," Patrick said. "I never want her from me again."

"*After you fetch Charlie back to Glenkirk,*" Henry said.

Patrick Leslie sighed deeply. "Verra well," he reluctantly agreed, "but ye must remain here at Glenkirk wi' my wife while I am gone, Henry. I canna leave Flanna wi' nay one but a houseful of servants and three young bairns. Angus Gordon hae nae the authority that ye do."

"I will stay," Henry said. "It should not take you that long, riding out alone."

"Aye," Patrick agreed. "I'll hae to go alone. If I traveled wi' a troop of my men, it might be believed that I was joining the king. I dinna want that. I am safer alone and can move more quickly. Once Charlie and I begin our return journey to Glenkirk, anyone watching will nae think us a threat, for we will be going in the wrong direction for a fight."

In the morning, the two brothers set off for Brae with their niece and two young nephews. As they exited the forest and came onto the shore of Loch Brae, they stopped for a moment to rest their mounts and to look across the blue water to the small, dark stone castle.

" 'Tis beautiful!" Brie cried, clapping her hands together. "No wonder Aunt Flanna wants to live there!"

"Is nae Glenkirk beautiful, Brie?" the duke asked.

"Yes, uncle, and bigger, too. Glenkirk is impressive and grand for all it is small, but Brae! 'Tis like something out of a knight's tale. I have never seen a castle on an island."

They rode around the loch until they finally reached the bridge connecting the island and the main shore. The bridge, which had been so rotted and rickety when he had last been at Brae, was now rebuilt. Their horses clopped slowly across the span. Patrick noted that much of the growth that had obscured his view several months prior was now gone. While some trees remained in the field between the bridge and the castle itself, one could now see the structure quite plainly. They rode from the bridge up a narrow road through those trees and into Brae.

A new stable had been constructed of timbers and stone with a sturdy slate roof. This stable would better stand the test of time than had the previous one. The courtyard was swept clean, and it was very quiet. There were no workmen in evidence. The duke looked up and could see from his vantage that the castle roof was also restored. He led his party up the stairs and into the castle itself. Ian More saw the duke and, bowing, hurried forward.

"Yer Grace," he greeted his master. "The lady is awaiting ye in her hall." He led them into the Great Hall of Brae where a fire burned this day in the fireplace.

Flanna arose slowly from her place, smiling at the look on her husband's face as he viewed her for the first time in several months. "Welcome to Brae, my lords," she saluted them. "Ian, fetch wine for our guests and some sweets for the bairns." She then held out her arms to the three children, who rushed to hug her.

"Aunt," Sabrina said, "you are so . . . so . . ."

"*Fat!*" Willy said.

Flanna laughed. "That is because I hae a bairn growing inside of me, Willy. When the bairn pops itself out, I shall be slender again."

"When will the bairn be ready, aunt?" Freddie wondered.

"Soon," Flanna told them. "Now, here is Aggie. Run to her, and she will show ye all of my wee Brae." She turned to Patrick when the children had left them, and said, "Well, sir, what hae ye to say to me? Or will ye continue to persist in yer foolishness?"

"Will ye accept my apology, lass?" he replied simply, thinking now that he had begun, the words were not hard at all to say.

"If ye will admit to being a jealous fool, I may," she responded.

"I love ye, Flanna. I lost both my temper and my wits when I saw another man admiring ye. Please forgie me, lass. I hae been miserable wi'out ye, and I want ye to come home," Patrick Leslie told his wife honestly. She was, he realized, more important to him than his injured pride.

Her eyes filled with quick tears, which immediately spilled down her cheeks. "I forgie ye, Patrick, wi' all my heart, for how can I nae when I love ye so verra much?"

He put his arms about her and kissed the salty tears from her pale face. "Ye'll come back?"

"Of course I will," she said, giving him a quick kiss on the lips. "Glenkirk's next duke should be born in his own home."

"*Ahem!*" The Marquis of Westleigh coughed discreetly.

The lovers broke apart, laughing, and the duke introduced his eldest brother to his wife.

"Ye're most welcome to Brae, sir, and to Scotland," Flanna said, thinking that he was very handsome. She particularly admired his turquoise eyes.

"And I, madame, am most delighted to meet the lady who has brought my little brother to both his knees and his senses," Henry Lindley teased her with a smile.

Flanna colored prettily, saying, "Now I hae met two of my husband's brothers. I am sorry I canna know yer mam."

"She'll come back one day," Henry promised her, "but come, madame, and sit down again. My wife has given me several children. I know what a woman needs at this point in her life, even if my dunderhead of a brother does not." He led Flanna back to her chair and seated her. "Now, tell me, when is the heir or the heiress due to enter this world? I should like to remain for the event so I may report it directly to our mother, whom your husband has yet to inform of his marriage to you. I assume only Charlie knew."

"Only because he came wi' his bairns last autumn," Patrick answered his brother. "How am I to send a message to our mother in the midst of all this strife, Henry? Few come visiting to Glenkirk. Perhaps a rare peddler, or tinker, but could I trust such a person to bring a letter, and where? At least there is some traffic between England and France. 'Tis easier for ye than 'tis for me. I'll send a letter wi' ye when ye return to Cadby. Ye can get it to our mam, for ye hae been corresponding wi' her all along."

Suddenly Flanna said quietly, "Why hae ye come to Glenkirk, my lord? And how did ye arrive unscathed? The little that we hear tells us that the English occupy Edinburgh, and that King Charles prepares to invade England and regain it. Why, then, are ye here? Should ye nae be wi' yer family?"

"I should," Henry Lindley agreed with a smile, "but I am instead here. Our mother is afraid for Charlie's life. She wants him at Glenkirk and not with King Charles. As an Englishman, I cannot be seen in the company of Charles Stuart's army, nor his person, lest I be accused of being a traitor to the current government. Patrick, however, can."

Ian More brought the gentlemen wine, and when he had served them, he handed Flanna a goblet of spring water which she now favored.

"Ye're an Englishman, sir, and yet ye canna be seen wi' yer king? I dinna understand," Flanna said, and then she took a sip from her goblet. "Do ye nae want yer king back, sir?"

"Cromwell is too strong, and the king not yet strong enough," Henry began his explanation. "The king has been told that those of us who support him, who are called Royalists, will rise up to champion him when he comes to England. It is not so, Flanna. The king's adherents in England have survived by remaining silent and invisible. We will continue to do so because the time is not right for the restoration of our monarchy. I do not know when that time will be. In the meantime, it would be foolish of us to lose our homes and everything we hold dear, or to beggar our families and endanger our friends by imprudent conduct. There are those who do not agree with me, but believe me, they are in a minority. I will support a legitimate government, but I will not lose my ancestral home, nor everything my family cherishes, in the cause of an absent king. I cannot.

"Our mother has written of her fears for Charlie. She appreciates his loyalty to the royal Stuarts, but she does not want to lose him in this quest of the king's. I lied to the authorities in order to obtain a pass to reach Glenkirk from England. Now Patrick must go to wherever the king has his encampment and make our brother see reason. Charlie must return to Glenkirk and his children. If the Parliamentary forces catch him with the king, they will execute him."

"I dinna think Charlie will leave his cousin," Flanna said slowly. "His loyalty to the king is great. So great he was able to dissuade me from my wifely duties, and I attempted to join the king's battle myself. He will nae come. But if he does nae come, then that is his decision, for he is a man grown. However, since his mam wishes it, Patrick must go to find Charlie and attempt to turn his heart. If she had known he was wed, and expecting a bairn, I dinna think she would hae asked such a thing of him; but she dinna know, and so he must go."

They were both astounded by her words. The brothers had expected Flanna to weep and cry. They had expected shrieking, and screaming, and all manner of womanly tactics. Instead, they had been given reluctant logic. She understood. She did not like it, *but she understood.*

The Marquis of Westleigh arose and took his sister-in-law's two hands in his. He kissed them. "Madame," he said, "you are the most sensible female I have ever encountered. I salute you!"

Flanna looked up at him with a serious demeanor, withdrawing her hands from his. "I am nae pleased by this situation," she said, "but I understand the importance of family, Henry." She turned to look at her husband. "When will ye go?" she asked him.

"Fairly soon," he said, and his green-gold eyes were filled with his love and admiration for her.

"Then, we hae best return to Glenkirk in the morning. I am at the point, I fear, where I must travel slowly, my lords. It will take us the day. If ye wish to leave me now, Patrick, and depart in the morning, ye hae my permission. Yer brother will escort me in safety."

"Nay," he quickly answered her. "I will remain the night wi' ye and take ye home myself tomorrow. I will leave the day after."

"If the children have had their curiosity satisfied," Henry said, "I shall return with them to Glenkirk today. Your man, Ian, can ride with us. I'll send back a cart and an escort for Flanna on the morrow, brother. Ye hae been separated and now are to be separated again. I know if it were me, I should like an evening alone with my wife."

Flanna smiled at him. "Ye're a tactful man, sir," she said.

The three Stuart children were gathered up along with Ian. It was decided that Aggie would depart, too, and she ran to fetch her belongings.

"We hae to eat," the duke murmured to his wife.

"The supper is in the kitchen," Flanna said. "I will serve ye myself. I dinna grow up being waited upon hand and foot, although I will admit to enjoying it," she chuckled.

The children came to protest, but Flanna waved them away.

"Now, bairns," she told the trio, "I'll be home tomorrow. Yer uncle and I hae nae seen each other in months. We want to spend a wee bit of time alone. Besides, I hae nae beds for ye to sleep in, and 'twould be a bit rough for ye. Willy is too young for it."

They departed reluctantly as Patrick and Flanna stood in the gates of Brae, waving them off.

"I remember the first day I set foot here," he told her. "Ye shot at me wi' yer bow and arrows. I think I loved ye then, though I knew it nae." His arm rested lightly about her shoulders.

"Is that why ye tied me up and brought me back to my da on yer saddle?" she teased him. "Come, and help me close the gates now."

" 'Tis too much for ye, lassie," he said.

Flanna threw him an exasperated look. "Patrick," she said, "I close these gates every evening by myself. It requires little but pushing, and Ian puts the bar across. Ye can do that for me."

"Even when the clansmen were working here ye closed the gates?" he inquired of her.

"Aye, I did. I fear no man, but I dinna want a badger in my pantry, ye understand," she explained. "When we arrived, we couldna get into the kitchen for a week for a wildcat hae her litter there. Fortunately she soon moved them."

He nodded. Then he lifted the big oak bar and set it into its place across the two great gates.

"Come along," she said briskly. "We'll eat in the kitchen. I'm nae of a mind to traipse up and down the stairs in my condition." She led him around the courtyard, through a small garden, and down a narrow flight of steps into the warm kitchen.

The room was neat, swept, and clean. A fire burned in the hearth where a lidded iron pot bubbled noisily over the flames. There was the scent of fresh bread baking. In the center of the room was a well-scrubbed oak table. The duke sat down while his duchess opened a cupboard and brought forth two pewter plates and mugs which she put upon the table. One set before him, and the other to his right. From a basket on the cupboard shelf, she pulled out two carved wooden spoons she added to the place settings. He watched her, fascinated. Patrick Leslie didn't ever recall having seen his mother in a kitchen.

Flanna went to the fireplace and, opening a little iron door to one side of it, peered in. Apparently satisfied, she shoved a wooden paddle into the oven and drew out a loaf of bread which she put, paddle, pan, and all, upon the table. Disappearing into the buttery, she soon returned with a little tub of butter and a half wheel of hard yellow cheese. These she set upon the table. She gathered up the plates from the table and went to the hearth. Using a two-tined toasting fork, she lifted the lid from the bubbling kettle. A plume of steam arose from the pot. Flanna smiled, and placing one of the plates on the floor, she dipped a spoon she had drawn from her pocket into the pot and filled the plate. Then, placing it before her husband, she returned to fill the second plate for herself. Sitting down at the table, she upended the bread pan, freeing the loaf, and cut two chunks of bread for them, shoving one at him. "Eat!" she instructed him.

Patrick dipped his spoon into his plate. The aroma of a rabbit stew assailed his nostrils. He realized how hungry he was as he began to eat. The stew had a fine brown gravy. It was filled with carrots and small onions. The meat was tender.

"Damn!" Flanna muttered irritably.

"What's the matter?" he asked her.

"The wine is on the high board in the hall," she said.

"There must be something down here," he replied.

"There's a keg of ale," she admitted.

"Where?" he queried.

"In the pantry," she told him.

He gathered up their mugs and went into the pantry, returning a moment later with two mugs of the foaming ale. "I like ale wi' my stew," he told her. "It makes the game tastier, lass." Then he grinned at her. " 'Tis a cozy supper we're haeing, Flanna Leslie. We must see that Henry returns to England wi' some of our fine whiskey. 'Twill travel better than salmon or haggis," Patrick said. He sliced two large pieces of cheese and offered her one.

"Aye. 'Twas most politic of him to leave us alone, although we surely canna play our lover's games wi' my great belly," Flanna responded. "Still, I will enjoy feeling yer bulk next to me tonight, Patrick. I hae missed ye. Why could ye nae come and apologize sooner?"

"Would ye hae forgiven me sooner?" he asked her.

"Aye," she drawled slowly. Her silver eyes met his, and he knew it to be so.

"Then, I am, indeed, a fool, Flanna," he told her softly.

"Aye," she agreed readily, mopping up the gravy on her plate with a piece of bread and eating it.

He laughed. "Ye're a brave lass considering yer girth. Ye canna outrun me now," he teased her.

"I take up a good part of the bed," she said, laughing.

"I'll be anxious to see just how much," he replied.

They finished their meal. Flanna poured hot water from a kettle on the hearth, mixing it with some cooler water from a bucket, into a basin in the stone sink and washed the dishes and spoons. Patrick, taking up a cloth, dried them and replaced them in the cupboard. He then set aside an iron basin of live coals in the ashes of the fireplace for the morning. Flanna was already slowly climbing the stairs to the hall, and then to the bedchamber on the floor above that. He came behind her with the bucket and the kettle, so they would have water in which to wash before retiring.

Outside, the sky was coloring with the sunset and the twilight to follow. It was a simple bedchamber they entered, with a large bed, a small bedside table, and a trunk at the bed's foot. There was a single tapestried chair by the fireplace, which had been lit by Aggie before her departure. Flanna sat wearily upon the large bed. It was hung with dark blue velvet draperies dangling from ancient brass rings.

"It isna the lord's chamber," she told her husband, "but I can see the loch from the windows," Flanna explained. "I love looking out on the water. It changes so often and so readily. Will ye help me get my boots off, Patrick?"

He knelt and, with some difficulty, drew each of her ankle-high boots from her feet which were very swollen. "Lord, lass!" he exclaimed.

"They get that way when I hae been on my feet all day," she told him matter-of-factly. Then she stood up. "Unlace me, please."

He quickly unlaced the back of the shapeless gown that she had been wearing and helped her out of it. Flanna then padded across the room in her bare feet and, filling the basin with a mix of the water, washed herself as best she could. Then, wearing only her chemise, she climbed into bed. Removing his clothing but for his shirt, which came down over his buttocks, he washed and joined his wife in the bed.

Her belly was huge. Propping himself up on an elbow, he studied her carefully. He tried to think back to when his mother had been full with his brothers. He didn't recall that she had gotten so big.

"Put yer hand on my belly," she said to him. "The bairn is moving about, and ye'll be able to feel it."

Reaching out, he touched her gently and was startled when his hand was distinctly pushed. Looking down, he could have sworn that he saw the outline of a foot, or at least the toes. "'Tis a laddie," he told her with a grin. "No lass would hae such a big foot."

She smiled. "He is healthy, and active, and that is all I want him to be," she replied.

He couldn't resist her fertile beauty. His big hand smoothed over and about her belly with the blue veining so prominent now, even through the thin fabric of her chemise. "I fear to leave ye until the bairn is safely born," he said honestly.

"Ye canna wait for me," she told him. "Any day the king will begin his trek down into England. Ye must bring Charlie back to Glenkirk if that is what yer mam desires. She must hae loved his father deeply to so fear losing him. I will hae my bairn whether ye are here or nae here, Patrick. Yer brother hae offered to remain. I hae the Brodies if I should need them. Ye must go."

"I thought ye would be angry," he said.

"I am nae happy about it," she admitted, "but ye canna go against yer mam in this, Patrick. What if Charlie were killed? At least if ye try to bring him back, yer conscience is clear. I dinna want to live wi' a man who will spend the rest of his life feeling regret."

"Ye're an amazing woman, Flanna Leslie," he responded. "And when I return, we willnae be parted again. Will ye agree to that, lass?"

"Aye, my lord, and my love, I will readily agree to it," Flanna told him. "Now, go to sleep. Ye've lulled the bairn, and he is quiet now. We should be, too."

He took her hand in his, and they slept.

Chapter

15

On the twenty-ninth of July, the Duke of Glenkirk departed his home, leaving his pregnant wife behind in the care of his eldest brother. He did not know that the king's army was already on the move. They crossed into England on the thirty-first of the month. The duke had no choice but to follow, and so he did. He had promised Henry that he would find Charlie and attempt to convince him to come back to Scotland. If he could reach Charlie before the army penetrated too deeply into England, or there was any significant battle, perhaps he might change his Stuart brother's heart and mind.

The duke was garbed simply in woolen breeks, a pair of old boots not worth stealing, a shirt, and leather jerkin. He didn't wish to attract anyone's attention, although his horse, a large dappled gray stallion with a coal black mane and tail, was magnificent. Only his clan badge, displayed on his tam, could identify him as a Scot. His length of dark green Leslie plaid was rolled up and tied behind his saddle.

The worn leather saddlebag he carried was packed with oatcakes. The duke wished to avoid public houses. There wasn't a Highlander alive who couldn't survive on oatcakes and whatever he could catch. Patrick also carried a small flask of wine and a larger flask of water. He had his flint and steel and would be able to make a fire should he want it. He was well armed with both pistols and sword. He was self-sufficient.

Patrick Leslie had spent almost all of his life in Scotland, unlike his more traveled siblings. He had been to France once as a child. It had been a brief visit, but he had met his scandalous grandmother, Lady Bothwell. His mother had taken him to England twice, but other than that, and the little time he had spent at the university in Aberdeen, and in Perth seeking his wife, Patrick Leslie had never been away from Glenkirk. Now he followed the rumors south, attempting to catch up with the king's forces, and with his brother, the not-so-royal Stuart.

Within a few days, he was dodging the scouts from Cromwell's army, which was but a week behind Charles II. Patrick had not bargained for this, and he grumbled silently to himself as he rode. It was to have been a simple errand. Go to the king's encampment and try to get Charlie to return with him. Now, instead, he found himself crossing over into England. Ahead of him rode the too few forces of the king. Behind him came the great army of Oliver Cromwell. And in the middle of it all rode Patrick Leslie, Duke of Glenkirk, on a fool's mission. Still, he pushed deeper into England. He had given his word. And then it hit him. He had given his word. *Just like his father!*

He wondered what his mother would have said, but then, it was his mother who had insisted he go after Charlie. Or had she? Was Henry just using their mother in an effort to get Charlie out of harm's way? In an attempt to protect his own family should the connection between the Duke of Lundy and the Marquis of Westleigh be made by someone in a position to cause difficulties? Then he put such thoughts from his head. Henry might be a careful man, but he would never deliberately put one of his siblings in danger to protect his own. It simply wasn't in his nature.

The king's army moved with unbelievable swiftness. Having departed his Scottish encampment, he was over the border in only six days. Once in England he called again upon his countrymen to join him, promising to reform the Church of England according to the Covenants he had agreed to in Scotland, promising a newly elected and free parliament, and recompense to all except those involved in his father's death. Having made these public promises on English soil, he was then proclaimed King of England and Scotland before his forces with a great flourish of trumpets and a volley of shots.

Although the city of Carlisle refused to open its gates to him, the king was cheered and welcomed in the other towns and villages through which he passed. In another ten days, he was deep into England, reaching the river Mersey. Behind him, the Duke of Glenkirk rode hard, but he was always just a day behind. When Patrick reached the bridge at Warrington, he learned that a small force of Cromwell's allies had put up but a token resistance. They then retired. The king claimed victory and again called upon his countrymen to hurry to his banner.

The king was now ready to move on to London, but he had few allies in this other than the Duke of Hamilton. They had moved very swiftly down from Scotland, and the men were tired, protested his other advisors. Better to rest a while where they would be safe. Security would be found at Worcester, the cathedral town in the west country. The populace was royalist, as was the countryside surrounding it. The western side of the town was protected by the river Severn and the river Teme. To the east, south, and north were the remains of the fortifications from the earlier civil war battle. These could be repaired and used again. So the king and his army moved south to Worcester, which Charles II entered in triumph, the mayor of Worcester carrying the city's sword before His Majesty. At the town cross, the mayor proclaimed Charles England's king. He was seconded by the sheriff of Worcester.

While neither the mayor nor the sheriff of Worcester were outright royalists, they had welcomed His Majesty graciously in order to protect the town from being sacked, which it undoubtedly would have been had they put up any sort of resistance. For the next week, the king's army went about the region collecting supplies of food, clothing, horses, and arms. Nothing more than a promise of remuneration was offered in exchange for all the inventory. Cromwell or king. It made no difference, many grumbled to themselves, although several men were hanged for looting.

Patrick Leslie arrived in Worcester on the twenty-seventh of August. Asking directions, he found his way to Charlie's favorite inn, The Swan, which was set on the riverbank. "Is the Duke of Lundy staying here?" he asked the innkeeper.

"And you are, my lord?" the innkeeper asked, bristling slightly at the Scot's accent.

"I am Lord Stuart's brother," Patrick replied, annoyed. "If my brother is here, I would like to know. I hae ridden all the way down from the north. I am anxious to find him. 'Tis a family matter."

"Aye, my lord, your brother is here," the innkeeper finally said, his tone a trifle more respectful now. "I'll take you to him if you will follow me." He moved off down a narrow hall, finally stopping before a door, knocking discreetly, and then opening the entry to usher the Duke of Glenkirk through into the chamber. Then he quickly withdrew.

Patrick's eyes adjusted themselves to the dimness. There were several gentlemen in the room, but he quickly picked out his brother. *"Charlie!"* he said.

The Duke of Lundy turned from the gentlemen with whom he had been conversing. His amber eyes widened with absolute surprise. "My God, Patrick, is that you?" he said. Then he grew pale. "My children!"

"The bairns are fine," Patrick quickly assured him.

"Mother?"

"In France planning a wedding for Autumn," was the answer.

"But why . . . ?" Charlie looked more than a little confused.

"We must speak in private," Patrick said. His tone was urgent.

"My lords," Charlie said, "this is my younger brother, Patrick Leslie, the Duke of Glenkirk. He has ridden down from Scotland to speak with me. Considering the times, I can only assume it is serious."

"Did you see any of the Roundheads as you came, my lord?" one of the men asked Patrick.

"There were scouts everywhere in advance of Cromwell and his army, which is but a day behind me, sir," Patrick answered.

"Good God! I had best get home while I can, and so should the rest of you," the gentleman said.

There were murmurs of assent, and the room quickly emptied of its occupants but for Charlie and Patrick.

The Duke of Lundy smiled sardonically, and then he poured two goblets of wine from the decanter tray by the door. Handing a goblet to his brother, he raised it in toast. "The king," he said.

"The king," Patrick replied.

"You look battered," Charlie noted. "Come, and let's sit by the fire. If the children are all right, and Mama is all right, I would learn why you are here, little brother. Knowing how strongly you feel, I realize it is not to add your sword to the king's defense."

"Henry is at Glenkirk," Patrick began, smiling at his brother's look of astonishment. "He told the local authorities a small lie in order to obtain the proper passes, and then he came. He is in correspondence with Mam, although how he manages it, I dinna know. Mam dinna want ye in the midst of yer cousin's struggle. She wants ye wi' me at Glenkirk."

"Patrick," his brother began, but the Duke of Glenkirk held up his hand to stay Charlie's protest.

"Let me say what I hae come to say," he told his elder. "I know I hae come on a fool's errand, but I promised Henry, who promised Mam. They both believe that the time isnae now for the royal Stuart to return to his English throne. After what I hae seen this last month as I came south, Charlie, I believe that they are right. Surely ye realize the truth. Yer friends tonight will nae fight for this king, will they? They scurried off to their homes at the mere mention of Cromwell, and they are English born."

"Why did not Henry come instead of sending you?" Charlie asked.

"Because Henry canna be seen in the company of the king or his army lest he endanger his own family and estates," Patrick replied. "I, however, am a Scot. It would be expected that I might endorse this king. Besides, I am an unknown quantity to the English authorities, while Henry is nae. Mam knew that, which is why she sent him to fetch me so I might come and fetch ye." Patrick took a swallow of his wine.

"Henry is always prudent," Charlie remarked, almost bitterly.

"So were ye until the Roundheads murdered yer wife," Patrick reminded his brother sharply.

"How could I remain in England without my Bess?" Charlie demanded. "And had I remained, Bess's parents would have taken my children from me, even as they attempted to do. Do you think the bastard-born son of Prince Henry Stuart, the king's own beloved cousin, would have been permitted by the Puritan courts to keep his sons and his daughter?"

"Ye did the right thing in bringing them home to Glenkirk, Charlie. Now come back wi' me yerself. 'Tis true ye're the royal bastard, the charming and wealthy duke, but ye hae nae power like the others who surround the king, nor hae ye ever wanted such power. Mam lost our father in this battle the Stuarts would wage. She does nae want to lose ye, Charlie." Patrick leaned forward and spoke even more earnestly. "Since ye hae nae power in this fight, what good are ye to yer cousin? Yer bairns hae lost their mother. Dinna throw yer life away so that they lose their father, too. Flanna and I are content to hae yer bairns wi' us, Charlie, but what they really need is their own da. And Flanna has probably already given birth to my heir while I hae been away seeking ye."

"Ah, Patrick, that I caused ye to miss the birth of yer first child," Charlie said, genuinely regretful.

" 'Twould be worth it if ye agreed to come back wi' me," the Duke of Glenkirk said to his elder sibling.

"I cannot," Charlie said almost sadly. "You must understand, Patrick, that while I have no power to influence my royal cousin in his decisions, and while I am no military strategist, I am his friend, his kin, and in these hard times, it makes me far more valuable to him than the others. I listen. I console. I tell him the truth. I share memories of our family. I serve a far different purpose than the others, which is why I am tolerated by these men of power. They do not perceive me as a threat to their own influence over the king. There will be no mention of me when the history of this time is written, which suits me, quite frankly. But I must be here for my cousin. I cannot, I will not, leave him."

Patrick sighed. "The army that follows me is almost three times the size of yers," he told Charlie. "Ye hae nae hope of winning here at Worcester, and if ye dinna win, what will happen next?"

"I don't know," Charlie replied.

"I do," Patrick said grimly. "They'll capture the king, and they'll capture ye. Ye'll both be executed, for ye're royal Stuarts, and this Cromwell is a man who, while hiding behind the merits of morality, righteousness, and virtue, is a power-hungry despot. He oppresses those who disagree wi' him. He sets himself up as judge and jury. If he were truly the man he claims to be, he would offer justice for all no matter their beliefs. But he is nae such a man, Charlie, and I canna believe ye would throw yer life away under such circumstances."

"If the battle goes against us, Patrick, we'll manage to escape," Charlie said with a small grin. "If there is one thing my cousin Charles is good at, 'tis escaping Cromwell and his ilk." He reached out a hand to comfort his brother. "Come, now, and tell me of my children."

"They are thriving. They hae their lessons each day but the Sabbath. Willy cut off his own curls, however. He snuck into the hall when nay one was there and took the shears from his sister's sewing basket to do the deed. Biddy cried for three days afterward. And then he refused to wear his dresses, so we breeked him. We hae nae other choice. He is a stubborn laddie." Patrick chuckled.

Charlie laughed. "Like Bess's father, I fear," he said. "And the lovely Flanna?"

"Spent the summer at Brae restoring it. She says she wants it for a second son one day, and she'll try to regain the title as well. Of course, the king will hae to be restored if that is to happen," Patrick remarked practically. "I think ye're in for a long haul, Charlie. Ye moved like lightning down from Scotland. Why did ye nae keep going? I would hae headed for London, but then, I am no strategist."

"The king and Hamilton wanted to continue on, but they were

overruled by yer kin, General Leslie, and his coterie," Charlie replied.

"So ye'll be caught here like rats in a trap," Patrick said. *"And, now, so am I."*

"We'll get you out first thing tomorrow," Charlie said. "Come, brother, and take my bed. A good night's sleep is what you need. I must go now and be with my cousin."

"I'll nae argue," Patrick responded. "I hae nae had a bed to sleep in since I departed Glenkirk several weeks ago."

The Duke of Lundy led his younger brother to a small room down the hall from where they had been speaking. Charlie pulled Patrick's boots off, and the Duke of Glenkirk fell gratefully into the bed.

"Where will ye sleep?" he demanded to know before unconsciousness claimed him.

"Trundle," Charlie said and, blowing out the candle, left the little chamber. He then exited The Swan and hurried to the house where the king was billeted to tell him what Patrick had said about Cromwell's forces, and that they would, in all likelihood, be at Worcester gates sometime on the morrow.

"He did not come down from that benighted land of his simply to give you a report on Cromwell's army," the king said astutely.

"Nay, cousin, he didn't," Charlie admitted.

"Then, why?" the king queried.

"It is typical of my family," Charlie began with a smile. "My mother, in France now, has had a correspondence with my eldest brother, the Marquis of Westleigh. She sent Henry up to Scotland to get Patrick to come down to England to fetch me to safety. She did not send Henry because if he were seen in the vicinity of Your Majesty's army, or person, it could reflect badly on him and on his family with the current government."

Now the king was smiling with amusement. "Your mother is a very clever woman. She always was. The Scots brother would be expected to be with me, and so if someone sees him, it is not considered unusual."

"Correct, Your Majesty. And even if Patrick were seen by

Cromwell himself, my brother would be an unknown quantity, for he has rarely ventured forth from his beloved Glenkirk. I do not believe that even his own kin, General Leslie, would know him if they came upon one another. So Patrick was sent to plead my mother's case. It has been a great sacrifice on his part, for his wife is expecting his heir and has undoubtedly had it by now. Patrick knew before he even came that I would refuse him his request. Still, he came, for our mother."

"Mothers have a profound effect on their sons," the king noted.

"I shall have to get Patrick out of the city as quickly as possible, for once Cromwell arrives, it will be difficult, if not impossible," the Duke of Lundy told his royal cousin.

"Go with him," the king said generously. "I would not have your mother think me heartless and selfish. She has lost her husband in my service. I cannot rob her of her sons. I did not know my uncle, Henry Stuart, but they say he was well liked by all who knew him and would have been a great king of England. It is also said that your mother loved him deeply, and had her own birth not been so mysterious, she might have been Queen of England, and you, now, its king."

"While I have always grieved my father's loss, cousin," Charlie told the king, "ruling England has never been my desire, as you well know. I have been quite content being a country gentleman, and one day when all this is over, I will be again. My Indian grandfather, the Emperor Akbar, believed that we were, each of us, wherever we ought to be at a given time. I believe that, too, although," he continued with a wry smile, "such thinking does not conform with the Solemn League of the Covenant, I fear. However, I think Your Majesty will not expose me to the kirk. Now, cousin, we are here because we are supposed to be here at this moment in time. Even my brother, Patrick. We will send him home as quickly as we can, but as for me, cousin, I will not leave you."

The king did not speak for a long moment, but then he said, "If this goes badly, Charlie, I may have to send you away, and if I do, you must promise me that you will go. Without argument. We share a name. If you were killed, Cromwell's people would trumpet the death of Charles Stuart. They would not bother to make the distinction between us. It could harm my cause."

The Duke of Lundy nodded slowly. "I am Your Majesty's most loyal servant," he said. "God forbid that time come, but if it does, I will obey you." Then Charlie knelt and, taking his cousin's hand, kissed it. When he arose again, the king waved him back into his chair.

"Tell me the news about the delicious Duchess of Glenkirk," he said with a twinkle in his amber eyes.

"She has probably delivered of her child by now. Patrick said little more than that. Ah, yes, she has spent the summer at her mother's family seat restoring it. She has high hopes that one day when Your Majesty has come into his own again that she may convince you to give the family's title to her second son."

"There are no male heirs?"

"No," Charlie explained. "Her grandfather Gordon was the last Earl of Brae. He had a son, but like me, bastard-born. Flanna's mama was the heiress of Brae and was able to pass that title on to her daughter, but my sister-in-law is ambitious. She wants the earldom back for the Leslies of Glenkirk. She says that since her own family, the Brodies of Killiecairn, and her husband would not allow her to run about the Highlands recruiting troops for Your Majesty, the only accomplishment she can offer my brother is the restoration of that earldom for one of his sons. The ladies of Glenkirk who have come before Flanna have been rather unusual in many ways. She seeks to be something other than, as she so quaintly puts it, the do-naught duchess."

The king laughed heartily, something he rarely did these days. "Cousin," he told the Duke of Lundy, "you have my promise that when the day comes that I sit upon England's throne again, I will restore the Earldom of Brae to your brother's wife for her second son. Flanna Leslie made me laugh in that dark place called Scotland. And her young heart was a good one. And such generosity will cost me nothing, eh?"

Now it was Charlie who laughed. "Our grandfather said almost the exact same thing to Jemmie Leslie when he conferred upon him the Dukedom of Glenkirk," Charlie explained. "He said that since the earldom already existed with its castle and lands, it cost him naught to make Jemmie a duke."

"Blood will tell," the king responded, wiping his tears of mirth away. "Ah, Charlie, I have not enjoyed myself so much in weeks. 'Odds fish, cousin, I cannot wait until we can restore the court and live decently once again."

"Everything will happen in its time, Majesty," Charlie promised.

In the morning, they discovered Cromwell at the gates of the town of Worcester. He had not been expected until late in the day, but the dawn came to reveal each of the city's locked gates but one small one guarded from the outside. For the moment, there was absolutely no way in which Patrick Leslie could escape. He cursed softly beneath his breath when he was told what had happened. He did not want to die for this king. He wanted to be on the road north to his wife and family at Glenkirk.

The Earl of Derby had escaped into the city the night before with the news that his forces in Lancastershire to the north had been destroyed. The local gentry had not risen in an effort to aid the king. Cromwell, through taxation, had more than enough monies to pay for all the troops who would follow his banner. England's king had nothing with which to pay his small army but the hope of his eventual restoration, at which time all those faithful would be rewarded. Men with possessions kept silent on their estates. Men with nothing flocked to Cromwell, who could reward them with each battle fought.

Cromwell's forces moved to the south and southeast in an effort to cut off the king's escape to London. The king countered by ordering the town's four bridges over the Severn blown up; but while three were destroyed entirely, the bridge at Upton to the south was only damaged, and Cromwell's forces were able to repair it in order to use it. The day after the Protector's arrival, the guns began to batter the town. The king kept the bulk of his men within the walled town, for there the narrow streets were a natural defense. To the

west he sent three Scottish regiments to guard the confluence of the
Severn and the Teme rivers. General Middleton forayed forth in a
bold try to quiet their opponents' guns. He failed, and lost many.

The Protector might have assaulted the city immediately, but he
was a superstitious man. He waited until the third of September, the
first anniversary of his victory at Dunbar, to mount an all-out assault.
Patrick Leslie, caught inside of Worcester, decided that he would
probably survive because it was not possible that he die on the same
day as his father had died. Or was his God a deity with a sense of
humor?

On the morning of September third, the king climbed to the top
of the great square tower of the cathedral. He sanguinely observed
Cromwell's thirty thousand men arrayed before the city of
Worcester. He gazed down on the town itself with its winding and
narrow streets bordered by ancient medieval houses. His forces consisted of just about twelve thousand men. Charles II sighed, resigned. It would, indeed, take a miracle to win this battle, and he
did not believe in miracles. Still, the battle must be fought.

He was the King of England and Scotland. He should have fifty
thousand men at his beck and call, yet he did not. Why had they not
told him that his own people were so frightened after the years of
civil war that they would not rise in his support? Why had no one
said that all that everyone wanted was simply peace? He did not understand, but he knew as he looked down from his observation post
that many good men on both sides were going to die today. He knew
that when the sun set over the Malvern Hills, he would still be king,
but in name only. And he would probably be running for his life
once again. *If, indeed, he survived.* He turned to his cousin, Charlie,
who was the only person he had allowed to make the ascent with
him.

" 'Tis impossible," the king said.

"Aye," Charlie agreed.

"We need to have a plan," the king began.

"When the time comes, sire, we will go through the Claps gate.
Cromwell's generals do not think that you will return north, and so
that little, unimportant gate is virtually unguarded in order to allow

the Scots who survive to be driven through it and back over the border," Charlie told the king.

"Hmmmm," the king murmured thoughtfully.

"You will have to go when they tell you to go, Your Majesty," the Duke of Lundy said quietly. "There can be no argument."

"And you must go when I tell you, Charlie," the king replied, "*and* you must take your brother with you." Charles II chuckled. "I do not imagine that Patrick Leslie is pleased to be caught here."

Charlie smiled. "Nay, he is not," he agreed.

Below them the guns boomed noisily. "We must go down," the king said. "And you must leave as quickly as you can. Let it not be said that Cromwell killed two Charles Stuarts today."

"I will make for France, cousin, and be in Paris ready to serve you when you arrive," Charlie said. "I believe I can get there before you. Cromwell will set all his forces to seeking you, sire. He will not be looking for me, but I would far rather that you go than I."

The two men descended the cathedral tower into the square where the king's generals were awaiting him. The two cousins embraced, each wishing the other good fortune this day. Then Charlie hurried back to The Swan to alert his brother that they would be leaving immediately.

"And how the hell are we supposed to escape this chaos?" Patrick demanded angrily of his brother. "Look about ye, man! Panic! Fires! Frightened civilians terrified for their lives."

"There's a gate to the north that's not well guarded," Charlie said calmly. "I've been advised to leave that way."

"So," Patrick almost shouted, "it hae all come down to this! Ye will leave the king even before the battle is begun and concluded. Why could ye nae hae come to this decision before we got trapped here?"

"*No Charles Stuart must die here today,*" Charlie said with emphasis. "Think of the propaganda value if Cromwell's people could claim that they killed Charles Stuart? It would make it a hundred times as difficult for the king to eventually return. He would have to prove he was whom he said he was and not some bloody imposter."

"Yer cousin and his advisors might hae come to this conclusion sooner," Patrick grumbled.

"If we depart now while the fighting is concentrated by the Fort Royal, we can escape through Claps gate and then turn west," Charlie told his brother.

"Why west?" Patrick demanded. "I would go north."

"And so will Cromwell's forces after the battle is won," Charlie said. "We go west because I have a friend who will shelter us until the worst is over. Then I intend going to Bristol and embarking on one of the family's ships for France. You can come with me and then cross back over to Scotland, or you can decide your own path back; but for the next few days, we must hide in a safe place."

Outside, they could hear the fighting beginning to spill over into the streets themselves. The Fort Royal fell. General Leslie, so discouraged as he remembered Dunbar, decided there was no hope and did not properly support the king's men. Some of the soldiers began to throw down their arms in despair. The king, stripped of his armor now, attempted to no avail to rally his men. He had fought bravely all the day through, never sparing himself danger, and gaining the admiration of everyone, even his enemies. Now, however, the streets were beginning to run red with the blood of the dead and the dying. At dusk the king was finally convinced to flee himself and did so through the same gate that his cousin and the Duke of Glenkirk had earlier departed through. Night was now falling, and behind him the killing was still continuing as Cromwell's forces rounded up the opposing forces and sought desperately to find the king.

Charlie and Patrick had left Worcester at mid-morning, taking advantage of the confusion and disorder about them. As they had been told, the Claps gate was unguarded, being a small gate. Several miles from the town, the brothers turned west toward Wales. Eventually the uproar behind them died, and there was only the sound of birdsong and animals as they rode cross-country. Charlie obviously knew exactly where he was going, and Patrick followed obediently alongside of his elder sibling. Finally, as the sun began to sink behind the hills ahead of them, they turned off the road. The barely visible track they now followed meandered on for several miles, ending before a dark stone house that appeared deserted.

They had just stopped when a shot rang out, and Patrick Leslie swore, grabbing at his shoulder in pain.

"*Barbara!*" Charlie shouted. "'Tis me, and you've just shot my brother, damnit!"

There was a long silence, and then finally the front door to the house opened. A woman ran out, flinging herself into the Duke of Lundy's arms. "Oh, God, Charlie, I am sorry!" she exclaimed, and then she kissed him.

Charlie Stuart enjoyed the kiss for a brief moment, and then he untangled the clinging woman. "You have always acted without thought for the consequences, Barbara," he said. "Now help my brother into the house, and I will stable our horses."

With some difficulty, and wincing with pain, Patrick Leslie slid off his stallion. The woman put an arm about him, instructing him to lean on her as she aided him to gain the house.

"Which brother are you?" she asked him as she settled him in chair by the fire in her parlor. "The Scot from the look of you."

"There are three Scots," Patrick half groaned. "I'm the eldest. Patrick Leslie, Duke of Glenkirk, at yer service, madame."

"Mistress Barbara Carver," the woman said. "Hold still now while I get your jerkin off, my lord."

"Do ye always shoot at yer visitors, madame?" Patrick demanded. He flinched as she removed his leather jerkin.

"The bullet is in your shoulder, my lord. I shall have to remove it," she answered him, and she began to unlace his shirt.

"Ye'll nae put a hand to me, madame, until my brother is here in this room," Patrick told her. "If ye hae some whiskey, I should welcome it. And ye hae nae answered my question."

"These are difficult times, my lord," Barbara Carver said softly. "It was dusk. I could not see who it was who approached my home. I am a woman alone but for an elderly servant." While she spoke, she had moved to a sideboard that held decanters and drinking vessels. She poured something into a pewter dram cup and, coming to his side, handed it to him.

Patrick drank the whiskey down, his eyes widening with surprise as he recognized his own brew. "This is Glenkirk whiskey," he said.

"Aye," she answered him quietly, "it is. Your brother is very particular and saw that I had it for when he visited."

"Yer husband?" Patrick asked.

"Dead for a number of years," she answered him. "My father was a well-to-do merchant in Hereford. I have known your brother since I was a child, for my father serviced Queen's Malvern, and I would often come with him when he delivered his goods. Lord and Lady de Marisco were very kind to me. When my father died, my mother remarried his senior apprentice. My stepfather did not want me. He planned to put me into service, but I was not raised to be a servant. Lady de Marisco learned of my plight. She arranged my marriage to Squire Randall Carver, a childless widower, some years my senior. He was very good to me, but sadly I produced no children for him. I was a good wife, my lord. Please, let me put a bit of whiskey on your wound. It will sting, but we must avoid infection." She carefully tore his shirt away around the bloody wound. "Well," she observed, "'twas a clean shot at least."

He laughed. He couldn't help himself. This was an absolutely ridiculous situation in which he found himself. "*Ouch!*" He blanched as she dabbed a small cloth on the open wound.

"Will he live?" Charlie demanded to know as he entered the room.

"The bullet must come out, but he would not have it until you were here," Barbara Carver said.

"It's going to hurt like hell, little brother," Charlie said almost cheerfully. "Give him lots of whiskey, Barbara, and then we'll get to work. The shoulder is nice and fleshy, Patrick, so nothing vital is in danger. You'll remain a few days with Barbara to heal, and then you had best be on your way home. I have no doubt that Cromwell's men will be out in force by the morrow, combing the countryside for royalists."

"And if they come here?" Patrick demanded irritably.

"I'll put you in the priest's hole, my lord," Barbara Carver said with a smile. She was, he noticed for the first time, a very pretty woman.

"The priest's hole?"

"I am a Catholic, my lord, which is why I remain here in my comfortable isolation. In this time, being a Catholic is even worse than being an Anglican." Then she laughed. "It is rare that any come here but those who are invited or know they will be welcome."

"Are there any ye might expect in the next few days?" Patrick asked her wryly. Having realized how lovely this woman was, he was now curious as to her real relationship to his brother. Surely Charlie hadn't been unfaithful to his Bess, whom he adored.

"Right now my friends are too busy chasing your friends," she told him with another smile. Then she handed him not a dram cup, but beaker full of whiskey. "When you've finished it, my lord, we will begin. It will, as Charlie says, hurt, but it must come out." She then turned to Charlie. "And where will you go now?"

"France," he said. "The searchers will be going north and east at first. That will give me time to make my dash to Bristol. There is always an O'Malley-Small trading company ship there. By the time Cromwell's people turn south and east, I'll be in Bristol aboard my vessel. The king sent me away before the worst of the battle. Patrick and I escaped through the Claps gate. Actually, my brother shouldn't have been there at all. While he does not support Cromwell, he does not support the king either. Mother sent him to fetch me," Charlie said with a small smile. "And my royal cousin feared if I was killed, Cromwell would claim the death of Charles Stuart and further muddy the waters of my family's eventual restoration, for while today was not their day, they will be restored in time."

"God save the king," Barbara Carver agreed. She turned back to Patrick. "Drink up, my lord. The sooner I get that bullet out of you, the sooner we can have a nice hot supper. My old Lucy is in the kitchen now preparing a meal for us."

The Duke of Glenkirk swallowed down the whiskey. It burned inside his belly, and he found himself becoming almost drowsy. He leaned back in his chair. The fire was warm, and he felt all the cares of the last few weeks slipping away from him. *Flanna.* He dared to let his thoughts turn to his beautiful wife. When he returned to Glenkirk, their bairn would be born, and he would have her in his bed again. A smile of anticipation lit his handsome features, and then the sensation of pain shot through him. "Hellfire and damnation!" he swore, attempting to pull away from the pain, his green-gold eyes flying open to behold Mistress Barbara Carver digging at his bloody shoulder with what appeared to be a very sharp knife.

"Drink some more whiskey," Charlie ordered him, and he saw that it was his brother who was holding him down.

"*Jesu!*" Patrick swore again. "'Tis glad I am 'tis nae vital, madame!" And then he fainted.

"Thank heavens," Mistress Carver said. "He was being so brave, but the damned bullet is buried farther than I anticipated. Now I can get at it." She worked her knife deeper into the wound, and then smiling, she slowly levered the round lead pellet up until she was able to pick it out of his shoulder with her two fingers. She stared at it a moment, and then she handed it to Charlie. "A souvenir," she told him. "Take it to your mother and tell her what your brother did for you in leaving his Scottish aerie and coming to help you."

"I think not," Charlie said with a chuckle, but he pocketed the bullet nonetheless.

Mistress Carver dressed Patrick's wound and bandaged it. "He'll live, but he'll feel the wound for weeks, I fear."

"Where do you want him?" Charlie asked her.

"Put him in the bedroom next to mine. I'll want to look in on him in the night and make certain there is no infection," she said.

Charlie picked up his brother, not some small feat, and exiting the parlor, carried him upstairs as he had been ordered. He gently removed Patrick's boots and drew a coverlet over him. "Thank you, little brother," he said softly, and then he returned down the narrow stairs to the parlor. Old Lucy, Barbara's servant, was just bringing in the meal to the small dining room off the parlor. He greeted her warmly, and she gave him an equally warm welcome.

"You must be starving," Barbara said. "Sit down. How long have you been back in England?"

"I came with my cousin," Charlie told her, helping himself to both trout and beef.

"The children?"

"In the north," was all he said. "Safe."

"You should hove remained with them until this was all over and settled," she said. "Why didn't the king understand that there would be no great popular rising for him?"

"No one told him," Charlie answered her, "and I am not certain that the lines of communication were even open between the English royalists and the Scottish lords. He might have succeeded but that they insisted upon resting their troops in Worcester. He wanted to go right for London."

"It's too soon," Barbara Carver said wisely. "Right now we are all frightened. In time we will be sick of these Puritans, but not quite yet."

"How have you survived?" he inquired.

"The Puritans are not as moral as they pretend to be. I keep my faith to myself, of course, but the local gentleman in charge of the district visits me. I make no difficulties, nor do I raise the specter of impropriety, and so Squire Randall's widow is left in peace out on her hillside," Barbara told him.

"Is there any danger of this man coming soon?" Charlie asked.

"He's not a soldier. It's unlikely he was involved in the battle at Worcester, but he will go there in the next day or two to be seen and to take part in the executions that will follow. I do not expect to see him until all is settled. Several weeks, probably."

They ate, and they drank as they had so many times in the past. And when they had finished, without a word, they went upstairs.

"Let me check your brother first," she whispered to him. She entered her second bedroom and, going over to Patrick, put a hand on his forehead. "He has a slight fever," she said. "It was to be expected. I had best get some watered wine for him."

"Later," Charlie said, drawing her out into the little hallway and into her own bedroom. He enfolded her into his arms and kissed her deeply, his tongue pushing between her lips to fence with her tongue. His hands began to unlace her gown in swift and expert fashion.

Barbara laughed and pulled away from him. "Your boots, my lord! I don't intend to have my fine linens muddied." She pushed him back into a chair, and kneeling down, she pulled the boots from his feet, and then his stockings, exclaiming as she did, "Whew! How long have you been wearing those, Charlie Stuart?"

"Too long," he told her, rising, and pulling her up to continue what he had started.

Soon Barbara's clothing lay in a heap upon the floor of her bedchamber, and she lay upon her back in her bed watching as he removed his own garments. Wickedly she pulled apart her nether lips to his gaze and played with herself before his blazing amber eyes. Her little pointed tongue licked suggestively along the outline of her lips, taunting him. She took the two fingers that had been used to arouse her now swollen lovebud and put them into her mouth, her blue eyes never leaving his. *"Hurry!"* she urged him, her lust plain for him to see.

He had to be careful of the clothes he wore, for he had little else, Charlie realized. But he couldn't stop looking at her, and he could feel his male member growing harder and harder as he did. His fingers were clumsy as he struggled to undo his garments. Barbara had always been a fascinating and inventive mistress, but he had certainly never wanted her like he wanted her now. Finally and successfully denuded, he wasted no time in joining her in bed. Their mouths mashed together in a passionate kiss again. He filled his hands with her wonderful big breasts, squeezing firm, yet soft flesh, rolling the large nipples between his fingers.

"Fuck me!" she husked into his ear. "We can play later, Charlie, but I want you filling me. *Now!*"

He obliged, and groaned with the incredible pleasure the simple act of thrusting into her gave him. "Ahhh, God, Barbara!" He began to piston her vigorously.

"Ohh, yes! Oh, yes, Charlie!" she cried, wrapping her thighs about his waist. "Ohhh, fuck me! Fuck me! *Fuck me!*" She almost screamed with the incredible sensations his hard love lance was giving her. She couldn't remember him ever having been so big before, or was it that she had just forgotten? She couldn't seem to get enough of his lust. Her hips pushed up to meet his every plunge.

His head was spinning. How long had it been since he had had a woman? He couldn't remember, and the knowledge shocked him. He was a man who had always enjoyed his bedsport. He had had a loving wife, and Barbara had always been a wonderful mistress. The warmth of her response to him, the warmth of her lush flesh, sent his senses reeling. He was like a boy with his first woman, and he was absolutely unable to control himself. "Oh, God'" he groaned, and his passions burst forth, filling her with a surfeit of his lusts.

"Ohhhh, yes!" she echoed his satisfaction as she felt his love juices rushing forth, and she released her own pent-up desires.

And afterward as they lay in each other's arms, Barbara Carver asked him bluntly, "How long has it been since you made love to a woman, my darling Charlie?"

"Months," he admitted with a weak grin.

"You have battered me," she told him, smiling. "I hope there is enough left in you for another round tonight. I have missed you."

"Perhaps more than a single round," he said with a chuckle. "I have missed you, you irreverent wench. Are you this wild with your Puritan lover? Or is the whispering of naughty words in his ear just enough to satisfy him?" Leaning over, he kissed her breast.

"We play a game, he and I," she told Charlie honestly. "I am a naughty schoolgirl with lewd and lascivious thoughts that I confess to him. Then I must bare my bottom to him for a spanking. Only then does he fuck me, and quickly afterward sneaks off back to his wife."

"'Odds fish, sweetheart, he doesn't hurt you, does he?"

Barbara laughed. "No, of course not. You know me better than that, Charlie. I would not permit such a thing. It is just that he feels so guilty about fucking me, or any woman for that matter, that he cannot become aroused in a normal fashion. I have tried with him; but he needs to play his little game, and he is grateful for my cooperation."

"Do you see him in the village?"

"Sometimes, but I never acknowledge him, for we are not supposed to know one another well enough," she explained. "His wife is a dreadful shrew. She may suspect him of such roguery, but she cannot prove it. He is terrified of her, so does not come too often. Once, however, when someone in the village suspected my loyalties, he defended me, and even got his wife to do so by suggesting that my accuser harbored lustful thoughts toward me or covetous thoughts for my small property. I was a respectable widow of a respected man who lived quietly in her mourning." Barbara laughed. "I was actually quite surprised he was so daring."

"He is obviously fond of you for your kindness," the Duke of Lundy observed. He took a tendril of her dark blond hair between his fingers and kissed it. "You have always been kind, Barbara."

"I had best go and get some cooling liquid for your brother," she said, arising from the bed and pulling her chemise back on.

"Hurry back," he said, a wicked twinkle in his eye.

Chapter

16

Patrick Leslie felt very groggy when he awoke just before dawn the next morning. Outside the window of the chamber, the sky was beginning to lighten. He moved slightly, groaning with the pain in his left shoulder. Almost immediately the door to the chamber opened, and Charlie came in. He was fully dressed. Pouring a goblet of watered wine, he brought it to his brother.

"Drink it. You've got a slight fever which Barbara tells me is to be expected, but the wound is clean, with no infection," the Duke of Lundy advised his younger brother.

Patrick eagerly swallowed down the cool liquid. When he had slaked his thirst, he said, "I heard ye last night. Jesu, Charlie, I dinna know ye had a mistress. Surely Bess dinna know. It would hae broken her heart, for she loved ye deeply."

"Nay," Charlie reassured his sibling, "Bess never knew. I loved her above all women, but Christ, man, I'm a Stuart! We have great appetites. Bess and I were married six years when Barbara and I renewed our acquaintance. Bess was with child, while Barbara had been a widow for several years."

"So ye slept wi' her?"

"I was Barbara's first lover, Patrick. When Madame Skye found out, she was furious at me, for Barbara was a respectable girl; but the future Duke of Lundy would not wed a merchant's daughter ac-

cording to her. Our great-grandmother first made certain that
Barbara was not carrying my child. Then she made the match for her
with Squire Carver. I never saw her again until the first of the civil
wars. I was in Worcester, and we met on the street. We spoke. I
learned she had been widowed for several years. One day I came up
here to visit her, and . . . well . . ."

"Ye couldn't resist fucking her?" Patrick inquired mockingly.

Charlie grinned. "Nay, I'm afraid I couldn't. Barbara is a most delicious armful, but more important to me she is a good friend.
Sheltering us like this is very generous of her, for if it is known that
she gave refuge to two royalists, she could be executed. And that,
little brother, is why I must leave now for Bristol. It is almost dawn,
and I do not want to be seen. Out here, even in this splendid isolation, one never knows who is watching or even why."

"Then, I should go, too," Patrick said, and he attempted to get to
his feet, but fell back against the pillows. "Damn, Charlie, I am as
weak as a kitten."

"Barbara wants you to remain until you are stronger," his brother
said. "And then, too, you will need to know what has happened in
its entirety before you make your plans to go north."

"And ye dinna?" Patrick demanded.

"Nay. I know what I need to know. The king's forces were badly
beaten yesterday. I expect my cousin has escaped, for he has always
been good at extricating himself from tight situations, but for how
long he is allowed to be at liberty is another matter. It will take all
his cunning to elude his enemies. Cromwell's people will be set to
finding him. A large reward will certainly be posted. I must get to
France to tell the queen what I know and to assure our mother that
I am safe, that we are all safe. If I were captured, Cromwell's people
would think nothing of shouting the capture of Charles Stuart from
the rooftops. Indeed, it would be no lie; but the fact it was the wrong
Charles Stuart would not be mentioned, and the king's forces would
lose heart. And even when the lie was fully proven, it would be difficult for the king. So I must be on my way, Patrick. Give me your
hand, little brother. I do not know when we will see each other
again, but we will one day. Shall I bring Mam your love?"

Patrick nodded. "Tell her about Flanna and the bairn," he said. "God speed, Charlie. Try not to get yerself killed."

"I won't," the Duke of Lundy promised, and then clasping his brother's hand a final time, he released it and was gone through the door.

Patrick Leslie felt the tears slip down his cheeks, and he impatiently wiped them away. Had that damned woman not shot him, he, too, would be ready to travel. As it was, he ached, and if the truth be known, he was absolutely exhausted with his travels and the fears they had all suffered in Worcester. Unable to help himself, his eyes closed, and he slept once again. When he finally awoke, the sun was setting to the west over the purple hills he saw through his bedchamber window. A figure seated by the small fireplace arose and came forward.

"How are you feeling, Patrick Leslie?" Barbara Carver asked him. She bent and felt his forehead. "Your fever is gone. Excellent! I obviously did a good job of surgery on you." She smiled a brilliant smile, and he was again aware of how lovely she was.

"I'm better than I was this morning," he told her. "Is Charlie really gone, or did I dream it?"

"Your brother is gone," she told him. "And we have seen no one else the whole day. That may not last, however, and I want you to be ready should we have visitors. While I do not expect my Puritan friend, he could come. The ideal situation would be for me to put you in the priest's hole. When you feel able to get up, I will show you where it is. And it would be better if you remained in the house where you cannot be seen; but that, too, may not be entirely practical, so we must have another plan. If someone comes and I cannot hide you, you will be Paddy, a stableman sent to me from Queen's Malvern by Mr. Becket, the majordomo. You can hear, but you are dumb, and when the duke dismissed all his servants and departed England, Becket felt sorry for you and sent you to me as he knew I was without a man to help around the place now. You must be dumb because your accent will surely give you away as a Scot, Patrick Leslie, and no one will believe that you were not with the king."

"I should leave as soon as I can," Patrick said. "Ye have been very kind, Mistress Carver, but I wouldna endanger my brother's *good friend*, who hae so graciously sheltered us."

Barbara Carver laughed. "You do not approve of me, do you, my lord? I am sorry, however, because Charlie and I are long-time friends from our childhood. I would be remiss if I allowed you to endanger yourself. You cannot leave until your shoulder is healed, nor can you leave until we learn the lay of the land. Now, if you think you can get up, you may have supper with me downstairs. I expect you are very hungry at this point. When did you last eat?"

"I canna remember," he said, feeling a bit guilty that she had seen his disapproval of her when she was being so generous. He sat up and put his long legs over the side of the bed. His head spun for a moment, but then cleared. He sat for a time, and then he arose. While his shoulder hurt like hell, he felt all right otherwise.

"Lucy has roasted a nice joint. I can smell it from here," she said with another smile. "Come along. If you feel any weakness, I will help you."

He slowly descended the staircase, and she led him into her little dining room, indicating he sit at one end of the table. Her old servant came forth from the kitchen carrying a platter upon which was a roast of beef. There was already bread, butter, and cheese upon the table along with a plate containing a roasted chicken. The servant didn't wait to ask. She simply piled his plate with food and ordered him to eat. He saw his hostess hide a smile. When he had finished everything that had been put upon his plate, she brought him a dish of egg custard and some strawberry jam. He greedily spooned it up. And all the while his glass was kept filled with good red wine that he recognized as coming from his family's estate at Archambault in France. He finally pushed himself back from the table.

"The old woman is a good cook," he remarked.

"Her name is Lucy," Barbara said. "You ate well, so I may assume you are on the road to recovery. Again, my lord, I do apologize for shooting you last night. I did not expect visitors, and certainly not Charlie. I hope you can forgive me."

The wine had mellowed him, and he thought, who was he to

stand in judgment of his brother and Barbara Carver? As Charlie had pointed out, he was a Stuart, and it was a well-known fact, at least in Scotland, that Stuarts had large appetites for life. "Ye couldna hae waited until ye received a hail?" he asked her.

"If I had not, you might be dead," she said. "I aimed for your heart, Patrick Leslie "

"Ye're a poor shot," he told her with a small grin. "God help us when a woman hae a gun. If ye hae been my wife, I would be dead, for Flanna is an excellent shot wi' a bow. Aye, I forgie ye, Barbara Carver. Ye hae nursed me well, and fed me even better."

"You are very different from Charlie," she noted.

"Aye," he agreed. "He's an Englishman, born and bred, but I am a Scot, born and bred. Still, we are brothers and love each other dearly. Our mam gave birth to five sons, two Englishmen and three Scots. I have two English sisters and one Scots sister, but we are all family and loyal to one another."

"You must be that you came down from Scotland to try and dissuade Charlie from being with the king," she noted.

Lucy bustled into the dining room. "Someone's coming!" she said. "Best to hide our visitor, mistress."

Barbara Carver arose quickly. "Come with me, Patrick Leslie." He followed her into the little parlor, watching with amazement as she went over to the fireplace and, reaching inside, touched the far wall, which immediately swung open. He needed no urging, and carefully avoiding the blaze in the hearth, he stepped over and around it to fit himself into the niche behind the fireplace wall. "I'll come and get you when our visitor is gone. Depending on who it is, it may be a while."

Old Lucy shoved a flask into his hand with a nod. Then she and Barbara closed the back wall of the fireplace on him. Patrick looked about him. The space was small, but not impossible. He could stand if he chose, or there was a trifooted stool to sit upon. To his surprise, the space was not stifling despite its location. He uncorked the flask and sniffed. *Wine.* Well, he didn't need it now, having just finished a good meal. He put the stool into a corner of the little space and, sitting down, closed his eyes.

Her musket in hand, Barbara Carver hailed the incoming visitor, and then cursed softly beneath her breath. It was her Puritan protector. Setting the gun by the door, she put on her most cheerful smile. Then, remembering the magnificent stallion in the stables, she hissed to Lucy, "Go and take his damned horse lest he see Lord Leslie's beast and ask questions."

Lucy hobbled out just as Sir Peter arrived and slid from his mount. "Give the beastie to me, yer worship," she said. "I'll take care of it." And she moved as quickly away from him as she could, clutching the horse's bridle.

"Darling!" Barbara cried softly, and opened her arms to him.

"My dear," he chided her, "go inside lest someone see you."

"Oh, Peter, it is already night," she protested prettily, but she obeyed him.

He entered the house and kissed her briefly. "I cannot stay, but I wanted to come and tell you what has happened."

"Oh"—she pouted—"and I have been so naughty, sir. I truly need a spanking." Then she sighed.

"Elsbeth knows I'm here. She insisted I come and warn you of the villains traversing the countryside right now. She invites you to our home for safety's sake. I told her you would not come, but she still was adamant that I come to make certain that the poor widow was safe. I must return almost immediately."

She pouted at him again. Her breasts were very visible over the top of her gown, and he could scarce take his eyes from them.

"So, madame," he said, "you are in need of some correction?"

She smiled seductively, putting a single finger in her mouth and sucking on it. She lowered her eyes to allow her eyelashes, which were dark in comparison with her hair, to brush her cheeks. Then she held out her hand to him. "Come upstairs with me," she tempted.

"I can't, but your parlor will do nicely, my dear. First I shall punish you for your naughtiness, and then I will tell you what has happened before I return home to my wife. Come, madame!"

Barbara Carver felt her cheeks grow pink as she considered just how much of what would go on in her parlor could be heard from behind the fireplace wall, but there was no help for it. She allowed Sir Peter to usher her into the room. He sat upon a chair, and she dutifully put herself over his knees. Her skirts were immediately, indeed eagerly, raised, and he began to punish her smooth white bottom with blows of his gloved hand. She squealed and wiggled as was her custom until finally he cried, *"Enough!"* She was then hustled across the room and bent across a tabletop, her skirts still uplifted. He entered her almost at once, sobbing, pumping her briefly before releasing his juices. Stepping away from her, he lowered her skirts and helped her to rise.

"Ah, my dear," he said as they now sat together upon the settle, "you are as always such a comfort to me."

"I am glad," she murmured. 'Odds fish! The man knew nothing of making love. "I know how difficult these times are for you, Sir Peter. But tell me now, for I am so very eager to learn what has happened. A peddler passed by last week and said the king's army was in Worcester. Is it true?"

"It was," Sir Peter replied. "The king has been justly beaten, and while his person is still at large, rest assured, my dear, that God will deliver him into our hands for execution shortly."

"Then, you know where he is?" Barbara pressed.

"Well, no, but we are on his trail," Sir Peter said pompously, "and we will certainly catch him. Who in England will shelter him but for possibly some of the traitorous Catholics? If those he believes are his adherents were English, would there not have been a popular uprising in his favor? But there was not. The man who calls himself King of England came over the border with a small troop of his Scots rabble. We will soon have Scotland under our thumb as well. Then there will be no place for this Charles Stuart to hide. The criminals who supported him, however, may be roaming the countryside, my dear, and so you must be vigilant. It is unlikely that they have come to the southwest, but these Scots are not very intelligent. They have probably, with their leader, fled north, but we are in pursuit. In a very short time we will catch this man. We have already begun executing those traitors in Worcester. We've torn down the city's walls in punishment and rounded up as many Anglicans and Catholics as

we could find. Depending on the nature of their crimes, they will either be jailed, transported, or executed." He arose. "I must be on
my way home, my dear. You should be safe, but be on your guard
nonetheless. It is unlikely anyone will come your way." Then Sir
Peter took his leave of Barbara Carver.

She watched him go from the doorway of her house, and when he
had disappeared over the hills, she hurried into the parlor to open
up the priest's hole. There she found Patrick dozing peacefully, his
back against the wall. She woke him, relieved that he had not been
a party to her embarrassment. Then she told him what Sir Peter had
disclosed.

Patrick nodded. "Charlie was right to leave before dawn for
Bristol," he said. "Now the question is when can I return north."

"I think we must wait until the furor has died down. Once the
king is either caught or successfully makes his way to France, then
you will be safe to depart. I have travel papers that just require the
filling in of a name. Sir Peter gave them to me months ago in the
event that I should want to make a journey of any sort. But you must
wait, Patrick Leslie. I could not face Charlie again one day if I got
you killed or imprisoned. Promise me that you will do nothing foolish. I know how you long to be back at your beloved Glenkirk with
your wife and new child, but you must be patient, if not for yourself,
for them."

"For a time, at least," he promised her. "I need to know more before I dare to venture home, Barbara Carver."

The king had, indeed, escaped Worcester, going through the
same gates his cousin had earlier exited through. The Duke of
Hamilton had been killed that day in the fighting, but the king was
accompanied by the Scottish Lord Lauderdale, the Earl of Derby,
and the Duke of Buckingham. The king's only contact with Roman
Catholics had been with the French priests who served his mother
and the Irish who occasionally peopled his father's court. Now, on
the advice of Derby, he put himself into the hands of the English
Roman Catholics and discovered while they were faithful to their
church, they were also the loyalest of the loyal to their king and to
their country.

Disguised as a laborer, he sheltered first with the Penderells, a family of yeoman farmers at their farm, Whiteladies, in Shropshire. They hid him in the woods and attempted to get him into Wales, but to everyone's distress, the local militia was holding all the bridges over the Wye. The king was then taken to Boscobel, where he was hidden first in the house, then the gardens, and finally he was forced to climb an oak tree where he hid as Cromwell's men searched all about below him. By the seventh of September, but four days after his defeat, he was at Moseley Hall. On the tenth of the month, disguised now as a tenant farmer's son, he escorted Mistress Jane Lane, a royalist's daughter, to visit a friend at Abbot's Leigh near Bristol. Mistress Lane had the proper passes for traveling.

He remained briefly at the manor of Abbot's Leigh, unrecognized by the family. He was, however, recognized by the family's butler. The butler, glad to be of service to his king, advised Charles to take Mistress Lane and ride across Somerset. Following the man's advice, the king reached Trent Hall on the sixteenth of September. He was now under the protection of his old friend Francis Wyndham and a group of royalists.

They could not find a ship at Dover. The ports all along that particular part of the coast were full of Cromwell's soldiers preparing to leave for Jersey to take it and the other Channel isles under their *protection*. The royalists set about to find a ship that could sail from the Hampshire or Sussex coast. Locating a suitable and sturdy vessel, they quickly brought the king aboard. On October fourteenth, he sailed from Shoreham, landing at Fecamp in Normandy two days later. By the twentieth of October, all of England knew that Charles Stuart had escaped Oliver Cromwell's grasp, and while he was not there, England still had a king.

Upon hearing the news as she shopped in the nearby village, Barbara Carver told Patrick Leslie that it was now safe for him to return home. She had enjoyed his company, but it was time. He departed before first light on the morning of October twenty-second. Old Lucy had baked him a supply of oatcakes and filled his flasks with both wine and water. He thanked her and bid her farewell.

Mistress Carver had told him the night before that she would not be up when he went, and so he had said his good-byes the previous evening, thanking her for her care. His shoulder was now healed but for the scar.

He rode north, and then north and east, over the next weeks, always taking the road less traveled, never stopping where he might have to speak with anyone lest they know him for a Scot and call the local authorities down upon him. It was lonely, and it was cold as the autumn began to near winter. He crossed the border just north of Otterburn, riding across the Cheviot hills. He avoided Edinburgh, taking a ferry across the Firth of Forth, riding across Fife and ferrying across the Firth of Tay. He crossed the South Esk, the North Esk, the rivers Dee and Don. The hills rose up all around him, and he stopped briefly to take his plaid from his saddle and wrap it about him for warmth, because now he would not be arrested if someone saw him or spoke to him. His heart began to beat faster as he suddenly realized that he was recognizing landmarks. He pushed the big dappled gray stallion harder. The cold air smelled of home. Then suddenly he exited the forest, and ahead of him stood Glenkirk Castle. He had been on the road for over a month, and he was tired, but tonight he would sleep in his own bed, with his beloved wife.

Flanna stood atop the battlements of Glenkirk as she did each afternoon, looking south, seeking him, willing him home. Her breasts were swollen with her milk that was even now beginning to seep through her gown. She sighed, and was about to turn away when she saw the rider. He was yet distant, *but she knew*. In her heart she knew it was her Patrick. Flanna, her pulses racing, forced herself to climb carefully down the ladder from the rooftop to the corridor below. Then she dashed down the several flights of stairs, racing into the hall, shouting, *"He's home! He's home!"*

She ran from the hall and out the door of the castle into the courtyard, shouting. She ran through the courtyard and beneath the iron portcullis across the oaken drawbridge. Her bodice was soaked through with her milk, her red hair was flying, and she smelled like a cow, but she ran directly toward him. And he jumped off his stallion before he had even pulled it to a stop and ran to her, enfolding her in his arms, swinging her about. They laughed as if they were mad. Then the laughter died as suddenly as it had begun, and Patrick Leslie kissed his wife as she had never been kissed before, and was kissed in return in the same fashion.

"I knew ye were nae dead!" she finally said as together they walked back to the castle.

"Who said I was dead?" he asked, surprised.

"Ye dinna come home, and we heard the king was beaten and fled to France. I hae never seen so many peddlers as I hae seen this autumn, all of them filled wi' news and eager to share it, though how much of it was true, I dinna know. What kept ye so long in England?"

"Welcome home, my lord!" Angus Gordon was beaming as Patrick entered the hall. He shoved a goblet of wine into the duke's hands.

"Ah, here ye are safe and sound, and us so fearful for ye," Mary More-Leslie said, and then she began to weep.

Patrick hugged his housekeeper. "Now, Mary, I only went down into England to fetch my brother," he soothed her.

"And where is that feckless laddie?" she demanded.

"In France, lo these many weeks." He laughed. "Where is Henry?"

"In England, lo these many weeks," Flanna parroted him. "Did ye think I was going to wait until ye returned to hae the bairns? I sent him home a week after I hae them. And a good thing, too. Do ye wish to see yer sons, my lord?" She took him by the hand, leading him across the Great Hall to two cradles by the fireplace above which hung the portrait of his ancestor, the first Earl of Glenkirk.

Patrick Leslie stared down in astonishment. *Two!* He had sired two sons!

"They're already baptized, so ye'll hae to be content wi' their names," she told him. "We couldna be waiting for ye to finally wend yer way home, Patrick Leslie."

"What are they called?" he asked. *Two. Two sons!*

"The next duke is James, and the Earl of Brae is Angus," she said quietly. "They were born on the nineteenth of August."

His sons stared up at him dispassionately. They were as alike as two peas in a pod. Each had a head full of black hair. Each had blue eyes, but then he remembered all babies began with blue eyes. They were plump and very alert.

"Well?" Flanna demanded.

"They're wonderful!" he exclaimed.

"Is that all ye hae to say to me? My family was delirious wi' delight when they learned I hae given ye twin sons, Patrick Leslie," she told him, "and all ye can say to me is *wonderful?*" Then she laughed, for from the moment she had said *sons*, he had gotten a dumbstruck look on his face that was yet there. Then she once again became aware of her now very wet bodice, and said, "The bairns must be fed."

And there was Aggie, unlacing Flanna's bodice and exclaiming with distress at the condition it was in, not to mention her chemise beneath. Flanna sat by the fire and undid the chemise. Aggie handed her first one child, and then the other. The children began immediately to suck noisily upon her breasts, the milk bubbling about their little mouths as they greedily nursed.

Patrick stared, fascinated, at his wife's white breasts with their pale blue veins. His sons obviously had voracious appetites. Drawing up a chair, he sat by her side. "How do ye tell which one is which?" he asked her.

"Jamie hae wee mole just above his left lip, but Angus does nae. Yer mam hae just such a mark in her portrait. I checked to see if it were nae a bit of dust, but it isna," Flanna told him.

"Nay, it isna dust," Patrick said. " 'Tis a family marking."

"Then, ye can certainly hae nae doubts anymore," Flanna said softly, and she looked directly at him.

"Did we nae settle this months ago?" he demanded of her.

"Aye, but I wanted to be certain," she said sweetly.

"Jesu, woman! They both look just like me!" he swore softly.

"Did ye think so?" she murmured with false innocence.

"Motherhood hae nae softened ye," he replied, but his eyes were dancing wickedly.

"The bairns will be full soon," she said. "Are ye hungry?"

"Aye!" His look was meaningful.

"I'll see that the cook hae a good supper for ye, my lord, and then ye'll want to sleep in yer own bed, I'm sure," she said.

"I'll want to sleep in yer bed," he told her, and chuckled when she colored. "So, ye can still blush like a lass, even though ye're a shameless hussy wi' bairns of yer own, Flanna Leslie."

She said nothing, but instead, after she had finished feeding her sons, she arose and told him, "I'll go and prepare a bath for ye, my lord, for ye'll nae get into my bed wi' the stink of yer journey on ye. Angus, see his lordship is fed after his long ride."

He sat by the fire, watching his sons sleep as the food was brought to the high board. Finally, at Angus's urging, he went to eat. "She's called young Brae after ye," he noted to the big man.

"I think she called him after the first Earl of Brae who was Angus," came the answer.

"I dinna know the first earl, but I do know ye," Patrick said. "I prefer to believe that my son is named for his great-uncle."

"Thank ye, my lord," Angus Gordon said, and he felt tears behind his eyelids.

"Sit wi' me, Angus," the duke said, "and tell me how it went wi' her. And why did Henry leave her?"

"She birthed yer sons easily. Her sister-in-law, Una Brodie, came to be wi' her and was quite outraged at how simple it was for her." Angus chuckled. "There was nae need for yer brother to remain after she hae had the bairns. She knew he was anxious to return to his own family at Cadby, and so she sent him off wi' a troop of Glenkirk men to see him as far as the border, for Cromwell's people hae been rooting about this summer."

"But Una stayed?" he asked anxiously.

"Aye, ye couldnae get rid of her, for she fell in love wi' yer sons. She was a great help to Flanna. We finally sent her home a month ago, when Aulay came complaining after his wife." Angus chuckled.

The two men spoke companionably while Patrick ate, and then

finally Aggie came to say that the duke's bath was ready. He arose and went upstairs to their apartment. The tub had been set up in the dayroom before the fire, and to his surprise, Flanna was in it awaiting him. Aggie was suddenly nowhere to be found. The Duke of Glenkirk grinned, delighted, and quickly pulled his clothes off, leaving them in a reeking pile upon the floor.

"They should be burned, and those boots will nae do ye again," Flanna noted pithily. She looked him up and down boldly. "Ye're thinner."

"Oatcakes dinna make a full meal," he said, climbing into the tub with her.

"Be careful!" she warned. "I'll nae hae the chamber flooded."

"Then, come over here, madame, so I may kiss ye properly," he ordered her.

"First ye wash," she replied, squealing as he yanked her to him, and the water sloshed over the top of the tall wooden tub. *"Patrick!"*

"Ye hae gotten out of the habit of obeying yer lord and master," he said. "I can see I must retrain ye." Then he attempted to kiss her.

Flanna swatted him with the washing rag. "Lord and master, indeed, husband!" she half shouted at him, but she was smiling. "Jesu! Yer hair is filthy! 'Tis a breeding ground for nits most likely!" She quickly dipped her hand into the jar of soap and then slapped it upon his dark head. Her two hands began to work up a good lather even as he pulled her into his arms, kissing her very thoroughly until she was breathless and rosy.

"I sheltered wi' Charlie's mistress these past few weeks," he told her. "She was most hospitable."

"Charlie hae a mistress?" Flanna was half surprised, remembering her brother-in-law's love for his wife, but then she was not entirely surprised, remembering his family's reputation. "And just how hospitable was this woman to ye, Patrick Leslie?" She yanked him forward and pushed his head beneath the water, rinsing the soap from it.

He came up sputtering and laughing. She was jealous. *She really did love him!* "Verra to Charlie, merely kind to me, particularly in light of the fact she shot me," he told his wife.

"*She shot ye?* What the hell did she shoot ye for, Patrick?" Now she saw the scar on his shoulder, and her fingers immediately went to it.

"It was dusk when we approached her house, which is verra isolated," he began. "Before Charlie could identify us, a shot rang out, and I was the one it hit. Barbara is, I fear, a verra poor shot," he chuckled.

"She could hae killed ye, the bitch!" Flanna exploded.

"Nay, she couldna, and she didna," he said, putting his arms about her to comfort her. "And here I am back home wi' ye, lassie, and safe in yer arms," he said, kissing her brow.

"How do I know ye're nae a ghostie?" she demanded.

He took her hand and drew it beneath the water to his burgeoning manhood. Her fingers closed about it, and it blossomed further beneath her touch. "Could a ghostie hae such a formidable and firm rod, lassie?"

She continued to caress him, her eyes half closing with her obvious pleasure. Her fingertips moved past his love lance to stroke at his twin jewels. "I need more proof," she murmured in his ear, her teeth nibbling upon the fleshy lobe.

His hands sought her buttocks, and finding them, he cupped her, lifting her up to impale her upon his manhood. He felt himself sliding deep inside her and groaned with the simple enjoyment of his action. Her two wet hands now clasped his face between them, and she kissed him passionately and yet tenderly as he began to slowly piston her.

"Ah, lassie," he groaned, "ye're almost as tight as ye were on our wedding night." He was going to die of delight.

She did not tell him that in her wanderings about the castle in his absence—while she waited for, and after the birth of their sons—she had found a small book of potions, salves, and amorous treatments to be used to keep one's husband content. She wasn't certain who had written the words down, but she was as pleased as he was that it was all working. Flanna closed her eyes, sighing with pleasure as they quickly reached their heaven together. "Oh," she said to him, "ye're surely nae a ghostie, Patrick Leslie, for nae ghostie could offer me such enjoyment." Then she took up the bath brush and began to scrub him free of his travels.

And when they were both clean and dry, they repaired to their bed, lying naked, the golden light of the fire playing over their bodies. Patrick kissed his wife deeply, his tongue playing hide and seek with hers. He found himself unable to satisfy his deep longings for her easily. His lips touched her breasts lovingly, licking at the nipples until they pearled with her milk, sucking upon her until she was crying out with her longing for him.

"Oh, ye're a wicked man!" she told him, half shocked, but also thrilled by his actions.

"And ye're a delicious armful, my darling lassie," he told her as he entered her again. This time, the edge off his carnal appetite, he moved slowly upon her, arousing her fires, bringing her almost to pleasure only to draw back. She cursed him much to his amusement. He reveled in the sharpness that her nails gave him as they raked down his long back in her desperation. He thrust deep and hard into her until she was practically screaming with the pleasure he was imparting. Her legs suddenly wrapped tightly about him, almost forcing the breath from him, and he slipped even farther into her than he ever had before. She tightened her love sheath about him in retaliation, knowing that he was about to explode his juices, and when she hotly whispered the single word, *"Now!"* into his ear, his passion for her erupted fiercely, flooding her secret garden and filling her womb with life.

Afterwards they lay together, her red-gold hair on his broad chest, and she told him, "We hae made another bairn, Patrick Leslie."

"Ye're certain?" he gently teased, dropping a kiss on that fiery head of hers and thinking how very much he loved her.

"Aye," she replied.

"Another son for Glenkirk, lassie. I will nae complain at that," he told her.

"Nae a son, my lord. A daughter. This time we hae made a lass! Of that I am absolutely certain," Flanna assured him.

"And what will we call her?" he asked, smiling.

"I dinna know yet, but I will on the day she is born," Flanna told him.

"Nae until then?" he teased her.

She raised her glorious head and looked down at him, her silvery eyes suddenly very serious. "Nae until then," she repeated. Then she kissed him, and Patrick Leslie thought none of it mattered at all because she loved him. They would know in time, and that was perfectly all right. He had by some miracle found the only lass he would ever really want. Whatever happened just beyond tomorrow was in the hands of the fates, and that was good enough for him. His hand wrapping about a hank of Flanna's beautiful hair, he pulled her down and kissed her with all the love that had ever been stored in his heart, and when Flanna kissed him back in the exact same way, Patrick Leslie knew that whatever happened to the world about them, his life would always be perfect because of that autumn afternoon that he had strayed onto the lands of Brae and met its heiress.

Epilogue

Queen's Malvern, Late Summer 1663

Jasmine, Dowager Duchess of Glenkirk, looked directly at her son Patrick and his wife, Flanna. "I want your daughter," she said bluntly to them.

"*Mam!*" Patrick said, surprised. What the hell was this all about? he wondered, They had been at Queen's Malvern six weeks.

"*Which one?*" Flanna asked, ever practical.

"Diana, of course," came the answer.

"Diana is our eldest daughter," Patrick protested. "What do ye want her for, Mam?"

"I want to save her from becoming any more of a wild creature than she already is," Jasmine replied quietly. "Because she is your eldest girl, Patrick, and quite obviously your favorite, you have allowed her far more freedom than any young girl should have. She must be civilized if we are to make a good marriage for her eventually. Neither you, nor Flanna, as much as I love you both, can do for Diana what I can do for her. What matches have you considered for her?"

"She is only going to be eleven!" Patrick said.

"How like my father you are. It is as I thought," Jasmine answered him. "You adore her so much that you do not consider the swift passing time. Suddenly she will be lying in the heather on some hillside with a perfectly unsuitable young man because she knows no better, and you have not bothered to make a good match for her. I cannot allow that to happen, nor can I see that exquisite child wasted on some rough Scot."

"Ye dinna agree wi' her?" Patrick turned in desperation to his wife.

"I do agree wi' her," Flanna answered him. "Diana is a Leslie, Patrick, but for all my title, I will always be Brodie-born. My mother died when I was Diana's age, and I ran wild. Poor Una could nae tame me. Only that ye wanted Brae we would hae nae found each other. I canna teach Diana the things she needs to know to make the kind of marriage a Duke of Glenkirk's eldest daughter should make. Yer mam can, and I am grateful to her that she is willing to take on the task. Do ye nae remember how wild Sabrina became in our care? Yet look what an elegant lady she has become now. See the fine marriage she made wi' her Earl of Lynmouth, the beautiful bairns she hae. I want that for Diana, and one day for Mair, too. They are pure Leslie, both of them. As for Sorcha, she is a Brodie. I see it already, though she barely hae even a year. She'll remain in our Highlands and wed wi' a good man. Or perhaps she'll go to the New World wi' her younger brothers one day. She will hae that kind of adventurous spirit." Flanna's silver eyes met the beautiful turquoise ones of her mother-in-law. "Aye, ye may hae Diana, and I am glad that ye would hae her."

Jasmine reached out and took Flanna's hand in hers, her gaze a steady one. "You may not have elegant manners, my daughter, but you have what many who practice such civilities do not. You have nobility of spirit, which I believe a far more valuable asset to a woman. We have only just met this summer, my dear, but I see what a fine wife you have been to my son. I see the children you have given him. Five sons and three daughters. How Glenkirk's walls must ring again with their laughter, and how much that means to their father. If I had picked a wife for Patrick myself, Flanna, I should not have done as well as he did by accident. Even if in the beginning it was for the wrong reasons."

"When do ye want Diana?" the Duke of Glenkirk asked his mother.

"Immediately," was the reply. "She does not need to return to Scotland when you do. Queen's Malvern will be her home from now on, and until she weds one day."

"Charlie is content with this?" Patrick queried. His mother could sometimes be a bit high-handed. She had never stopped being the Mughal's daughter in all her seventy-three years.

"Charlie is delighted, as is Barbara," Jasmine assured her son. "With Freddie at Oxford, and Willy serving the king as a page at court, they welcome a young relative in the house. Besides, Diana will be a fine companion for Cynara. They are so close in age, and gracious, you can certainly see they are cousins. Charlie's wife is a very elegant woman, and Diana can learn much from her."

"Charlie told me once that ye said a Duke of Lundy should nae wed wi' a Hereford merchant's daughter," Patrick teased his mother.

"Not for a first marriage," Jasmine returned, "but Bess is long dead these many years, and her children are grown. Charlie loves Barbara enough that he has formally legitimatized their daughter. Neither is in the first flush of youth any longer. I fully approved their marriage in June, for their own sake, and certainly for Cynara's. She must, like Diana, take her proper place in society," the dowager replied.

"So ye hae it all settled, eh, Mam? Autumn wi' her Gabriel and their twin bairns. Twins obviously run in the Leslie line. Did nae my Leslie grandmother hae twins? Aye, she did, I remember. Henry and his family hae survived Cromwell's rule, as hae the rest of us, now in our mid life and content. No more adventuring, Mam, eh?" The Duke of Glenkirk chuckled. "I wonder what Madame Skye would have thought if she could hae seen all her descendants here at Queen's Malvern last month trampling over her lawns, meeting for the first time, making matches, discovering how much alike many of us are. Would she hae been pleased?"

"I think she would have been," Jasmine said. "She was a woman who loved her family. Now, Patrick, I don't want you to worry yourself about Diana. She will be perfectly happy here, and I will provide for her. With all your brood, you will not notice she is even gone."

"Aye, I will," the Duke of Glenkirk said softly, but he knew what his mother was doing for his eldest daughter was the right thing. Lady Diana Leslie was a very beautiful child who would grow up one day to be a beautiful woman. She didn't belong in his Highland aerie. She belonged at court where she would attract a rich and powerful husband. *Or a king.* "Ye'll teach her to refuse an improper advance from even the most powerful gentleman in the realm, will ye nae, Mam?" he said nervously.

Flanna laughed and patted her husband's big hand. "She'll nae be a naïve goosie like her mam, Patrick. Nae wi' yer mother guiding her," the Duchess of Glenkirk assured her husband.

Jasmine laughed too for she now knew the true story of Flanna's meeting with a young King Charles in Perth twelve years back. They had not met since, nor were they likely ever to meet again; but the king had restored the earldom of Brae to the Leslies of Glenkirk for Angus Gordon Leslie, the second born of Flanna's twin sons. Angus delighted in teasing his slightly elder sibling that while he would one day be the Duke of Glenkirk, he was only Lord Leslie, while Angus was already the holder of his own title. Such mockery did not please the future duke.

The next day on the ninth of August both Jasmine, and her granddaughter, Diana, celebrated their birthdays. Several days after that the Leslies of Glenkirk along with their sons, James, Angus, Malcolm, Ian, and Colin; and their two remaining daughters, Mairghread and Sorcha, departed Queen's Malvern for Scotland. Her brothers were hardly unhappy to leave Diana behind, but Mair, who was almost five, wept.

Diana stood next to her grandmother in the graveled drive watching as her family disappeared from her view. The shoes on her feet hurt, but her grandmother and Lady Barbara had both assured her that a lady wore shoes in public. She would miss her father most of all, and then Mair, but her grandmother had promised that Mair would eventually join them at Queen's Malvern. Still, her cousin, Cynara Stuart, was already proving to be an interesting companion.

"Well," Jasmine said when the dust from the Glenkirk party had finally dissipated, "we shall now begin." She looked at her granddaughters with a twinkle in her beautiful eyes.

Diana smiled back a brilliant smile. "I cannot wait to meet the king," she said,

"Nor I," Cynara echoed.

Jasmine burst out laughing. I shall not be bored with these two headstrong vixens in my charge, she thought. Then she said, "In time, my ladies. In due time." And taking the two girls by the hands she walked them back into the house.